THE OLD-HOUSE JOURNAL 1982
CATALOG

COMPILED BY THE EDITORS OF THE OLD-HOUSE JOURNAL

Cover Photo: *Everett Ortner*

The Old-House Journal
CATALOG

Published by The Old-House Journal Corporation,
69A Seventh Avenue, Brooklyn, N.Y. 11217
Tel. (212) 636-4514

Published in Association with

The Overlook Press
Lewis Hollow Road
Woodstock, N.Y. 12498

Distributed to the trade by The Viking Press

Library of Congress Catalog Card Number 81-641968
ISBN 0-87951-137-0

ISSN 0271-7220

© Copyright 1981 by The Old-House Journal Corporation. All rights reserved. No part of this publication may be reproduced or transmitted in any form or by any means, electronic or mechanical, including photocopying, recording, or by any information storage and retrieval system, without permission in writing from The Old-House Journal Corporation.

Every effort has been made to provide dependable data. However, the publisher does not warrant that the data herein are complete or accurate.

WARNING: Lists herein have been seeded to detect unauthorized use of this information for sales promotion and other direct mail solicitation purposes in violation of the copyright.

Cover and Book Design: *Charles Eanet*

THE OLD-HOUSE JOURNAL 1982 CATALOG

CONTENTS	
Introduction	5
HOW TO USE THIS CATALOG	6
Key To State Abbreviations	10
PRODUCT & SERVICE DIRECTORY	11
Exterior Building Materials & Supplies	12
Exterior Ornament & Architectural Details	19
Exterior Hardware	27
Other Exterior Ornament & Details	31
Building Materials For Interiors	34
Decorative Interior Materials & Supplies	41
Furniture & Furnishings	49
Interior Hardware, Plumbing & House Fittings	54
Heating Systems, Fireplaces & Stoves	70
Lighting Fixtures & Parts	72
Paints, Finishes, Removers & Supplies	82
Tools & Other Supplies	89
Antique & Recycled House Parts	93
Renovation & Restoration Supply Stores	97
Restoration Services	98
Decorating Services	102
COMPANY DIRECTORY	105
About The Old-House Journal	161
Books About Period Houses	162
ORDER FORM	166
ALPHABETICAL INDEX	168
ADVERTISERS' INDEX	176

Compiled and Edited by the staff of The Old-House Journal

INTRODUCTION

THIS CATALOG is your roadmap to the fascinating world of old-house services and supplies. Every day, more and more people are discovering the joys of fine craftsmanship and excellent design to be found in old houses. And if you are restoring one of these old gems, you want to use products and services that are appropriate and authentic.

FORTUNATELY, more than 1,000 companies are now selling products that are tailored to the special needs of old-house lovers. With this Catalog, you have the most complete and up-to-date set of "Yellow Pages" for this fast-changing market.

FOR DIRECTIONS on how to use this Catalog most effectively, consult the diagram on the following two pages.

HINTS ON CONTACTING COMPANIES

ONCE YOU'VE used the Catalog to find the companies you wish to contact, consider these points of mail-order manners. Being aware of these hints will help avoid misunderstandings—and will make shopping by mail more fun.

1. BEFORE WRITING and saying "send catalog," check the write-up in the Company Directory to see if they have literature —and if there's a charge. It wastes your time and theirs if the company has to write back to tell you that there's a charge for their literature.

2. DON'T SEND form-letter inquiries to dozens of companies. Many companies will ignore these. Besides, since most companies have a charge for literature, you at least have to tailor the letter so that the proper fee is enclosed.

3. WRITE "Catalog Request", "Order", or similar clarifying phrase on the outside of your envelope to aid in accurate handling.

4. IF YOU ARE ASKING for more information than a catalog can provide, telephoning is usually the fastest and most satisfactory way to get the answer.

5. IF YOU DECIDE to write to a company asking a non-routine question, a self-addressed, stamped envelope (SASE) is a thoughtful gesture. And be sure to be concise, specific—and legible—in asking your question.

6. BE PATIENT. With mail being what it is, it can take 4 weeks or longer for catalogs or merchandise to arrive.

7. BE AWARE THAT prices change. Prices quoted in this Catalog were accurate as of mid-year 1981. If you are using the Catalog in 1982 or later, expect that some prices may have gone up.

8. ALWAYS MENTION The Old-House Journal Catalog when you write. It helps identify you as part of the "family."

WHY SOME COMPANIES AREN'T LISTED

THIS CATALOG does not claim to be a complete directory of the field. Rather, it is a sourcebook of companies that have answered a detailed questionnaire sent to them by the editors of The Old-House Journal. Only those companies that replied—and provided suitable backup literature—have been included. There may be other companies that are worthy of inclusion. But since they did not provide the requested information to the editors, we have no way of knowing what their products are like—and whether they are responsive to the needs of old-house owners.

THERE ARE ALSO some companies that did answer our questionnaire and submit product literature—and that still are not listed in this Catalog. That's because, in the opinion of the editors, the products were not appropriate for pre-1930 houses.

AND FINALLY, there are some companies that aren't listed because the editors have found them to be scoundrels. When the editors get a complaint about a company, we give the com-

pany every opportunity to rectify the problem. (And most of them do.) Every once in a while, however, we encounter a company that is quite indifferent to customer complaints—or who plays fast and loose with deposit money sent in advance for orders.

ALL COMPANIES that prove to be scoundrels are barred from the Catalog listings. To date, there are 17 firms that have been eliminated from the Catalog on these grounds.

IF A COMPANY GIVES YOU PROBLEMS

THE CATALOG EDITORS have made every effort to screen out companies that we feel have shoddy products or shady business ethics. Of course, the editors can't guarantee the

How To Use
The Old-House Journal Catalog

Step 1

LOOK UP the product or service you are seeking in the Alphabetical Index that starts on page 168. The Index contains numerous cross-references that take into account common synonyms for the same item.

The Alphabetical Index refers you to the proper page in the Product & Service Directory.

```
Blinds, Shutters, & Shades, Interior..........53, 68
Blinds, Wood Venetian ......................53
Bluestone ..................................13
Boards, Salvage ........................34, 36
   (see also Salvage Building Materials, Barnboard)
Bollards and Stanchions ....................33
Brackets ...............................20, 41
Braided Rugs...............................52
Brass Beds.................................52
Brass Lacquer .............................82
Brass Polish...............................82
Brick Cleaners.............................12
Bricks, Handmade ..........................13
Bricks, Salvage............................13
   (see also Salvage Building Materials)
```

Step 2

IN THE Product & Service Directory, you'll find a heading for the item you are seeking. Under that heading will be the names of all the companies that the editors have validated as providing that product or service.

As a further convenience, on the same page you'll find related product headings. In addition, there are useful display advertisements for companies supplying that type of item.

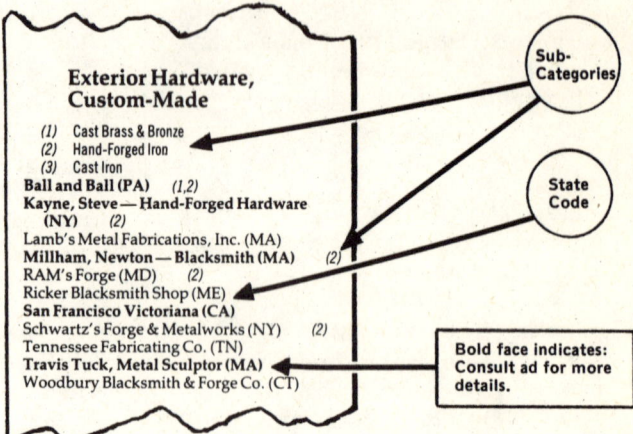

After each company name is a two-letter state abbreviation. This helps you find nearby suppliers when there are many companies in a category. If you have any difficulty deciphering these standard Post Office abbreviations, you will find the key on page 10.

The small numbers after the company name in some categories tell which of the sub-categories they sell.

A company's name in **bold face** means that it has placed an advertisement in this Catalog that you can consult for more information. If the ad doesn't appear on the same page, then consult the Advertisers' Index on page 176 for location of the company's ad.

Step 3

AFTER LOCATING a company that looks interesting, consult the firm's full listing in the Company Directory that starts on page 105. Here you'll find a lot of information about the company compressed into a small space:

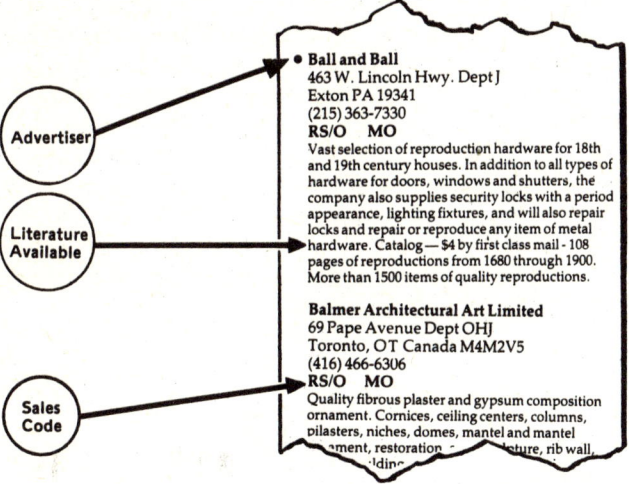

The Sales Code in each company listing tells how the firm sells its products or services. Some will sell nationwide via mail order (MO). Others will sell only through distributors (DIST); you can't buy from them directly. Some companies sell directly from a retail store or office (RS/O). A few companies will sell only to interior designers and architects (ID).

Key to Abbreviations

MO = sells by Mail Order
RS/O = sells through Retail Store or Office
DIST = sells through Distributors
ID = sells through Interior Designers only

A bold-face bullet (●) next to the company name means that the company has placed an ad in the Catalog to provide you with more information.

Step 4

WHEN YOU'VE SPOTTED a company with an advertiser code (●) that interests you, refer to the Advertisers' Index on page 176. This page tells you where you'll find their display ad. Often, the company will provide additional ordering information right in the ad.

AA-Abbingdon	39
A-Ball Plumbing Supply	60
A.E.S. Firebacks	70
A.S.L. Associates	88
Abatron, Inc.	87
Able/Stanley Wood Carving Co.	41
Abraxas International, Inc.	65
Addco Architectural Antiques	35, 93
Agape Antiques	70
Alcon Lightcraft Co.	76
American Delft Blue, Inc.	43
American General Products	39
Antique Street Lamps	80
Architectural Antiques Exchange	94
Architectural Iron Co.	29
Architectural Paneling, Inc.	48
Architectural Restoration & Design Assoc.	98
Architectural Terra Cotta & Tile	44
Arriaga, Nelson	50
Art Directions	94
Ascherl Studios	80
Ball and Ball	69
Barclay Products Co.	55
Beall, Barbara Vantrease Studio	44
Beauti-home	68
Benjamin Moore Co.	85
Berridge Manufacturing Co.	15
Biggs Company	49

The Old-House Journal 1982 Catalog

performance of every company listed in this Catalog. But we can follow up on any problems that you might have. If someone doesn't reply to your inquiry... or you aren't happy with the way your order was handled, please let us know.

HAVING PERSONALLY screened their applications, and having given them free space for their editorial listings, the editors want to make sure that each company lives up to the representations it has made to us.

THE EDITORS can do two things when you are not satisfied with a company's performance:

(1) We will follow up on your behalf and attempt to bring about a satisfactory solution.

(2) If the company does not make a good-faith effort to resolve the problem, and its bad performance seems part of a pattern, the firm will be barred from all future editions of the Catalog.

AS MENTIONED ABOVE, there are 17 companies now barred from the Catalog because of the editors' dissatisfaction with their business practices and ethics.

HAPPILY, customer complaints have been few. And most of those that are brought to our attention are quickly resolved as soon as the problem is brought to the companies' attention.

IF YOU HAVE A PROBLEM with any company listed in this Catalog, please let us hear from you. Contact:

Catalog Editor
The Old-House Journal
69A Seventh Avenue
Brooklyn, N.Y. 11217

GIVE US THE SPECIFICS of your problem and tell what corrective action you've already taken. If it's an order and money has already changed hands, Xerox copies of your checks—plus any previous correspondence—would be helpful.

IF YOUR LETTER IS RETURNED TO YOU

PEOPLE frequently complain that letters to Catalog companies are returned stamped "No Longer At This Address," or the person is unable to get a response from the company. Upon investigation, we find that the vast majority of these complaints result from people using Catalogs that are two or three years out of date.

THE ADDRESSES and telephone numbers in this Catalog were up-to-date as of mid-1981—the date when the Catalog went to press. If you are using this Catalog in late 1982 (or later) you will find that:

(a) A few companies listed have gone out of business; and

(b) Several dozen companies will have moved.

BECAUSE things change so rapidly, the editors have found that we must update the Catalog at least once a year. When the 1983 edition comes out in November of 1982, we'll delete those few companies that have gone out of business and will have caught up with the new addresses of those several dozen companies that have moved.

WHO'S LISTED

EDITORIAL LISTINGS in the Catalog are provided free to qualifying companies. To be listed, the companies had to meet several criteria established by the editors:

● PRODUCTS OR SERVICES must be suitable, in the opinion of the editors, for houses built before 1930;

● COMPANIES must show a desire to serve the special interests of old-house lovers. This interest is evidenced by their willingness to answer a detailed questionnaire sent to them by the editors.

● COMPANIES also had to submit samples of their product literature to assist the editors in evaluating their products and services.

SCOPE OF THE CATALOG

COMPANIES LISTED in this Catalog are mainly those that sell nationally and whose products are not widely available. Our Catalog does not attempt to include items that are commonly available at hardware stores, building supply centers and department stores.

ALSO, this Catalog does not attempt to be a comprehensive Directory of local services and craftsmen. To do so would be to create a book so thick that no one could afford to buy it. We have included, however, individual craftsmen when we have been able to obtain first-hand information about them—and when their skills seemed out-of-the-ordinary.

IN NO WAY does this Catalog purport to be all-inclusive. By restricting listings to companies from whom we have first-hand information, we feel we have created a more selective and useful product for you, the reader.

IF A GOOD COMPANY ISN'T LISTED

IF YOU KNOW about other good sources for old-house products and services, please let us know about them. We'll send them a questionnaire and give them the opportunity to be listed in the next edition.

THE EDITORS have spent several hundred hours struggling with the massive amount of information compiled for this Catalog. When so much data is processed, it's inevitable that a few errors will creep in. But with the amount of proof-reading and double-checking that we've done, we're confident that the errors are minimal.

WE BELIEVE that you'll find this 1982 Catalog the most complete and up-to-date Directory available...and that it will help you get added pleasure from the old house you love!

Katharine Conley
Stephanie Croce
Carolyn Flaherty
Cole Gagne
Clem Labine
Joni Monnich
Patricia Poore
Barbara Schiller

Cataloguers for the 1982 Edition

A Note About State Abbreviations

After each company name in the Product & Service Directory you'll find a two-letter state code. This indicates the state in which the company is located. The state code helps you find nearby suppliers when there is a long list of companies within a category.

The full name, address and telephone number of every company can be found in the Company Directory starting on page 105.

Alabama	AL	Nebraska	NE
Alaska	AK	Nevada	NV
Arizona	AZ	New Hampshire	NH
Arkansas	AR	New Jersey	NJ
California	CA	New Mexico	NM
Canada	CAN	New York	NY
Colorado	CO	North Carolina	NC
Connecticut	CT	North Dakota	ND
Delaware	DE	Ohio	OH
District of Columbia	DC	Oklahoma	OK
Florida	FL	Oregon	OR
Georgia	GA	Pennsylvania	PA
Hawaii	HI	Puerto Rico	PR
Idaho	ID	Rhode Island	RI
Illinois	IL	South Carolina	SC
Indiana	IN	South Dakota	SD
Iowa	IA	Tennessee	TN
Kansas	KS	Texas	TX
Kentucky	KY	United Kingdom (England)	UK
Louisiana	LA	Utah	UT
Maine	ME	Vermont	VT
Maryland	MD	Virginia	VA
Massachusetts	MA	Washington	WA
Michigan	MI	West Virginia	WV
Minnesota	MN	Wisconsin	WI
Mississippi	MS	Wyoming	WY
Missouri	MO		
Montana	MT		

THE PRODUCT & SERVICE DIRECTORY

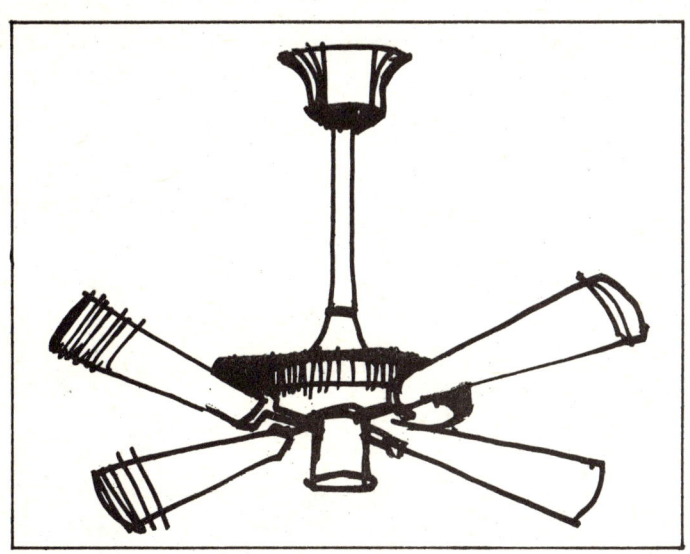

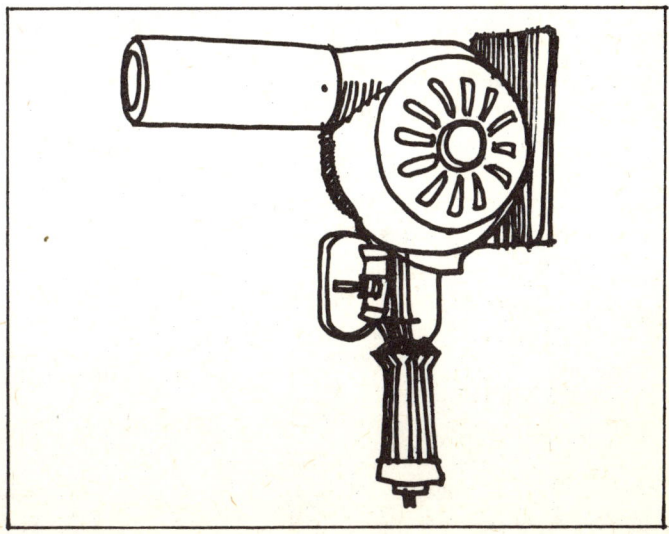

PRODUCT & SERVICE DIRECTORY

Exterior Building Materials & Supplies

THE EXTERIOR

Water is the worst enemy of old masonry buildings and protection from its depradations—scaling, crumbling, disintegration—should be high on an owner's priority list.

Repointing—replacing the old deteriorated mortar with new—is one of the most common masonry repairs. A few tips: Study the profile of an existing joint and match the shape. Use a hammer and cold chisel rather than power tools to cut out mortar joints.

Don't use ready-mix or cement mortars on buildings constructed before the 1880's when Portland cement came into general use. Soft lime-based mortars were used before then, and can be duplicated.

If bricks must be replaced, use bricks from other parts of the building or replace with salvage bricks or new handmade bricks that match in color and texture.

When cleaning masonry buildings is necessary the oldest method is often the best—water and a stiff bristle brush. Chemical cleaning is another choice. Sandblasting and water blasting should never be used. Soft stone will be eroded, polished stone pockmarked and brick stripped of its protective outer skin and left vulnerable to deterioration. Once the surface is thoroughly clean, a sealer is normally not recommended because it can cause additional problems.

If your house was painted originally, and many brick buildings were, then stay with a painted surface and renew it every three to five years. The building will be historically correct and protected against moisture.

Bare exterior wood, new and old, should be treated with a water-repellent preservative solution to guard against damage caused by rot and mildew.

Natural wood or grained wood exterior doors need a good coat of varnish to protect them from attack by the elements, the sun in particular. Use a varnish that is clearly labelled for exterior use such as spar varnish—a heavy varnish designed for severe weather conditions.

See Company Directory for Addresses & Phone Numbers

Building Maintenance Materials & Supplies

Basement Waterproofing Paints & Compounds

Benjamin Moore Co. (NJ)
Standard Dry Wall Products (FL)
U.S. Gypsum Company (IL)
United Gilsonite Laboratories (PA)

Bird & Pest Control Products

Bird — X (IL)
Nixalite of America (IL)
Paramount Exterminating Co. (NY)

Masonry Cleaners & Paint Strippers

Diedrich Chemicals-Restoration Technologies, Inc. (WI)
North Coast Chemical Co. (WA)
ProSoCo, Inc. (KS)

Restoring America's Landmarks with

RESTORATION TECHNOLOGIES, INC.

- Remove flaking and unsightly paint from masonry (brick and stone), metal, and wood (clapboards and trim) with Diedrich 606 Multi-layer Paint Remover.

- Remove accumulated pollution grime, carbon dirt, mildew, smoke stains, etc. from all brick, stone, terra cotta and other masonry with Diedrich 101 Masonry Restorer.

- Avoid the abrasive damage caused by sandblasting.

- Over 800 contractors have used our product nationwide—individuals can call for name of nearby contractor.

- Movie available—A super 8, narrated, color film demonstrating the use of our restoration chemical products.

- Sold only to contractors, architects and preservation groups. Seeking dealers-distributors — Write for free brochure.

300A East Oak Street, Dept. OHJC, Oak Creek, WI 53154
(414) 761-2591

Masonry Sealers

Diedrich Chemicals-Restoration Technologies, Inc. (WI)
Hydrozo Coatings Co. (NE)
ProSoCo, Inc. (KS)
Standard Dry Wall Products (FL)
U.S. Gypsum Company (IL)
United Gilsonite Laboratories (PA)
Watco - Dennis Corporation (CA)
Wood and Stone, Inc. (VA)

Paints, Exterior—Masonry

Standard Dry Wall Products (FL)
U.S. Gypsum Company (IL)

Preservatives, Wood

Cabot Stains (MA)
E & B Marine Supply (NJ)
Hydrozo Coatings Co. (NE)
Minwax Company, Inc. (NJ)
Savogran Co. (MA)
U.S. Gypsum Company (IL)
Watco - Dennis Corporation (CA)

Stains, Exterior

Barnard Chemical Co. (CA)
Cabot Stains (MA)
U.S. Gypsum Company (IL)

Varnishes, Exterior

Barnard Chemical Co. (CA)
E & B Marine Supply (NJ)
North Coast Chemical Co. (WA)
United Gilsonite Laboratories (PA)

Masonry & Supplies

Bricks, Handmade

(1) New
(2) Salvage

Colonial Brick Co. (IL) 2
Cushwa, Victor & Sons Brick Co. (MD) 1
Glen — Gery Corporation (PA) 1
Kensington Historical Co. (NH) 2
Old Carolina Brick Co. (NC) 1

Stone

(1) Bluestone
(2) Granite
(3) Limestone
(4) Marble
(5) Sandstone (Brownstone)
(6) Slate
(7) Other Stone

"Mr. Slate" Smid Incorporated (VT) 6
Delaware Quarries, Inc. (PA) 2,3,4,5,6
Evergreen Slate Co. (NY) 6
Hilltop Slate Co. (NY) 6
Rising & Nelson Slate Co. (VT) 6
Sculpture Associates, Ltd. (NY) 4,7
Structural Slate Company (PA) 6
Tatko Bros. Slate Co. (NY) 6
Vermont Soapstone Co. (VT) 7
Vermont Structural Slate Co. (VT) 5,6

Stucco Patching Materials

Standard Dry Wall Products (FL)
U.S. Gypsum Company (IL)

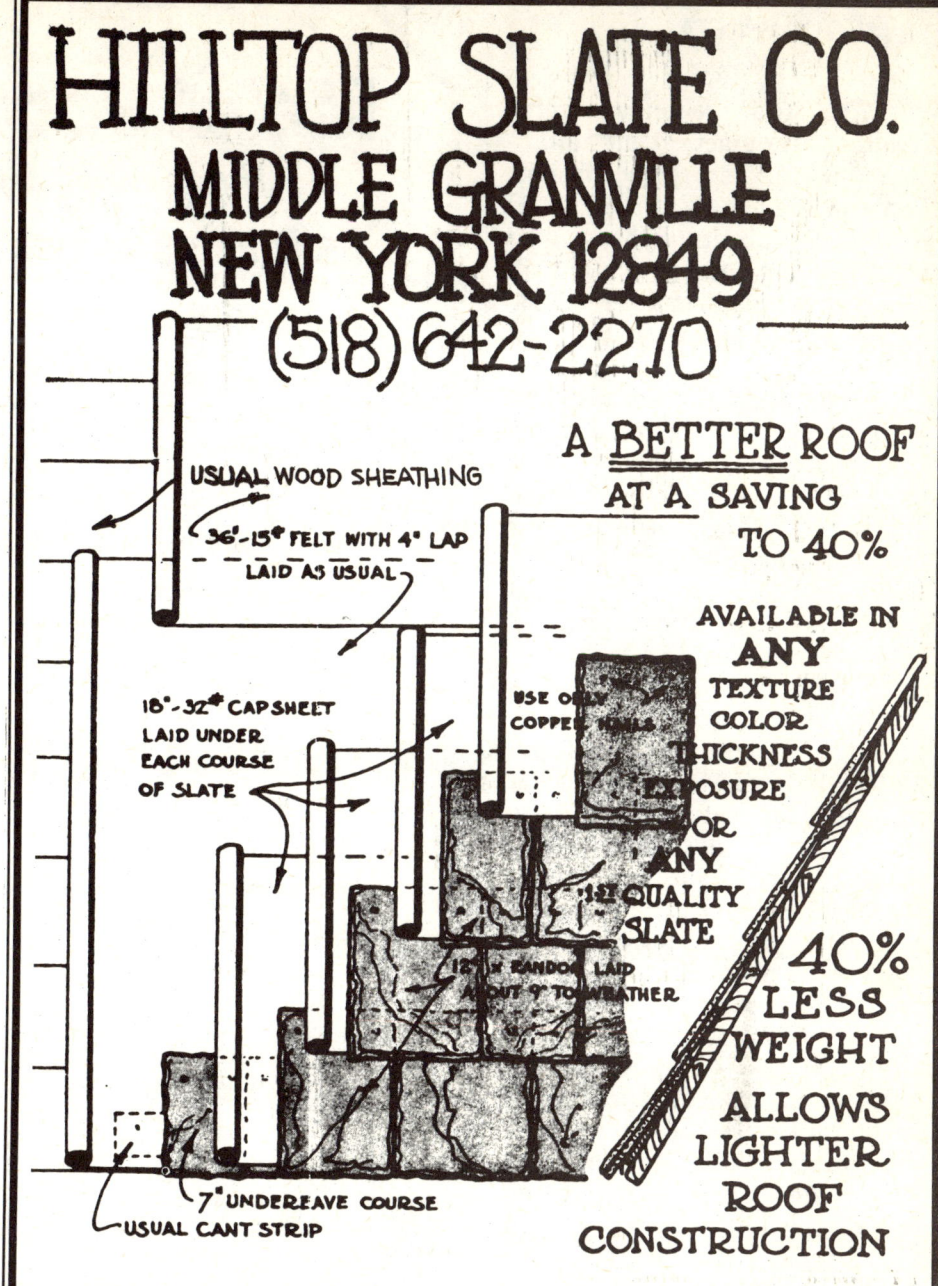

The best book about slate roofs is:

SLATE ROOFS

It's full of well-organized information — historical, scientific, and practical. It is required reading for any roofer or homeowner. The price (ppd.) is $7.95.

Order file 12-D from:
Vermont Structural Slate Company, Inc.
P.O. Box 98, Fair Haven, Vermont 05743
(802) 265-4933

The Old-House Journal 1982 Catalog

YOUR SPECIAL ROOF

The roof requires careful treatment for practical and aesthetic reasons. Whenever possible retain the orginal material, restore it or use a substitute that was in use when the house was built. If a new material has to be used, match the old in size, shape, color and texture.

Cedar shingles were the standard roofing material in America throughout colonial days. The Queen Anne and Stick and Shingle styles are distinguished by their use of shingles, often cut in special shapes. When properly applied cedar shakes and shingles will last appreciably longer than asphalt.

Metal shingles were popular in the late 19th and early 20th centuries. They are an appropriate and less expensive replacement material than slate on a Mansard roof. Terne is one of the oldest types of metal roofing. Suitable for many 19th century buildings, it is dark grey in color, durable and easy to maintain.

Slate is superlative in looks and durability. Although expensive, it is cost efficient over the long term. The one problem is finding a contractor familiar with slate roofs. Although similar to other shingling, slate roofing requires special know-how.

Ceramic tile roofs are a distinguishing feature of the Spanish Colonial and the Mission Revival styles.

Roofing Materials & Supplies

Metal Roofing

(1) Galvanized
(2) Terne
(3) Other

Berridge Manufacturing Co. (TX) 1,2,3
Conklin Tin Plate & Metal Co. (GA) 1,2,3
Follansbee Steel (WV) 2
Norman, W.F., Corporation (MO)

Metal Roof Shingles
W.F. Norman Re-Introduces Its Original Turn-of-the-Century Line

Again...W.F. Norman is making its complete line available. Beautiful in every detail and galvanized to last for years.

- **SPANISH TILE**   • **MISSION TILE**

- Style A Shingle (Victorian)
- Style C Shingle (Victorian)
- Normandie Style Shingle

Also Available! Roof cresting and finials. 4 styles of galvanized exterior metal siding.

W.F. Norman Corporation

P.O. Box 323 • Nevada, Missouri 64772
Toll free (800) 641-4038 • In Missouri call collect (417) 667-5552
Manufacturers of the celebrated Hi-Art® metal ceilings.

Shakes & Shingles, Wood

(1) Handsplit
(2) Machine Cut

Carlisle Restoration Lumber (NH) 2
Crawford's Old House Store (WI) 2
Hendricks Tile Mfg. Co., Inc. (VA)
Koppers Co. (PA) 2
Mad River Wood Works (CA) 2
Puget Sound Shake Brokers (WA)
Renovator's Supply (MA)
Shakertown Corporation (WA) 2
Shingle Mill (MA) 2
South Coast Shingle Co. (CA) 2

Shingles, Metal

Berridge Manufacturing Co. (TX)
Conklin Tin Plate & Metal Co. (GA)

Tiles, Asbestos

Supradur Mfg. Corp. (NY)

Tiles, Slate

"Mr. Slate" Smid Incorporated (VT)
Buckingham Slate Co. (VA)
Evergreen Slate Co. (NY)
Hilltop Slate Co. (NY)
Millen Roofing Co. (WI)
Rising & Nelson Slate Co. (VT)
Structural Slate Company (PA)
Supradur Mfg. Corp. (NY)
Vermont Structural Slate Co. (VT)
Walker, Dennis C. (OH)

Tiles, Terra Cotta & Ceramic

Architectural Terra Cotta and Tile, Ltd. (IL)
Gladding, McBean & Co. (CA)
Hendricks Tile Mfg. Co., Inc. (VA)
International Architecture (TX)
Ludowici-Celadon Co. (OH)

Other Roofing

Hendricks Tile Mfg. Co., Inc. (VA)

See Company Directory for Addresses & Phone Numbers

The Shingle Mill

High Quality
Natural Siding
and
Roofing Shingles

Special End Cuts
Available

Custom Shingles
for Restoration
on Request

Factory:
170 Mill Street Gardner, Mass.

Office/Mail:
Box 134
6 Cote Avenue
South Ashburnham, Mass. 01466
(617) 827-4889

Berridge Manufacturing Co.
Roofs of Distinction

BERRIDGE VICTORIAN SHINGLE
- Traditional appearance
- Ideal for reroofing and new construction
- No special tools required

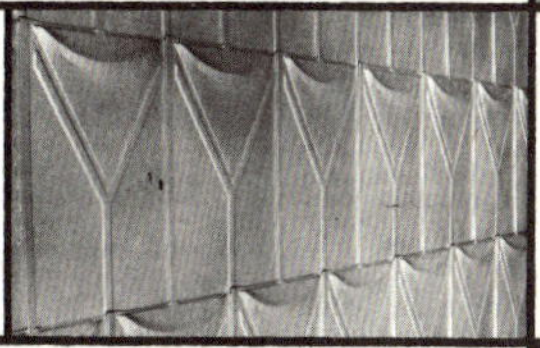

BERRIDGE CLASSIC SHINGLE
- 19th century roof in 20th century materials
- Light weight
- Easy to install

BERRIDGE FISH-SCALE SHINGLE
- Unique curved edge
- Deep relief
- Ideal for gable walls

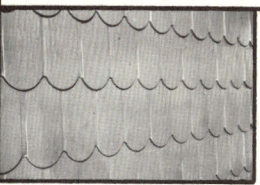

Popular colors available in prefinished galvanized steel; plus natural weathering materials, Galvalume, copper and terne-coated stainless steel.

1720 Maury/Houston, Texas 77026/(713) 223-4971

Old-Fashioned Roofing with Old-Fashioned Quality

FIREPROOF ROOFING SHINGLES
SUPRA-SLATE • DUTCH LAP
HEXAGONAL • TWIN LAP
AMERICAN TRADITIONAL

If you're planning to renovate an older building, the choice of roofing material is an important consideration. Supradur mineral fiber roofing shingles, which are covered by a 30-year warranty, provide maximum protection from the elements while contributing to the beauty of the structure.

Please send me more information on Supradur Fireproof Roofing Shingles.

Name _____
Address _____
City _____
State _____ Zip _____
Phone _____

Mail to: SUPRADUR MANUFACTURING CORP.
122 East 42nd Street, New York, N.Y. 10168
or call (212) 697-1160

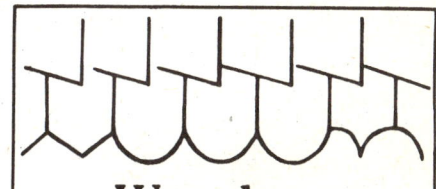

Wooden Ornaments

MAD RIVER
wood works

4935 Boyd Rd. P.O. Box 163 Arcata, CA 95521
(707) 826-0629 or (707) 822-2155

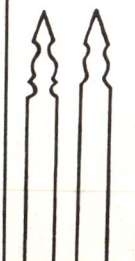
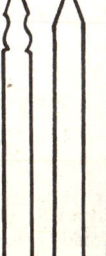

RESTORATION
HOUSE PARTS
in
CALIFORNIA
REDWOOD

The Old-House Journal 1982 Catalog

KNOW YOUR SIDING

Nothing will ever look better or be less disruptive than the siding material that was originally on your house. Fortunately there are now sources for authentic siding materials—clapboards, shakes and shingles. This being the case, it is truly alarming that there is an increase in the use of synthetic siding materials in older residential neighborhoods. These asbestos, aluminum and vinyl concoctions are not maintenance free. They will almost certainly destroy the architectural integrity of the building and may even contribute to the structure's deterioration.

Synthetic siding hides physical deterioration. Rot and insect attack may proceed unnoticed. Many sidings act as exterior vapor barriers, trapping excess water vapor which condenses and damages the wood; if installation is incorrect or if the siding is subsequently damaged, actual runoff water may enter behind the siding and be trapped. Such problems are undetectable because the siding makes a visual inspection impossible. And finally, artificial sidings offer no structural support, so that if continued deterioration leads to failure, the siding will buckle and separate from the building.

Synthetic sidings lose their pristine appearance. Aluminum is prone to dents and scratches. Solid vinyl is vulnerable to punctures and tears. Vinyl becomes brittle in cold weather and liable to shatter on impact. Color coatings can peel and fade. The solution to siding problems is repair, restoration and maintenance of the authentic siding material. When properly cared for wood siding will last for centuries. The overwhelming enemy of wood is rot. Wood that is kept totally free from water will be totally free from rot. Wood preservatives, paint, properly applied putty and caulk are the ammunition used in the battle to keep water out of exterior wood.

Siding Materials & Supplies

Clapboards, Beaded Edge and Other Old Styles

(1) Salvage
(2) New

Carlisle Restoration Lumber (NH) 2
Craftsman Lumber Co. (MA) 2
Kensington Historical Co. (NH) 1
Saltbox (PA) 2
Silverton Victorian Millworks (CO) 2
Sky Lodge Farm (MA) 2

Shingles, Special Architectural Shapes

Kingsway (CO)
Mad River Wood Works (CA)
Old'N Ornate Wooden Reproductions (OR)
Puget Sound Shake Brokers (WA)
San Francisco Victoriana (CA)
Shakertown Corporation (WA)
Shingle Mill (MA)

Shakes & Shingles, Custom-Cut

Mad River Wood Works (CA)
Puget Sound Shake Brokers (WA)
Shakertown Corporation (WA)
Shingle Mill (MA)

See Company Directory for Addresses & Phone Numbers

Siding, Barn

(1) Salvage
(2) New

Barn People, The (VT) 1
Belcher, Robert W. (GA) 1
Carlisle Restoration Lumber (NH) 1
Castle Burlingame (NJ) 1
Craftsman Lumber Co. (MA) 2
Farm Builders, Inc. (MD) 1
Saltbox (PA) 2
Sloane, Hugh L. (MA) 1
Structural Antiques (OK) 1
Vermont Weatherboard, Inc. (VT) 2
Vintage Lumber Co. (MD) 2
Walker, Dennis C. (OH) 2

Screen Doors, Wood

Cascade Mill & Glass Works (CO)
Combination Door Co. (WI)
Creative Openings (WA)
JMR Products (CA)
Mad River Wood Works (CA)
Moser Brothers, Inc. (PA)
Nord, E.A. Company (WA)
Old'N Ornate Wooden Reproductions (OR)
Remodelers' & Renovators' Supply (ID)
Renovation Products (TX)
Robillard, Dennis Paul, Inc. (ME)
Strobel Millwork (CT)
The Restoration Fraternity (PA)

Reminiscent of America's Past
Historical Restoration
Supply & Contracting Service

Farm Builders Inc. offers a wide range of Weathered Barn Siding, Timbers, and Milled Barn Lumber in Oak, Chestnut and Pine.

- **Random width Tongue & Groove Flooring in Oak and Long Leaf Heart Pine.**

- **Complete Milling Service**

- **Architectural Woodwork, Stain Glass and Hardware**

- **Hand Wrought Primitive Hardware**

Farm Builders unique services are the Relocation & Restoration of Historical Log Cabins, Post and Beam Barn Frame Conversions, or *any Historical Building Renovation.*

Farm Builders Historical Consulting Service will Research and Provide background information for any Restoration Project.

FREE Sample and Catalog available on Request

for more information call

Farm Builders Inc.
4708 Roland Avenue
Baltimore, Maryland 21210
(301) 235-4260

Treat Yourself

and your house to a taste of the great outdoors...

The Open Doors

"Open Doors" are beautiful #1 clear redwood screen doors exquisitely designed and patterned after Victorian and period styles. In 4 decorative patterns. Write for free brochure.

Dealer and wholesale inquiries invited.

JMR Products
1335 Main Street, Dept. JC
St. Helena, CA 94574

Designers guide to fancy cut cedar shingles.

Create unique interiors or exteriors with Fancy Cuts cedar shingles. Choose from 9 distinctive styles to design a limitless variety of traditional or contemporary patterns with textural effects. Nationally distributed. For sample, design guide and specs., write: Shakertown Corp., Dept. OH, Winlock, WA 98596.

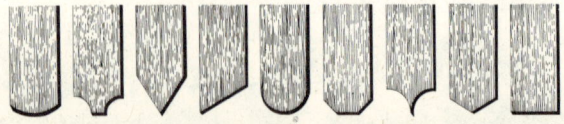

FISH SCALE HALF-COVE DIAMOND DIAGONAL ROUND OCTAGON ARROW HEXAGON SQUARE

Other Exterior Restoration & Maintenance Materials

Salvage Building Materials (Boards, Beams, Posts, etc.)

Addco Architectural Antiques (LA)
Barn People, The (VT)
Belcher, Robert W. (GA)
Carlisle Restoration Lumber (NH)
Castle Burlingame (NJ)
Croton, Evelyn — Architectural Antiques (NY)
Farm Builders, Inc. (MD)
Pelnik Wrecking Co., Inc. (NY)
Sloane, Hugh L. (MA)
Vintage Lumber Co. (MD)
Walker, Dennis C. (OH)

See Company Directory
for
Addresses & Phone Numbers

PRETTY AND PLAIN

In restoring an old house that is historically significant or architecturally distinctive, the repair or replacement of architectural features and ornamental details should be as close to the original as possible.

Many an old house can be called an honest bread-loaf of a building, built with simple integrity for a plain function by plain people. Others were embellished with fancy porches or decorative brackets late in the 19th century. Still others would not be compromised by the addition of a bit of tasteful ornament today.

Keep in mind that the original owner may just not have had the money or inclination to add those few enriching details to the exterior. Keep in mind, too, that whatever you add will become part of the house's history. Quality is in the workmanship, the materials, and the appropriateness. Your work should elicit delight—not chuckles or sneers—fifty years down the road.

Exterior Ornament & Architectural Details

Architectural Millwork
(1) Stock Items
(2) Custom Fabrication

Addco Architectural Antiques (LA) 2
Amherst Woodworking & Supply (MA) 2
Architectural Components (MA) 2
Architectural Woodworking (CT) 2
Art Directions (MO) 2
Berman, B.K. Victorian Millshop (CO) 2
Breakfast Woodworks Louis Mackall & Co. (CT) 2
C—E Morgan (WI) 1
Campbell, Douglas Co. (RI) 2
Campbell, Marion (PA) 2
Carpenter Assoc., Inc. (NH) 2
Center Lumber Company (NJ) 1,2
Crawford's Old House Store (WI) 1
Cumberland Woodcraft Co., Inc. (PA) 1
Curvoflite (NH) 2
Dimension Lumber Co. (NY) 2
Dixon Bros. Woodworking (MA) 2
Driwood Moulding Company (SC) 1,2
Drums Sash & Door Co., Inc. (PA) 1
Elliott Millwork Co. (IL) 1
F M P (TX) 1,2
Hallelujah Redwood Products (CA) 1,2
Henderson Black & Greene, Inc. (AL) 1
House Carpenters (MA) 2
Island City Wood Working Co. (TX) 2
Kingsway (CO) 1
Mad River Wood Works (CA) 2
Maurer & Shepherd, Joyners (CT) 2
Michael's Fine Colonial Products (NY) ... 2
Miles Lumber Co, Inc. (VT) 2
Millworks Inc. (VT) 2
Moose Creek Restoration, Ltd. (VT) 2
Mountain Lumber Company (VA) 2
Newby, Simon (MA) 2
Nord, E.A. Company (WA) 1
North Pacific Joinery (CA) 2
Old'N Ornate Wooden Reproductions (OR) 2
Period Productions, Limited (VA) 2
Pyramid Woodcraft Corp. (TX) 2
Robillard, Dennis Paul, Inc. (ME) 2
San Francisco Renaissance (CA) 2
San Francisco Victoriana (CA) 1
Silverton Victorian Millworks (CO) 2
Somerset Door & Column Co. (PA) 2
Strobel Millwork (CT) 2
The Restoration Fraternity (PA) 2
Turnbull's Custom Mouldings (MI) 2
Victorian Millshop (CO) 1,2
Victorian Reproductions, Inc. (MN)
Vintage Wood Works (TX) 1,2
Weir, R. & Co. (MA) 2
Wood Designs (OH) 1
Woodstone Co. (VT) 2

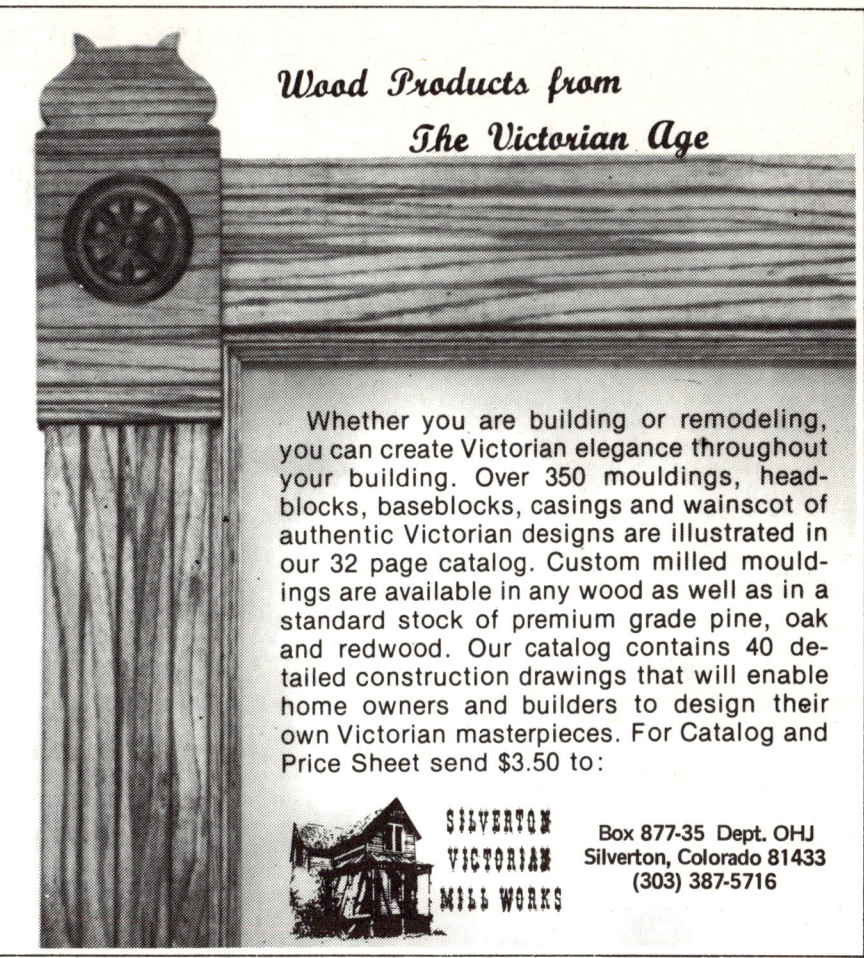

Wood Products from The Victorian Age

Whether you are building or remodeling, you can create Victorian elegance throughout your building. Over 350 mouldings, headblocks, baseblocks, casings and wainscot of authentic Victorian designs are illustrated in our 32 page catalog. Custom milled mouldings are available in any wood as well as in a standard stock of premium grade pine, oak and redwood. Our catalog contains 40 detailed construction drawings that will enable home owners and builders to design their own Victorian masterpieces. For Catalog and Price Sheet send $3.50 to:

SILVERTON VICTORIAN MILL WORKS
Box 877-35 Dept. OHJ
Silverton, Colorado 81433
(303) 387-5716

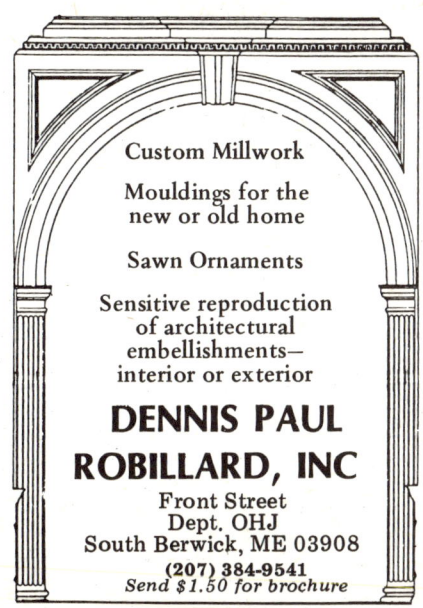

Custom Millwork

Mouldings for the new or old home

Sawn Ornaments

Sensitive reproduction of architectural embellishments— interior or exterior

DENNIS PAUL ROBILLARD, INC
Front Street
Dept. OHJ
South Berwick, ME 03908
(207) 384-9541
Send $1.50 for brochure

..a collection of polyurethane corbels, finials, and brackets by

Peter Wolf Concepts
For

Renovation Products
5302 Junius Dallas, Texas 75214 214-827-5111

Send $2.00 for a complete catalogue.

Brackets, Buttresses & Corbels—Exterior

(1) Stone
(2) Stamped Metal
(3) Wood

Art Directions (MO)
Berman, B.K. Victorian Millshop (CO) 3
ByGone Era (GA)
Croton, Evelyn — Architectural Antiques (NY) 1
Cumberland Woodcraft Co., Inc. (PA) 3
Hallelujah Redwood Products (CA) 3
International Architecture (TX) 1
Kenneth Lynch & Sons, Inc. (CT) 2
Old'N Ornate Wooden Reproductions (OR) .. 3
Period Productions, Limited (VA) 3
Pyramid Woodcraft Corp. (TX) 3
Renovation Products (TX) 3
Robillard, Dennis Paul, Inc. (ME) 3
Silverton Victorian Millworks (CO) 3
Victorian Millshop (CO) 3
Vintage Wood Works (TX) 3
Wrecking Bar, Inc. (TX)

Columns & Capitals—Exterior

(1) Wood
(2) Stone
(3) Plaster
(4) Iron
(5) Fiberglass
(6) Metal

American Wood Column (NY) 1
Architectural Sculpture (NY) 5
Biagiotti, L. (NY) 3
ByGone Era (GA)
Campbellsville Industries (KY) 6
Chilstone Garden Ornament (UK) 2
Croton, Evelyn — Architectural Antiques (NY)
Decorators Supply Corp. (IL) 3
Elk Valley Woodworking Company (OK) ... 1
Felber, Inc. (PA) 3
Hartman — Sanders Company (GA) 1,5
Henderson Black & Greene, Inc. (AL) 1
International Architecture (TX) 2
Lachin, Albert & Assoc., Inc. (LA) 2
Nord, E.A. Company (WA) 1
Period Productions, Limited (VA) 1
Saldarini & Pucci, Inc. (NY) 1
San Francisco Victoriana (CA) 1,3
Schwerd Manufacturing Co. (PA) 1
Somerset Door & Column Co. (PA) 1
Tennessee Fabricating Co. (TN) 4
Verine Products & Co. (UK) 5
Wrecking Bar, Inc. (TX)

Cornices—Exterior

(1) Wood
(2) Stamped Metal
(3) Fiberglass

Architectural Sculpture (NY) 3
Campbellsville Industries (KY) 2
Cumberland Woodcraft Co., Inc. (PA) 1
Fypon, Inc. (PA) 3
Hallelujah Redwood Products (CA) 1
Kenneth Lynch & Sons, Inc. (CT) 2
Period Productions, Limited (VA) 1
Saldarini & Pucci, Inc. (NY) 3
Wagner, Albert J., & Son (IL) 2

See Company Directory for Addresses & Phone Numbers

Gingerbread Trim—Wood

(1) Stock Items
(2) Custom Fabrication

Cumberland Woodcraft Co., Inc. (PA) 1
Hallelujah Redwood Products (CA) 1,2
Mad River Wood Works (CA) 2
Millworks Inc. (VT) 2
North Pacific Joinery (CA) 2
Old'N Ornate Wooden Reproductions (OR) 2
Rejuvenation House Parts Co. (OR)
Renovation Products (TX) 1
San Francisco Victoriana (CA) 1
Silverton Victorian Millworks (CO) 1,2
Victorian Building & Repair (IL) 2
Vintage Wood Works (TX) 1,2

Gutters, Leaders & Leader Boxes

(1) Wood
(2) Copper
(3) Lead
(4) Other

Alte, Jeff Roofing, Inc. (NJ) 2
Conklin Tin Plate & Metal Co. (GA) 2,4
Kenneth Lynch & Sons, Inc. (CT) 2,3
Wagner, Albert J., & Son (IL) 2

Mouldings, Exterior Wood

(1) Stock Items
(2) Custom-Made

Architectural Components (MA) 2
Bendix Mouldings, Inc. (NJ) 1
Berman, B.K. Victorian Millshop (CO) 2
Center Lumber Company (NJ) 2
Driwood Moulding Company (SC) 1
Drums Sash & Door Co., Inc. (PA) 2
Elliott Millwork Co. (IL) 1
Hallelujah Redwood Products (CA) 1
Mad River Wood Works (CA) 2
Michael's Fine Colonial Products (NY) 2
Millworks Inc. (VT) 2
North Pacific Joinery (CA) 2
Period Productions, Limited (VA) 2
Robillard, Dennis Paul, Inc. (ME) 2
Silverton Victorian Millworks (CO) 1,2
Turnbull's Custom Mouldings (MI) 2
Victorian Millshop (CO) 1
Weir, R. & Co. (MA) 2
Wood Designs (OH) 1

ALUMINUM PRODUCTS
Custom Fabrication
CORNICES
LOUVERS
CUPOLAS
COLUMNS
BALUSTRADES
SHUTTERS
URNS & BALLS
Baked on finishes available
call or write

CAMPBELLSVILLE INDUSTRIES, INC.
P.O. Box 278, Dept. OHJ
Campbellsville, KY 42718
502-465-8135

MAKING GINGERBREAD

Sawn wood ornament was originally popular because it was inexpensive: A carpenter could cut and install it at the building site.

While it might no longer be inexpensive, sawn wood ornament does have the virtue of being quite easy to restore and duplicate. Seemingly complex gingerbread detail can often be built up from simple pieces. If you can't match the orginal exactly, the important thing with exterior trim is to duplicate the mass and rhythm of the original. As long as you can fill in vacant spaces with reasonable facsimiles, very few people will ever detect the new work.

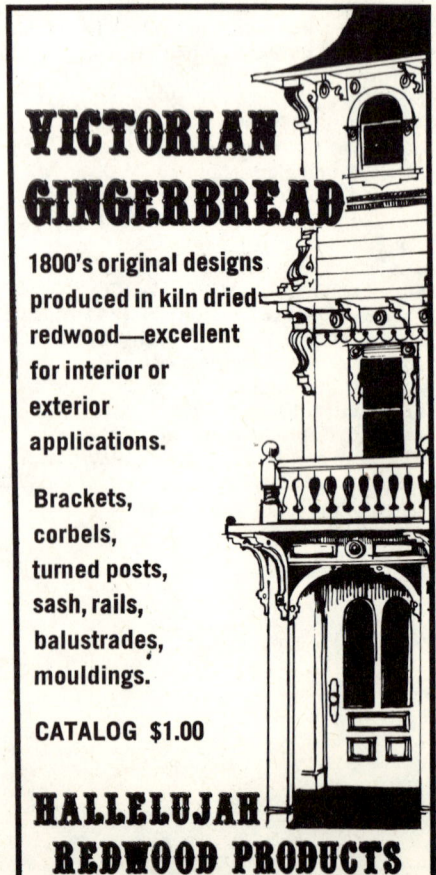

VICTORIAN GINGERBREAD

1800's original designs produced in kiln dried redwood—excellent for interior or exterior applications.

Brackets, corbels, turned posts, sash, rails, balustrades, mouldings.

CATALOG $1.00

HALLELUJAH REDWOOD PRODUCTS
PO Box 669, Mendocino CA 95460

SCHWERD'S
Quality Wood Columns
the standard of quality since 1860

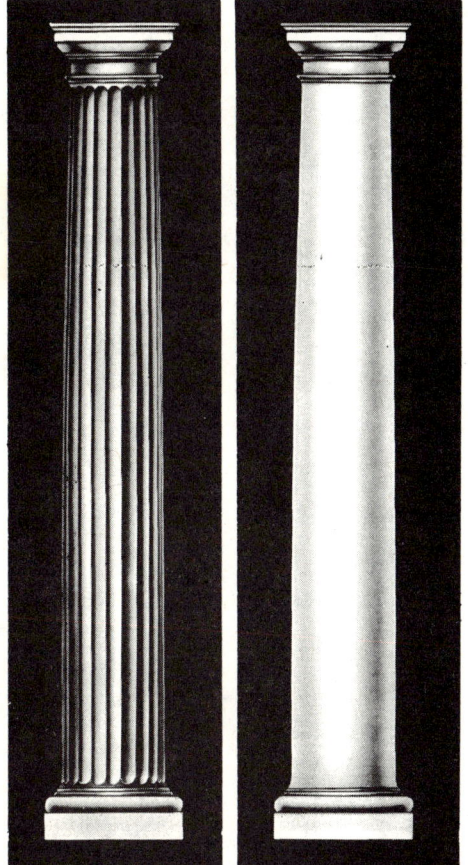

COLUMNS—Schwerd columns are durable. Our 100 + years of experience in manufacturing wood columns has proven that the durability of a wood column depends upon the strength of the joint and the quality and thickness of the wood. Schwerd column construction was developed to meet each specific requirement. The wood is the highest quality,, thoroughly seasoned Northern White Pine. The pride of craftsmanship and skilled techniques acquired by 100 years of specialized experience is applied. The resulting product is a "Schwerd Quality Column" specified by architects with complete confidence. Both standard and detail columns can be furnished from 4 in. to 50 in. in diameter and up to 40 ft. in length with matching pilasters.

If you are one of our old customers during the many years since our beginning in 1860 you know our product, if not, send us your inquiries and orders and join our list of satisfied customers.

Schwerd's complete aluminum bases
are available for 8, 10, 12, 14, 16, 20, 22, and 24 in. dia. columns.

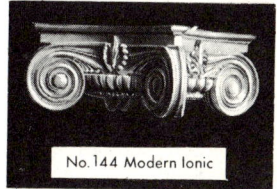

Schwerd's—Aluminum ventilated plinth and aluminum turned member base recommended for all exterior columns in the above diameters to provide a maintenance free, seamless base which is guaranteed against deterioration for a lifetime. Manufactured of 1/4 in. thick metal and a load-bearing capacity of 22,000 lbs.

A. F. SCHWERD MANUFACTURING COMPANY
telephone: 412-766-6322
3215 McClure Avenue   Pittsburgh, Pa. 15212

Mouldings, Exterior

(1) Ceramic
(2) Fiberglass
(3) Plaster
(4) Terra Cotta
(5) Stone
(6) Other

Architectural Sculpture (NY) 2,3
Architectural Terra Cotta and Tile, Ltd. (IL)
.... 4
Biagiotti, L. (NY) 3,6
Decorators Supply Corp. (IL) 3
Felber, Inc. (PA) 2,3
Fypon, Inc. (PA) 6
Gladding, McBean & Co. (CA) 4
International Architecture (TX) 5
Lachin, Albert & Assoc., Inc. (LA) 5
Saldarini & Pucci, Inc. (NY) 3
Up Country Enterprise Corp. (NH)

Porch Parts

(1) Stock Items
(2) Custom Work

Cumberland Woodcraft Co., Inc. (PA) 1,2
Dixon Bros. Woodworking (MA) 2
Hallelujah Redwood Products (CA) 1,2
Henderson Black & Greene, Inc. (AL) 1
Michael's Fine Colonial Products (NY) 2
Michael-Regan Wood Turnings (CA) 1
Nord, E.A. Company (WA) 1
North Pacific Joinery (CA) 2
Old'N Ornate Wooden Reproductions (OR) 2
Period Productions, Limited (VA) 2
Robillard, Dennis Paul, Inc. (ME) 2
Vintage Wood Works (TX) 1

Stamped Metal Ornament

Capitals • *Wreaths* • *Brackets*

Shown above are just some of the 3,000 pieces of stamped metal ornament offered in big 128-pg. catalog. These are not reproductions; stampings are made from original dies. This is the same metalwork that decorated thousands of late 19th and early 20th century buildings. For Catalog #7474 and price lists, send $3.50 to:

KENNETH LYNCH & SONS
78 Danbury Road
Wilton, CT 06897

Classic Grandeur In Wood

Somerset Columns

ANY SIZE—up to 40 inches in diameter and 40 feet long.

ANY DESIGN—built to architects specifications. Custom scale drawings are available.

VARIETY OF WOODS—the very finest seasoned pines, redwood and poplar in stock.

HIGHEST QUALITY MATERIALS AND TECHNIQUES—assure strong, permanent columns.

USED IN—residences, churches, colleges, inns, convalescent homes, funeral homes.

SOMERSET DOOR & COLUMN CO.
Box 328 Somerset Pa. 15501 (814) 445-9608
—*Send for our 8-page brochure*—

The Original Official 1916 Wood Moulding Guide

Featuring:
• Hundreds of actual turn of the century Wood Moulding Profiles.

• Complete section of Exterior and Interior Wood Moulding Profiles in use in 1916 and earlier.

Only $9.95 Postage Paid

Zillman Associates
Dept. OHJC
P. O. Box 370
Danville, IL 61832

Your complete source for VICTORIAN MILLWORK

Replicas of 19th century originals in kiln dried, premium grade *solid* Oak or Poplar.

Our expanded line includes designs for all interior and exterior applications; rails and balustrades, brackets, corbels, posts, grilles, fretwork, and much, much more!

- Precision manufactured so that product groups are compatible with each other for total design unity.
- Unlimited quantities for total design freedom.
- Factory direct affordable pricing.
- Custom millwork available for unusual requirements.

Send $3.50 for complete 24 page, full color catalog and Price List.

CUMBERLAND WOODCRAFT COMPANY, INC. Dept. 40
2500 Walnut Bottom Road
Carlisle, PA 17013   (717) 243-0063

---

period gingerbread, fretwork & gable treatments • period screen doors, porch swings & double facing glider turnings, finials, posts & columns plain & fancy wood stair parts & fancy cut cedar shingles • cupboard & door trim kits & moldings decorative wood & fibre carvings wood, styrene & urethane moldings & brackets • wood, brass & porcelain bath accessories & switchplates cupolas, weathervanes & fauna faucets • wood & brass house numbers & letters • cast table bases, park benches & lamp posts gargoyles & cenotaphs • steel ceiling & ceiling medallions

RENOVATION PRODUCTS
5302 Junius Dallas, Texas 75214 214-827-5111

SHUTTERS OR BLINDS ?

If the panels are solid they are called blinds. If they are slatted they are shutters. Originally they were used for protection or ventilation. Nowadays they are used all too often to confer instant antiquity. But properly used, wooden shutters or blinds can enhance the appearance of an old house. They might not always serve their original function, but they must look as if they could.

Shutters & Blinds, Exterior Wood

(1) New (Stock Items)
(2) Custom-Made

A.R.D. (NY) 1
Addco Architectural Antiques (LA) 2
Architectural Components (MA) 2
Beauti-home (CA) 2
Cumberland Woodcraft Co., Inc. (PA)
Iberia Millwork (LA) 2
Island City Wood Working Co. (TX) 2
Maurer & Shepherd, Joyners (CT) 2
Michael's Fine Colonial Products (NY) ... 2
Miles Lumber Co, Inc. (VT)
National Shutters and Millwork (NY)
Nord, E.A. Company (WA) 1
Period Productions, Limited (VA) 2
The Restoration Fraternity (PA) 2

See Company Directory for Addresses & Phone Numbers

Replacement Sash, any size, layout, circle, oval, gothic, cottage. Sash or complete window unit. Custom mouldings, doors, Raised panel shutters, millwork to detail. Send sketch, specifications for price.

Michael's Fine Colonial Products
Custom Millwork
Rte. 44, Box 179A, Salt Point, NY 12578
(914) 677-3960

The Old-House Journal 1982 Catalog 23

THE FRONT DOOR

A well-known restoration architect compared the main entrance of a house to the human mouth as an indicator of character. Carrying the analogy further he compares such metal additions as raw aluminum storm doors to dental braces in their visual appeal.

Even more than windows, doorways have been the victims of the unthinking remuddler seeking an instant up-date or quick Colonial effect. Replacing a clownish front door with an appropriate salvaged or reproduction exterior door will restore dignity to an old house with gratifying ease.

Exterior Doors, Reproduction

(1) Early American
(2) Victorian
(3) Turn-of-Century
(4) Custom-Made
(5) Other

Architectural Components (MA)
Bel-Air Door Co. (CA) 1,2,3,5
Carlisle Restoration Lumber (NH) 1
Cascade Mill & Glass Works (CO) 4
Driwood Moulding Company (SC) 4
Drums Sash & Door Co., Inc. (PA) 1,2,3,4
Elliott Millwork Co. (IL)
Feather River Wood and Glass Co. (CA) 2
Gibbons, John — Cabinetmaker (WI) 3,4
Kingsway (CO) 2
Landmark Doors (NY) 2,3
Maurer & Shepherd, Joyners (CT) 4
Nord, E.A. Company (WA) 1
North Pacific Joinery (CA) 4
Period Productions, Limited (VA) 4
Pocahontas Hardware & Glass (IL) 2
Robillard, Dennis Paul, Inc. (ME) 4
Spanish Pueblo Doors (NM) 4
Strobel Millwork (CT) 4
The Restoration Fraternity (PA) 4
Victorian Millshop (CO) 4
Wood Designs (OH)
Woodstone Co. (VT) 4

Exterior Doors, Antique (Salvage)

Architectural Antique Warehouse, The (CAN)
Architectural Antiques Exchange (PA)
Bare Wood Inc. (NY)
ByGone Era (GA)
Canal Co. (DC)
Castle Burlingame (NJ)
Ley, Joe/Antiques (KY)
Olde Bostonian Architectural Antiques (MA)
Red Baron's Antiques (GA)
Sloane, Hugh L. (MA)
United House Wrecking Corp. (CT)
Wrecking Bar, Inc. (TX)

YESTERDAY'S QUALITY TODAY

• Entry Systems • Doors • Sidelights • Decorative Glass •

Feather River Wood & Glass Co.

P.O. Box 444
Durham CA
95938

Reproduction Work For 18th Century Homes
Raised Panel Walls, 18th Century Windows and Entranceways

Authentic Colonial Joinery

Maurer & Shepherd, Joyners

122 naubuc ave., glastonbury, ct. 06033

(203) 633-2383

The Cascade Mill & Glass Works Presents...

*THE SAN JUAN COLLECTION

The Cascade Mill & Glass Works offers a select collection of highest quality, handcrafted entry, interior and screen doors. Constructed of only the finest wood and glass materials. Elegantly visible reminders of gracious living and quality craftsmanship of the "days of yesteryear."

SELECT WOODS ranging from Red Oak and Honduras Mahogany, custom orders of Walnut, Rosewood, Teak, Cherry and Pine.

EXPOSED MORTISE & TENON JOINTS wedged to achieve lasting quality that only hand-craftsmanship can ensure.

DOUBLE TONGUE & GROOVE GLUE JOINTS on all laminated panels.

HAND SHAPED MOLDING precisely mitred.

ROSETTES, HALF TURNINGS & SPINDLES created by hand.

HAND GROUND & POLISHED BEVELLED GLASS. Glass inserts may be all patterned bevelled glass, bevelled glass in combination with European stained glass, or clear glass with a 1" bevelled border.

Catalog $2.50

*The doors in the San Juan Collection are named after 19th Century gold and silver mines located in the San Juan Mountains of Colorado.

CASCADE MILL & GLASS WORKS • P.O. BOX 316 • OURAY, COLORADO 81427
TELEPHONE (303) 325-4780

Entryways & Door Framing Woodwork—Reproduction

(1) Early American
(2) Victorian
(3) Stock Items
(4) Salvage
(5) Custom-Made

Bare Wood Inc. (NY)
Berman, B.K. Victorian Millshop (CO) 5
C—E Morgan (WI) 3
Drums Sash & Door Co., Inc. (PA) 1,2,5
Fypon, Inc. (PA) 1
Gibbons, John — Cabinetmaker (WI) 5
Henderson Black & Greene, Inc. (AL) 1,3
Island City Wood Working Co. (TX) 5
Kensington Historical Co. (NH) 4
Kingsway (CO) 2
Maurer & Shepherd, Joyners (CT) 5
Michael's Fine Colonial Products (NY) 5
Period Productions, Limited (VA) 5
Somerset Door & Column Co. (PA) 5
Strobel Millwork (CT) 5
The Restoration Fraternity (PA) 5
United House Wrecking Corp. (CT) 4
Woodstone Co. (VT) 5
Wrecking Bar, Inc. (TX) 4

THE RIGHT WINDOWS

Fenestration—the art of placing window openings in a building wall—is one of the most important elements controlling the appearance of a house. Among the factors affecting the appearance of windows are size, shape and spacing of the window opening; type of sash—the framework in which the panes of glass or lights are set; number of lights in the sash; ornamentation surrounding the sash.

When sash cannot be restored with caulk, wood preservative, putty and paint, it should be replaced with sash that is consistent with the original design of the house. If ornamentation is missing or beyond repair and it is impossible to totally duplicate the original detailing, replace with a unit that duplicates the dimensions of the original. Thus, to the eye the rhythm and line of the structure will remain unchanged.

Window Balances (Replacement Channels)

Crawford's Old House Store (WI)
Quaker City Manufacturing Co. (PA)

Window Sash Weights—Cast Iron

Waterbury Foundry Co. (CT)

Window Frames & Sash—Period

(1) Early American
(2) Victorian
(3) New (Stock Items)
(4) Salvage
(5) Custom-Made

Air-Flo Window Contracting Corp. (NY) 3
Architectural Components (MA) 5
Crawford's Old House Store (WI) 1,2,5
Dovetail, Inc. (MA) 3
Drums Sash & Door Co., Inc. (PA) 3,5
Gibbons, John — Cabinetmaker (WI) 5
Hallelujah Redwood Products (CA) 3
Island City Wood Working Co. (TX) 5
Kensington Historical Co. (NH) 4
Kingsway (CO) 2
Lavoie, John F. (VT)
Manchester Lite (MA) 1
Maurer & Shepherd, Joyners (CT) 5
Michael's Fine Colonial Products (NY) 1,5
Moose Creek Restoration, Ltd. (VT) 5
Period Productions, Limited (VA) 1,2,5
Robillard, Dennis Paul, Inc. (ME) 5
Silverton Victorian Millworks (CO) 5
Smith, R.W. — Sashmaker (MA) 1
Somerset Door & Column Co. (PA) 5
Strobel Millwork (CT) 5
The Restoration Fraternity (PA) 5
Victorian Millshop (CO) 3

Crawford's Old House Store

Old Fashioned Windows

If you're looking for authentic wood windows for your old house, you've found them! We have a complete selection... and made to order!

Send $1.50, refundable, for our complete catalog. We have what you're looking for!

301 McCall Waukesha, Wisconsin 53186

See Company Directory for Addresses & Phone Numbers

Windows, Special Architectural Shapes (Rounds, Ovals, Fanlights, Transoms, Etc.)

Bare Wood Inc. (NY)
Bendheim, S.A. Co., Inc. (NY)
Crawford's Old House Store (WI)
Kraatz Hand Blown Glass (NH)
Lavoie, John F. (VT)
Manchester Lite (MA)
Pompei Stained Glass (MA)
Woodstone Co. (VT)

Window Glass, Clear—Handmade

(1) New
(2) Antique (Salvage)

Bendheim, S.A. Co., Inc. (NY) 1
Bienenfeld Ind. Inc. (NY) 1
Castle Burlingame (NJ) 2
Kensington Historical Co. (NH) 2
Kraatz Hand Blown Glass (NH)
Sloane, Hugh L. (MA) 2
Vintage Lumber Co. (MD) 2
Whittemore-Durgin Glass Co. (MA) 1

Window Glass, Curved

Shadovitz Bros. Distributors, Inc. (NY)

FOR THOSE WHO APPRECIATE **HISTORICAL WINDOWS**

Gracefully enhance your restoration or new construction with finely detailed transoms, quarter circles or round and oval windows.

John F. Lavoie
P.O Box 15
Springfield, VT 05156  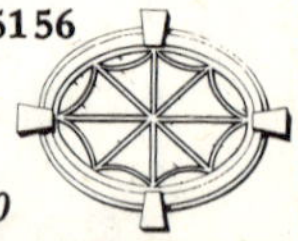
802-886-8253

Brochure $2.00

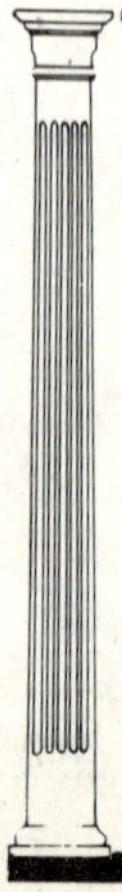

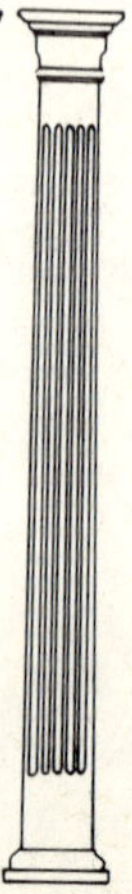

Quality Millwork Since 1926

- Columns
- Turned Porch Posts
- Entrance Features
- Sidelights (1/8" Temp. & I.G.)
- Spindles & Balusters
- Handrail & Newel Posts
- Fireplace Mantels
- Ironing Board Cabinets

Henderson, Black & Greene, Inc.
Post Office Box 589/Troy, Alabama 36081/(205) 566-5000

26 The Old-House Journal 1982 Catalog

THE RIGHT HARDWARE

Before 1800 the local blacksmith was the hardware man. In country houses the simple Suffolk thumb latch and the later, more elaborate Norfolk latch with a rolled sheet-iron back plate continued to be used through the 19th century. Surface mounted spring latches and box locks were used on the better buildings. Wrought iron bolts provided added security. Imported English hardware and brass hardware were used in urban areas and on the main entrances of the finer rural buildings.

By 1860 manufacturer's catalogs featured full lines of machine-made hardware, plain and fancy. But handwrought items continued to be made and used. Outbuildings and less important doors tended to have older or simpler hardware and thus it is not unusual to find a variety of hardware on one building.

Period hardware can be found in antique and salvage shops. Authentic reproductions are now readily available. When stylistically appropriate, fine blacksmith-made latches are worthwhile for exterior doors.

Hardware, Exterior

Door Hardware, Exterior

(1) Brass & Bronze
(2) Wrought Iron
(3) Door Knockers
(4) Rim Locks
(5) Mortised Locks
(6) Latches, Hand Forged
(7) Mail Slots
(8) Hinges
(9) Strap Hinges

18th Century Hardware Co. (PA) *3,6,9*
Abraxas International, Inc. (CA) *3*
Baldwin Hardware Mfg. Corp. (PA)
.... *1,3,4,5,6,7*
Ball and Ball (PA) *1,2,3,4,5,6,8,9*
Barnett, D. James — Blacksmith (IL) *6,8*
Bona Decorative Hardware (OH) *1,3,5*
Broadway Collection (MO) *1,3,4*
Canal Co. (DC) *1*
Castle Burlingame (NJ) *4,6,8,9*
Cohasset Colonials (MA) *8*
Colonial Lock Company (CT) *2,4*
Custom House (ME) *1,3*
Dover Furniture Stripping (DE)
Folger Adam Co. (IL) *1,4,8*
Guerin, P.E. Inc. (NY) *1,3*
Hartland Forge (NH) *6,9*
Horton Brasses (CT) *3*
Howland, John — Metalsmith (CT) *1,2,8*
Hunrath, Wm. Co., Inc. (NY)
Kayne, Steve — Hand-Forged Hardware (NY) *1,2,3,6,9*
Kingsway (CO) *1,3,7,8*
Millham, Newton — Blacksmith (MA)
.... *2,3,6,8,9*
Old English Brass, Ltd. (MO) *1,3,7,8*
Pfanstiel Hardware Co. (NY) *1,3*
Renovator's Supply (MA)
Ritter & Son Hardware (CA) *3*
San Francisco Victoriana (CA) *1,8*
Sign of the Crab (CA) *1*
Smithy, The (VT) *2,3,6,8,9*
Wallin Forge (KY) *2,3,6,8,9*
Weaver, W. T. & Sons, Inc. (DC) *1,3,4*
Williamsburg Blacksmiths, Inc. (MA)
.... *2,3,6,8,9*
Wolchonok, M. and Son, Inc. (NY) *1,4,5*

The Old-House Journal 1982 Catalog

Exterior Hardware, Custom-Made

(1) Cast Brass & Bronze
(2) Hand-Forged Iron
(3) Cast Iron

Arrowhead Forge (ME) 2
Ball and Ball (PA) 1,2,3
G. Krug & Son (MD) 3
Hartland Forge (NH) 2
Kayne, Steve — Hand-Forged Hardware (NY) 1,2
Leo, Brian (MN) 1
Millham, Newton — Blacksmith (MA) 2
RAM's Forge (MD) 2
Ricker Blacksmith Shop (ME) 2
San Francisco Victoriana (CA) 1
Schwartz's Forge & Metalworks (NY) 2
Smithy, The (VT) 2
Tennessee Fabricating Co. (TN) 3
Travis Tuck, Metal Sculptor (MA) 2
Woodbury Blacksmith & Forge Co. (CT) 2

Doorbells—Period Designs

(1) Electric
(2) Mechanical

Ball and Ball (PA)
Bona Decorative Hardware (OH) 2
Cumberland General Store (TN) 2
Dover Furniture Stripping (DE) 2
Period Furniture Hardware Co. (MA) 1
Renovator's Supply (MA)
Restoration Works, Inc. (NY) 2
Sign of the Crab (CA)

Shutter Hardware (Hinges, Holdbacks, Etc.)

Ball and Ball (PA)
Castle Burlingame (NJ)
Crawford's Old House Store (WI)
Dover Furniture Stripping (DE)
Millham, Newton — Blacksmith (MA)
Renovator's Supply (MA)
Smithy, The (VT)
Weaver, W. T. & Sons, Inc. (DC)
Williamsburg Blacksmiths, Inc. (MA)
Wrightsville Hardware (PA)

Other Exterior Hardware

18th Century Hardware Co. (PA)

Rim Deadbolt Lock

Laminated Steel Bolt
No. 1776 Knob Inside — Key Outside
No. 1776½ Key Inside — Key Outside
■ Cast Iron Case and Keeper — Black
$19.95 ppd. each

Colonial Lock Company
172 Main St., Terryville, Conn. 06786

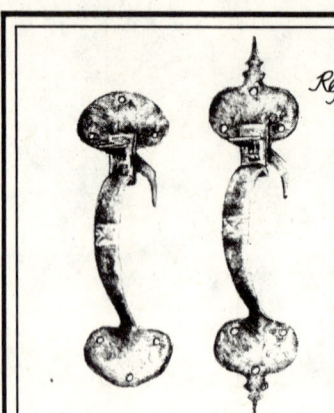

Reproductions of Early American Hardware

WILLIAMSBURG BLACKSMITHS, INC.

1 Buttonshop Rd. Dept. OHJ
Williamsburg, MA 01096

Catalog $2.50   (Brochure $.50)

AUTHENTIC *Williamsburg*®

BRASS RIM LOCKS & HINGES

Cast from an authentic brass formula which duplicates the mix used in original locks.

"Williamsburg" brass rim locks are authentic reproductions of genuine antiques which are preserved in the buildings in the colonial village of Williamsburg, Virginia. These locks and hinges meet all required standards and are approved by The Colonial Williamsburg Foundation.

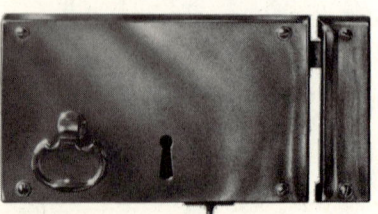
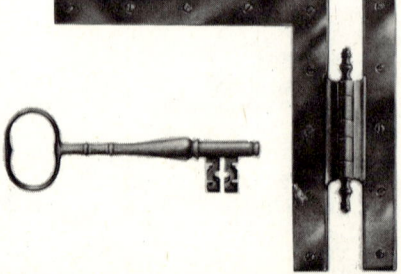

 Please call or write:

FOLGER ADAM CO.   P.O. Box 688 • Joliet, IL 60434 • Tel. 815/723-3438

CARING FOR IRON

By the mid 19th century cast iron had largely taken the place of wrought iron, and architectural ironwork had become readily available throughout most of the country. The Victorians made everything they could out of iron—stairs, fences, gates, grilles, crestings, railings and balconies, urns, fountains, furniture, pagodas and verandahs.

Replacing missing iron is not impossible, though it can be expensive. Ironwork is very much an active craft today. If the piece is not structural, consider aluminum castings—often a satisfactory substitute for iron. Aluminum is easier to ship and, once painted, is undistinguishable from iron.

Ornamental ironwork can last a very long time with the correct care and maintenance. Rust is the enemy and the key to its prevention is proper painting.

The first step is to remove all rust, grime and scaling paint with a wire brush, scraper and heavy sandpaper. It is often advisable to strip off all the old paint to bring out the fine details of the ironwork. Chemical removers and burning with an electric hot air gun or an inexpensive propane gas gun are do-it-yourself methods. Sandblasting the iron should be done only by professionals.

Once clean, the surface must be primed immediately with a coat of rust-retarding primer. Joints and bolt holes, which hold moisture, must be caulked. The primer should be left to cure according to the instructions on the label. Oil based paint used with a compatible primer will prevent most bonding problems. The finish paint should go on a clean, dust-free surface in two thin (not thinned) coats, with a proper drying time in between. Exterior enamel—glossy—offers the most resistance to dirt and abrasion. The most popular colors for ornamental ironwork have always been black, dark green and brown.

America's historic legacy includes many homes and public buildings. An integral part of those built between 1820 and 1900 was usually some distinctive form of wrought or cast iron, or a combination thereof.

Whether the ironwork of your home has been destroyed by an accident, is losing the battle of time with rust, or was removed in an attempt to 'modernize,' we will work with you to restore or recreate historically accurate interior or exterior ironwork.

We utilize the original methods and materials of the craft wherever possible. We make our own patterns, and cast our own iron.

Our goal, as always, is restoration.

Architectural Iron Company

Restorations in Cast and Wrought Iron

Box 674
Milford, Pennsylvania 18337

(717) 296-6371

Ironwork, Exterior

Balusters & Handrails, Iron—Period Designs

(1) Cast Iron
(2) Wrought Iron

G. Krug & Son (MD) 1,2
Gorsuch Foundry (IN) 1
Schwartz's Forge & Metalworks (NY) 2
Tennessee Fabricating Co. (TN)
Travis Tuck, Metal Sculptor (MA) 2

Cast Aluminum, Exterior Ornamental

Campbellsville Industries (KY)
Moultrie Manufacturing Company (GA)

Cast Iron, Exterior Ornamental

Oliver, Bradley C. (PA)
Robinson Iron Corporation (AL)
Stewart Manufacturing Company (KY)
Tennessee Fabricating Co. (TN)

Cast Iron, Custom Casting

Architectural Iron Company (PA)
Clarksville Foundry & Machine Works (TN)
G. Krug & Son (MD)
Gorsuch Foundry (IN)
Robinson Iron Corporation (AL)
Tennessee Fabricating Co. (TN)

Cresting

(1) Cast Iron
(2) Fiberglass

Rejuvenation House Parts Co. (OR) 1
Robinson Iron Corporation (AL) 1
Tennessee Fabricating Co. (TN) 1

Railings, Balconies & Window Grilles

(1) Cast Iron
(2) Wrought Iron

Architectural Antique Warehouse, The (CAN) 1
Architectural Antiques Exchange (PA)
Gorsuch Foundry (IN) 1
Mexico House (CA) 2
RAM's Forge (MD) 2
Robinson Iron Corporation (AL) 1
Schwartz's Forge & Metalworks (NY) 2
Tennessee Fabricating Co. (TN) 1
Travis Tuck, Metal Sculptor (MA) 2

Wrought Iron Ornaments, Stock Items

Claymont Forge (WV)
Tennessee Fabricating Co. (TN)

See Company Directory for Addresses & Phone Numbers

The Old-House Journal 1982 Catalog

The Courtyard: Montgomery, Alabama.
The Courtyard is an outstanding re-creation of the French Quarter in New Orleans. Over 26 tons of ornamental brackets, runners, column bases and capitals, lampposts, furniture, and fountains went into the construction of the office-shopping complex.

Robinson Iron is the source for cast iron originals. Choose from an extensive collection of unique designs, all aesthetically beautiful, all intricately detailed, many manufactured from exclusive pre-Civil War patterns. For traditional or contemporary environments, Robinson's ornamental cast iron products are an invaluable resource of incomparable durability. Whether creating new patterns from architectural drawings, or restoring partially destroyed metal work, Robinson Iron is the source. Catalog available, $3.00.

Robinson Iron
Robinson Road
Alexander City, Alabama 35010
Telephone: (205) 329-8484
Telex: 593-499

SCHWARTZ'S FORGE & METALWORKS

Architectural Iron Work
Custom Designed and Created
Gates — Railings — Grilles
Stairways

For Portfolio Send $3.50
Schwartz's Forge & Metalworks
P. O. Box 205, Deansboro, NY 13328
Telephone (315) 841-4477

Wrought Iron, Custom Fabrication

Antares Forge and Metalworks (NY)
Architectural Iron Company (PA)
Arrowhead Forge (ME)
Blacksmith Shop, Inc. (VT)
Cambridge Smithy (VT)
Claymont Forge (WV)
Ephraim Forge (IL)
Fiebiger, Inc. (NY)
G. Krug & Son (MD)
Hartland Forge (NH)
Kayne, Steve — Hand-Forged Hardware (NY)
Millham, Newton — Blacksmith (MA)
RAM's Forge (MD)
Ricker Blacksmith Shop (ME)
Schwartz's Forge & Metalworks (NY)
Smithy, The (VT)
Tennessee Fabricating Co. (TN)
Travis Tuck, Metal Sculptor (MA)
Wallin Forge (KY)
Williamsburg Blacksmiths, Inc. (MA)
Woodbury Blacksmith & Forge Co. (CT)

Other Exterior Ironwork

See Company Directory for Addresses & Phone Numbers

Other Exterior Ornament & Details

Awnings
Astrup Company (OH)

Awning Hardware
Astrup Company (OH)

Balustrades, Roof
Campbellsville Industries (KY)
Lachin, Albert & Assoc., Inc. (LA)

Chimney Pots
Architectural Terra Cotta and Tile, Ltd. (IL)
Superior Clay Corporation (OH)
Victorian Reproductions, Inc. (MN)

Cupolas
Campbellsville Industries (KY)
Cape Cod Cupola Co., Inc. (MA)
International Building Components (NY)
Kenneth Lynch & Sons, Inc. (CT)
Kool-O-Matic Corp. (MI)
Pyramid Woodcraft Corp. (TX)
Sun Designs (WI)
Sundials, Inc. (MA)
Tennessee Fabricating Co. (TN)
Westmoreland Cupolas (PA)

Fences & Gates—Period Designs

(1) Cast Iron
(2) Wrought Iron
(3) Wood
(4) Antique
(5) Cast Aluminum

1890 Iron Fence Co. (IN) 2
Architectural Antique Warehouse, The (CAN) 1
Architectural Antiques Exchange (PA)
Belcher, Robert W. (GA) 3
ByGone Era (GA) 4
Canal Co. (DC) 4
Canal Works (OH) 4
Claymont Forge (WV) 2
Kenneth Lynch & Sons, Inc. (CT) 1
Ley, Joe/Antiques (KY) 4
Mad River Wood Works (CA) 3
Moultrie Manufacturing Company (GA) 5
Oliver, Bradley C. (PA) 4
Robinson Iron Corporation (AL) 1
Saltbox (PA) 3
Salvage One (IL) 4
Schwartz's Forge & Metalworks (NY) 2
Stewart Manufacturing Company (KY) 2
Tennessee Fabricating Co. (TN) 1,2
Travis Tuck, Metal Sculptor (MA) 2
Wrecking Bar, Inc. (TX) 4

The Old-House Journal 1982 Catalog

Garden Ornament

(1) Fountains
(2) Statuary
(3) Planters
(4) Urns & Vases
(5) Other

Bench Manufacturing Co. (MA) 3
Biagiotti, L. (NY) 4
Chilstone Garden Ornament (UK) 2,3,4,5
Felber, Inc. (PA) 1
International Architecture (TX) 1,2
Kenneth Lynch & Sons, Inc. (CT) 1,2,4
Lachin, Albert & Assoc., Inc. (LA) 1
Ley, Joe/Antiques (KY)
Moultrie Manufacturing Company (GA) . 1,3,4
Richardson, Matthew Coppersmith (MA) ... 1
Robinson Iron Corporation (AL) 1,2,3,4
Roman Marble Co. (IL) 2,3
Silver Dollar Trading Co. (CO) 1
Spring City Electrical Mfg. Co (PA) 1
Sundials, Inc. (MA) 5
Tennessee Fabricating Co. (TN) 1,2,3,4
Topiary Frames by John Wallace (IL)
Verine Products & Co. (UK) 3
Victorian Reproductions, Inc. (MN)
Wilson, Dan (NC) 3

Gazebos

Bench Manufacturing Co. (MA)
Cedar Gazebos, Inc. (IL)
Sun Designs (WI)
Welsbach (CT)

Lawn and Porch Furniture

(1) Cast Iron
(2) Wood
(3) Wicker
(4) Wrought Iron

Kenneth Lynch & Sons, Inc. (CT) 1
Mexico House (CA) 4
Robinson Iron Corporation (AL) 1
Rocker Shop (GA) 2
Santa Cruz Foundry (CA) 1
Tennessee Fabricating Co. (TN) 1
Welsbach (CT) 1,4
Wilson, Dan (NC) 2

Lightning Rods, Old-Fashioned

Victorian Reproductions, Inc. (MN)

FLORA & FAUNA FAUCETS

Add a touch of perennial beauty to your garden with our solid brass quail. One of eight animal figures mounted on first quality ¾" hose bibbs. Available in bright brass, antique bronze, or verdegris. Visa, Mastercharge, prepay, C.O.D.

$28. ppd.

Flora & Fauna Faucets
Dept. OHJ
Gualala, CA 95445

CEDAR GAZEBOS

A gazebo is a charming addition to the grounds of a period home. Now you can buy a pre-fabricated gazebo kit in modular units of 100% heartwood cedar. Cedar resists decay, warping, twisting and checking— the ideal wood for outdoor structures.

Each wall and roof panel is hand crafted and comes pre-assembled for easy installation. The gazebos are available with either permanent or removable screening. Pre-fabricated decks are available with all of our models.

Three styles are available:
Pagoda—6 or 8 sided with Oriental roof.
South Seas Classic—6, 8, or 10 sided with lattice roof
Midwestern Classic—6, 8 or 10 sided with solid roof, suitable for areas where snow loads occur.

Suggested retail prices start at $793.00.

Custom gazebos are also available by sending us the proper diameter desired, number of slides, and a picture or sketch of the gazebo. We will manufacture it in a pre-fab kit.

Kits assemble in 2 hours or less by 2 people.

Dealer inquiries invited.

Send for free brochure and price list.

**Cedar Gazebos Inc.
10432 Lyndale Avenue
Dept. OHJ
Melrose Park, IL 60164
(312) 455-0928**

Mail Boxes — Period Designs

Restoration Works, Inc. (NY)
Sign of the Crab (CA)
Silver Dollar Trading Co. (CO)

Plaques & Historic Markers

Historic Buildings Group (NY)
Jaxon Co., Inc. (AL)
Lake Shore Markers (PA)
Meierjohan — Wengler, Inc. (OH)
Moultrie Manufacturing Company (GA)
Orthographic Engraving Co. (NY)
Saldarini & Pucci, Inc. (NY)
Smith-Cornell Homestead, Inc. (IN)
Sweet William House (IL)
Weaver, W. T. & Sons, Inc. (DC)

Sheet Metal Ornament, Exterior

Campbellsville Industries (KY)
Flam Sheetmetal Specialty Co. (NY)
Kenneth Lynch & Sons, Inc. (CT)

Signs, Old-Fashioned

Shelley Signs (NY)
Ship 'n Out (NY)
Vintage Wood Works (TX)

Turnbuckle Stars

Ainsworth Development Corp. (MD)

Weathervanes—New & Reproduction

Cambridge Smithy (VT)
Campbellsville Industries (KY)
Cape Cod Cupola Co., Inc. (MA)
Copper House (NH)
Cumberland General Store (TN)
Kayne, Steve — Hand-Forged Hardware (NY)
Kenneth Lynch & Sons, Inc. (CT)
Kingsway (CO)
Metals by Maurice (MA)
Period Furniture Hardware Co. (MA)
RAM's Forge (MD)
Renovator's Supply (MA)
Richardson, Matthew Coppersmith (MA)
Ship 'n Out (NY)
Sign of the Crab (CA)
Smithy, The (VT)
Travis Tuck, Metal Sculptor (MA)
United House Wrecking Corp. (CT)
Victorian Reproductions, Inc. (MN)
Wallin Forge (KY)
Washburne, E.G. & Co. (MA)

See Company Directory for Addresses & Phone Numbers

Streetscape Equipment

(1) Bollards and Stanchions
(2) Promenade Benches
(3) Street Clocks
(4) Tree Grates
(5) Street Lamps

Antique Street Lamps (TX) 5
Bench Manufacturing Co. (MA) 2
Canterbury Designs, Inc. (CA) 2,3,4
Chilstone Garden Ornament (UK) 2
Kenneth Lynch & Sons, Inc. (CT) 1,2,4
Santa Cruz Foundry (CA) 2
Spring City Electrical Mfg. Co (PA) 1,5
Valley Iron & Steel Co. (OR) 5
Vermont Iron Stove Works (VT) 2
Welsbach (CT) 1,2,5

Other Exterior Ornament

Gargoyles — New York (NY)
Topiary Frames by John Wallace (IL)

One of a kind Weathervanes

Designed on order and constructed in the early 19th century manner. Truly an investment as well as a pleasure to live with. From $800.

Also the finest custom metal work of all kinds. No stock items and no brochure. All inquiries answered personally.

TRAVIS TUCK
Metal Sculptor & Blacksmith

Martha's Vineyard
Mass. 02568 USA

(617) 693-3914 or 693-4076

Master Charge and Visa Accepted

CURL UP with a Catamount™
WARM UP with an Elm™

Catamount Park Benches are made to be used indoors or out, in contemporary or traditional settings. Constructed of cast iron supports, hardwood slats, bronze medallions, and held together with stainless steel fasteners, the Catamount offers years of comfortable seating.

Elm woodstoves feature the unique design of a round combustion chamber for a cleaner burn and a warp free lifespan. Fully baffled, ¼" cast iron, airtight efficiency, and a double viewing window set us apart from the competition. We also have a rotating flue and hardwood handles that stay cool to the touch.

VERMONT IRON
1211 Prince Street, Box 299
Waterbury, Vermont 05676
802/244-5254

For information   ☐ Catamount
enclose $1   ☐ Elm

CAST IRON BENCHES

Decorative iron and oak benches combine ultimate seating comfort with the finest elegance in design. Wood prefinished with Danish oil stain, ends in wrought iron black or forest green.
Write for free brochure.

SANTA CRUZ FOUNDRY
Courthouse Square, Dept. OHJ
Hanford, CA 93230 (209) 584-1541
Dealer inquiries invited

WEATHERVANES
ROOSTER DEER
SULKY EAGLE
FISH HORSE
WHALE
COW

GRASSHOPPER & MORE!
from solid copper

THE GOOD OLD
FASHION KIND
Send $.50
for brochure.
DEALER INQUIRIES INVITED

914 • 855-5947

Ship'n Out
8W Charles St.
Pawling, N.Y. 12564

The Old-House Journal 1982 Catalog

Building Materials For Interiors

Baseboards

Bangkok Industries, Inc. (PA)
Bendix Mouldings, Inc. (NJ)
Dixon Bros. Woodworking (MA)
Drums Sash & Door Co., Inc. (PA)
F M P (TX)
Old World Moulding (NY)
Silverton Victorian Millworks (CO)

Beams, Hand-Hewn

(1) Antique (Recycled)
(2) New

Barn People, The (VT) 1
Belcher, Robert W. (GA) 1
Broad-Axe Beam Co. (VT) 2
ByGone Era (GA) 1
Castle Burlingame (NJ) 1
Hubbard Folding Wood Box Co., Ltd. (WI) 2
Industrial Woodworking, Inc. (IL) 2
Kensington Historical Co. (NH) 1
Mountain Lumber Company (VA) 1
Old World Moulding (NY) 2
Period Pine (GA) 1
Saltbox (PA) 2
Sloane, Hugh L. (MA) 1
Walker, Dennis C. (OH) 2

Boards, Salvage

Barn People, The (VT)
Farm Builders, Inc. (MD)
Kensington Historical Co. (NH)
Mountain Lumber Company (VA)
Period Pine (GA)
Vintage Lumber Co. (MD)

Casings & Frames for Doors & Windows

(1) Stock Items
(2) Custom Made

Architectural Components (MA) 2
Drums Sash & Door Co., Inc. (PA) 1,2
Elliott Millwork Co. (IL) 1
F M P (TX)
Michael's Fine Colonial Products (NY) .. 2
Period Productions, Limited (VA) 2
Silverton Victorian Millworks (CO) 2
The Restoration Fraternity (PA) 2

Ceilings, Wood—Custom Manufactured

Architectural Paneling, Inc. (NY)

Chair Rails

(1) Stock Items
(2) Custom Made

Bendix Mouldings, Inc. (NJ) 1
California Heritage Wood Products, Ltd. (CA) 2
Cumberland Woodcraft Co., Inc. (PA)
Dimension Lumber Co. (NY) 2
Dixon Bros. Woodworking (MA) 2
Drums Sash & Door Co., Inc. (PA) 2
Elliott Millwork Co. (IL)
Industrial Woodworking, Inc. (IL) 1,2
Maurer & Shepherd, Joyners (CT) 2
Michael's Fine Colonial Products (NY) .. 2
Old World Moulding (NY) 1
Period Productions, Limited (VA) 2
Silverton Victorian Millworks (CO)
Turnbull's Custom Mouldings (MI) 2

Doors, Interior

(1) Antique (Salvage)
(2) Reproduction
(3) Early American
(4) Victorian
(5) Turn-of-Century
(6) Custom-Made
(7) Other

Addco Architectural Antiques (LA) 1
Architectural Antique Warehouse, The (CAN) 1
Architectural Antiques Exchange (PA)
Architectural Components (MA) 2
Architectural Heritage (CAN) 1
Art Directions (MO) 1
Bank Architectural Antiques (LA) 1,4
Bare Wood Inc. (NY) 1
ByGone Era (GA) 1
C—E Morgan (WI) 3
Canal Co. (DC) 1
Cascade Mill & Glass Works (CO) 2,6
Castle Burlingame (NJ) 1
Driwood Moulding Company (SC) 6
Drums Sash & Door Co., Inc. (PA) 6
Hubbard Folding Wood Box Co., Ltd. (WI) 6
Landmark Doors (NY) 2,4,5
Ley, Joe/Antiques (KY) 1
Maurer & Shepherd, Joyners (CT) 6
Nord, E.A. Company (WA)
Olde Bostonian Architectural Antiques (MA) 1
Pat's Etcetera Company (TX) 1
Period Productions, Limited (VA) 6
Salvage One (IL) 1
Second Chance (GA) 1
Sloane, Hugh L. (MA) 1
Somerset Door & Column Co. (PA) 6
Structural Antiques (OK) 1
The Restoration Fraternity (PA) 6
United House Wrecking Corp. (CT) 1
Wrecking Bar, Inc. (TX) 1

HAND HEWN BEAMS

Send $1.00 for complete information

The Broad-Axe Beam Co.
RD 2   Box 181-J
W. Brattleboro, Vermont 05301
802-257-0064

BASEBOARDS
DOOR / WINDOW FACINGS
ROSETTES
CORNER BLOCKS
write for information

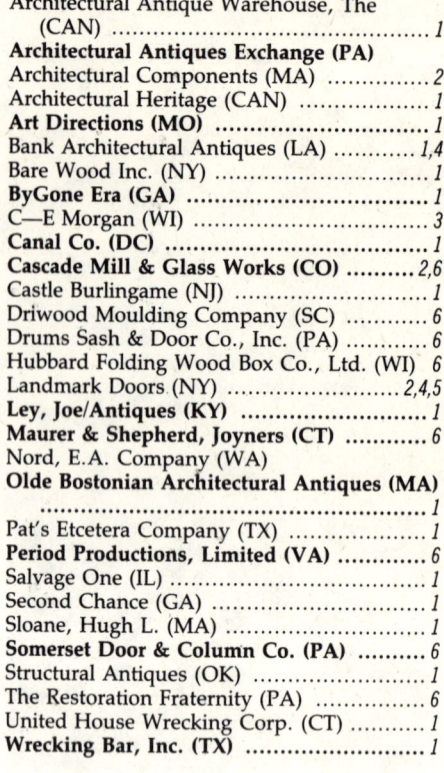

Frank Mullins
327 S. EDGEFIELD
DALLAS, TEXAS 75208
214-9428316

Dumbwaiters & Built-Ins

Dorz Mfg. Co. (WA)
Henderson Black & Greene, Inc. (AL)
International Building Components (NY)
Iron-A-Way, Inc. (IL)
Sedgwick Machine Works, Inc. (NY)
Vincent — Whitney Co. (CA)

Flooring, Wood

(1) Hardwood Strip
(2) Heart Pine
(3) Parquet
(4) Wide Board
(5) Other

A.R.D. (NY)
Addco Architectural Antiques (LA) 2,4
Allstate Flooring (NY) 3
Bangkok Industries, Inc. (PA) 1,3,4
ByGone Era (GA) 2
Carlisle Restoration Lumber (NH) 4
Castle Burlingame (NJ) 4
Craftsman Lumber Co. (MA) 4
Farm Builders, Inc. (MD) 2
Harris Manufacturing Company (TN) 3,4
Hartco (TN) 3
Kensington Historical Co. (NH) 4
Kentucky Wood Floors, Inc. (KY) 1,3,4
Lee Woodwork Systems (PA) 1
Maurer & Shepherd, Joyners (CT) 5
Memphis Hardwood Flooring Co. (TN) 1
Mountain Lumber Company (VA) 2,4
Nassau Flooring Corp. (NY) 1,3,4
Natural Wood Floors - Inlaid Wood Mosaic Div. (IL) 3
Period Pine (GA) 2
Period Productions, Limited (VA) 1,2,4
Saltbox (PA) 4
Sundials, Inc. (MA) 1
Vintage Lumber Co. (MD) 2
Wrecking Bar, Inc. (TX) 3

ANTIQUE FLOORING

100 year old vintage heart red pine lumber. Tongue and groove flooring, stair treads, risers and beams. *Nationwide delivery.*

Architectural Antiques

2601 Chartres St., New Orleans, LA. 70117
(504) 945-4879   945-4890

See Company Directory
for
Addresses & Phone Numbers

Whether for luxury or necessity...

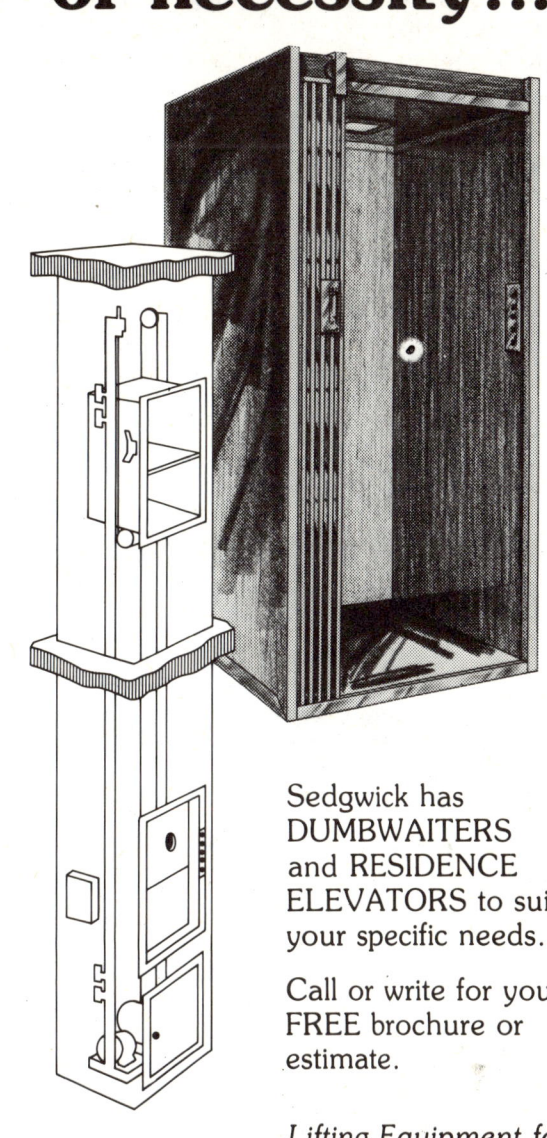

Sedgwick has DUMBWAITERS and RESIDENCE ELEVATORS to suit your specific needs.

Call or write for your FREE brochure or estimate.

Lifting Equipment for Home and Industry

 since 1893

Foot of Prospect Street
P.O. Box 630X
Poughkeepsie, N.Y. 12602
Telephone: (914) 454-5400

The Old-House Journal 1982 Catalog

FLOORING

Most floors have three major components: supporting joists, subflooring laid at right angles to the joists, and finish flooring at right angles to the subfloor.

Floors were made of softwood, usually pine, during the 18th and much of the 19th centuries. Typically they were left bare or painted—sometimes in solid colors—often in stencilled, wood-grained, or spatterdashed patterns.

Many mid-Victorian houses had no finish flooring at all. Since wall-to-wall carpeting was then fashionable it could be laid directly over the subflooring. By the 1870's when all-over carpets became *passé* and exotic rugs came into vogue, oak finish flooring was used for the more important rooms. The rich favored parquet designs—"wood carpeting of oak, beautifully polished."

By the 1890's middle class homes had standardized strip-oak flooring in the front hall, living room, and dining room. Odd-lot planks and mass-produced parquet continued to be popular, too. Plain softwood floors were often still used in the less public rooms.

Flooring, Stone & Ceramic

(1) Slate, Marble & Other Stone
(2) Ceramic Tile

"Mr. Slate" Smid Incorporated (VT) 1
A.R.D. (NY)
American Olean Tile Company (PA) 2
Bank Architectural Antiques (LA)
Brooklyn Tile Supply (NY) 2
Country Floors, Inc. (NY) 2
Evergreen Slate Co. (NY) 1
International Architecture (TX) 1,2
Marble Technics Ltd. (NY) 1
Structural Slate Company (PA) 1
Tatko Bros. Slate Co. (NY) 1
Tile Distributors, Inc. (NY) 2
Vermont Structural Slate Co. (VT) 1
Wrecking Bar, Inc. (TX)

Fretwork & Grilles, Wood

Architectural Arts (IN)
ByGone Era (GA)
Croton, Evelyn — Architectural Antiques (NY)
Cumberland Woodcraft Co., Inc. (PA)
North Pacific Joinery (CA)
Old'N Ornate Wooden Reproductions (OR)
Period Productions, Limited (VA)
Pyramid Woodcraft Corp. (TX)
Victorian Reproductions, Inc. (MN)
Vintage Wood Works (TX)

Grilles for Hot-Air Registers

(1) New
(2) Antique (Original)

A-Ball Plumbing Supply (OR) 1
Bow & Arrow Stove Co. (MA) 1
Bryant Steel Works (ME) 2
Reggio Register Co. (MA) 1
Renovator's Supply (MA) 1

Hardwoods Suppliers

Amherst Woodworking & Supply (MA)
Center Lumber Company (NJ)
Constantine, Albert and Son, Inc. (NY)
Craftsman Lumber Co. (MA)
Morgan Woodworking Supplies (KY)
Mountain Lumber (VA)
Weird Wood (VT)

MOUNTAIN LUMBER

RARE & SPECIAL WOODS

Old Heart Pine • Random width & wide plank flooring
Wormy Chestnut & South American Wormy Mahogany Paneling
Rough sawn & hand-hewn beams
Custom-made cabinets, doors & trim

All Wood Kiln Dried • Finest Quality Millwork Available

MOUNTAIN LUMBER COMPANY
1327 CARLTON AVENUE, P.O. BOX 285, CHARLOTTESVILLE, VA 22902
TELEPHONE: (804) 295-1922

WIDE PINE FLOORING
& PANELING (12" TO 22" WIDE)

Wide Oak Boards   Ship-lapped Pine

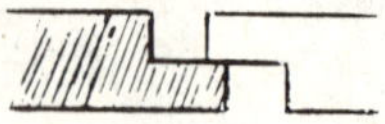

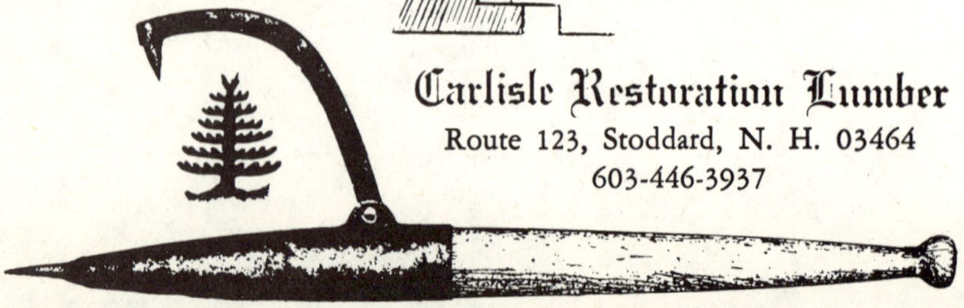

Carlisle Restoration Lumber
Route 123, Stoddard, N.H. 03464
603-446-3937

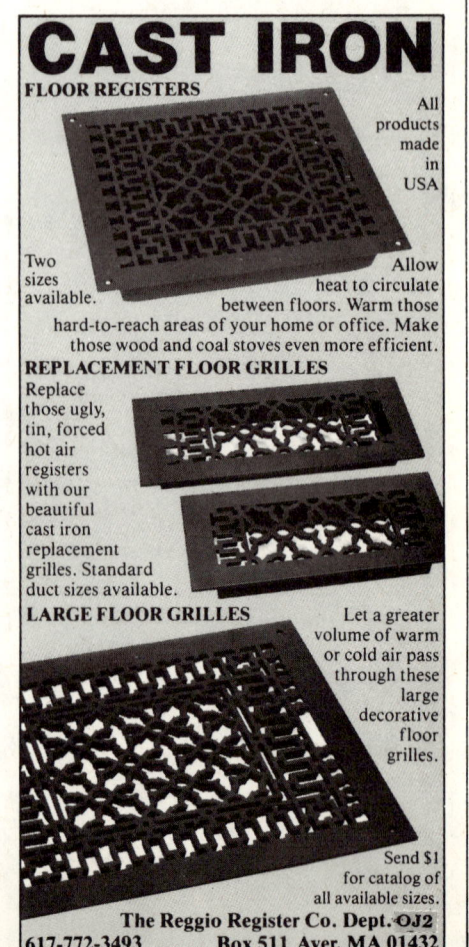

CAST IRON

FLOOR REGISTERS

All products made in USA

Two sizes available. Allow heat to circulate between floors. Warm those hard-to-reach areas of your home or office. Make those wood and coal stoves even more efficient.

REPLACEMENT FLOOR GRILLES

Replace those ugly, tin, forced hot air registers with our beautiful cast iron replacement grilles. Standard duct sizes available.

LARGE FLOOR GRILLES

Let a greater volume of warm or cold air pass through these large decorative floor grilles.

Send $1 for catalog of all available sizes.

The Reggio Register Co. Dept. OJ2
617-772-3493   Box 511 Ayer, MA 01432

SOUTHINGTON Specialty Wood Co.

FOR YOUR REPRODUCTION OR RESTORATION

We're **WOOD SPECIALISTS** with years of experience who are known for our fine quality, wide assortment and reasonable prices. Because wood is our only product, we're qualified to help you select materials that best suit your personal needs and tastes. **We're a little hard to find so call (203) 621-6787 for directions.**

A Few Examples Of The Numerous Items We Stock

Wide Board Flooring

Premium Pine $1.45 sq. ft.
Kiln Dried, Random Width 12" to 18"

Select Red or White Oak $3.50 sq. ft.
Kiln Dried, Random Width 8" to 14"

Select White Ash $3.50 sq. ft.
Klin Dried, Random Width 8" to 14"

Plank Flooring and Wall Paneling

Kiln Dried, Tongue and Groove Boards,
Random Width 3" to 7"

Cherry $2.20 sq. ft.
Butternut $2.40 sq. ft.
Red Oak $2.25 sq. ft.
Elm $2.20 sq. ft.
Maple $2.50 sq. ft.
Ash $2.20 sq. ft.

Wood Roofing and Siding

Eastern White Cedar Shingles
Western Red Cedar Shingles
Clapboards, Cedar, Cypress and Pine

Etcetera

Posts and Beams of All Sizes
4" Thick Mantels 8" to 14" Wide
Natural Edge Tree Slabs For Tables,
Bar Tops, Signs etc.

Write For Complete Brochure And Price List

100 West Main Street
Plantsville, CT 06497

Overdoor Treatments

Bel-Air Door Co. (CA)
California Heritage Wood Products, Ltd. (CA)
Driwood Moulding Company (SC)
Fypon, Inc. (PA)
International Building Components (NY)
Verine Products & Co. (UK)

Staircases

C—E Morgan (WI)
Cooper Stair Co. (IL)
Curvoflite (NH)
Dean, James R. (NY)
Dixon Bros. Woodworking (MA)
Driwood Moulding Company (SC)
Drums Sash & Door Co., Inc. (PA)
Mylen Spiral Stairs (NY)
Period Productions, Limited (VA)
Taney Supply & Lumber Corp. (MD)
United Stairs Corp. (NJ)
Woodstone Co. (VT)

See Company Directory for Addresses & Phone Numbers

ALL OAK SPIRAL STAIRS AND WOOD RAILING SYSTEMS... INSTALLED EASILY.

UNITED STAIRS CORPORATION
Highway 35
Keyport, New Jersey 07735
(201) 583-1100   Telex 642861

James R. Dean
ARCHITECTURAL STAIRBUILDING AND HANDRAILING

Providing a source for custom stair and handrail work and access to over 20 years experience in the trade. Offering individualized services to meet your particular building or remodeling requirements.

- Builders of straight, curved, eliptical and circular interior wood stairs and solid wood handrail work of all description.
- All woods, all work by special order only.
- Fabricators of one of a kind stairwork, reproductions of old designs, matching of existing work, solid wood handrail work for existing stairs.
- Fully assembled stairs and knocked down, handrail work shipped anywhere freight collect Cooperstown, New York.
- Consultation, architectural drawings, stair and balustrade repair information available.

15 Delaware St.   Cooperstown, New York 13326
607-547-2262

Professional Workmanship Guaranteed

The Old-House Journal 1982 Catalog

Spiral Staircases

(1) Wood
(2) Metal

A.R.D. (NY)
American General Products (MI)
American Ornamental Corporation (TX) 2
Cooper Stair Co. (IL) 1
Curvoflite (NH) 1
Duvinage Corporation (MD) 1,2
International Building Components (NY) ... 1
Midwest Spiral Stair Company (IL) 1,2
Mylen Spiral Stairs (NY)
Remodelers' & Renovators' Supply (ID) 2
San Francisco Victoriana (CA)
Schwartz's Forge & Metalworks (NY)
Stair-Pak Products Co. (NJ) 1
Stairways, Inc. (TX) 1,2
Steptoe and Wife Antiques Ltd. (CAN) 2
Taney Supply & Lumber Corp. (MD) 1
United Stairs Corp. (NJ) 1
Victorian Revival (MD) 2
Whitten Enterprises, Inc. (VT) 2
Woodbridge Ornamental Iron Co. (IL) 2
York Spiral Stair (ME) 2

SPIRAL STAIRWAYS...
THE UNCOMMON ACCENT

- Decorator Designed
- Adds graceful access to your lofts, mezzanines, attics, or any area
- Models for space saving or for a more integral part of your overall effect
- Models for the do-it-yourself buff

SEND FOR DESCRIPTIVE BROCHURES

WOODBRIDGE
ORNAMENTAL IRON COMPANY
2725 N. CLYBOURN AVE.
CHICAGO, IL 60614
(312) 935-1500

See Company Directory
for
Addresses & Phone Numbers

THE STEPTOE™ CAST IRON SPIRAL STAIRCASE IN MODULAR FORM*

A fine reproduction of an original Victorian styled spiral staircase. Delivered in kit form, to fit a 4' diameter opening, for easy on-site assembly. (8" treads, fourteen to a circle) Please write for brochure and nearest dealer to:

THE STEPTOE™ CAST IRON STAIRCASE

3626 Victoria Park Ave. Willowdale, Ontario, Canada M2H 3B2. Tel. (416) 497-2989.

*A product of Steptoe and Wife Antiques Ltd.

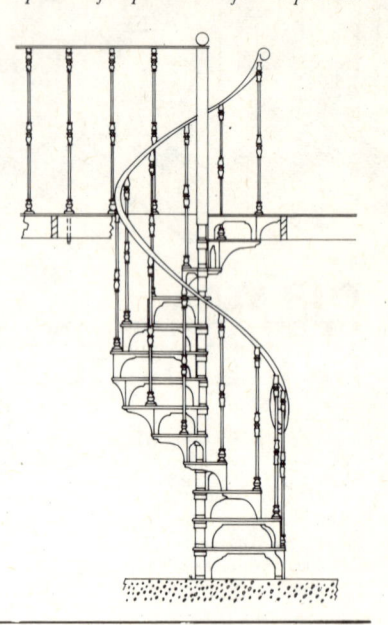

You can discuss THE STEPTOE CAST IRON STAIRCASE at any of these regional dealers:

ATLANTA, GA
The Wrecking Bar of Atlanta, Inc.
404/525-0468

BALTIMORE, MD
Victorian Revival
301/225-0649 462-2959

BOISE, ID
Remodelers' & Renovators' Supply
208/377-5465

CHICAGO, IL
Woodbridge
312/935-1500
Creative Interior Sources
312/661-1475

CLEVELAND, OH
The Emporium
216/522-0044

DALLAS, TX
The Wrecking Bar, Inc.
214/826-1717

HOUSTON, TX
The Emporium
713/528-3808

JACKSON, NJ
Amar Steel Corp.
201/928-3000

KINGSTON, MA
The Perseverance
617/585-8009

LITTLE ROCK, AR
Victorian Supply Co.
501/372-6999

MALIBU, CA
Phineas Fogg & Co.
213/465-8104

MINNEAPOLIS, MN
Mayfair
612/338-1802

NEW YORK, NY
Urban Archaeology
212/431-6969

OKLAHOMA CITY, OK
Architectural Specialties
405/843-3583

PHILADELPHIA, PA
Gargoyles, Ltd.,
215/629-1700

RICHMOND, VA
Greendale Railing Co.
804/266-2664

ST. LOUIS, MO
Art Directions
314/863-1895

SAN DIEGO, CA
Architectural Emporium
714/234-6083

SAN FRANCISCO, CA
S. F. Victoriana
415/648-0313

STAMFORD, CT
United House Wrecking
203/348-5371

WESTFIELD, MA
Main Sail
413/562-9562

WILMINGTON, NC
Colony Iron & Brass Co.
919/762-9112

YPSILANTI, MI
Materials Unlimited
313/483-6980

CANADA

MONTREAL
Architectural Antiques
514/849-3344

OTTAWA
The Architectural Antique Warehouse
613/224-5530

VICTORIA, B.C.
Attica Ltd.
604/382-4214

Staircase Parts

(1) Balusters, Antique (Original)
(2) Balusters, New
(3) Balusters, Custom-Made
(4) Handrails
(5) Newel Posts
(6) Other

Bank Architectural Antiques (LA) 4,5
Bare Wood Inc. (NY)
Bedlam Brass Beds — Denver (CO) 4
ByGone Era (GA) 1,4,5
C—E Morgan (WI) 2,4,5
Canal Co. (DC) 1,5
Croton, Evelyn — Architectural Antiques (NY) 1,5
Cumberland Woodcraft Co., Inc. (PA) ...2,4,5
Curvoflite (NH) 3
Dean, James R. (NY)
Dixon Bros. Woodworking (MA) 3,4
Drums Sash & Door Co., Inc. (PA) 6
Elk Valley Woodworking Company (OK) ... 2
Haas Wood & Ivory Works (CA) 3,4,5
Harris Manufacturing Company (TN) 6
Henderson Black & Greene, Inc. (AL) ...2,4,5
Industrial Woodworking, Inc. (IL) 4
Island City Wood Working Co. (TX) 3,4
Kingsway (CO) 2,5,6
Ley, Joe/Antiques (KY) 5
Mansion Industries, Inc. (CA) 2,4,5
Michael's Fine Colonial Products (NY) ..3,4,5
Michael-Regan Wood Turnings (CA) 2,4
Miles Lumber Co, Inc. (VT) 3
Nord, E.A. Company (WA) 2
North Pacific Joinery (CA) 3,4,5
Olde Bostonian Architectural Antiques (MA) 5
Second Chance (GA) 1,5
Somerset Door & Column Co. (PA) 3,5
Taney Supply & Lumber Corp. (MD)
Wrecking Bar, Inc. (TX) 5

KINGSWAY

VICTORIAN RESTORATION MATERIALS

- Brass Hardware
- Decorative Moulding
- Panelling & Wainscoting
- Porcelain Doorknobs
- Stair Parts
- Fancy Cut Shingles
- Victorian Gingerbread and Millwork

4723 Chromium Drive
Colo. Springs, CO 80918
(303) 599-4512

Catalog Available $2.00 plus 50¢ postage

TIN CEILING

Stamped metal ceilings, popular from 1895—1915, can introduce a strong design element in a room, and for this reason should be used with care. An important fact to remember is that metal ceilings were never widely used as the original finish in formal halls and parlors. A much overlooked way to utilize tin ceiling panels is to create a dado in halls, kitchens and bathrooms. To simulate the look of Lincrusta-Walton, the painted stamped metal can be glazed in a tan-brown leather-like shade.

Tin Ceilings

A.R.D. (NY)
AA-Abbingdon (NY)
Antique Reproduction Co. (TX)
Ceilings, Walls & More, Inc. (TX)
Chelsea Decorative Metal Co. (TX)
Hi-Art East (GA)
Klinke & Lew Contractors (CO)
Norman, W.F., Corporation (MO)
Ohman, C.A. (NY)
Remodelers' & Renovators' Supply (ID)
Shanker Steel Corp. (NY)
Steptoe and Wife Antiques Ltd. (CAN)
Structural Antiques (OK)
Victorian Revival (MD)

Add flair with Studio Stair®

CIRCULAR and SPIRAL STAIRS

- Any Height
- Various Sizes
- Several Styles
- Easy Installation

Add excitement and beauty, reduce cost of remodeling with SPACE SAVING All Wood or Wood-Steel combination.

WRITE or CALL for complete information:
AMERICAN GENERAL PRODUCTS, INC.
P.O. Box 395, Ypsilanti, Michigan 48197
Telephone: (313) 483-1833

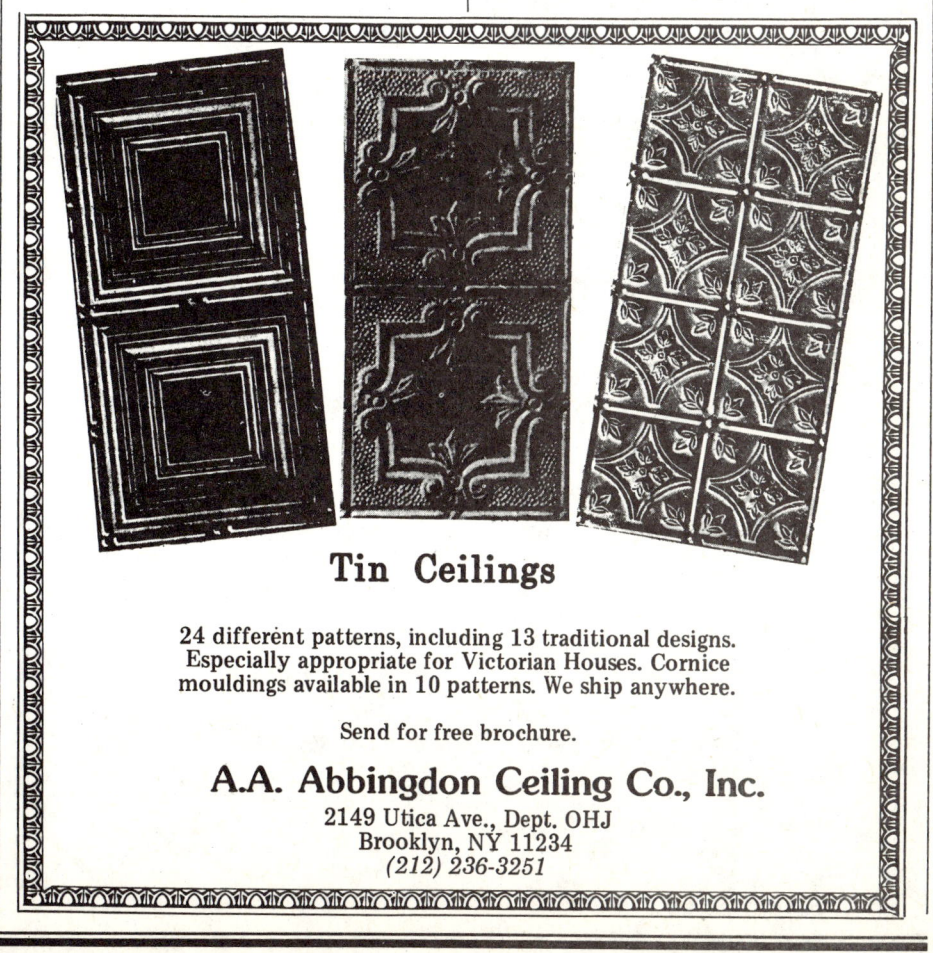

Tin Ceilings

24 different patterns, including 13 traditional designs. Especially appropriate for Victorian Houses. Cornice mouldings available in 10 patterns. We ship anywhere.

Send for free brochure.

A.A. Abbingdon Ceiling Co., Inc.
2149 Utica Ave., Dept. OHJ
Brooklyn, NY 11234
(212) 236-3251

Our metal ceilings and wall coverings are produced from original patterns from the early 1900's. Our company has been producing the ceilings since 1912 and we are currently the only major manufacturer in the country. Catalog free.

Shanker Steel Co., Inc.
70-32 83rd St., Glendale, NY 11385
(212) 326-1100

FREE!
VENEER CRAFT CATALOG PLUS SIMPLIFIED INSTRUCTIONS

90 varieties world's rarest veneers, pre-joined veneers, checkerboards, broad choice wood band and art inlays. Illustrated in full color — at reasonable prices. Learn how to create beautifully veneered furniture quickly, easily. Re-veneer old tables, chests, cabinets, clocks, with ease. Transform cracked and chipped veneered surfaces instantly! Illustrated catalog shows new contact cement technique that you learn fast. Send for FREE simplified instructions plus color catalog today.
MORGAN, Dept. OO3K1
1123 Bardstown Rd., Lou., Ky. 40204

Veneers & Inlays

Artistry in Veneers, Inc. (NY)
Boseman Veneer & Supply Co. (TX)
Constantine, Albert and Son, Inc. (NY)
Dover Furniture Stripping (DE)
Gaston Wood Finishes, Inc. (IN)
Homecraft Veneer (PA)
Morgan Woodworking Supplies (KY)
Woodworkers' Store, The (MN)

Wainscotting

(1) Antique (Salvage)
(2) New

Art Directions (MO) 1
Bare Wood Inc. (NY) 2
Canal Works (OH) 1
Carlisle Restoration Lumber (NH) 2
Castle Burlingame (NJ) 1
Craftsman Lumber Co. (MA) 2
Cumberland Woodcraft Co., Inc. (PA) 2
Dixon Bros. Woodworking (MA) 2
Elliott Millwork Co. (IL) 2
Hubbard Folding Wood Box Co., Ltd. (WI) 2
Kingsway (CO) 2
Landmark Doors (NY) 2
Lee Woodwork Systems (PA) 2
Maurer & Shepherd, Joyners (CT)
Old World Moulding (NY) 2
Olde Bostonian Architectural Antiques (MA)

Restoration Hardware (CA) 2
Silverton Victorian Millworks (CO) 2
The Restoration Fraternity (PA) 2
Victorian Reproductions, Inc. (MN)

Decorative Metal Ceilings
Original turn-of-the-century patterns

NOW AVAILABLE!

Using eighty year old dies, the W. F. Norman Corporation is once again producing metal plates for the design of ceilings and wall coverings. Their growing popularity stems not only from nostalgia but from their beauty, permanence, fireproofing and economy.

The fullness of the Hi-Art™ line — including center plates, corner plates, border plates, cornice and filler plates — permits classic designs to be produced that are architecturally proportioned for an exact fit.

Write for reproduction copy of 72 page illustrated catalog. Price $3.

W. F. Norman Corporation
P.O. Box 323 • Nevada, Missouri 64772 • 417-667-5552

Quality Veneers and related supplies

Good selection of crotches, burls and quarter sawn veneer

Catalog Free

Boseman Veneer & Supply Company
403 Laurel, Dept. OHJ
Friendswood, TX 77546
(713) 482-5730

Wall Panelling, Wood—Period

(1) Antique (Salvage)
(2) New—Stock Items
(3) Custom-Made

Architectural Antique Warehouse, The (CAN) 1
Architectural Antiques Exchange (PA)
Architectural Components (MA) 3
Architectural Paneling, Inc. (NY) 3
Art Directions (MO) 1
Bangkok Industries, Inc. (PA) 2
Bare Wood Inc. (NY) 3
Campbell, Douglas Co. (RI) 3
Canal Works (OH) 1
Carlisle Restoration Lumber (NH) 3
Cooper Stair Co. (IL) 2
Craftsman Lumber Co. (MA) 3
Cumberland Woodcraft Co., Inc. (PA) 2
Curvoflite (NH) 3
Dixon Bros. Woodworking (MA) 3
Driwood Moulding Company (SC) 2
Elliott Millwork Co. (IL)
Floors By Juell (IL) 3
Industrial Woodworking, Inc. (IL) 2,3
Kensington Historical Co. (NH) 1
Maurer & Shepherd, Joyners (CT) 3
Mountain Lumber Company (VA) 1
Old World Moulding (NY) 2,3
Period Pine (GA) 2
Period Productions, Limited (VA) 3
Restorations Unlimited, Inc. (PA) 3
Salvage One (IL) 1
Sloane, Hugh L. (MA) 3
Somerset Door & Column Co. (PA) 3
The Restoration Fraternity (PA) 3
Up Country Enterprise Corp. (NH)
Vermont Weatherboard, Inc. (VT) 2
Walker, Dennis C. (OH) 3
Wrecking Bar, Inc. (TX) 1

Other Interior Structural Materials

Ceilings, Walls & More, Inc. (TX)
Giles & Kendall, Inc. (AL)

See Company Directory for Addresses & Phone Numbers

Decorative Interior Materials & Supplies

Brackets & Corbels—Interior

Able/Stanley Wood Carving Co. (NY)
ByGone Era (GA)
Croton, Evelyn — Architectural Antiques (NY)
Cumberland Woodcraft Co., Inc. (PA)
Decorators Supply Corp. (IL)
Elk Valley Woodworking Company (OK)
Haas Wood & Ivory Works (CA)
Hallelujah Redwood Products (CA)
Period Productions, Limited (VA)
Vintage Wood Works (TX)

Ceiling Medallions & Ornaments

(1) Composition
(2) Plaster

Architectural Sculpture (NY)	2
Balmer Architectural Art Limited (CAN)	1,2
Biagiotti, L. (NY)	2
Classic Illumination (CA)	2
Decorators Supply Corp. (IL)	2
Felber, Inc. (PA)	2
Focal Point, Inc. (GA)	1
Garbe's (OK)	
Giannetti Studios (MD)	1,2
Lachin, Albert & Assoc., Inc. (LA)	2
Old World Stucchi Decor (PA)	2
Ornamental Plaster-Works (NY)	2
Saldarini & Pucci, Inc. (NY)	1,2
San Francisco Victoriana (CA)	2
Weaver, W. T. & Sons, Inc. (DC)	1

PLASTERWORK

Ornamental plasterwork is one of the finishing touches that make old houses so distinctive. If you don't have your own custom mouldings made, you can order new plaster ornaments, or you can buy authentic, high quality reproductions moulded of lightweight polymers. This material is approximately the density of white pine and can be worked with carpenter's tools. It's very easy to install and takes paint well.

PLASTER ORNAMENTS
Ceiling pieces • Niche Shells
Cornices • Domes • Capitals
Mouldings • Models

COMPOSITION ORNAMENTS FOR WOODWORK
Scrolls • Wreaths • Cornices
Rosettes • Beading • etc.

FIBRE GLASS CASTINGS RESTORATIONS

Saldarini & Pucci Inc.
156 Crosby Street
Dept. OHJ
New York, N.Y. 10012
Telephone: (212) 673-4390

Able/Stanley Wood Carving Co.

Replacement parts and custom work

Brackets - Capitals - Cornices
Statues - Mouldings - Rosettes

Send SASE (legal size) for FREE brochure

368 Atlantic Ave.
Brooklyn, NY 11217
(212) 834-9679

Your complete source for VICTORIAN MILLWORK

Replicas of 19th century originals in kiln dried, premium grade *solid* Oak or Poplar.

Our expanded line includes designs for all interior and exterior applications; rails and balustrades, brackets, corbels, posts, grilles, fretwork, and much, much more!

- Precision manufactured so that product groups are compatible with each other for total design unity.
- Unlimited quantities for total design freedom.
- Factory direct affordable pricing.
- Custom millwork available for unusual requirements.

Send $3.50 for complete 24 page, full color catalog and Price List.

CUMBERLAND WOODCRAFT COMPANY, INC. Dept. 40

2500 Walnut Bottom Road
Carlisle, PA 17013   (717) 243-0063

The Old-House Journal 1982 Catalog

FOR CEILINGS WITH CLASS

To use with chandeliers and overhead fans or for eyecatching wall accents.

- ★ plaster reinforced with glass fiber
- ★ lightweight and durable
- ★ easy to install
- ★ fire-safe; noncombustible, no toxic fumes
- ★ prices begin at $35.00

Complete color brochure $1.00. Includes medallions, cornices, friezes, ceiling and door panels.

Dovetail, Incorporated

BOX 1569-102, LOWELL, MA 01853 • (617) 454-2944

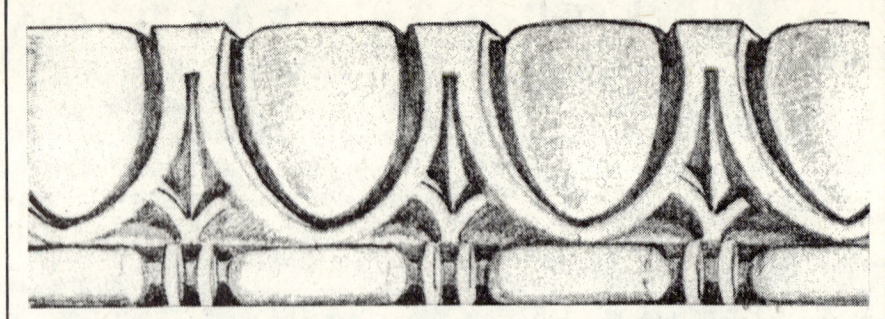

When you need authentic molded plaster architectural shapes for restoration or period ornamentation—Call Felber

- ❦ we have a huge inventory of period ornaments
- ❦ we use real plaster not plastic
- ❦ our moldings are flame proof and smokeless
- ❦ we do custom restoration and matching

felber, inc.
110 Ardmore Ave., PO Box 551
Ardmore, PA 19003
(215) 642-4710

A Revolution in Tradition... Because our product is made of modern polymers, you can saw it, flex it, nail it, paint it or stain it. And because it's Focal Point brand...you can expect it when it's promised, receive it in one piece, install it within your budget, and call us for background knowledge and personal, professional support. And if you've enjoyed looking at these few samples in black-and-white, we can't wait till you see our full-color brochure. Installation photos. Decorating ideas. The full collection of cornice moldings, recessed domes, medallions, niche caps, mantels, overdoor pieces and stair brackets. Only the finest quality design becomes part of The Collection.

The Collection from FOCAL POINT INC.

Send $1.50 for our new full-color brochure. Dept. **Y2-2a,** 2005 Marietta Rd. N.W. Atlanta, GA 30318. (404) 351-0820

42   The Old-House Journal 1982 Catalog

Columns & Capitals—Interior

(1) Composition
(2) Plaster
(3) Wood

Able/Stanley Wood Carving Co. (NY)	3
American Wood Column (NY)	3
Architectural Sculpture (NY)	2
Balmer Architectural Art Limited (CAN)	1,2
Bare Wood Inc. (NY)	
Biagiotti, L. (NY)	1,2
ByGone Era (GA)	3
Cumberland Woodcraft Co., Inc. (PA)	3
Decorators Supply Corp. (IL)	2,3
Elk Valley Woodworking Company (OK)	3
Felber, Inc. (PA)	2
Giannetti Studios (MD)	1,2
Haas Wood & Ivory Works (CA)	3
Hartman — Sanders Company (GA)	3
Kingsway (CO)	1
Lachin, Albert & Assoc., Inc. (LA)	2
Period Productions, Limited (VA)	3
Saldarini & Pucci, Inc. (NY)	1,2,3
Second Chance (GA)	3
Wrecking Bar, Inc. (TX)	

See Company Directory for Addresses & Phone Numbers

Only the finest in tiles and earthenware

For authentic Delft Blue Ltd. earthenware...

- each piece must be a one-of-a-kind 100% handpainted work of art.
- each piece must have the Peter Van Rossum signature.
- each piece must be dated.

American Delft Blue Ltd.
787 Oella Ave.
Ellicott City, Maryland 21043
(CATALOG $1.00)

PLASTER
- Cornice
- Ceilings
- Medallions

COMPOSITION ORNAMENTS (13,000)

CAPITALS & BRACKETS

TRADITIONAL FIREPLACE MANTELS

CUSTOM REPRODUCTION & WOOD COLUMNS QUOTED

THE *Decorators Supply* CORP.
3610-12 South Morgan
Chicago 60609
Est. 1892

CERAMIC TILE

Unglazed quarry tiles and encaustic tiles (tile with inlaid color similar to marquetry in wood) were often used in the vestibules of late 19th century houses. They can also give a dramatic Victorian character when used for a kitchen floor.

Small white hexagonal tiles and little white and black tiles were popular choices for bathroom floors until about 1930. These small tiles come pre-spaced on paper backing for easy installation.

Ceramic Tile

(1) Antique
(2) Dutch
(3) Encaustic
(4) Hand-Painted
(5) Period Styles—New
(6) Small White Hexagonal (Bathroom)
(7) Custom-Made

American Delft Blue, Inc. (MD) 2,4,7
American Olean Tile Company (PA) 5
Architectural Terra Cotta and Tile, Ltd. (IL) 3
Beall, Barbara Vantrease Studio (CA) 4,7
Berkshire Porcelain Studios (MA) 4,7
Brooklyn Tile Supply (NY) 6
Country Floors, Inc. (NY) 5
Dutch Products & Supply Co. (PA) 2,4
Elon, Inc. (NY) 4
FerGene Studio (IN) 5
Hearthstone Tile Co. (NY) 7
Jonathan Studios, Inc. (MN) 4,7
Mercer Tile & Pottery Works (NJ) 5,7
Second Chance (GA) 1
Tile Distributors, Inc. (NY) 6
Up Your Alley (PA) 1
Williams, Helen (CA) 1,2
Winburn Tile Manufacturing Co. (AR) 5,6
Wrecking Bar, Inc. (TX) 1

Architectural
Terra Cotta and Tile Ltd.

DESIGN AND MANUFACTURE
OF ARCHITECTURAL CERAMICS:

— Terra Cotta
— Encaustic Tiles

PRESERVATION
RESTORATION

727 S. DEARBORN
CHICAGO, IL
60605
312-786-0229

Genuine
Handpainted
Delft Tiles

26 different series
in Delft Blue or
Polychrome,
Plain Tiles to
match for fireplace,
kitchen, backsplash, coffee tables.

Send $1.00 for brochure and
name of your nearest dealer to:

Dutch Products & Supply Co.
P.O. Box 269, Dept. OHJ
Yardley, PA 19067

COUNTRY FLOORS®

300 East 61st Street,
New York, N.Y. 10021
(212) 758-7414

For handmade authentic
reproduction tiles for
floors and walls, from
Holland, France, Spain,
Portugal, Italy and
Mexico.

Country Floors® tiles are
available through
representatives in most
major cities around the
U.S. Send $5.00 for 60-
page color brochure and
the name of your nearest
representative.

BARBARA VANTREASE BEALL STUDIO

CUSTOM
HANDPAINTED CERAMIC TILES

23727
HAWTHORNE BOULEVARD
TORRANCE, CA 90505
213/378-1233

See Company Directory
for
Addresses & Phone Numbers

Corner Bead Moulding

Crawford's Old House Store (WI)

Glass, Curved—For China Cabinets

Furniture Revival and Co. (OR)
Morgan & Company (NY)
Pat's Etcetera Company (TX)
Shadovitz Bros. Distributors, Inc. (NY)
Squaw Alley, Inc. (IL)

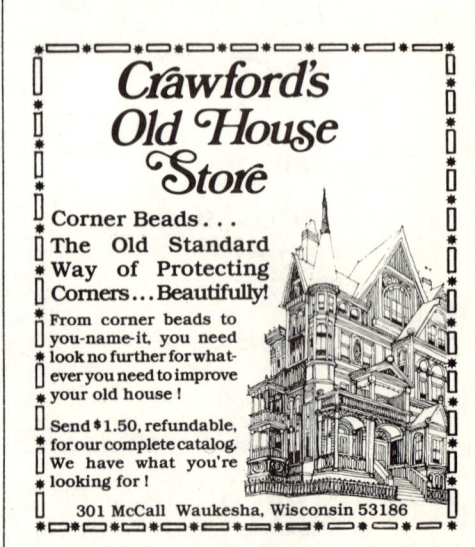

Crawford's Old House Store

Corner Beads...
The Old Standard
Way of Protecting
Corners...Beautifully!

From corner beads to
you-name-it, you need
look no further for what-
ever you need to improve
your old house!

Send $1.50, refundable,
for our complete catalog.
We have what you're
looking for!

301 McCall Waukesha, Wisconsin 53186

THE ART GLASS REVIVAL

One of the more spectacular elements of Victorian architecture is the use of "fancy glass" for doors and windows.

The use of stained and leaded glass emerged rather tentatively in the 1840's as a result of the popularity of the Gothic Revival style. Residential stained glass of a simple geometric quality was used in the 1860's and 1870's. But the high point artistically and in popularity was the twenty years between 1880 and 1900. By the end of World War I, stained glass had become an expensive extra in the plans of increasingly cost conscious builders.

Eclectic placement of stained glass is a hallmark of late Victorian architecture. Wherever there is a window of unusual shape or location there most likely will be stained glass. The front doorway has always been the most popular place, with complete entryway sets composed of door transom and matching side lights. Bay and oriel windows often have stained glass transom lights above the window openings. Except for bathroom windows stained glass was not customarily used above the second storey in houses. Inside use of stained glass was also popular. The stairway space with its ample wall areas and landings was used for the most exotic windows. Many homes have inside entryways fancier than those visible only to passers-by. Besides windows, stained glass is also found as a part of interior doors, bookcase doors, skylights and even fireplace screens.

Etched glass is particularly appropriate for doors and transoms in the Italian style houses that were built from the 1840's to the late 1800's. Stained glass with its medieval effect was antithetical to the classical themes.

Fancy beveled glass was the last of the decorative window and door treatments to come into fashion, mainly because it wasn't until the end of the 19th century that mass-produced plate glass could be made thick enough to have its edges ground down.

Beveled glass was often used in bookcase and cabinet doors as well.

Today with the increasing interest in 19th century decoration the repair, restoration and design of art glass is a burgeoning field. Many old techniques are being revived and new ones are being devised to create traditional motifs.

Glass, Art—Antique (Stained, Bevelled, Etched, Etc.)

Addco Architectural Antiques (LA)
Architectural Antiques Exchange (PA)
Architectural Heritage (CAN)
Art Directions (MO)
Bank Architectural Antiques (LA)
ByGone Era (GA)
Canal Co. (DC)
Canal Works (OH)
Condon Studios — Stained Glass (MA)
Electric Glass Co. (VA)
Golden Movement Emporium (CA)
Master's Stained and Etched Glass Studio (CA)
Pelnik Wrecking Co., Inc. (NY)
Red Baron's Antiques (GA)
Reflections (PA)
Salvage One (IL)
Spiess, Greg (IL)
Structural Antiques (OK)
Such Happiness, Inc. (MA)
United House Wrecking Corp. (CT)
Wilson, H. Weber, Antiquarian (MD)
Wrecking Bar, Inc. (TX)

Glass, Leaded & Stained—New

(1) New Work
(2) Restoration & Repair

Beirs, John (PA) 1
Bel-Air Door Co. (CA) 1
Bill's Beauts (MS) 1
Boulder Art Glass Co., Inc. (CO) 1,2
Brauer, Sandra (NY) 1,2
Condon Studios — Stained Glass (MA) ... 1,2
Elegant Accents Incorporated (CA) 1
G. Brittain M. Co. Stained Glass Studios (HI) 1,2
Glass Menagerie Designs Ltd. (CA) 1
Glassmasters Guild (NY) 1
Greenland Studio, The (NY) 1,2
Jonathan Studios, Inc. (MN) 1
Lamb, J & R Studios (NY) 1,2
Louisville Art Glass Studio (KY) 1
Manor Art Glass (NY) 1
Master's Stained and Etched Glass Studio (CA) 1
Melotte-Morse Studios (IL) 1,2
Meredith Stained Glass Studio, Inc. (VA) . 1,2
Morgan Bockius Studios, Inc. (PA) 1,2
Nast, Vivian (NY) 1
Newburyport Stained Glass Studio (MA) .. 1,2
Old Hickory Stained Glass Studio (WI) 1,2
Pompei Stained Glass (MA) 1,2
Porcelli, Ernest (NY) 1,2
Rambusch (NY) 2
Reflections (PA) 2
Ring, J. Stained Glass, Inc. (MN) 1,2
Rohlf's Stained & Leaded Glass (NY) 2
Savoy Studios (CA) 1,2
Spiess, Greg (IL) 1
Studio Design, Inc. t/a Rainbow Art Glass (NJ) 1
Studio Stained Glass (IN) 1,2
Such Happiness, Inc. (MA) 2
Sunburst Stained Glass Co. (IN) 1,2
Victoriana Glass Works, Inc. (NJ) 1,2
Walton Stained Glass (CA) 1
Willet Stained Glass Studio, Inc. (PA) .. 1,2
Wilson, H. Weber, Antiquarian (MD) 1,2
Windowcraft (GA) 1

STAINED GLASS | The finest original designs exquisitely articulated
Special effects
V. Nast
49 Willow Street
Brooklyn, N.Y.
(212) 596-5280

Glass, Etched—New

(1) Stock
(2) Custom

Bel-Air Door Co. (CA)	1
Bill's Beauts (MS)	2
Boulder Art Glass Co., Inc. (CO)	2
CW Design, Inc. (MN)	2
Condon Studios — Stained Glass (MA)	
Elegant Accents Incorporated (CA)	1,2
Glass Etch Designs (TX)	1,2
Glass Menagerie Designs Ltd. (CA)	2
Ice Nine Glass Design (MN)	1,2
Jonathan Studios, Inc. (MN)	2
Louisville Art Glass Studio (KY)	2
Master's Stained and Etched Glass Studio (CA)	2
Meredith Stained Glass Studio, Inc. (VA)	1
Morgan Bockius Studios, Inc. (PA)	2
Nast, Vivian (NY)	2
Ostrom Studios (OR)	2
Pocahontas Hardware & Glass (IL)	1,2
Pompei Stained Glass (MA)	2
Savoy Studios (CA)	2
Victoriana Glass Works, Inc. (NJ)	2

See Company Directory for Addresses & Phone Numbers

Glass, Specialty—New

(1) Bevelled
(2) Carved & Cut
(3) Engraved
(4) Glue-Chip
(5) Slumping & Bending

Acme Bent Glass (CN)	5
Architectural Emphasis (CA)	1
Beirs, John (PA)	1
Bel-Air Door Co. (CA)	1
Bevel Right Mfg. (NJ)	1
Beveled Glass Industries (CA)	1
Beveling Studio (WA)	1,2,4
Boulder Art Glass Co., Inc. (CO)	4,5
CasaBlanca Glass, Ltd. (GA)	1
Century Glass Inc. of Dallas (TX)	1,4
Cherry Creek Ent. Inc. (CO)	1
Condon Studios — Stained Glass (MA)	5
Electric Glass Co. (VA)	1
Elegant Accents Incorporated (CA)	1
Louisville Art Glass Studio (KY)	1
Master's Stained and Etched Glass Studio (CA)	1
Meredith Stained Glass Studio, Inc. (VA)	1
Morgan & Company (NY)	5
Morgan Bockius Studios, Inc. (PA)	1,2,5
Ostrom Studios (OR)	4
Pat's Etcetera Company (TX)	1
Pompei Stained Glass (MA)	1,5
Ring, J. Stained Glass, Inc. (MN)	1,3,5
Rohlf's Stained & Leaded Glass (NY)	1
Savoy Studios (CA)	2
Shadovitz Bros. Distributors, Inc. (NY)	1,5
Spiess, Greg (IL)	1
Studio Stained Glass (IN)	1
Sunburst Stained Glass Co. (IN)	1
Victoriana Glass Works, Inc. (NJ)	1,2,5
Walton Stained Glass (CA)	1
Windowcraft (GA)	1

ICE NINE
glass design

MIDWEST'S FINEST

Etched Glass

Authentic Designs For Restoration

Residential   Commercial

CATALOG only $2.00

1507 S. 6th St.
Minneapolis, MN 55454
Phone (612) 375-9669

Ernest Porcelli/Stained Glass

123 Seventh Avenue, Brooklyn, New York 11215 — (212) 857-6888

Custom designed, leaded and stained glass windows, door panels, side lights, skylights
For Commercial and Residential Use

Repairs and Restoration — Estimates with SASE, send dimensions

Mantels

(1) Antique (Original)
(2) New (Reproduction)
(3) Cast Iron
(4) Marble
(5) Slate
(6) Wood
(7) Other

Addco Architectural Antiques (LA)	1,6
Amerian Woodworking (CA)	2,6
Architectural Antiques Exchange (PA)	1,6
Architectural Heritage (CAN)	1
Architectural Paneling, Inc. (NY)	2,6
Art Directions (MO)	1
Bank Architectural Antiques (LA)	1
Bare Wood Inc. (NY)	1,6
ByGone Era (GA)	1,3,4,5,6
C—E Morgan (WI)	6
Canal Co. (DC)	1
Canal Works (OH)	1
Castle Burlingame (NJ)	1
Crawford's Old House Store (WI)	2,4,6
Decorators Supply Corp. (IL)	2
Driwood Moulding Company (SC)	2
Drums Sash & Door Co., Inc. (PA)	2
Feather River Wood and Glass Co. (CA)	2,6
Henderson Black & Greene, Inc. (AL)	2
International Building Components (NY)	6
Island City Wood Working Co. (TX)	4,5,6
Jonathan Studios, Inc. (MN)	1
Ley, Joe/Antiques (KY)	1
New York Marble Works (NY)	4
Old World Moulding (NY)	2
Olde Bostonian Architectural Antiques (MA)	1
Period Productions, Limited (VA)	6
Purcell, Francis J., II (PA)	1
Readybuilt Products, Co. (MD)	2,6
Remodelers' & Renovators' Supply (ID)	2
Restoration Hardware (CA)	2
Roman Marble Co. (IL)	1,4
Salvage One (IL)	1
Second Chance (GA)	1
Spiess, Greg (IL)	1
The Restoration Fraternity (PA)	2
United House Wrecking Corp. (CT)	1,6
Verine Products & Co. (UK)	2
Wrecking Bar, Inc. (TX)	1

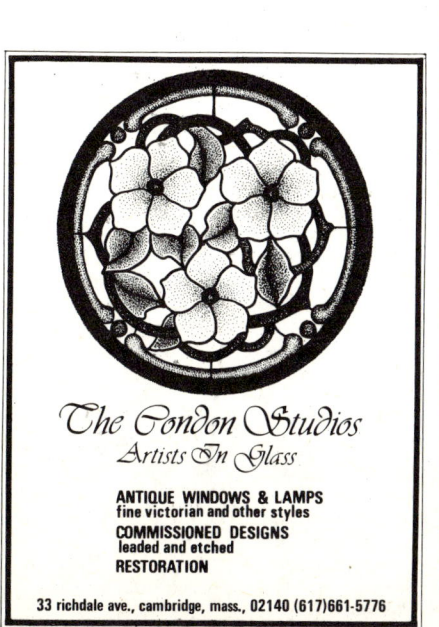

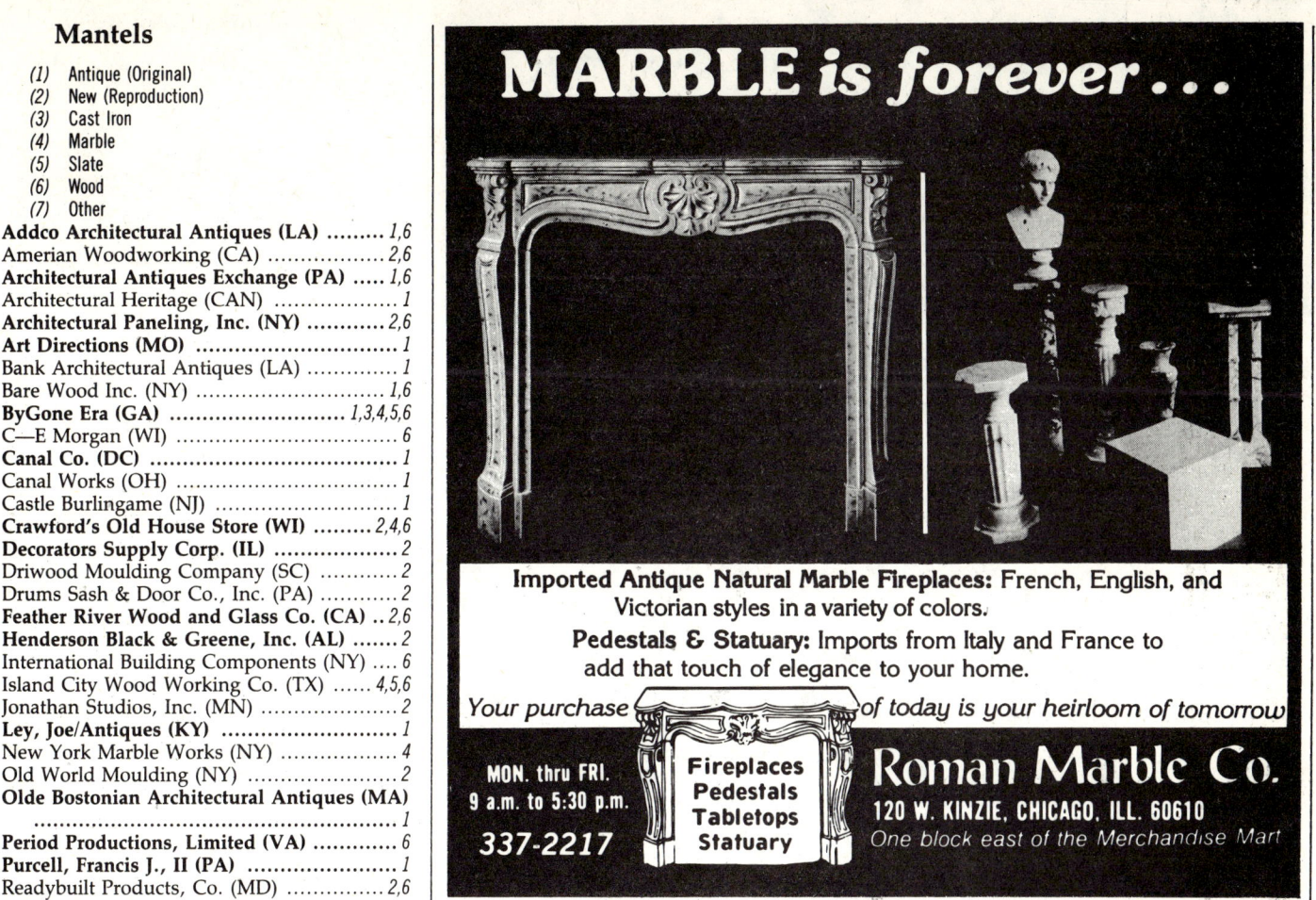

MARBLE is forever...

Imported Antique Natural Marble Fireplaces: French, English, and Victorian styles in a variety of colors.

Pedestals & Statuary: Imports from Italy and France to add that touch of elegance to your home.

Your purchase of today is your heirloom of tomorrow

MON. thru FRI. 9 a.m. to 5:30 p.m.
337-2217

Fireplaces
Pedestals
Tabletops
Statuary

Roman Marble Co.
120 W. KINZIE, CHICAGO, ILL. 60610
One block east of the Merchandise Mart

ETCHED GLASS
The Quality, Design & Workmanship in our glass has No Substitute

SEND $1.50 for Illustrated information on the most exacting copies of old glass available today!

DOORS
Raised Panel Entrance Doors Available In Custom Made & Stock Sizes

We Ship Direct To You

For new construction or restoration work this glass provides the finishing touch

Send $1.50 to

Pocahontas Hdwe. & Glass
Box 127. Dept. OHJ
Pocahontas, IL 62275
(618) 669-2880

The Condon Studios
Artists In Glass

ANTIQUE WINDOWS & LAMPS
fine victorian and other styles
COMMISSIONED DESIGNS
leaded and etched
RESTORATION

33 richdale ave., cambridge, mass., 02140 (617)661-5776

Marble, Replacement (Finished Pieces)

Marble Technics Ltd. (NY)
New York Marble Works (NY)

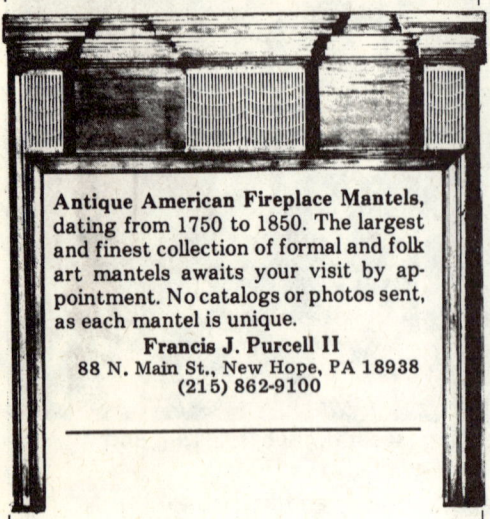

Antique American Fireplace Mantels, dating from 1750 to 1850. The largest and finest collection of formal and folk art mantels awaits your visit by appointment. No catalogs or photos sent, as each mantel is unique.

Francis J. Purcell II
88 N. Main St., New Hope, PA 18938
(215) 862-9100

See Company Directory for Addresses & Phone Numbers

FIREPLACES, MOULDINGS & CARVINGS
IMMEDIATE DELIVERY

Send $5.00 for Brochure. Sample included. Deductible on Orders.

Architectural Paneling
979 Third Ave., Suite 1518
New York, N.Y. 10022

ARCHITECTURAL PANELING INC.

USING WOOD TRIM

In houses of the 18th and 19th centuries, the wood trim was hand carved and based on pattern books and the carpenter's own aesthetic judgement. By the Victorian era, standardized moulding was commercially milled in eight classic shapes, which are still used to this day.

A simple moulding can be replaced from stock. More complex patterns can be built up by combining stock parts—just as our predecessors did. If the trim is totally missing, its shape can sometimes be discovered by looking for old paint profiles at the edge of door frames or in the corner of walls. When the rooms have been completely reduced to bare boxes, trim can be used to good effect if it is true to the original architectural style of the house. For example, moulding can be used on modern flush doors to give the appearance of the original panel doors.

Mouldings & Cornices—Interior Decorative

(1) Composition
(2) Plaster
(3) Wood
(4) Custom Cast

A.R.D. (NY)
Addco Architectural Antiques (LA) 2
Architectural Sculpture (NY) 4
Balmer Architectural Art Limited (CAN) .. 1,2
Bendix Mouldings, Inc. (NJ) 3
Biagiotti, L. (NY) 1,2,4
California Heritage Wood Products, Ltd. (CA) 3
Casey Architectural Specialties (WI) 2
Cumberland Woodcraft Co., Inc. (PA) 3
Decorators Supply Corp. (IL) 1,2,3
Dixon Bros. Woodworking (MA) 3
Dovetail, Inc. (MA) 4
Driwood Moulding Company (SC) 3
Elliott Millwork Co. (IL) 3
Englewood Hardware Co. (NJ)
Felber, Inc. (PA) 2
Focal Point, Inc. (GA) 1
Garbe's (OK) 2
Giannetti Studios (MD) 1,2
Haas Wood & Ivory Works (CA) 3
Hallelujah Redwood Products (CA) 3
Kingsway (CO) 3
Klise Manufacturing Company (MI) 3
Lachin, Albert & Assoc., Inc. (LA) 2,4
Millworks Inc. (VT) 3
Morgan Woodworking Supplies (KY) 3
Old World Moulding (NY) 3
Old World Stucchi Decor (PA) 2
Ornamental Plaster-Works (NY) 2
Period Pine (GA) 3
Saldarini & Pucci, Inc. (NY) 1,2,3,4
Schaefer, Rick — Plasterer (CA) 4
Silverton Victorian Millworks (CO) 3
Turnbull's Custom Mouldings (MI) 3
Weir, R. & Co. (MA) 3
Wood Designs (OH) 3

Ornaments

(1) Composition
(2) Wood
(3) Plaster

Addco Architectural Antiques (LA) 2
American Wood Column (NY) 2
Balmer Architectural Art Limited (CAN) 1
Bendix Mouldings, Inc. (NJ) 2
Biagiotti, L. (NY) 1,3
Casey Architectural Specialties (WI) 3
Decorators Supply Corp. (IL) 1,3
Felber, Inc. (PA) 3
Focal Point, Inc. (GA) 1
Gargoyles — New York (NY) 1
Giannetti Studios (MD) 1,3
Haas Wood & Ivory Works (CA) 2
Hallelujah Redwood Products (CA) 2
Kingsway (CO) 1
Lachin, Albert & Assoc., Inc. (LA) 3
Old World Stucchi Decor (PA) 3
Ornamental Plaster-Works (NY) 3
Saldarini & Pucci, Inc. (NY) 1,2,3
Silverton Victorian Millworks (CO) 2
Weaver, W. T. & Sons, Inc. (DC) 1
Woodworkers' Store, The (MN) 2

Strobel Millwork

ARCHITECTURAL MILLWORK

We Specialize in the duplication of Early Millwork

•

Old style Doors and Windows with Insulated Glass

Corner Block

Victorian

Salem

Entrances
Raised Panel Walls

•

Many Other Styles of
INTERIOR TRIM
AVAILABLE

STAIRS

•

Brochure $2.00

•

Established 1953

STROBEL MILLWORK

ROUTE 7,
CORNWALL BRIDGE, CT 06754
(203) 672-6727

Plasterwork, Decorative

(1) Precast Mouldings
(2) Custom Mouldings

Addco Architectural Antiques (LA) 2
Architectural Sculpture (NY) 2
Balmer Architectural Art Limited (CAN) 1
Biagiotti, L. (NY) 1,2
Casey Architectural Specialties (WI) 1,2
Decorators Supply Corp. (IL) 1
Felber, Inc. (PA) 1,2
Giannetti Studios (MD) 1,2
Lachin, Albert & Assoc., Inc. (LA) 2
Mangione Plaster and Tile and Stucco (NY) 2
Old World Stucchi Decor (PA) 2
Ornamental Plaster-Works (NY) 2
Saldarini & Pucci, Inc. (NY) 1,2
San Francisco Victoriana (CA) 2
Schaefer, Rick — Plasterer (CA) 2

Furniture & Furnishings

Bed Hangings

(1) Netted Bed Canopies
(2) Bed Curtains
(3) Quilts & Coverlets

Antique Quilt Repair (CA) 3
Bedlam Brass Beds — Denver (CO) 3
Biggs Co. (VA) 1
Brown, Carol (VT) 3
Cohasset Colonials (MA) 1
Cole, Diane Jackson (ME) 3
Colonial Weavers (ME) 3
Country Curtains (MA) 2,3
Ephraim Marsh Co. (NC) 1
Gurian's (NY) 3
Huber, S. & C. — Accoutrements (CT) 1,2
Pandora's Quilt Museum (PA) 3
Sunshine Lane (OH) 3

Candlestands & Holders

(1) Candlestands
(2) Candelabra
(3) Candlesticks

Barnett, D. James — Blacksmith (IL) 1
Claymont Forge (WV) 3
Cohasset Colonials (MA) 1
Colonial Casting Co. (CT) 3
Craft House, Colonial Williamsburg (VA)
.... 1,2,3
Ephraim Marsh Co. (NC) 1
Essex Forge (CT) 1
Greenfield Village and Henry Ford Museum (MI) 1
Guild of Shaker Crafts (MI) 1,3
Historic Charleston Reproductions (SC) 3
Huber, S. & C. — Accoutrements (CT)
Hurley Patentee Lighting (NY) 1,2,3
Kayne, Steve — Hand-Forged Hardware (NY) 1
Loose, Thomas — Blacksmith/ Whitesmith (PA) 3
Millham, Newton — Blacksmith (MA) 1
Olde Village Smithery (MA) 3
Renovator's Supply (MA)
Saltbox (PA)
Sign of the Crab (CA) 2
Washington Copper Works (CT) 2
Wolchonok, M. and Son, Inc. (NY) 3

Clocks

(1) Traditional (Assembled)
(2) Kits

Adirondack Hudson Arms (NY) 1
Armor Products (NY)
Cornucopia, Inc. (MA) 1
Greenfield Village and Henry Ford Museum (MI) 1
Magnolia Hall (GA)
Mason & Sullivan Co. (MA)
Miller, Howard Clock Co. (MI) 1
Ogren & Trigg Clock Service (MN)
Olde Timer Watch & Clock Shoppe (CA) ... 1
Pendulum Shop (PA) 1
Selva — Borel (CA) 1,2
Sign of the Crab (CA)
Viking Clocks (AL) 2

Chairs, Early American Reproduction

(1) Colonial Wooden Side Chairs
(2) Rockers
(3) Other

Cornucopia, Inc. (MA) 1,2
Craft House, Colonial Williamsburg (VA) ... 1
Ephraim Marsh Co. (NC) 1,2
Greenfield Village and Henry Ford Museum (MI) 1
Guild of Shaker Crafts (MI) 2
Heritage Design (IA) 2
Hitchcock Chair Co. (CT)
Lea, James — Cabinetmaker (ME) 1
Rocker Shop (GA) 2
Saltbox (PA) 1
Shaker Workshops (MA) 1,2
Whitley Studios (PA) 2
Yield House, Inc. (NH)

BIGGS brings you the 18th century today.

HANDTIED FISHNET CANOPIES
In authentic 18th century designs made to fit single, double, Queen and King sizes. Available in white or off-white. Shown above is the lovely double diamond design. For information please write to:

MRS. F.W. STREET, BIGGS DIRECT MAIL
105 E. Grace St., Richmond, VA 23219
FURNITURE CATALOGUE $6.00

The Old-House Journal 1982 Catalog

Chairs, Victorian Reproduction

(1) Morris
(2) Turn-of-Century Oak
(3) Rockers
(4) Other

Amerian Woodworking (CA) 2
Dover Furniture Stripping (DE) 2
Magnolia Hall (GA) 2,3
Museum Enterprises, Inc. (WA)
Thomastown Chair Works (MS) 3
Victorian Reproductions, Inc. (MN) 3

Clothing, Period

(1) Patterns
(2) Custom-Made
(3) Ready-To-Wear

Arriaga, Nelson (NY) 2,3
Past Patterns (MI) 1

Victoriana Reborn!

Specializing in Edwardian and contemporary attire

Custom made to order by

NELSON ARRIAGA
418 Grand Avenue
Brooklyn, New York 11238
(212) 783-1221

Catalog $3.00

Nelson Arriaga is tailor to The Old-House Journal Staff

Drapery Hardware

(1) Wood Poles & Brackets
(2) Metal Poles & Brackets
(3) Decorative Tie-Backs

Ball and Ball (PA) 2,3
Cohasset Colonials (MA) 1
Constance Carol, Inc. (MA) 1
Country Curtains (MA) 1
Craft House, Colonial Williamsburg (VA) ... 3
Gould-Mesereau Co., Inc. (NY) 1,2,3
Guerin, P.E. Inc. (NY) 2,3
Hunrath, Wm. Co., Inc. (NY) 2

Drapery Trimmings

Craft House, Colonial Williamsburg (VA)
Scalamandre, Inc. (NY)

Drapery & Curtains

(1) Curtains, Ready-Made
(2) Curtains, Custom-Made
(3) Drapes, Custom-Made

Beck, Nelson of Wash. Inc. (DC) 2,3
Cohasset Colonials (MA) 1
Constance Carol, Inc. (MA)
Country Curtains (MA) 1
Dorothy's Ruffled Originals (NC) 1,2
Grilk Interiors (IA) 2,3
Home Fabric Mills, Inc. (MA) 2,3
Mather's (MD) 1

Drapery & Curtain Patterns—Period Designs

Colonial Weavers (ME)

Fabric, Reproduction

(1) Early American
(2) Victorian
(3) Turn-of-Century

Brunschwig & Fils, Inc. (NY) 1,2,3
Clarence House Imports, Ltd. (NY) 1,2
Cohasset Colonials (MA)
Cowtan & Tout, Inc. (NY) 1,2,3
Craft House, Colonial Williamsburg (VA) ... 1
Hexter, S. M. Company (OH) 1
Historic Charleston Reproductions (SC)
Johnson, R.L. Interiors (MT)
Scalamandre, Inc. (NY) 1,2,3
Waverly Fabrics (NY) 1,2

Fabric, Traditional

(1) Tapestry
(2) Crewel
(3) Handwoven
(4) Linen, Cotton
(5) Horsehair
(6) Silk, Velvet, Damask
(7) Other

Brown, Carol (VT) 4,7
Brunschwig & Fils, Inc. (NY) 1,4,5,6
Cowtan & Tout, Inc. (NY) 6
Craft House, Colonial Williamsburg (VA) .. 4,6
Cyrus Clark Co., Inc. (NY) 4
Gill Imports (CT) 2
Gurian's (NY) 2
Heirloom Rugs (RI)
Home Fabric Mills, Inc. (MA) 6
Homespun Weavers (PA) 4
Huber, S. & C. — Accoutrements (CT) .. 2,3,4
Johnson, R.L. Interiors (MT)
Liberty of London (NY)
Lovelia Enterprises, Inc. (NY) 1
Scalamandre, Inc. (NY) 2,4,5,6
Waverly Fabrics (NY) 4

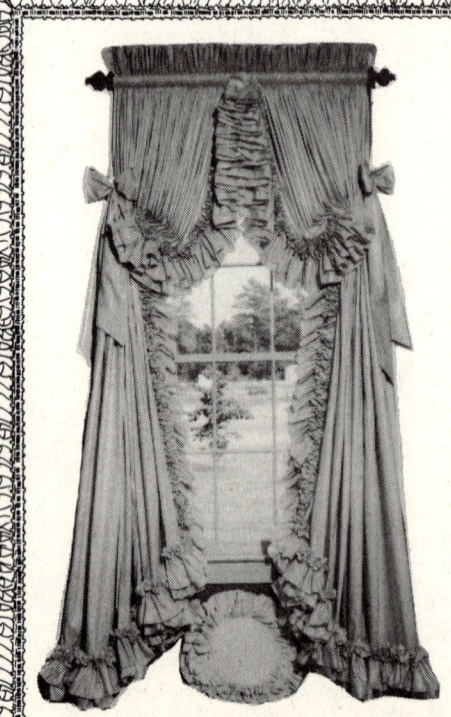

Designer Curtains by Dorothy

Exquisite! Our Custom-made Ruffled Curtains featuring lavish 8" Ruffles • 28 yds. of Perma-Press or All lace fabric per 96" length • Bow Tiebacks • available in a large variety of fabrics — Solid Ecrus, Whites, Creams; All lace; Chintz, Pastels, Calicoes, Ginghams, Dotted Swiss; untrimmed, or trimmed with Rickrack, Ribbon or Lace. Many Curtain Styles.

Ruffled Accessories made to order, too, including Coverlets, Dust Ruffles, Shams, Lampshades, Pillows, Placemats, Napkins, Chairpads, Wreaths and Tea Aprons.

Unusual Giftware and Accessories — Wrought-iron Lamps, Tinware, Candlesticks, "Pewter-look" metal Tableware, Baskets, Braided Rugs, String Canopies.

36-Page Color Catalog & Swatches $4.00

Dorothy's Ruffled Originals, Inc.
6721 Market Street, Wilmington, NC 28405 (Dpt. OHJ)
(919) 791-1296 Toll-free 1-800-334-2593 In NC: 1-800-672-2947
Master Charge • Visa

COUNTRY CURTAINS®
FREE FALL CATALOG

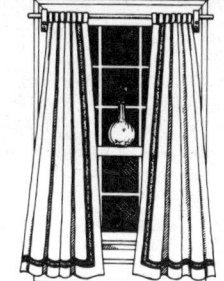

Country Curtains are a tradition... years of old-fashioned quality and conscientious service. Curtains in cotton muslin and carefree permanent press, some with ruffles, others with fringe or lace trim. Also tab curtains, bed ensembles, tablecloths, wooden rods and other accessories. Free catalog and color flyer... fabric swatches available to help you decide. Please call 413-298-3921 or write us. Satisfaction guaranteed.

☐ PLEASE SEND FREE CATALOG
Name
Address
City
State   Zip

COUNTRY CURTAINS
At The Red Lion Inn
Dept. OHJ, Stockbridge, Mass. 01262

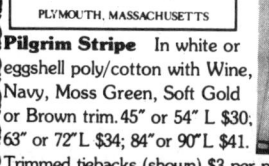

Constance Carol
PLYMOUTH, MASSACHUSETTS

Pilgrim Stripe In white or eggshell poly/cotton with Wine, Navy, Moss Green, Soft Gold or Brown trim. 45" or 54" L $30; 63" or 72" L $34; 84" or 90" L $41. Trimmed tiebacks (shown) $3 per pair, plain tiebacks free. Also available lined. Custom sizes available. Brackets and ¾" x 48" rod (unfinished) $5. Add $2 shipping. Add sales tax for MA (5%), PA (6%), VA (4%). Check, money order, MC, or VISA.
Constance Carol, Dept. OHJ
Box 899, Plymouth, Mass. 02360
Call Toll Free Mon - Fri 9 - 4: 1-800-343-5921.
(From Mass: 1-800-242-5815.)

See Company Directory for Addresses & Phone Numbers

For More Information About Traditional Fabric See SCALAMANDRE Ad Inside Back Cover

The leading collections of documentary American wallcoverings... the new "Greenfield Village" Volume III and the "Countryside" collections.

GREENFIELD VILLAGE
HENRY FORD MUSEUM
DEARBORN MICHIGAN

S.M. HEXTER COMPANY

The Old-House Journal 1982 Catalog

Furniture, Reproduction — Custom-Made

Biggs Company (VA)
Boston Cabinet-Making Inc. (MA)
Campbell, Douglas Co. (RI)
Campbell, Marion (PA)
Carolina Leather House, Inc. (NC)
Crowfoot's Inc. (AZ)
Curry, Gerald — Cabinetmaker (ME)
Custom Woodworking (CT)
Dixon Bros. Woodworking (MA)
Gaudio Custom Furniture (NY)
Hanscom's Corner Shop (ME)
Lea, James — Cabinetmaker (ME)
Master Wood Carver (NJ)
Mead Associates Woodworking, Inc. (NY)
Millbranth, D.R. (NH)
Newby, Simon (MA)
Nutt, Craig, Fine Wood Works (AL)
Orr, J.F., & Sons (MA)
Whitley Studios (PA)

DIXON BROS. WOODWORKING

- ROLL TOP DESKS -
SOLID WHITE OAK
MAHOGANY, WALNUT
$1,200 to $2,000
617-445-9884

See Company Directory
for
Addresses & Phone Numbers

PIONEER RUGS

Restore to original look
by using
"WOVEN PIONEER RAG RUGS"

Deseret Industries Manufacturing
1680 South Industrial Road
Salt Lake City, Utah 84104
Phone (801) 531-4094

Furniture & Accessories — Period Styles

(1) Country Primitive
(2) Wicker
(3) Early American
(4) Victorian
(5) Turn-of-Century
(6) Brass Beds
(7) Kits
(8) Other

Amerian Woodworking (CA) 3
Bedlam Brass Beds (NJ) 4,6
Bedlam Brass Beds — Denver (CO) 6
Berea College Student Craft Industries (KY) 3
Cane & Basket Supply Company (CA) 7
Capitol Victorian Furniture (AL) 4
Cohasset Colonials (MA) 1,3
Corner Legacy (AR) 5
Cornucopia, Inc. (MA) 1,3
Country Loft (MA) 1,3
Craft House, Colonial Williamsburg (VA) ... 3
Custom House (ME) 4
Davis Cabinet Co. (TN) 3,4
Ephraim Marsh Co. (NC) 3
Golden Movement Emporium (CA) 6
Greenfield Village and Henry Ford Museum
 (MI) 3,7
Guild of Shaker Crafts (MI) 3
Hanscom's Corner Shop (ME) 3
Hardwood Craftsman, Ltd. (IL) 7
Heritage Design (IA) 7
Hickory Chair Company (NC) 3
Historic Charleston Reproductions (SC) 3
Hitchcock Chair Co. (CT) 3
Hooterville Manufacturing Co. (GA) 6
Jennifer House (MA)
Kimball Furniture Company (IN) 4
Kittinger Company (NY) 3
Lea, James — Cabinetmaker (ME) 1,3
Lisa — Victoria Brass Beds (VA) 6
Magnolia Hall (GA) 4,5
Martha M. House (AL) 4,6
Mazza Frame and Furniture Co., Inc. (NY)
Outer Banks Pine Products (PA) 3
Renovators Co. (NY)
Rocker Shop (GA) 1
Saltbox (PA) 3
Seraph, The (MA)
Shaker Reproductions (NY) 3
Shaker Workshops (MA) 3,7
Swan Brass Beds (CA) 6
The Bartley Collection, Ltd. (IL) 3,7
Unique Brass Foundry, Inc. (NY) 6
Up Country Enterprise Corp. (NH)
Victorian Reproductions, Inc. (MN) 4
Viking Clocks (AL) 1,7
Vintage Oak Furniture (CA) 5
Western Reserve Antique Furniture Kit (OH)
 3,7
Yield House, Inc. (NH) 3

Lamp Shades — Period Styles

Bedlam Brass Beds — Denver (CO)
Burdoch Silk Lampshade Co. (CA)
Custom House (ME)
Holcomb, Tracy (CA)
Lundberg Studios (CA)
Victorian Reproductions, Inc. (MN)

Needlework Kits

(1) Crewel Chair Kits
(2) Rug Braiding & Hooking
(3) Needlepoint
(4) Quilt Patterns

Braid-Aid (MA) 1,2,3
Craft House, Colonial Williamsburg (VA) . 1,3
Cumberland General Store (TN)
Historic Charleston Reproductions (SC) ... 1,3

Pedestals & Plant Stands

(1) Cast Iron
(2) Marble
(3) Wood
(4) Wrought Iron

Magnolia Hall (GA) 3
New York Marble Works (NY) 2
Santa Cruz Foundry (CA) 1
Wolchonok, M. and Son, Inc. (NY) 1,3,4

Picture Hangers — Period Styles

S & W Framing Supplies, Inc. (NY)

Prints & Original Art

Baren, Joan (NY)
Creatus (PA)
Facemakers, Inc. (IL)
Gifford, D.K. (GA)
Harmon, Ruth (CA)
Kohler Co. (WI)
McGivern, Barbara — Artist (WI)
Michels, Dale/Illustrator (WV)

Rugs & Carpets

(1) Ingrain
(2) Oriental
(3) Traditional
(4) Documentary Reproductions
(5) Custom-Made
(6) Other

Greenfield Village and Henry Ford Museum
 (MI) 4,5
Jacobsen, Charles W., Inc. (NY) 2
Johnson, R.L. Interiors (MT) 3
Newbury Carpets (MA) 4,5
Scalamandre, Inc. (NY) 1,3
Stark Carpet Corp. (NY) 2,6

Rugs, Folk

(1) Braided
(2) Floorcloths
(3) Straw Matting
(4) Hooked
(5) Needlework
(6) Woven
(7) Other

Brown, Carol (VT) 6
Cole, Diane Jackson (ME) 6
Country Braid House (NH) 1
Deseret Industries Manufacturing (UT) ... 1
Floorcloths Incorporated (MD) 2
Good Stenciling (NH) 2
Greenfield Village and Henry Ford Museum
 (MI) 4
Heirloom Rugs (RI) 4
Heritage Rugs (PA)
Historic Interiors, Ltd. (MI) 2
Huber, S. & C. — Accoutrements (CT) 1,4,5,6
Import Specialists, Inc. (NY) 3

Shades & Blinds—Period Styles

Bare Wood Inc. (NY)
Devenco Louver Products (GA)
Iberia Millwork (LA)

Old-Fashioned Restaurant Fittings

Architectural Antique Warehouse, The (CAN)
Art Directions (MO)
Bedlam Brass Beds (NJ)
Bona Decorative Hardware (OH)
Brass Menagerie (LA)
Canal Works (OH)
Gargoyles, Ltd. (PA)
Ley, Joe/Antiques (KY)
Ship 'n Out (NY)
Spiess, Greg (IL)

Umbrella Stands & Coat Racks

(1) Umbrella Stands
(2) Coat Racks

Bedlam Brass Beds (NJ) 2
Kayne, Steve — Hand-Forged Hardware (NY) 2
Lemee's Fireplace Equipment (MA) 1
Magnolia Hall (GA)
Outer Banks Pine Products (PA) 2
Renovator's Supply (MA) 2
Swan Brass Beds (CA) 2
Unique Brass Foundry, Inc. (NY) 2

Wallcoverings (Other than Wallpaper)

(1) Anaglypta
(2) Leather, Genuine
(3) Leather, Imitation
(4) Embossed Vinyl
(5) Other

Bradbury & Bradbury Wallpapers (CA) 1
Brown, Carol (VT) 5
Flexi-Wall Systems (SC) 5
Hexter, S. M. Company (OH) 4
Rejuvenation House Parts Co. (OR) 1
Remodelers' & Renovators' Supply (ID) 1
San Francisco Victoriana (CA) 1
Scalamandre, Inc. (NY) 2,3
Thibaut, Richard E., Inc. (NY) 3,4

Wallpaper, Early American

(1) Documentary Reproduction
(2) Scenic Antique
(3) Scenic Reproduction
(4) Other

Brunschwig & Fils, Inc. (NY) 1
Cowtan & Tout, Inc. (NY) 1
Craft House, Colonial Williamsburg (VA) ... 1
Greenfield Village and Henry Ford Museum (MI) 1
Hexter, S. M. Company (OH) 1
Scalamandre, Inc. (NY) 1
Schumacher (NY) 1
Thibaut, Richard E., Inc. (NY) 1,3

Wallpaper, Custom Duplication & Restoration

CW Design, Inc. (MN)
Cowtan & Tout, Inc. (NY)
Hexter, S. M. Company (OH)
Old Stone Mill Corp. (MA)
Scalamandre, Inc. (NY)
Victoria Wallpaper Co. (CAN)

Wallpaper, Specialty

(1) Murals
(2) Imported Oriental
(3) Borders & Panels
(4) Custom-Made
(5) Other

Bradbury & Bradbury Wallpapers (CA) 3
Brunschwig & Fils, Inc. (NY) 3
CW Design, Inc. (MN) 4
Cowtan & Tout, Inc. (NY) 3,4
San Francisco Victoriana (CA) 3
Scalamandre, Inc. (NY) 3
Thibaut, Richard E., Inc. (NY) 1,2
Victorian Collectibles (WI) 5

HANDPRINTED VICTORIAN WALLPAPERS

Available by mail order.
Please send $1.00 for brochure.
BRADBURY & BRADBURY WALLPAPERS
P.O. Box 155 Benicia, CA 94510
707/644-0724

For More Information About Period Wallpaper See SCALAMANDRE Ad Inside Back Cover

Wallpaper, Traditional

(1) Early American Patterns
(2) Victorian Design
(3) Art Nouveau
(4) Other

Bradbury & Bradbury Wallpapers (CA) 2
Brunschwig & Fils, Inc. (NY) 2
Cowtan & Tout, Inc. (NY) 1,2
Craft House, Colonial Williamsburg (VA) ... 1
Greenfield Village and Henry Ford Museum (MI) 1
Hexter, S. M. Company (OH) 1
Johnson, R.L. Interiors (MT)
Old Stone Mill Corp. (MA) 1
Scalamandre, Inc. (NY) 1,2,3
Schumacher (NY) 1,2
Thibaut, Richard E., Inc. (NY) 1,2,3
Victoria Wallpaper Co. (CAN) 2,3
Warner Company (IL)
Wolf Paints And Wallpapers (NY) 1,2

Wallpaper, Victorian

(1) Documentary Reproduction
(2) Hand-Printed Reproduction
(3) Other

Bradbury & Bradbury Wallpapers (CA) ... 1,2
Brunschwig & Fils, Inc. (NY) 2
Cowtan & Tout, Inc. (NY) 2
Scalamandre, Inc. (NY) 1,2
Schumacher (NY) 1
Stamford Wallpaper Co., Inc. (CT) 1
Thibaut, Richard E., Inc. (NY) 1,2
Victoria Wallpaper Co. (CAN) 1

Other Decorative Accessories

Doll Depot (IN)
Lewis, John N. (PA)

Custom made WOODEN VENETIAN BLINDS DEVENCO PRODUCTS INC.

All of our blinds are made expressly for your windows in the traditional style (2")
Choice of Stain or Paint
To match your trim with coordinating tape and cord colors.
Call us today or write for more information and cost.
BOX 700
Decatur, GA 30030
404-378-4597

Interior Hardware, Plumbing & House Fittings

Alarm Systems—Fire & Security
Restoration Works, Inc. (NY)

Bathroom Accessories
(1) Soap Dishes, Etc.
(2) Towel Racks, Etc.
(3) Medicine Cabinets
(4) Other

A-Ball Plumbing Supply (OR) 1
Barclay Products Co. (IL) 1,2,4
Bona Decorative Hardware (OH) 2
Brass Menagerie (LA) 2
Broadway Collection (MO) 2
Canal Co. (DC) 3
Corner Legacy (AR) 3
Guerin, P.E. Inc. (NY) 2
Hunrath, Wm. Co., Inc. (NY) 2
Jennings Lights of Yesterday (CA) 2
Kayne, Steve — Hand-Forged Hardware (NY) ... 2
Kingsway (CO) 4
New England Brassworks (CT) 2
Pfanstiel Hardware Co. (NY) 2
Renovator's Supply (MA) 1,2
Restoration Works, Inc. (NY) 3
Shaker Reproductions (NY) 2
Sign of the Crab (CA)
Smithy, The (VT) 2
Southern Accents Architectural Antiques (AL) ... 3
Sunrise Salvage (CA) 1,2
Twanky Dillo Forge (VT) 2,4

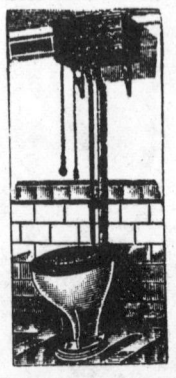

BRASS TOWEL BARS

12" bar ... $15
18" bar ... $18
24" bar ... $20
30" bar ... $22.50
add $3 for shipping
VISA and MasterCard accepted

Hand crafted, polished brass, U.S.A. made, center reinforced with steel rod.

JENNINGS
1523 San Pablo Ave.
Berkeley, CA 94702
(415) 526-1008

8" tissue holder
$15 each

See Company Directory for Addresses & Phone Numbers

Classic American Brass

Bathroom Hardware and Decorative Accessories, handcrafted of solid brass in our historic 1840 foundry.

Brochure 50¢ (refundable)

New England BrassWorks
220 Riverside Avenue
Bristol, Connecticut 06010

OLD PLUMBING FIXTURES: High-tank toilets, claw foot tubs pedestal bases, porcelain handle faucets, radiators. Visit our shop for a large selection of old-fashioned used bathroom and plumbing fixtures.

P & G New and Used Plumbing Supply Co.
155 Harrison Ave.
Brooklyn, New York 11206
(212) 384-6310

One Product You Can Bet Your Assets On Is Our Oak Commode Seat.

Since 1976 our company has manufactured a line of high-end oak bathroom accessories, the nucleus of which is our oak toilet seat.

Our seats have a quality appearance and indeed they are built to last for years. The components, solid oak lumber and solid brass hinges, and the workmanship come together to make our oak seats something special.

Upgrade your bathroom just as you have upgraded the rest of your home. Seats are $47.50 postpaid, and are available in standard or elongated sizes, dark oak or golden oak finishes, and with lacquered brass or chrome-plated hinges.

We also have a 30-day no hassle refund policy. Send check, money order, VISA or Masterchange with expiration date, to:

DeWeese Woodworking Company
Dept. OHJ
P.O. Box 576
Philadelphia, MS 39350

Our phone number is (601) 656-4951.
Our brochure is available on request.

---

54 The Old-House Journal 1982 Catalog

Bathroom Faucets & Fittings

(1) Antique (Salvage)
(2) Reproduction
(3) Old Faucet Parts

A-Ball Plumbing Supply (OR)	2
Barclay Products Co. (IL)	2
Bona Decorative Hardware (OH)	2
Broadway Collection (MO)	2
Dentro Plumbing Specialties (NY)	3
Domestic Environmental Alternatives (CA)	2
Englewood Hardware Co. (NJ)	2
Guerin, P.E. Inc. (NY)	2
Hunrath, Wm. Co., Inc. (NY)	2
Kingsway (CO)	2
Kohler Co. (WI)	2
P & G New and Used Plumbing Supply (NY)	1
Pfanstiel Hardware Co. (NY)	2
Porcelain Restoration (NC)	2
Remodelers' & Renovators' Supply (ID)	2
Renovator's Supply (MA)	2
Rheinschild, S. Chris (CA)	2
Ritter & Son (CA)	2
Sign of the Crab (CA)	
Southern Accents Architectural Antiques (AL)	
Sunrise Salvage (CA)	2
Tennessee Tub (TN)	1,2,3
Walker Industries (TN)	2
Wolchonok, M. and Son, Inc. (NY)	2

Nostalgia

Nostalgic plumbing products charmingly recreated by Kohler. Pedestal lavatories. Antique faucets. Rolled-rim cast iron bathtubs with feet. High-tank, pull-chain toilets. Send $1.00 for brochures. **Kohler Co., Box OH, Kohler, WI 53044.**

For More Information
About Faucets & Fixtures
See
RENOVATOR'S SUPPLY
Ad Inside Front Cover

BARCLAY
PRODUCTS COMPANY
QUALITY BATH ACCESSORIES

Barclay Products Company
P.O. Box 12257
Chicago, Illinois 60612
(312) 243-1444

The Old-House Journal 1982 Catalog

Bathroom Toilets & Seats — Period Styles

(1) High-Tank Toilets (New)
(2) High-Tank Toilets (Salvage)
(3) Toilets, Period Styles
(4) Toilets, Period Styles (Salvage)
(5) Toilet Parts
(6) Wooden Toilet Seats

Addco Architectural Antiques (LA)	2,4
Brass Menagerie (LA)	3
Deweese Woodworking (MS)	6
Jennings Lights of Yesterday (CA)	1,6
Kohler Co. (WI)	1
P & G New and Used Plumbing Supply (NY)	2
Renovator's Supply (MA)	1
Restoration Works, Inc. (NY)	1
Rheinschild, S. Chris (CA)	1
Southern Accents Architectural Antiques (AL)	4
Sunrise Salvage (CA)	1
Tennessee Tub (TN)	2,3
Walker Industries (TN)	1,6

PULL CHAIN TOILET

*Handcrafted oak tank with durable stainless steel liner, brass pipe and fittings
*Designed by licensed plumber and craftsman

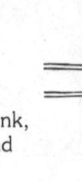

*Also available: copper kitchen sink, oak bath sink, and copper bathtub

Send $1.35 for brochure

S. Chris Rheinschild
2220 Carlton Way
Santa Barbara
California 93109
(805) 962-8598

See Company Directory for Addresses & Phone Numbers

Distinctive Hardware With Class

Solid Brass Reproduction Hardware with the Durability and Beauty of Bygone Years

**Door & Drawer Hardware
Switchplates, Plumbing Fixtures, Latches
Lamps, Light Fixtures, Fireplace Accessories, Locks
Wind Vanes, Ice Box Hardware
Hooks, Hangers & Brackets**

Her Majesty's Brass Works Ltd., Division of:
Sign of the Crab
Department 132
8101 Elder Creek Road • Sacramento, CA 95824 • (916) 383-2722

FREE FULL COLOR CATALOG
for Retailers, Interior Decorators, Architects & Contractors

☐ Please send me your Free Catalog
☐ Please advise me of the nearest place where products can be seen.

My name is _____

Company name _____

Street or Box No. _____

City _____ State _____ Zip _____

Resale No. _____

Sunrise Salvage

Purveyors of fine Victorian home accessories, we at Sunrise Salvage are proud to present both original fixtures and craftsmanlike replicas designed to accent your home with the elegant flavor of a bygone era.

The bathtub shown in this photo is an original clawfoot tub with brass plated legs and a custom made oak rim. Tubs of this type are available in our Berkeley store or by special order. Our tub/shower fitting is the finest available and offers the utmost in convenience and reliability.

The pullchain toilet is back! Sunrise Specialty manufactures this classic commode, a functional vessel of Victorian history. Quality constructed of oak, solid brass fittings and copper-lined tank assembly.

Sunrise Specialty is proud to offer the 'Berkeley' model vitreous china pedestal sink, an exact reproduction of an original sink manufactured circa 1900. Choose from our exciting array of faucets and fixtures.

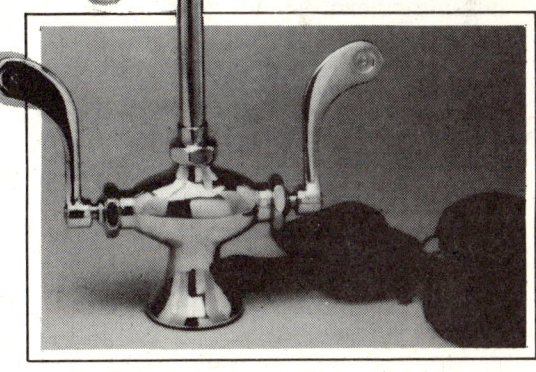

An exact reproduction of a pantry faucet manufactured by Chicago Faucet Co. many years ago is now brought back for you by Sunrise.

Also available are such functional memorabilia as: brass plumbing fixtures, wood and marble mantels, marble mantels, marble washstands, and much, much more. Send $1.00 for our new 16-page full color catalog.

Stop by our showroom when visiting the Bay Area.

415-845-4751
2210 San Pablo Avenue   Berkeley   CA 94702   Dept. COHJ

THE BATHROOM

A bathroom in an Early American house is either a much later addition or a converted bedroom with plain twentieth-century fixtures. Therefore decoration is the only way to relate the bathroom to the rest of the house.

Walls can be papered with one of the many good reproduction wallpapers, some of which are now vinyl coated for durability. Stencilling gives an Early American look to plaster walls. If the present bathroom includes unattractive painted cabinets, they can be grained to simulate wood. Reproductions of simple Colonial lighting fixtures and hardware will add to the traditional look. Window curtains can be a simple arrangement of white or documentary print fabric in a tie-back or Shaker style.

In houses built after 1850 it's possible to recreate a late 19th century bathroom. The essentials of a good bathroom are simplicity, style, and cleanliness. Early bathrooms had as much attention paid to floor, wall, and lighting as to the fixtures themselves.

Wood mouldings can be added at the top of the wallpaper, or to divide the walls into parts. If there is existing wainscotting it will probably be made of softwood—not worth stripping. But it can be painted, grained, or antiqued. Wallpaper borders can lend an old-fashioned effect. Textures play an important role...real marble or slate lavatory tops, tile, wood. Painted imitations of these materials were also quite common. Stained glass or leaded windows afforded privacy and decorative interest in Victorian and Edwardian bathrooms. Wood floors were spatterpainted and varnished until just before the turn of the century when small hexagonal tiles and little black and white tiles became popular. Bathrooms tiled in pastel colors were not common until the late 1920's.

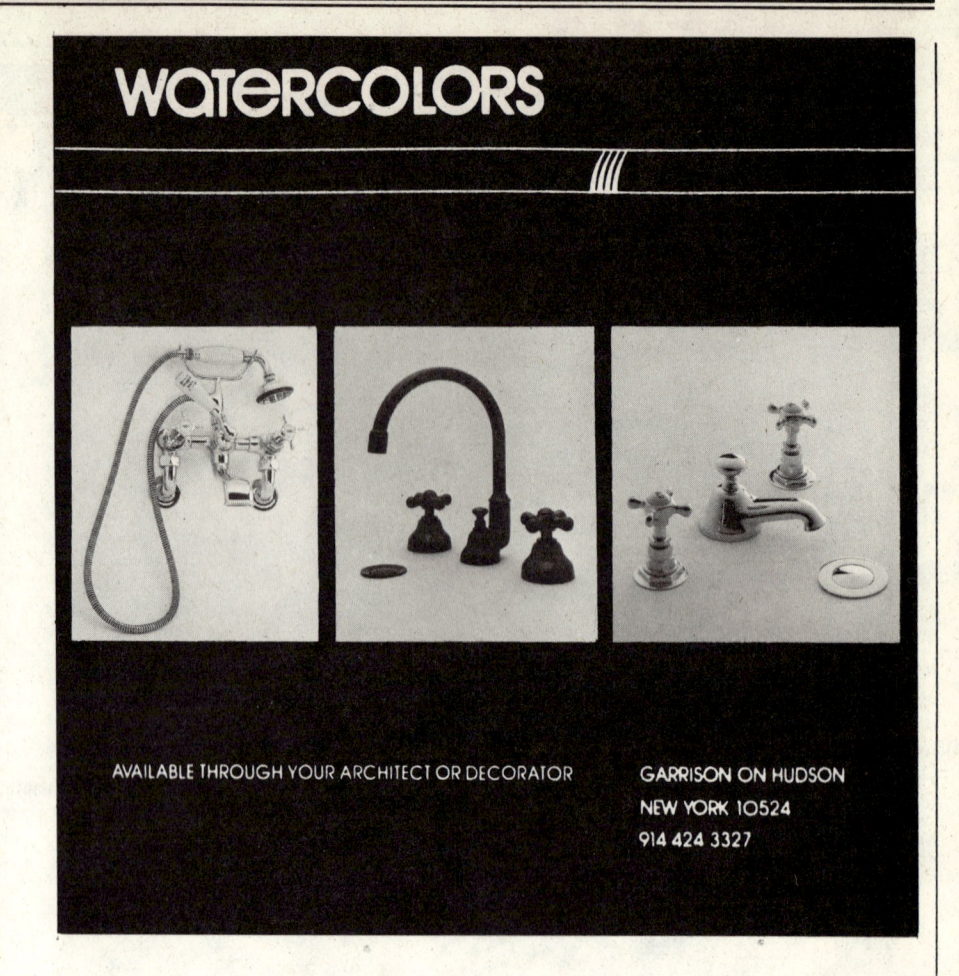

WATERCOLORS

AVAILABLE THROUGH YOUR ARCHITECT OR DECORATOR

GARRISON ON HUDSON
NEW YORK 10524
914 424 3327

Attractive, authentically styled period fittings, fixtures, and accessories are now readily available. When adding a new bathroom to an old house, white fixtures are the best choice since colored ones are a recent innovation, as is the glass shower enclosure.

THE EASIEST, CLEANEST WAY TO REMOVE PAINT
THE MASTER APPLIANCE HEAT GUN
MORE THAN 4,000 IN USE BY OLD-HOUSE JOURNAL SUBSCRIBERS

There's no PLEASANT way to remove paint. But if you have a large amount of paint to strip, the fastest, safest and most economical way is with the Master Appliance electric heat gun.

The Master heat gun has been collecting raves from readers ever since Patricia and Wilkie Talbert's original letter in the April 1976 issue of The Old-House Journal. Since then, more than 4,000 OHJ subscribers have purchased heat guns. And the raves are still coming in.

Master Appliance is the #1 maker of heat guns in the U.S.; they sell more because their heat gun has a proven track record of long life and reliability. When The Old-House Journal decided to make these hard-to-find tools available directly to our readers, we naturally turned to the #1 heat gun.

Of special interest are the safety factors. The heat gun avoids the hazards of methylene chloride vapors that are given off by most paint removers. And because it operates at a lower temperature than a propane torch, there's no danger of vaporizing lead the way a torch will. (Of course, you should observe normal precautions in handling the scrapings of any lead-based paint.) Too, the fire danger is lower than with a propane torch or blowtorch. (But because it is a heat-generating tool, caution should be observed with wall partitions that contain dust.)

The heat gun is ideal for stripping paint from interior woodwork where a clear finish is going to be applied. There's none of the scorching such as you get with a propane torch. Use the heat gun for stripping paint from such places as: (1) Doors; (2) Wainscotting; (3) Window and door frames; (4) Exterior doors; (5) Porch columns and woodwork; (6) Baseboards; (7) Shutters; (8) Panelling. In addition, the heat gun can be used for such purposes as thawing pipes in winter, loosening synthetic resin linoleum paste, and softening old putty when replacing window glass.

The heat gun is NOT recommended for: (1) Removing shellac and varnish; (2) Stripping paint on window muntins (possible cracking of the glass from heat); (3) Stripping the entire exterior of a house (too slow); (4) Stripping Early American milk paint (only ammonia will do that).

The electric heat gun softens paint in a uniform way so that it can be scraped off with a knife. Some clean-up with chemical remover is required, but the heat gun will remove about 98% of the paint—vastly reducing the amount of chemical needed and the consequent mess. See article in the November 1979 OHJ for additional details on operation.

Because it is a high-quality industrial tool, the Master heat gun isn't cheap. But with paint remover around $12 per gallon, the gun only costs as much as 5-6 gallons of remover. In some communities, groups of neighbors are buying a heat gun to share.

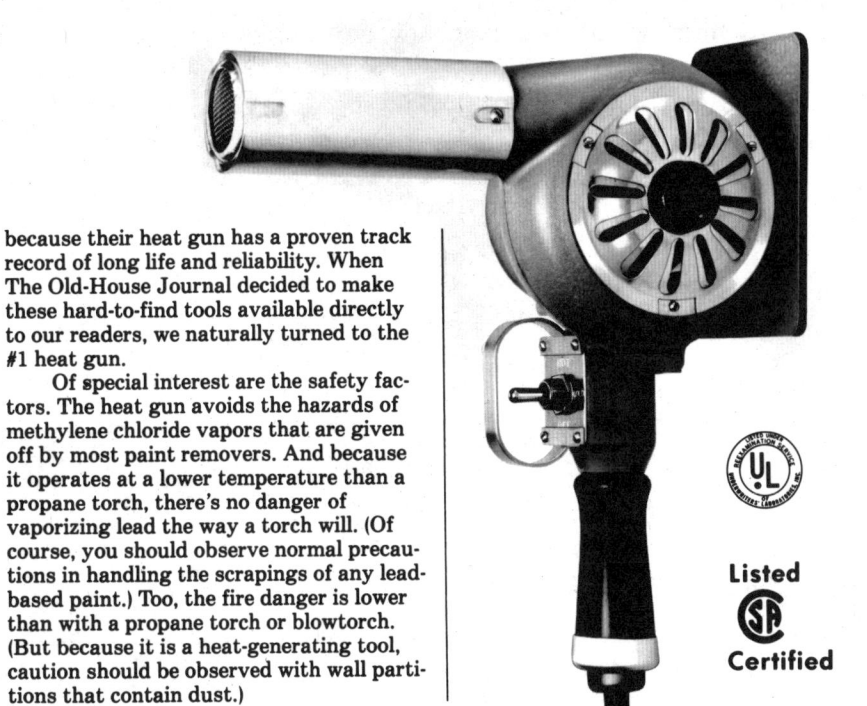

CHECK THESE FEATURES

- Approved by Underwriters Laboratories
- Adjustable air intake regulates temperature between 500 F. and 750 F.
- Rated at 120 v. and 14 amps
- Rugged die-cast aluminum body—no plastics
- Double-jacketed heater
- 8-ft. 3-wire oil-resistant grounded cord with moulded plug
- Pistol-grip handle; 3-position fingertip switch with guard for added safety
- No asbestos used in construction
- Rubber-backed stand swivels 90°; contains keyhole for hanging
- Heavy-duty industrial construction for long life
- Guaranteed by The Old-House Journal. If a unit should malfunction for any reason within two months of purchase, return it to The Old-House Journal and we'll replace it free.

ORDER FORM
Please send one of the HG-501 Heavy-Duty Master Appliance Heat Guns.

☐ Enclosed is **$66.95**

☐ Charge my VISA card: Card Exp._____ No. _____

Signature _____

NOTE:
- N.Y. State residents must include applicable sales tax;
- Because heat guns are shipped via United Parcel Service, please give a STREET ADDRESS—Not a P.O. Box number.

Name _____
(please print)

Street Address _____

City _____ State _____ Zip _____

Mail to: Old-House Journal, 69A Seventh Ave., Brooklyn, N.Y. 11217 (212) 636-4514

The Old-House Journal 1982 Catalog

Bathtubs & Sinks — Period Styles

(1) Tubs & Sinks, Antique (Salvage)
(2) Sinks, Period Styles — New
(3) Sink Replacement Bowls
(4) Tubs, Period Styles — New
(5) Tub Parts & Fittings
(6) Sink Parts & Fittings
(7) Shower Rings
(8) Shower Curtains, Extra-Size

A-Ball Plumbing Supply (OR)	5,7
Addco Architectural Antiques (LA)	1
Barclay Products Co. (IL)	5,7,8
Brass Menagerie (LA)	2,3
Broadway Collection (MO)	2,3
Great American Salvage (VT)	1
Guerin, P.E. Inc. (NY)	2
Kohler Co. (WI)	2,3,4
P & G New and Used Plumbing Supply (NY)	1
Period Furniture Hardware Co. (MA)	3
Remodelers' & Renovators' Supply (ID)	2
Rheinschild, S. Chris (CA)	2,4
Southern Accents Architectural Antiques (AL)	1,5,7
Sterline Manufacturing Corp. (IL)	5,7
Stringer's Environmental Restoration & Design (CA)	2,3
Sunrise Salvage (CA)	1,5,7
Surrey Shoppe Interiors (MA)	8
Tennessee Tub (TN)	1
Walker Industries (TN)	2,4
Weaver, W. T. & Sons, Inc. (DC)	3

HORTON BRASSES
Nooks Hill Road, P.O. Box 95-OJ
Cromwell, CT 06416 (203) 635-4400

HORTON BRASSES are authentic copies of 17th, 18th, 19th & early 20th century pulls.

Mfrs. of Cabinet & Furniture Hardware for Homes & Antiques.

Send $1.50 for a Catalogue.

NEW THINGS FOR CLAW-FOOTED TUBS
AND RESTORED BATHROOMS

- TUB SHOWER CONVERSIONS • SUCCESSFUL TUB REFINISHING KITS
- WASTE OVERFLOW ASSEMBLIES • BRASS TOILET SEAT HINGES
- HIGH TANK FLUSH TUBES • ORNATE REGISTER GRATES
- OVER RIM BASKETS • BATH SUPPLIES • FAUCETS

A•BALL PLUMBING SUPPLY
1703 West Burnside Street
Portland, Oregon 97209
phone (503) 228-0026

Write for Free Brochure

See Company Directory for Addresses & Phone Numbers

Finally . . HARD-to-FIND Hardware!

Send for our catalog of high quality, hard-to-find hardware, tools, plumbing, and specialty items for your restoration, rehab, or redecorating projects.

$2.00 refundable with 1st purchase

RESTORATION WORKS INC.
412½ Virginia Street
Buffalo, New York 14201

716/ 881-1159

BONA
Decorative Hardware

Fine Solid Brass All Periods
Doors, Bathrooms & Furniture

also

Porcelain Crystal Iron
Wood Pewter Lucite

Send for free catalog

2227 Beechmont Avenue
Cincinnati, OH 45230
513-232-4300

LOST HARDWARE

In Early American buildings imported or fancier hardware was used in the more important rooms while locally made items were considered sufficient for lesser rooms. In replacing missing hardware search for clues in the paintwork and for evidence of earlier nailholes to determine the size and shape of the missing originals. In replacing or remounting hardware always match the finish of the screws to that of the hardware.

CABINET FITTINGS

Nothing detracts more from a piece of furniture than wrong handles and fittings. Fortunately there are excellent and authentic reproductions available.

In the 17th century and again in the early Victorian era (1840–1865) wooden knobs and handles were used. The period in-between favored brass fittings: teardrop for William and Mary, bat's wing for Queen Anne, rosettes with bail handle and willow design for Chippendale, oval plate for Hepplewhite, oblong plate, lion's head with pendant ring and embossed rosette knobs for Empire.

Pressed glass and mushroom shaped knobs were also used on Eastlake pieces. A pendant pear-shaped knob combining brass and wood was used on the better Eastlake furniture.

H-shaped hinges usually made of cast brass but sometimes of wrought iron were used from about 1720-1755. Cast brass feet are found on tables, sofas and some chairs of the Sheraton and Empire periods.

Cabinet & Furniture Hardware — Period

1874 House (OR)
18th Century Hardware Co. (PA)
19th Century Company (CA)
Abraxas International, Inc. (CA)
Anglo-American Brass Co. (CA)
Antique Hardware Co. (CA)
Ball and Ball (PA)
Bona Decorative Hardware (OH)
Broadway Collection (MO)
Crawford's Old House Store (WI)
Dover Furniture Stripping (DE)
Englewood Hardware Co. (NJ)
Furniture Revival and Co. (OR)
Garbe's (OK)
Gaston Wood Finishes, Inc. (IN)
Guerin, P.E. Inc. (NY)
Guild, The (CA)
Horton Brasses (CT)
Hunrath, Wm. Co., Inc. (NY)
Keystone Furniture Stripping (CA)
Klise Manufacturing Company (MI)
Old English Brass, Ltd. (MO)
Paxton Hardware Co. (MD)
Period Furniture Hardware Co. (MA)
Pfanstiel Hardware Co. (NY)
Renaissance Decorative Hardware Co. (NJ)
Renovator's Supply (MA)
Ritter & Son Hardware (CA)
Shaker Reproductions (NY)
Squaw Alley, Inc. (IL)
Weaver, W. T. & Sons, Inc. (DC)
Williamsburg Blacksmiths, Inc. (MA)
Wolchonok, M. and Son, Inc. (NY)

Carpet Rods

Baldwin Hardware Mfg. Corp. (PA)
Ball and Ball (PA)
Guerin, P.E. Inc. (NY)
Pfanstiel Hardware Co. (NY)
Renovator's Supply (MA)
Wolchonok, M. and Son, Inc. (NY)

Coat Hooks

Anglo-American Brass Co. (CA)
Baldwin Hardware Mfg. Corp. (PA)
Claymont Forge (WV)
Custom House (ME)
Kayne, Steve — Hand-Forged Hardware (NY)
Renovator's Supply (MA)
Sign of the Crab (CA)
Smithy, The (VT)
Twanky Dillo Forge (VT)
Weaver, W. T. & Sons, Inc. (DC)

Sterline MANUFACTURING CORPORATION

CONVERTOS

CONVERTS ORDINARY TUBS INTO MODERN SHOWERS

Economical
•
Easy to install
•
No Walls to break

There's a Converto for every tub

Dept. OHJ
410 N. Oakley Blvd.
Chicago, IL 60612
Phone (312) 226-1555

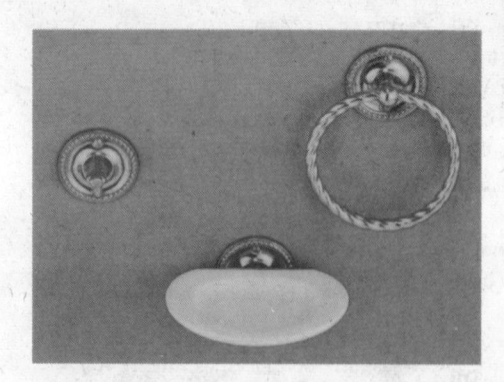

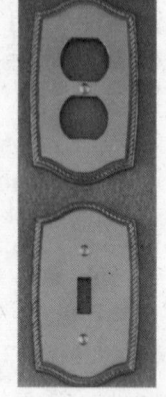

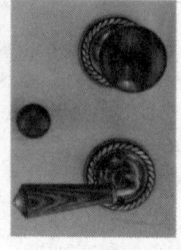

We're Recreating The Past.

... in solid brass ...
decorated porcelain ...
shimmering crystal ...
acrylics ... and wood.

Send $5.00 for our four-color catalog. Refundable with $100 purchase.

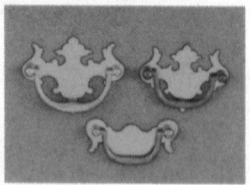

the Broadway Collection

of Fine Hardware and Bath Accessories

The Broadway Collection
Broadway Home Center
601 W. 103rd Street • Kansas City, MO 64114

Door Hinges

- (1) Brass & Bronze
- (2) Iron
- (3) Early American
- (4) Victorian
- (5) Turn-of-Century
- (6) Custom-Cast Brass & Bronze
- (7) Custom-Wrought Iron
- (8) Other

18th Century Hardware Co. (PA)	8
Antares Forge and Metalworks (NY)	7
Baldwin Hardware Mfg. Corp. (PA)	1
Ball and Ball (PA)	1,2,3,4,5
Barnett, D. James — Blacksmith (IL)	2
Bona Decorative Hardware (OH)	1,3
Broadway Collection (MO)	1
Cohasset Colonials (MA)	3
Folger Adam Co. (IL)	1
Guerin, P.E. Inc. (NY)	1
Hartland Forge (NH)	2,7
Horton Brasses (CT)	2
Howland, John — Metalsmith (CT)	1,2
Kayne, Steve — Hand-Forged Hardware (NY)	2,3
Leo, Brian (MN)	6
Millham, Newton — Blacksmith (MA)	2,3,7
Old English Brass, Ltd. (MO)	1
Period Furniture Hardware Co. (MA)	1,2
Pfanstiel Hardware Co. (NY)	1,5
Renovator's Supply (MA)	2,3
Ritter & Son Hardware (CA)	1
Sign of the Crab (CA)	1,3,4
Smithy, The (VT)	7
Wallin Forge (KY)	7
Williamsburg Blacksmiths, Inc. (MA)	2,3
Wolchonok, M. and Son, Inc. (NY)	1
Woodbury Blacksmith & Forge Co. (CT)	7

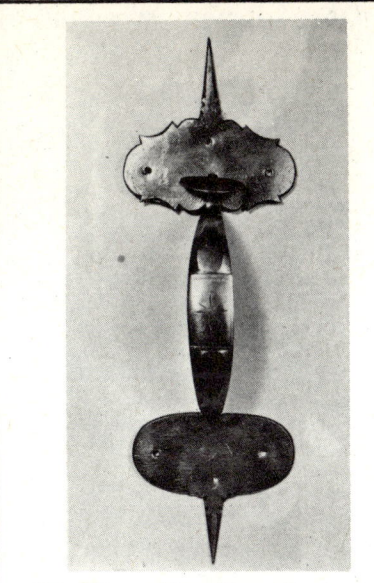

Hand Forged Iron House Hardware and furnishings: H-L hinges, straps, butterflies, shutter hardware, interior and exterior latches — candlestands, rushlights, betty lamps, andirons, cranes, spits, broilers, toasters.

Catalogue $1.00

Newton Millham
672 Drift Road
Westport, Mass. 02790

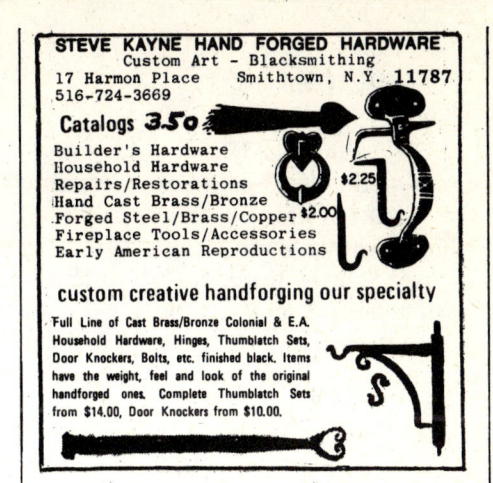

STEVE KAYNE HAND FORGED HARDWARE
Custom Art - Blacksmithing
17 Harmon Place   Smithtown, N.Y. 11787
516-724-3669

Catalogs $3.50

- Builder's Hardware
- Household Hardware
- Repairs/Restorations
- Hand Cast Brass/Bronze
- Forged Steel/Brass/Copper
- Fireplace Tools/Accessories
- Early American Reproductions

custom creative handforging our specialty

Full Line of Cast Brass/Bronze Colonial & E.A. Household Hardware, Hinges, Thumblatch Sets, Door Knockers, Bolts, etc. finished black. Items have the weight, feel and look of the original handforged ones. Complete Thumblatch Sets from $14.00, Door Knockers from $10.00.

See Company Directory for Addresses & Phone Numbers

Accessories so exceptional, an entire home could be designed around them.

The decorative hardware and accessories you choose can be the finishing touch. Or the finish.

For well over a century, P.E. Guerin has specialized in the former. Offering faucet sets, door knobs, pulls, finials, fixtures and more...in thousands of variations. Many of which you've never seen before and will never see anywhere else.

We'll even work with you to custom-design whatever you have in mind. But first, see what we have in mind...in our catalog. Send $4, your name and address, to: P.E. Guerin, Inc., Box BD-1, 23 Jane St., N.Y., N.Y. 10014.

When it comes to artful design and superb craftsmanship, we wrote the book.

P.E. GUERIN, INC.
At home in the finest homes... for 120 years.

The Old-House Journal 1982 Catalog

KNOBS & LATCHES

By the mid-19th century machine-made latches were replacing the work of local craftsmen. The white ceramic knobs found in Greek Revival houses were used with these latches into the Victorian age. As the 19th century progressed a variety of knobs became popular—mercury glass, black ceramic, wood, stamped brass, bronze, painted porcelain, milk and sandwich glass. Cut glass knobs were used into the 20th century. Door hardware should be kept in working order. Missing or broken parts can often be restored by using a piece from an upstairs closet or utility room, then replacing that one with a new or reproduction model.

See Company Directory for Addresses & Phone Numbers

Door Latches—Wrought Iron

(1) Antique (Original)
(2) New—Stock Items
(3) Custom-Made

18th Century Hardware Co. (PA)	2
Antares Forge and Metalworks (NY)	3
Arrowhead Forge (ME)	3
Ball and Ball (PA)	1,2,3
Barnett, D. James — Blacksmith (IL)	2
Bona Decorative Hardware (OH)	2
Broadway Collection (MO)	2
Ephraim Forge (IL)	3
Hartland Forge (NH)	2,3
Kayne, Steve — Hand-Forged Hardware (NY)	2
Millham, Newton — Blacksmith (MA)	2,3
Period Furniture Hardware Co. (MA)	2
RAM's Forge (MD)	3
Renovator's Supply (MA)	2
Ricker Blacksmith Shop (ME)	3
Smithy, The (VT)	3
Wallin Forge (KY)	3
Williamsburg Blacksmiths, Inc. (MA)	2
Woodbury Blacksmith & Forge Co. (CT)	3

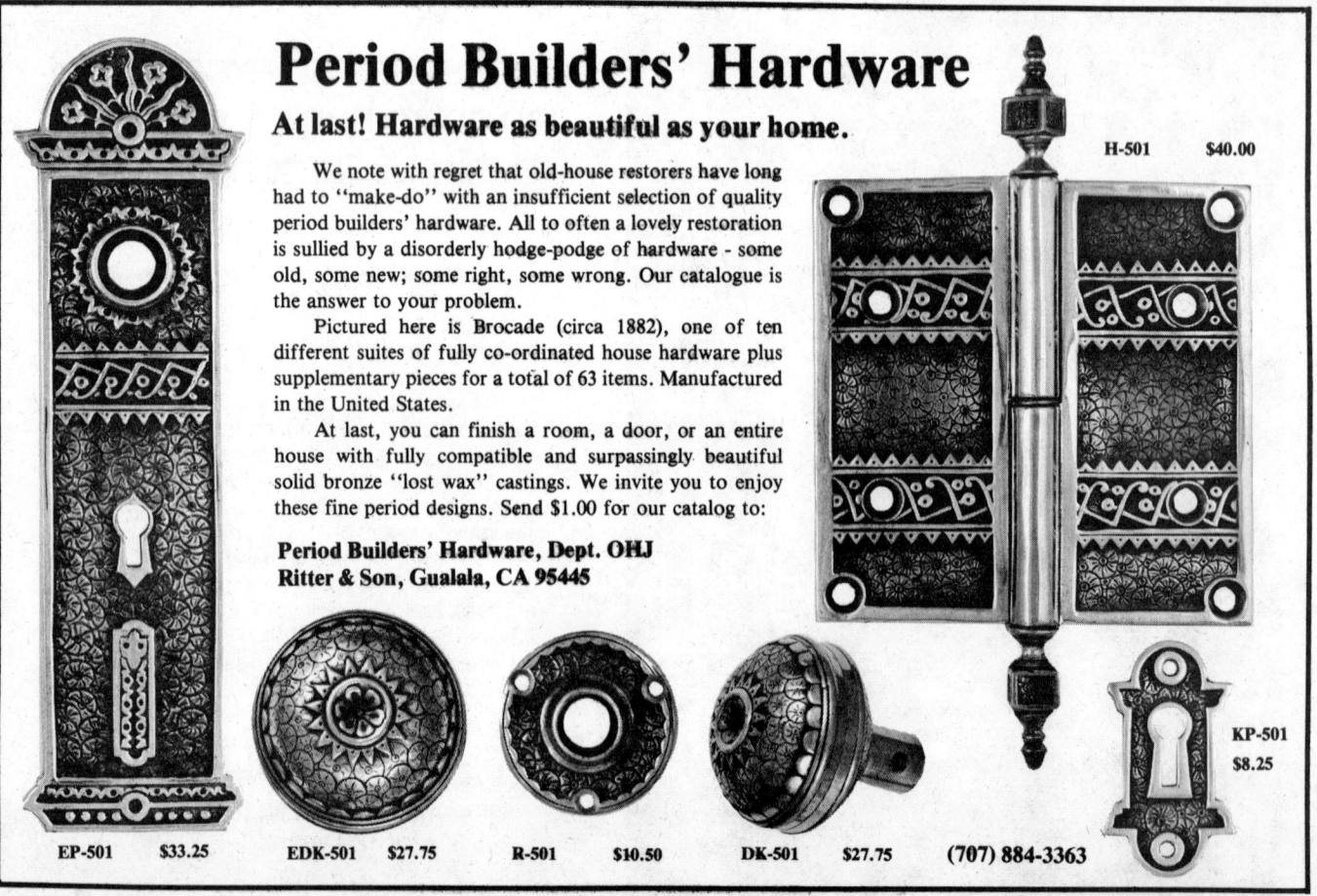

SOLID BRASS & GLASS KNOBS $6.75 pair
SOLID BRASS PLATES $9.50 pair
add 10% UPS ($2.00 Min) California Residents add 6% tax

Catalogue $3.00 Postpaid
VISA, MC, AM Express
(707) 443-3152

One source for bath fittings, door and cabinet hardware, lighting, millwork, mantels and more.

Restoration Hardware
438 SECOND STREET, EUREKA, CA 95501

Period Builders' Hardware

At last! Hardware as beautiful as your home.

We note with regret that old-house restorers have long had to "make-do" with an insufficient selection of quality period builders' hardware. All to often a lovely restoration is sullied by a disorderly hodge-podge of hardware - some old, some new; some right, some wrong. Our catalogue is the answer to your problem.

Pictured here is Brocade (circa 1882), one of ten different suites of fully co-ordinated house hardware plus supplementary pieces for a total of 63 items. Manufactured in the United States.

At last, you can finish a room, a door, or an entire house with fully compatible and surpassingly beautiful solid bronze "lost wax" castings. We invite you to enjoy these fine period designs. Send $1.00 for our catalog to:

Period Builders' Hardware, Dept. OHJ
Ritter & Son, Gualala, CA 95445

(707) 884-3363

| EP-501 | $33.25 | EDK-501 | $27.75 | R-501 | $10.50 | DK-501 | $27.75 | H-501 | $40.00 | KP-501 | $8.25 |

---

64 The Old-House Journal 1982 Catalog

Door Knobs & Escutcheons

(1) Brass & Bronze
(2) Porcelain & Glass Knobs

Abraxas International, Inc. (CA)
Baldwin Hardware Mfg. Corp. (PA) 1
Broadway Collection (MO)
Crawford's Old House Store (WI) 1
Englewood Hardware Co. (NJ)
Guerin, P.E. Inc. (NY)
Litchfield House (CT) 2
Old English Brass, Ltd. (MO) 1
Renaissance Decorative Hardware Co. (NJ) 1
Renovator's Supply (MA)
Restoration Hardware (CA)................1,2
Ritter & Son Hardware (CA).................1
San Francisco Victoriana (CA) 1
Sullivan's Antiques (CA) 2
Weaver, W. T. & Sons, Inc. (DC) 1

Door Locks

(1) Brass & Bronze
(2) Iron
(3) Rim Locks
(4) Mortised Locks
(5) Early American
(6) Victorian
(7) Turn-of-Century
(8) Other

Abraxas International, Inc. (CA) 1
Baldwin Hardware Mfg. Corp. (PA) 1,3,4
Ball and Ball (PA) 1,2,3,4,5,6,7,8
Bona Decorative Hardware (OH) 1,2,3,4,5
Brass Menagerie (LA) 1
Broadway Collection (MO) 1,3
Colonial Lock Company (CT) 2,3
Crawford's Old House Store (WI)
.... 1,2,3,4,5,6,7,8
Folger Adam Co. (IL) 1,3
Garbe's (OK) 3
Millham, Newton — Blacksmith (MA) 2,5
Old English Brass, Ltd. (MO) 1
Period Furniture Hardware Co. (MA) .. 1,3,4,5
Pfanstiel Hardware Co. (NY) 1
Renovator's Supply (MA) 1,2,4,5
Sign of the Crab (CA) 1,4,5,6
Weaver, W. T. & Sons, Inc. (DC) 3
Williamsburg Blacksmiths, Inc. (MA) 2,5

Dry Sinks & Liners

Orr, J.F., & Sons (MA)
Outer Banks Pine Products (PA)

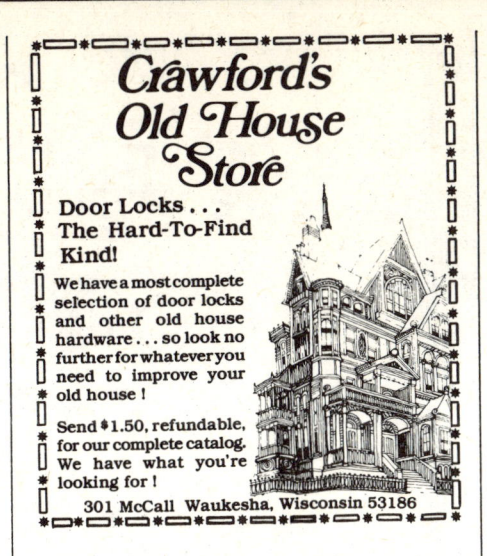

Crawford's Old House Store

Door Locks...
The Hard-To-Find Kind!

We have a most complete selection of door locks and other old house hardware...so look no further for whatever you need to improve your old house!

Send $1.50, refundable, for our complete catalog. We have what you're looking for!

301 McCall Waukesha, Wisconsin 53186

GLASS KNOBS NEVER USED

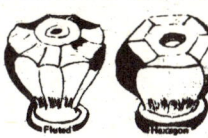

FLUTED
Color Choice: Crystal or Black

Size	Dia.	Lgth	Price
Sm.	7/8"	3/4"	$1.00 ea.
Lg.	1-3/8"	1-5/8"	$2.00 ea.

Bolts included, 15% Freight + $2.50 packing. Check or M.O.

P. Sullivan
P.O. Box 132
Santa Ana, CA 92702

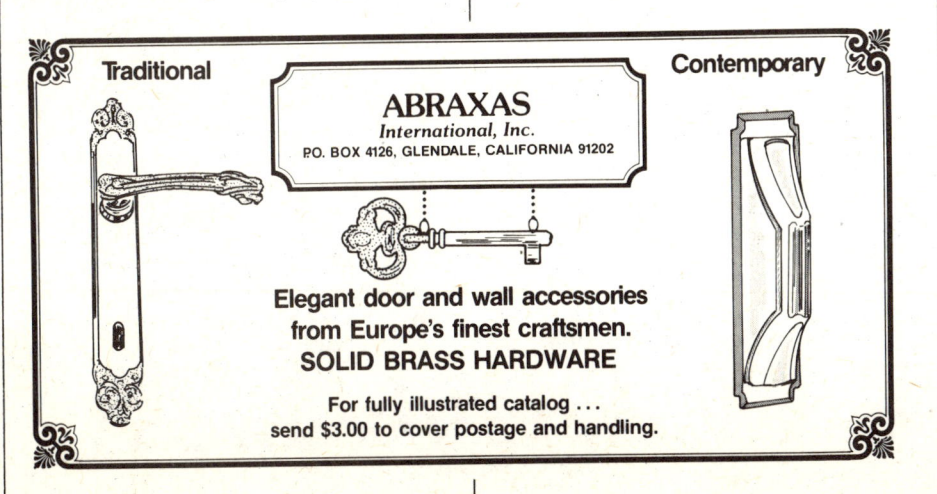

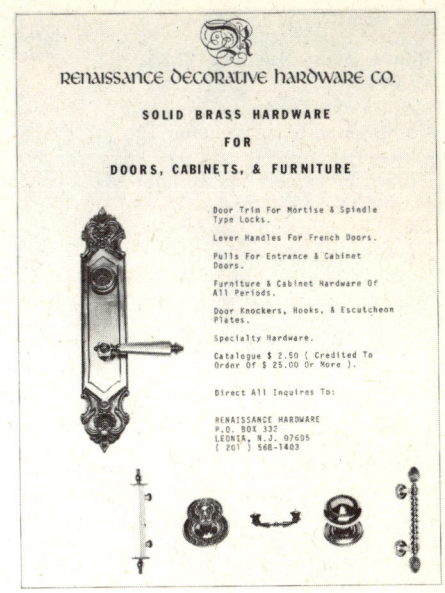

RENAISSANCE DECORATIVE HARDWARE CO.

SOLID BRASS HARDWARE
FOR
DOORS, CABINETS, & FURNITURE

Door Trim For Mortise & Spindle Type Locks.
Lever Handles For French Doors.
Pulls For Entrance & Cabinet Doors.
Furniture & Cabinet Hardware Of All Periods.
Door Knockers, Hooks, & Escutcheon Plates.
Specialty Hardware.
Catalogue $2.50 (Credited To Order Of $25.00 Or More).

Direct All Inquiries To:

RENAISSANCE HARDWARE
P.O. BOX 332
LEONIA, N.J. 07605
(201) 568-1403

PRACTICAL CEILING FANS

1890—1910 was the heyday of the classic four-blade electrically propelled ceiling fan, although they continued to be used until the advent of air conditioning in the mid 1930's. Today's rising utility bills have brought renewed interest in a cooling device that circulates air for approximately the cost of running a 100 watt light bulb. Ceiling fans are also useful in cold weather. Operated at a low speed, a ceiling fan recirculates warm air, reducing heat loss through the ceiling and walls. Although some experts feel these fans work best in rooms with high ceilings, many are designed for standard 8 foot ceilings.

For More Information
About Hardware, See
RENOVATOR'S SUPPLY
Ad Inside Front Cover

Traditional — Contemporary

ABRAXAS
International, Inc.
P.O. BOX 4126, GLENDALE, CALIFORNIA 91202

Elegant door and wall accessories from Europe's finest craftsmen.
SOLID BRASS HARDWARE

For fully illustrated catalog...
send $3.00 to cover postage and handling.

Fans, Ceiling

Bow & Arrow Stove Co. (MA)
CasaBlanca Fan Co. (TX)
Ceiling Fan Company, Inc. (FL)
Cumberland General Store (TN)
Fan — Attic, Inc. (OH)
Golden Movement Emporium (CA)
Hunter Div. - Robbins & Myers (TN)
McAvoy Antique Lighting (MO)
Newstamp Lighting Co. (MA)
Royal Windyne Limited (VA)
Southern Accents Architectural Antiques (AL)
Worthington Trading Company (MO)

Hardware, Interior—Custom Duplication

(1) Cast Brass & Bronze
(2) Cast Iron
(3) Wrought Iron

18th Century Hardware Co. (PA)
Anglo-American Brass Co. (CA) 1
Antares Forge and Metalworks (NY) 3
Ball and Ball (PA) 1
Blaine Window Hardware, Inc. (MD) 1
Brass Menagerie (LA) 1
Ephraim Forge (IL) 3
Experi-Metals (WI) 1
Guerin, P.E. Inc. (NY) 1
Howland, John — Metalsmith (CT) 1,3
New England Brassworks (CT) 1
Ricker Blacksmith Shop (ME) 3
San Francisco Victoriana (CA) 1
Smithy, The (VT) 2
Stringer's Environmental Restoration & Design (CA)
Travis Tuck, Metal Sculptor (MA) 3
Wallin Forge (KY) 3

Hunter The Original Olde Tyme CEILING FANS

This is the ORIGINAL. A standard of excellence since 1886. An attractive fixture that's a functional year-round energy saver. Available in 36" and 52" sizes with wooden blades. Light optional.
Send for free full-color catalog.

FAN-ATTIC, INC.
P.O. Box 628
Delaware, Ohio 43015
(614) 369-2626

THE KEYWESTER COLLECTION™

Key Wester Palm Fan protected by U.S. Patent No. D256614.

All decorative components of the Key Wester Collection Fans are copyright designs. All rights reserved.

Handcrafted Cool

Since 1975 we have been making America's only Hand-Crafted old time ceiling fan. A marriage of modern electrical efficiency and art castings of jewelry quality. Genuine Turn-of-the-Century styling and craftsmanship. Heavy cast housings with coordinated motor covers and blade brackets. In traditional or contemporary designs. These fans are built to be the heirlooms of the future. We take an old fashioned pride in our products and assure their quality and authenticity to be second to none.

All fans are available in two motor types: The old style oil lubricated two speed motor which provides downward airflow, or our three speed reverse air flow model with sealed, permanently lubricated bearings. Either offers the same solid old-fashioned quality, beauty and comfort.

Available in a variety of colors and metal finishes as well as with solid brass components. With a choice of genuine hardwood paddles, balanced to perfection to provide years of whisper-quiet operation. Each backed by our exclusive 7 year limited warranty.

Whether you require one fan for your parlor or a dozen custom fans for a restaurant, our order department will be happy to discuss your requirements. We promise knowledgeable, courteous service and prompt delivery. We invite your inquiries. Our color brochure is available for a $1.00 charge, refundable with your order.

THE CEILING FAN COMPANY
A Division of Ganstir Inc.
4220 S.W. 75th Avenue, Dept. OHJ   Miami, Fla. 33155   (305) 266-5899

When The Old-House Journal Selected Ceiling Fans For Their Offices, They Chose "America's Finest"—Royal Windyne. Maybe You Should Too.

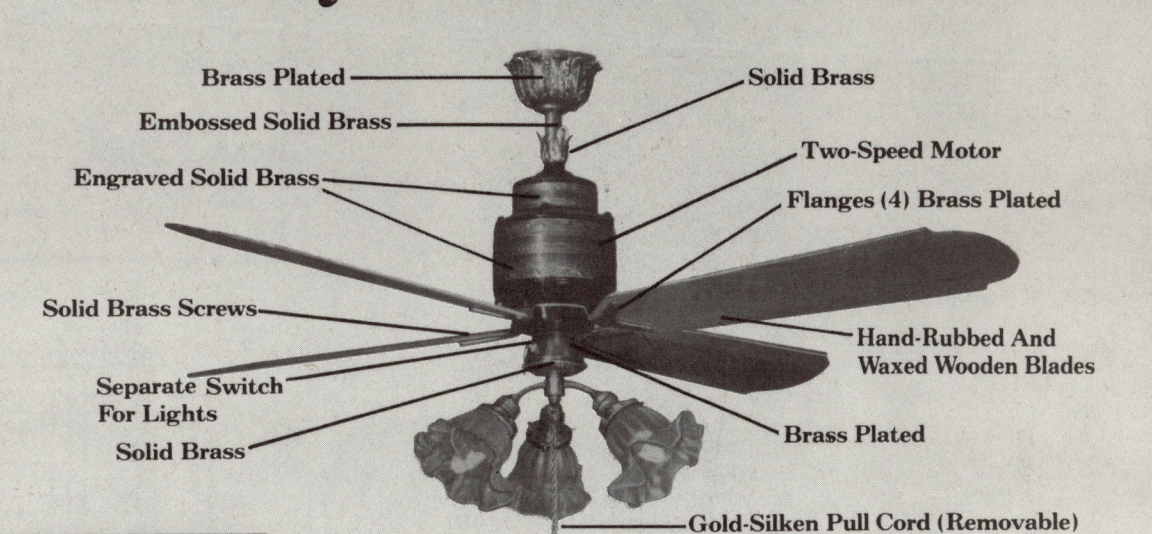

- Brass Plated
- Embossed Solid Brass
- Engraved Solid Brass
- Solid Brass Screws
- Separate Switch For Lights
- Solid Brass
- Solid Brass
- Two-Speed Motor
- Flanges (4) Brass Plated
- Hand-Rubbed And Waxed Wooden Blades
- Brass Plated
- Gold-Silken Pull Cord (Removable)

The Old-House Journal Offices

Not Available In Stores.

If your home is worth $100,000 or more, experience shows that there is only one ceiling fan for you—the handbuilt Royal Windyne, "America's Finest Ceiling Fan."

All the other ceiling fans are mass produced—for the masses. And they look it. Royal Windyne Ceiling Fans are *hand-built*—and *they look it*.

Now you can own a beautiful rarity that reflects your individuality and appreciation for fine workmanship. When your friends admire your Royal Windyne Ceiling Fan, you can tell them, "It was custom built for me."

The Royal Windyne is hand-built with many features not found on *any other* ceiling fan. For example, *only* with a Royal Windyne do you enjoy the charm and elegance of engraved *solid brass* appointments—not just an inexpensive coating that looks like plastic.

Only with a Royal Windyne do you receive furniture quality blades cut from a *solid* piece of wood, not strips of wood glued side by side. These blades are thicker, furniture finished, hand-rubbed and hand-waxed and precision balanced—attributes of fine craftsmanship not available on any other ceiling fan.

The beautiful broad wooden blades quietly circulate a large volume of air. Incredibly pleasant in the summer, with or without the use of air conditioning. In the winter, reclaim heated air that rises to the ceiling. Year round comfort and beauty. And the energy savings will actually help pay for your ceiling fan—it uses about as much electricity as a light bulb.

Why not decide for yourself? Order one and inspect it. Try it for 30 days. If you are not satisfied, return it for a full refund, including return shipping charges. Guaranteed in writing for five years. Easy installation; fits all standard ceiling heights of eight feet or more. Longer drop rods available for high ceilings.

Enjoy the incredibly relaxing breeze, the elegance and the frugality of yesterday. The choice of discriminating restorationists, architects, interior designers and people who know and appreciate fine quality. *Not available elsewhere*. Our custom production for this summer is limited, so order now.

To order, send check or M/C, VISA or American Express information. Please specify your choice of Golden Oak or Dark Walnut finished blades. Telephone, if you like, for additional information, advice or ordering.

53" Supreme (shown) $497 53" Regular—$389
39" Supreme— $432 39" Regular—$297
Solid Brass Victoria Light (shown) add $84.50.
Please add $4.50 per fan for shipping. Virginia residents add sales tax. Literature $1.

Royal Windyne Limited
1316 West Main Street—Dept. OH-3
Richmond, Virginia 23220 (804) 358-1899

Please custom build the following Royal Windyne Handbuilt Ceiling Fan(s) for me:

_____
_____
_____

ROYAL WINDYNE LIMITED
1316 West Main Street—Dept. OH-3
Richmond, Virginia 23220 (804) 358-1899

Ship to:
Name_____
Address_____
City/State/Zip_____
☐ Check or Money Order ☐ VISA
☐ Master Charge ☐ American Express
Acc't. #_____ Exp._____
Signature_____

The Old-House Journal 1982 Catalog

Ice Box Hardware

A.R.D. (NY)
Anglo-American Brass Co. (CA)
Renovator's Supply (MA)
Ritter & Son Hardware (CA)

Key Blanks—For Antique Locks

Abraxas International, Inc. (CA)
Ball and Ball (PA)

Kitchen Cabinets

A.R.D. (NY)
Dixon Bros. Woodworking (MA)
Moser Brothers, Inc. (PA)
Rich Craft Custom Kitchens, Inc. (PA)
Wood-Hu Kitchens, Inc. (MA)

Kitchen Faucets & Fittings, Old Styles

(1) Antique (Salvage)
(2) Reproduction
Sunrise Salvage (CA) 2

Kitchen Sinks, Old Styles

(1) Antique (Salvage)
(2) Reproduction
1874 House (OR) 1
Rheinschild, S. Chris (CA) 2

Library Ladders

Putnam Rolling Ladder Co., Inc. (NY)

Radiators — Period Styles

(1) Antique (Salvage)
(2) New
A.A. Used Boiler Supply Co. (NY) 1
P & G New and Used Plumbing Supply (NY) 1

Shutters & Blinds, Interior

(1) New—Stock Items
(2) Custom-Made
A.R.D. (NY) 1
Addco Architectural Antiques (LA) 2
Architectural Components (MA) 1
Bank Architectural Antiques (LA) 1
Beauti-home (CA) 2
Dixon Bros. Woodworking (MA) 2
Historic Windows (VA) 2
Iberia Millwork (LA) 2
Maurer & Shepherd, Joyners (CT) 2
Michael's Fine Colonial Products (NY) ... 2
National Shutters and Millwork (NY)
Period Productions, Limited (VA) 2
Perkowitz Window Fashions (IL) 1
The Restoration Fraternity (PA) 2

Shutter Hardware

(1) Brass & Bronze
(2) Iron
(3) Custom-Made
Ball and Ball (PA) 1,2,3
Barnett, D. James — Blacksmith (IL) ... 2
Crawford's Old House Store (WI) 2
Kayne, Steve — Hand-Forged Hardware (NY) 2
Millham, Newton — Blacksmith (MA) 2
Period Furniture Hardware Co. (MA) 1
Renovator's Supply (MA)
Smithy, The (VT) 2
Wallin Forge (KY) 3

Sliding Door Tracks & Hardware

BWH Stamping, Inc. (PA)
Blaine Window Hardware, Inc. (MD)
Grant Hardware Company (NY)
Renovator's Supply (MA)
Sanders, David & Co. (NY)
Woodworkers' Store, The (MN)

Switch Plates, Period Designs

A-Ball Plumbing Supply (OR)
Old English Brass, Ltd. (MO)
Renovator's Supply (MA)
Sign of the Crab (CA)
Weaver, W. T. & Sons, Inc. (DC)
Wolchonok, M. and Son, Inc. (NY)

Trunk Hardware

Antique Trunk Supply Co. (OH)
Charolette Ford Trunks (TX)
Dover Furniture Stripping (DE)
Furniture Revival and Co. (OR)
Renovator's Supply (MA)

Window Hardware

(1) Brass & Bronze
(2) Iron
(3) Custom-Made
Ball and Ball (PA) 1,2,3
Blaine Window Hardware, Inc. (MD) 1
Bona Decorative Hardware (OH) 1
Guerin, P.E. Inc. (NY) 1
Leo, Brian (MN) 3
Period Furniture Hardware Co. (MA) 1
Quaker City Manufacturing Co. (PA)
Renovator's Supply (MA) 1
Smithy, The (VT) 2

SOLID BRASS ICE-BOX HARDWARE

IB-2 $8.50

Just 2 of our 160 beautiful 19th Century furniture Replicas

Send $1.00 for our catalog of solid brass hathooks, knobs, dresser pulls, etc. to:

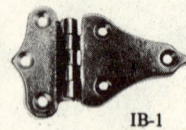

Ritter & Son Hardware
Dept. OHJ
Gualala, CA 95445

IB-1 $6.50

Beauti-home

3088-F WINKLE AVE.
Santa Cruz, CA 95065

(408) 462-6452

Manufacturers of
Custom Louvre
Shutters

for over 20 yrs.

Movable, standard, wide
Flat or Raised Panels
Fixed - Vertical
Shojis

For WINDOWS & DOORS

Solid Oak Rolling Ladders For Libraries, Lofts And Stores.

Write for a free price list and catalog.

PUTNAM
ROLLING
LADDER Co. Inc.
32 Howard Street
Dept. GNP
N.Y., NY 10013
(212) 226-5147

See Company Directory
for
Addresses & Phone Numbers

EVERYTHING for your restoration!

House, cabinet and furniture hardware, lighting fixtures, fireplace equipment and decorative accessories. Produced from brass, bronze, handforged or cast iron, from stock or made to order. Repair and copy work done per quotation. Send $4.00 for our 1978, 108 page catalog showing over 1000 stock items.

Exton, Pennsylvania 19341
Tel. (215) 363-7330

Our "Golden Glow" Brass Polish is shipped in minimum lots of two (2) one pint cans for $5.00, which includes postage, add $1.00 west of the Mississippi.

The Old-House Journal 1982 Catalog 69

Heating Systems, Fireplaces & Stoves, and Energy-Saving Devices

Auxiliary Fireplace Devices to Increase Heat Distribution

Cumberland General Store (TN)
Envirostyle Direct (MN)
Shenandoah Manufacturing Co. (VA)

Central Heating Systems

(1) Wood Fired
(2) Coal Fired
(3) Combination
(4) Other Fuels

Cumberland General Store (TN)
Energy Marketing Corporation (VT) 1,2,3
Heckler Bros. (PA) 2
Shenandoah Manufacturing Co. (VA) 1,2,3
Ultimate Energy Systems (NY) 3,4

Chimney Brushes

Ace Wire Brush Co. (NY)
Woodmart (WI)

Chimney Linings

Bow & Arrow Stove Co. (MA)
Superior Clay Corporation (OH)

Coal Grates

(1) Coal-Burning
(2) Simulated

Bryant Steel Works (ME) 1
Cumberland General Store (TN) 1
Heckler Bros. (PA) 1
Lemee's Fireplace Equipment (MA) 1
Litchfield House (CT) 1

Fireplaces, Manufactured

Acme Stove Company (DC)
Cumberland General Store (TN)
Fireplaces by Martin (AL)
Jotul U.S.A., Inc. (ME)
Portland Stove Foundry, Inc. (ME)
Preway, Inc. (WI)
Readybuilt Products, Co. (MD)

Fireplace Dampers & Structural Parts

Cumberland General Store (TN)
Lyemance International (KY)

Gas Logs

Peterson, Robert H., Co. (CA)
Readybuilt Products, Co. (MD)

Heat Shields For Free-Standing Stoves

Hearth Shield/Berry Metal (NJ)

Fireplace Accessories

(1) Andirons
(2) Bellows
(3) Coal Scuttles
(4) Cranes
(5) Fenders
(6) Firebacks
(7) Firegrates
(8) Firescreens
(9) Pokers & Fireplace Tools
(10) Wood Baskets

A.E.S. Firebacks (CT) 6
Acme Stove Company (DC)
Adams Company (IA) 1,10,3,8,9
Auto Hoe, Inc. (WI) 9
Ball and Ball (PA) 1,4,5,8,9
Barnett, D. James — Blacksmith (IL) 1
Blacksmith Shop, Inc. (VT) 1,10,7,8,9
Bryant Steel Works (ME) 7
Buck Creek Bellows (VA) 2
Claymont Forge (WV) 9
Craft House, Colonial Williamsburg (VA)
Ephraim Forge (IL) 4,8,9
Essex Forge (CT) 1,9
Hartland Forge (NH) 1,4
Howland, John — Metalsmith (CT) 1
Hurley Patentee Lighting (NY) 8
Itinerant Reproductions, Inc. (CT) 8
Kayne, Steve — Hand-Forged Hardware (NY) 1,4,5,7,8,9
Lehman Hardware & Appliances (OH) 3,9
Lemee's Fireplace Equipment (MA)
.... 1,2,3,4,6,7,8,9
Litchfield House (CT) 7
Mexico House (CA) 8
Millham, Newton — Blacksmith (MA) .. 1,4,9
Old English Brass, Ltd. (MO) 2
Pennsylvania Firebacks (PA) 6
Period Furniture Hardware Co. (MA)
.... 1,2,3,5,6,8
Peterson, Robert H., Co. (CA) 7
RAM's Forge (MD) 1,4,9
Renovator's Supply (MA) 1,4,8,9
Ricker Blacksmith Shop (ME) 1,4,9
Schwartz's Forge & Metalworks (NY) ... 1,9
Smithy, The (VT) 9
Twanky Dillo Forge (VT) 9
Wallin Forge (KY) 1,4,5
Washington Stove Works (WA) 3
Williams, Helen (CA) 6
Woodbury Blacksmith & Forge Co. (CT) 1,4,9

A. E. S. FIREBACKS

Fine quality reproduction firebacks taken from original designs. Placed in the rear of the fireplace, the fireback protects the masonry and, in turn, radiates heat. Add antique charm and efficiency to your fireplace with ease. Send for free brochure-

A. E. S. FIREBACKS
27 Hewitt Road, Dept. OHC
Mystic Connecticut 06355
(203) 536-0295

See Company Directory for Addresses & Phone Numbers

AGAPE ANTIQUES

Box 43, Saxtons River, VT 05154
(802) 869-2273   Dave & Ruth Wells

Original one of a kind restored antique wood, coal or gas, kitchen ranges and parlor stoves.

An extensive inventory of newly cast grates and liners and misc. parts especially for Glenwood stoves, plus many old parts for stoves.

We recommend a phone call to discuss fuel requirements, size of area to be heated, style preferred, etc.

Furnace Parts

A.A. Used Boiler Supply Co. (NY)
Heckler Bros. (PA)
Standard Heating Parts, Inc. (IL)

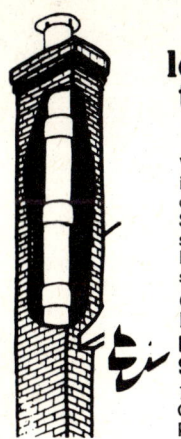

Now! A low-cost way to line your chimney

Vitroliner chimney liner inserted in old flues cuts chimney fire risks. Starters, caps, offsets and special shapes provide layout flexibility and secure installation.

Call or write for brochure.

BOW & ARROW STOVE CO.
11 Hurley Street
Cambridge, Mass. 02141
Phone 617/492-1411

THE ORIGINAL CUMBERLAND GENERAL STORE

THESE GOODS REALLY FOR SALE? YOU BET! Items include everything from ceiling fans to hand pumps, windmills to wood stoves; period furniture and hardware to Homestead hams and mountain cheddar; stockman's canes and horse drawn carriages to log cabin building tools and honest kitchen utensils. Order your copy of our big, new "WISH AND WANT BOOK" Catalogue. 250 pages of merchandise you thought would never be available again. Only $3.75 ppd., and worth it. In fact, we guarantee it.

CUMBERLAND GENERAL STORE
Dept. OH82, Route 3, Crossville, Tn. 38555

Stoves

(1) Heating
(2) Cooking (Kitchen)
(3) Wood-Burning
(4) Coal-Burning
(5) Antique

Acme Stove Company (DC) 3
Adirondack Hudson Arms (NY) 1
Agape Antiques (VT) 5
Antique Stove Imports (OH) 5
Bow & Arrow Stove Co. (MA) 3,4
Bryant Steel Works (ME) 2,5
Country Catalog (CA) 3
Cumberland General Store (TN) 2,4
Empire Stove & Furnace Co. (NY) 3,4
Energy Marketing Corporation (VT) 1
Fourth Avenue Stove & Appliance Corp. (NY) 1,2,3,4
Hayes Equipment Corp. (CT) 1,3
House of Webster (AR)........................ 2
Jotul U.S.A., Inc. (ME) 1,3,4
Lehman Hardware & Appliances (OH) 1,2,3,4
Portland Stove Foundry, Inc. (ME) 1,2,3,4
Shenandoah Manufacturing Co. (VA) 1,3,4
Upland Stove Co., Inc. (NY) 1,3
Vermont Castings, Inc. (VT) 1,3,4
Vermont Iron Stove Works (VT) 3
Victor-Renee Assoc. (NY) 5
Washington Stove Works (WA) 1,2,3,4
Woodstock Soapstone Co., Inc. (VT) 3
Worthington Trading Company (MO) 3,4

An Early American Kitchen can be yours with a

COUNTRY CHARM ELECTRIC RANGE

...**CAST IRON** reproduction from original patterns. Combined with the Early American charm of this antique is the convenience of automatic oven and burner controls, and easy-care porcelain top. Coffee mill houses clock, oven timer and minute minder. Fits modern range space. Prices start at $875.00, plus freight charges.

Send 25¢ for your "Country Charm" Appliance Folder and Gift Catalog.

Quality backed by 35 years of Skilled Craftsmanship.

Made and Sold Only by
THE HOUSE OF WEBSTER
"Old Fashioned Gifts"
BOX OH1181 ROGERS, ARK. 72756

SHIVERING?
WINDOWS LEAK?

Stop that Shivering with

"WOOD INSIDE STORM WINDOWS"

Do-It-Yourself

For Info., send 50¢ for Brochure to:
John McNair Construction Co., Inc.
Box 6414, Baltimore, Maryland 21230

Stove Parts

(1) Stove Pipe & Fittings
(2) Isinglass For Stove Doors
(3) Other Stove Parts

Bow & Arrow Stove Co. (MA) 1
Bryant Steel Works (ME) 2,3
Cumberland General Store (TN) 1
Empire Stove & Furnace Co. (NY) 2,3
Hearth Shield/Berry Metal (NJ)
Heckler Bros. (PA) 3
Jotul U.S.A., Inc. (ME) 1
Thompson & Anderson, Inc. (ME) 1,3
Twanky Dillo Forge (VT) 3
Wrightsville Hardware (PA) 1,3

Other Heating Equipment

A.A. Used Boiler Supply Co. (NY)
Campbell-Lamps (PA)
Cumberland General Store (TN)
Peterson, Robert H., Co. (CA)

Solar Heating Systems

North American Solar Development Corp. (VA)
Pedersen, Arthur Hall — Design & Consulting Engineers (MO)

Ventilating Equipment

Kool-O-Matic Corp. (MI)

Water Heaters—Alternate Fuels

Cumberland General Store (TN)
Energy Marketing Corporation (VT)

Window Coverings, Insulating

Appropriate Technology Corp. (VT)
Bow & Arrow Stove Co. (MA)
Home Fabric Mills, Inc. (MA)
North American Solar Development Corp. (VA)
Window Blanket Company, Inc. (TN)

Storm Windows, Wood

(1) Outside Mounting
(2) Inside Mounting

Air-Flo Window Contracting Corp. (NY) .. 1,2
Combination Door Co. (WI) 1
Cusson Sash Company (CT) 1
Drums Sash & Door Co., Inc. (PA) 1
HowAll Products, Inc. (IN) 1
McNair Construction Co. (MD) 2
Moser Brothers, Inc. (PA) 1,2
Smith, R.W. — Sashmaker (MA) 1

Storm Windows, Metal & Plastic

(1) Outside Mounting
(2) Inside Mounting

Air-Flo Window Contracting Corp. (NY) .. 1,2
Plaskolite, Inc. (OH) 2

Lighting Fixtures & Parts

THE RIGHT LIGHT

To light the old house in an appropriate manner it is necessary to become familiar with the lighting devices used from the 17th through the early 20th centuries. For function as well as decorative light, electrified period fixtures can be combined with unobtrusive contemporary lighting.

Colonial: Up to 1790

Tallow candles were for the rich—grease-soaked rushes for the poor. Early chandeliers were suspended candlesticks. Later ones were elegant imports from Europe. Lamps were basically a wick in a tin, iron or pottery container filled with grease, oil or lard.

Early American: 1790—1850 (Federal and Greek Revival)

After Independence, popular taste was influenced less by Europe and more by the classical styles of ancient Greece and Rome. A well-furnished parlor dining room would have a girandole—a large convex mirror surmounted by an eagle and with candle brackets on either side—an elegant chandelier and additional candle brackets on the walls. The innovative, expensive and handsomely decorated Argand, Astral and Solar lamp with their increased draft were great improvements over the simple glass or pewter whale oil lamps, sparking lamps and peg lamps used by the less affluent.

Mid to Late Victorian (1851-1901)

The first important change in lighting after mid-century was the use of kerosene as a fuel. As lamps were developed specifically for use with kerosene the variety of burners, lamp chimneys and globes was enormous. A kerosene lamp will be appropriate in any setting after 1860. Student lamps were most popular from 1875—1900. Hanging kerosene lamps with colorful glass globes were commonly used in the front hall and library.

Chandeliers were made to use all the various fuels and came in an endless variety from plain to fancy. Glass or metal bracket lamps set in a swinging iron frame attached to the wall were favored for kitchens and bedrooms. During the latter part of the 19th century gas lighting was piped into many houses in the larger urban areas. The most commonly used fixture was the gasolier with colored, frosted and milk glass globes, domes and shades. Gas bracket lights, often quite elaborate, were used throughout the house. During the 1890's the fanciful parlor lamp had its golden age.

The Edwardian Era (1902—1914)

Combination electric and gas fixtures, introduced during the last decade of the 19th century, were used in both chandelier and bracket form after the turn of the century. The first widely manufactured type of electric fixtures were simulated candles. Until the 1920's, electric chandeliers, wall sconces and some lamps simulated the 18th century candle-holding lighting devices. The domed leaded glass lamp popularized by Louis Comfort Tiffany and the box-shaped, often wood framed lamps of the Arts and Crafts style were the first lamps designed specifically for the electric bulb.

Lighting Fixtures & Lamps—Antique

1874 House (OR)
Addco Architectural Antiques (LA)
Antiquary, The (PA)
Art Directions (MO)
Brass Menagerie (LA)
Brasslight Antique Lighting (WI)
ByGone Era (GA)
Canal Co. (DC)
City Barn Antiques (NY)
City Knickerbocker, Inc. (NY)
City Lights (MA)
Condon Studios — Stained Glass (MA)
Cosmopolitan International Antiques (NY)
Greg's Antique Lighting (CA)
Hexagram (CA)
Illustrious Lighting (CA)
Jennings Lights of Yesterday (CA)
Jo-El Shop (MD)
Ley, Joe/Antiques (KY)
London Venturers Company (MA)
Mattia, Louis (NY)
McAvoy Antique Lighting (MO)
Moriarty's Lamps (CA)
Neri, C./Antiques (PA)
Ocean View Lighting and Home Accessories (CA)
Old Lamplighter Shop (NY)
Olde Bostonian Architectural Antiques (MA)
Reflections (PA)
Rejuvenation House Parts Co. (OR)
Roy Electric Co., Inc. (NY)
Sarah Bustle Antiques (IL)
St. Louis Antique Lighting Co. (MO)
Stanley Galleries (IL)
Wilson, H. Weber, Antiquarian (MD)
Wrecking Bar, Inc. (TX)
Yankee Craftsman (MA)

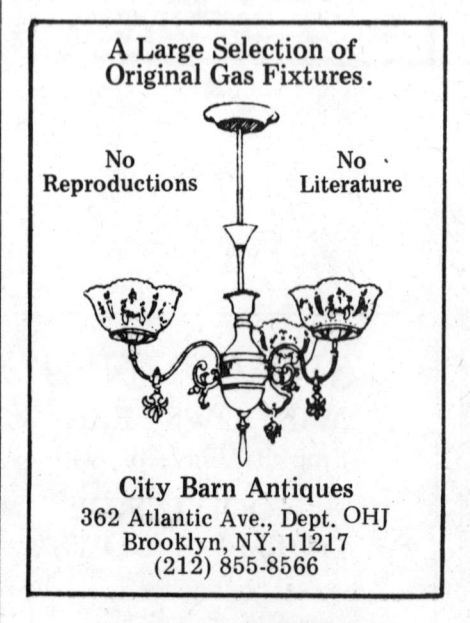

A Large Selection of Original Gas Fixtures.

No Reproductions   No Literature

City Barn Antiques
362 Atlantic Ave., Dept. OHJ
Brooklyn, NY. 11217
(212) 855-8566

See Company Directory for Addresses & Phone Numbers

ORIGINAL ANTIQUE LIGHTING

Four Arm Gas & Electric Circa 1880

Roy Electric Co. Inc.
1054 Coney Island Ave.
Dept. OHJ
Brooklyn, NY 11230

Sat. 12-6 or by appointment
1-212-339-6311

Catalog $3

City Lights
Antique Lighting

TABLE LAMPS
CEILING FIXTURES
FLOOR LAMPS
WALL LIGHTS AND SCONCES

all lights and shades are old
circa 1860-1930

2226 Mass Ave. • Cambridge,
(617) 547-1490 MA 02140
Hours: Tuesday thru Saturday 12-6
Thursday until 7:30

DON'T SETTLE FOR A COPY WHEN YOU CAN HAVE AN ORIGINAL...
A PIECE OF HISTORY.

Restored American Antique Lighting Fixtures

Original Shades of the period
Circa 1850 • 1925

no brochures or catalogues,
specific requests answered promptly.

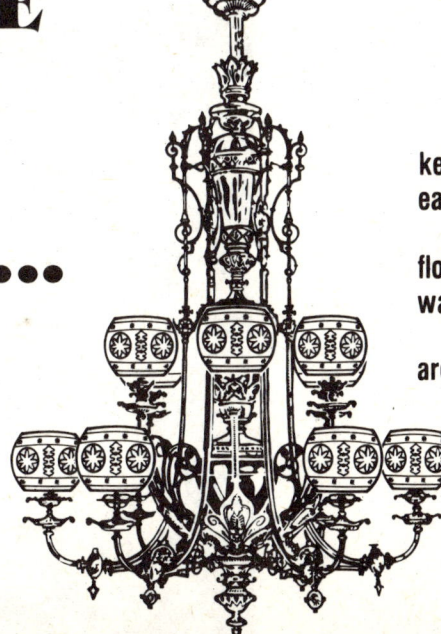

kerosene • gas • transition
early electric fixtures

floor, table and desk lamps
wall sconces

architectural hardware

STANLEY GALLERIES

2118 NORTH CLARK • CHICAGO, IL 60614 • 312 • 281 • 1614

The Old-House Journal 1982 Catalog

Lighting Fixtures, Reproduction—Early American

(1) Ceiling & Wall Fixtures
(2) Lamps

A.J.P. Coppersmith (MA)	1
Aladdin Lamp Mounting Co. (NJ)	2
Authentic Designs (NY)	1
Baldwin Hardware Mfg. Corp. (PA)	1,2
Ball and Ball (PA)	1
Brass Lion (TX)	1
Brass Menagerie (LA)	
Cohasset Colonials (MA)	1,2
Colonial Casting Co. (CT)	1
Colonial Tin Craft (OH)	1,2
Copper House (NH)	1
Country Loft (MA)	1,2
Craft House, Colonial Williamsburg (VA)	1
Dutch Products & Supply Co. (PA)	1
Ephraim Marsh Co. (NC)	2
Essex Forge (CT)	1
Gates Moore (CT)	1
Georgia Lighting (GA)	1
Greene's Lighting Fixtures (NY)	1
Heritage Lanterns (ME)	1
Historic Charleston Reproductions (SC)	2
Hurley Patentee Lighting (NY)	1,2
Kayne, Steve — Hand-Forged Hardware (NY)	1
King's Chandelier Co. (NC)	1
Lamplighter Shoppe (VA)	1
Loose, Thomas — Blacksmith/Whitesmith (PA)	1
MarLe Company (CT)	1
New England Brassworks (CT)	1
Newstamp Lighting Co. (MA)	1
Olde Village Smithery (MA)	1
Period Furniture Hardware Co. (MA)	1
Period Lighting Fixtures (CT)	1,2
Renovator's Supply (MA)	1
Ricker Blacksmith Shop (ME)	1
Saltbox (PA)	1,2
Village Forge (NC)	1,2
Village Lantern (MA)	1
Wallin Forge (KY)	1
Washington Copper Works (CT)	1,2
Worthington Trading Company (MO)	2

See Company Directory for Addresses & Phone Numbers

Beautiful and Unusual Lighting Catalog

- Colonial and Traditional Styles
- For indoor and outdoor use.
- Visit our factory store.
- Send $2.00 for idea-packed 28 page catalog

NEWSTAMP LIGHTING
Dept. OH82
227 Bay Road, N. Easton, MA 02356

Colonial Chandeliers and Wall Sconces in Solid Brass.

Also available with Delft Blue or Multi-color ceramic parts.

Send $1 for brochure and name of nearest dealer to:

Dutch Products & Supply Co.
P.O. Box 269, Dept. OHJ
Yardley, PA 19067

Restore or decorate with fine old gas, electric or combination fixtures. Exquisitely handcrafted solid brass reproduction ceiling fixtures, sconces and lamps; along with an excellent shade selection. We also have added a fine Mission style oak and art glass ceiling fixture.
Wholesale/Retail — Catalogue $3.00

St. Louis Antique Lighting Co.
25 N. Sarah, St. Louis, MO 63108
314-535-2770

CHANDELIER
Handcrafted to the drip on the tapered candles
Two-tier, 4 arms over 8 arms
Pewter coated or painted.
15" from Ring to Hook.
Diameter 27"

Catalogues $2.00 refunded with 1st purchase

Gates Moore

RIVER ROAD, SILVERMINE
NORWALK, CONNECTICUT 06850

Liting the Way™, a tradition at **THE SALTBOX**™

Authentic Reproductions

Brochure $1.00

2229 Marietta Pike, Lancaster, PA 17603
608 North Green St., Greensboro, NC 27401
859 East High St., Lexington, KY 40502
3808 Riverside Dr., Green Bay, WI 54301

GREG'S ANTIQUE LIGHTING
And Fine Collectables

An outstanding selection of Original Victorian Chandeliers, Wall Sconces and other Lighting.

Specializing in American Gas & Electric Fixtures from 1850 to 1910.

American 5-Arm Gas Fixture c. 1856

12005 Wilshire Blvd., Los Angeles, CA 90025   213/478-5475

Ocean View LIGHTING
1810 FOURTH ST.
BERKELEY, CA 94710
415·841·2937

authentic reproduction — Griffin Wall Sconce

Handcrafted Victorian Nostalgia

Fire polished crystal prisms; handwrought brass and brass plate. Fine hand blown glass; Rose bouquet and banding in October's golden, brown and green colors, fired for permanency. Tucked under the 14" shade are color enhancing fluorescent bulbs that require 54 watts of elect. 3-way switch. Approx. 20" wide x 34" long.
Direct from factory prices -- One year warranty. Check or Money Order. $268.00 postpaid. Available in plain Opaline White -- $228.00 Brochure $1.50.....

WINDY LANE™ FLUORESCENTS, INC.
35972 Hwy. 6, OHC-82 Hillrose, Colo. 80733
©WINDY LANE FLUORESCENTS, INC.
—Pat. Pend.

HANDMADE PERIOD LIGHTING REPRODUCTIONS

Entirely handmade 17th and 18th century lanterns, chandeliers and sconces in copper, pewter, distressed tin and wood. Carefully researched designs and detailed craftsmanship reflect the original warmth and charm of early lighting.

Our reproductions have been selected by the Newport Restoration Foundation and several other major historical societies and national landmarks.

•catalogues (refundable) $2.00

PERIOD LIGHTING FIXTURES
1 Main Street, Dept. OJ2
Chester, CT 06412
203-526-3690

ELEGANCE YOU CAN AFFORD

Direct from us, the designers and makers $1.50 for 96-page catalog of our crystal chandeliers, etc. Victorian and genuine Strass—also brass Colonial. Satisfaction guaranteed. Shipped prepaid.

KING'S CHANDELIER COMPANY
Dept. OHJ, Eden, NC 27288

Lighting Fixtures, Reproduction—Victorian

(1) Ceiling & Wall Fixtures
(2) Lamps

Aladdin Lamp Mounting Co. (NJ)	1,2
Alcon Lightcraft Co. (TX)	1
Baldwin Hardware Mfg. Corp. (PA)	1
Ball and Ball (PA)	1
Brass Menagerie (LA)	
Brasslight (NY)	1,2
City Knickerbocker, Inc. (NY)	1,2
Classic Illumination (CA)	1,2
Dutch Products & Supply Co. (PA)	1
Faire Harbour Ltd. (MA)	2
Fenton Art Glass Company (WV)	2
Golden Movement Emporium (CA)	1,2
Greene's Lighting Fixtures (NY)	1
Hurley Patentee Lighting (NY)	1
Illustrious Lighting (CA)	1
Jennings Lights of Yesterday (CA)	1
King's Chandelier Co. (NC)	1
Lamplighter Shoppe (VA)	1
London Venturers Company (MA)	1
Luigi Crystal (PA)	1,2
Magnolia Hall (GA)	2
Nowell's, Inc. (CA)	1,2
Ocean View Lighting and Home Accessories (CA)	1
Old Lamplighter Shop (NY)	1,2
Pendulum Shop (PA)	1,2
Progress Lighting (PA)	1
Rejuvenation House Parts Co. (OR)	1
Remodelers' & Renovators' Supply (ID)	
Renovator's Supply (MA)	1
Robin's Roost (CA)	2
Roy Electric Co., Inc. (NY)	1,2
San Francisco Victoriana (CA)	1
Sign of the Crab (CA)	2
St. Louis Antique Lighting Co. (MO)	1,2
Unique Brass Foundry, Inc. (NY)	2
Victorian D'Light (CA)	1,2
Victorian Lightcrafters, Ltd. (NY)	1
Victorian Reproductions, Inc. (MN)	1,2
Windy Lane Fluorescents (CO)	1

---

alcon Lightcraft Co.

Antique and reproduction
Victorian and
Turn Of The
Century
Fixtures and Sconces.

Inquiries with S.A.S.E. will be answered.

ALCON LIGHTCRAFT CO.
1424 West Alabama
Houston, Texas 77006
(713) 526-0680

See Company Directory for Addresses & Phone Numbers

Solid Brass
Reproduction
Victorian Lighting

Please send $2.00 for mail order catalog

VICTORIAN LIGHTCRAFTERS LTD.

(formerly Stansfield's Lamp Shop)
P.O. Box 332, Dept. OHJ82
Slate Hill, NY 10973
Phone: (914) 355-1300

ORIGINAL GAS, OIL AND EARLY ELECTRIC LIGHTING FIXTURES
1800 - 1910

restored, wired, and ready to hang

catalog $2.00

we ship anywhere

THE LONDON VENTURERS COMPANY
ROCKPORT, MASSACHUSETTS 01966
(617) 546-7161

Antique or reproduction?

Does it really matter? Here's why we are proud to bring to you our superb line of solid brass reproduction hanging, table, floor and wall lamps. Excellence in quality of design, detail and construction. Using the best materials available. Each fixture is handmade one at a time, using the best of the old techniques of 100 years ago, so we may give you the best in lighting for your needs, whether residential or commercial. Or, let us build a fixture for you.

Many of our lamps are available in kerosene for home or cabin. To complement your elegant fixture choose from over 100 authentic domestic, imported, cased and hand-blown glass shades to enhance each fixture. For our full line of excellent lighting and shades send $5.00 specifying Edition 1 catalogue "C."

Or, for a representation of our full line ask for the "NEW CENTURY COLLECTION" brochure — free on request.

Wholesale to Trade.

VICTORIAN REPRODUCTIONS INC.
1601 PARK SOUTH, MINNEAPOLIS MN 55404   612/338-3636

COMBINATIONS UNLIMITED

Victorian D'Light has available over 5000 different combinations of portables, wall brackets and hanging fixtures, accented by glass shades in cased, etched and frosted styles. All lamps are solid brass, turn-of-the-century reproductions, U.L. listed. Full-color catalogue available, send $3.00, refundable.

OFFICES:
533 West Windsor Rd.
Glendale, CA 91204
(213) 956-5656
Factory:
532 West Windsor Rd.
Glendale, CA 91204

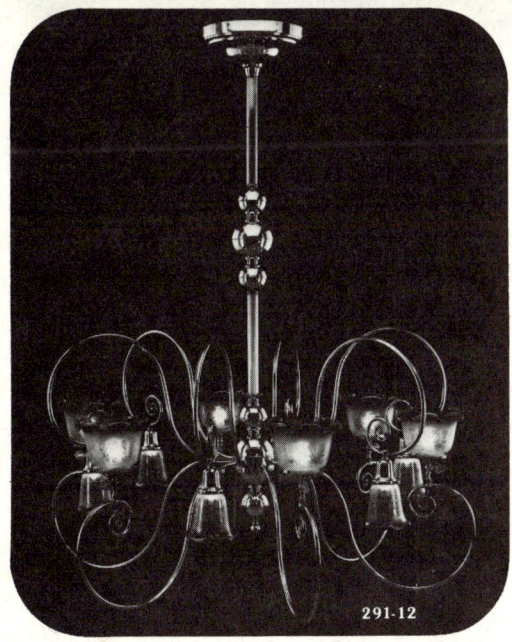

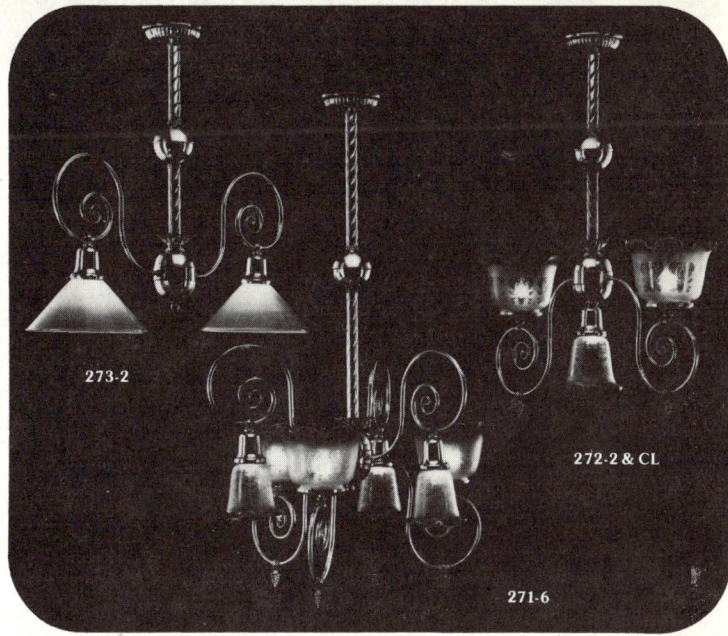

291-12 273-2 272-2 & CL 271-6

Represented nationwide; Contact us for your nearest representative

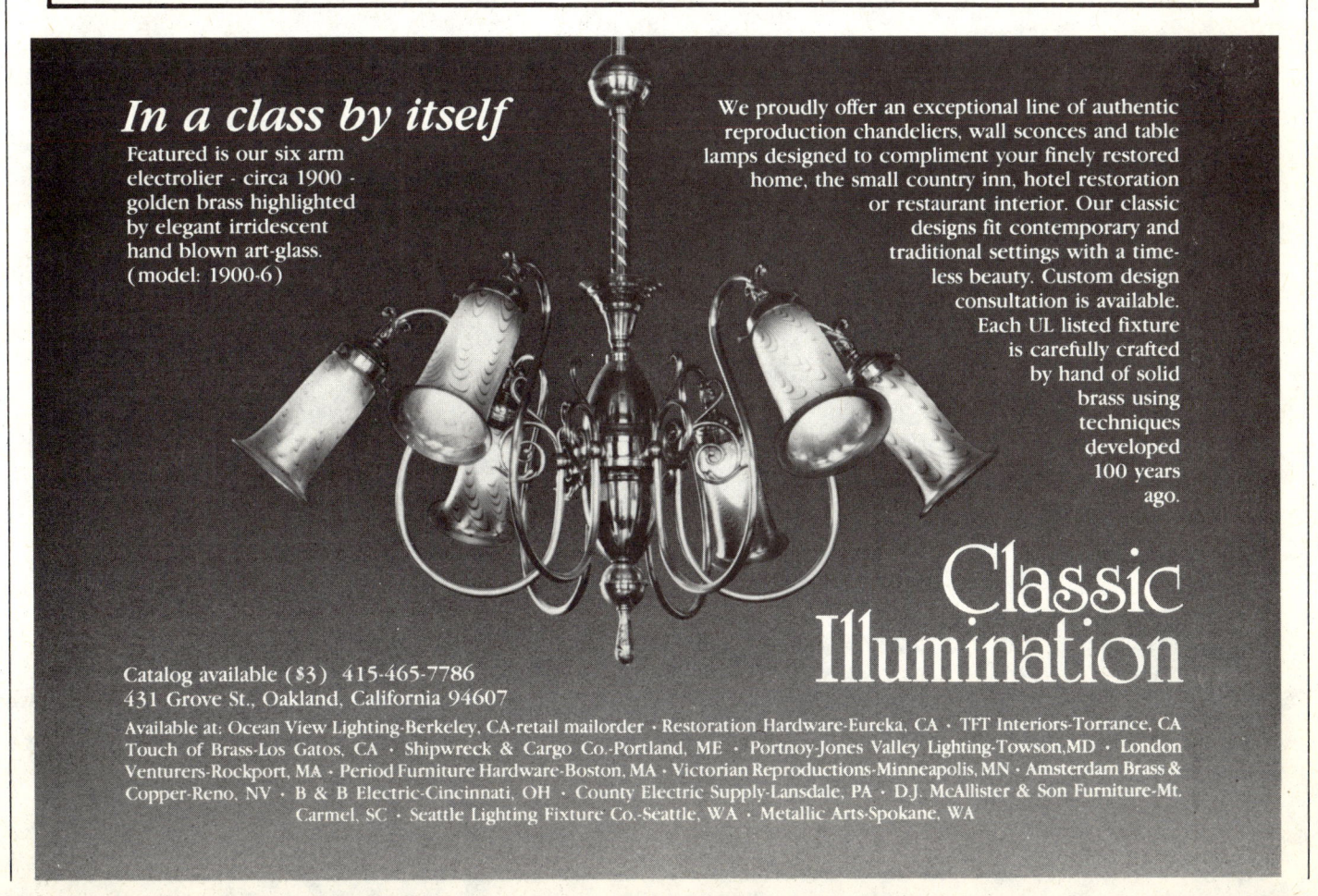

In a class by itself

Featured is our six arm electrolier - circa 1900 - golden brass highlighted by elegant irridescent hand blown art-glass. (model: 1900-6)

We proudly offer an exceptional line of authentic reproduction chandeliers, wall sconces and table lamps designed to compliment your finely restored home, the small country inn, hotel restoration or restaurant interior. Our classic designs fit contemporary and traditional settings with a timeless beauty. Custom design consultation is available. Each UL listed fixture is carefully crafted by hand of solid brass using techniques developed 100 years ago.

Classic Illumination

Catalog available ($3) 415-465-7786
431 Grove St., Oakland, California 94607

Available at: Ocean View Lighting-Berkeley, CA-retail mailorder · Restoration Hardware-Eureka, CA · TFT Interiors-Torrance, CA Touch of Brass-Los Gatos, CA · Shipwreck & Cargo Co.-Portland, ME · Portnoy-Jones Valley Lighting-Towson, MD · London Venturers-Rockport, MA · Period Furniture Hardware-Boston, MA · Victorian Reproductions-Minneapolis, MN · Amsterdam Brass & Copper-Reno, NV · B & B Electric-Cincinnati, OH · County Electric Supply-Lansdale, PA · D.J. McAllister & Son Furniture-Mt. Carmel, SC · Seattle Lighting Fixture Co.-Seattle, WA · Metallic Arts-Spokane, WA

The Old-House Journal 1982 Catalog

Progress Lighting creates the first collection of authentic American Victorian Reproductions

Dr. Roger Moss, nationally recognized authority on American architecture and decorative arts, has authenticated this collection of historically accurate American Victorian Reproductions, for Progress Lighting, the world's largest manufacturer of home lighting fixtures.

Diligently researched, attention has been given to the accuracy of the smallest details. Forgotten manufacturing techniques were rediscovered, old dies and glass molds found, restored or recreated. Ranging in date from 1840 to 1900, the collection includes a selection of styles:

Classical Revival, Rococo Revival, Colonial Revival, Art Nouveau and matching wall, hall and street light adaptations.

Minor modifications necessary to meet modern electrical codes have been subtly concealed. The overall scale, the finely detailed castings and the blown glass shades conform so closely to the originals that the many people who formerly sought antiques in vain can use them with confidence. For full color "American Victorian" catalog, send $1.00 to Progress Lighting, G Street and Erie Avenue, Philadephia, Pa., 19134

progress lighting®
Subsidiary of Kidde, Inc. KIDDE Philadelphia, PA 19134

Illustrious Lighting

Gas & Electric
Chandeliers
Sconces
Art Nouveau/Deco
Floor Lamps
Oil Lamps
Etched &
Cut Crystal
Shades

OVER 200 FIXTURES ON DISPLAY!

1812 DIVISADERO
SAN FRANCISCO, CA 94115

We invite you to a unique experience of authentic Victorian lighting.

(415) 922-3133

See Company Directory for Addresses & Phone Numbers

Lighting Fixtures, Reproduction—Early 20th Century

(1) Ceiling & Wall Fixtures
(2) Lamps

Alcon Lightcraft Co. (TX) 1
Ascherl Studios (OH) 2
Brass Menagerie (LA)
Brasslight (NY) 1,2
Classic Illumination (CA) 1,2
Dutch Products & Supply Co. (PA) 1
Greene's Lighting Fixtures (NY) 1
London Venturers Company (MA) 1
Lundberg Studios (CA) 2
Mexico House (CA) 1
Ocean View Lighting and Home Accessories (CA) 1
Old Lamplighter Shop (NY) 1,2
Pendulum Shop (PA) 1,2
Progress Lighting (PA) 1
Robin's Roost (CA) 2
Roy Electric Co., Inc. (NY) 1
San Francisco Victoriana (CA) 1
St. Louis Antique Lighting Co. (MO) 1,2
Victorian D'Light (CA) 1,2
Victorian Lightcrafters, Ltd. (NY) 1
Victorian Reproductions, Inc. (MN) 1,2
Yankee Craftsman (MA) 1

Gas Mantles

Nowell's, Inc. (CA)
Old Lamplighter Shop (NY)

Three Nostalgic-Look Table Lamps

Victorian gooseneck stands 20½" tall. Frosted tulip-shaped glass shade on weathered brass base.
$19⁹⁵ + $3⁰⁰ ppd.

Electric 'oil' lamp has antique polished brass finish with opal glass shade and hurricane chimney - stands 23" high
$39⁹⁵ + $4⁰⁰ ppd.

Classic desk lamp with swivel shade of heavy molded plastic has the look of old-fashioned case glass. Stands 16½" tall on a polished brass base. Your choice of green, amber or white.
$24⁹⁵ + $3⁰⁰ ppd.

SEND TO: **Robin's Roost**
167 Maynard Avenue, Dept. OH
Newbury Park, CA 91320
California residents add 6% sales tax

Kerosene Lamps & Lanterns

Aladdin Industries, Inc. (TN)
Campbell-Lamps (PA)
Cumberland General Store (TN)
Faire Harbour Ltd. (MA)
Heritage Lanterns (ME)
Lamplighter Shoppe (VA)
Lehman Hardware & Appliances (OH)
London Venturers Company (MA)
Moriarty's Lamps (CA)
Nowell's, Inc. (CA)
Old Lamplighter Shop (NY)
Sign of the Crab (CA)
Victorian Reproductions, Inc. (MN)
Washington Copper Works (CT)

Lamp Posts & Standards, Reproduction

Antique Street Lamps (TX)
Georgia Lighting (GA)
Kenneth Lynch & Sons, Inc. (CT)
MarLe Company (CT)
Niland, Thomas M. Company (TX)
Saltbox (PA)
Schwerd Manufacturing Co. (PA)
Silver Dollar Trading Co. (CO)
Spring City Electrical Mfg. Co (PA)
Tennessee Fabricating Co. (TN)
Welsbach (CT)

Lamps & Lanterns, Exterior—Reproduction

A.J.P. Coppersmith (MA)
Ball and Ball (PA)
Colonial Tin Craft (OH)
Essex Forge (CT)
Gates Moore (CT)
Georgia Lighting (GA)
Heritage Lanterns (ME)
MarLe Company (CT)
Metals by Maurice (MA)
Newstamp Lighting Co. (MA)
Niland, Thomas M. Company (TX)
Period Lighting Fixtures (CT)
Renovator's Supply (MA)
Richardson, Matthew Coppersmith (MA)
Saltbox (PA)
Sign of the Crab (CA)
Silver Dollar Trading Co. (CO)
Travis Tuck, Metal Sculptor (MA)
Village Lantern (MA)
Washington Copper Works (CT)
Welsbach (CT)

Lighting Fixtures—Gas Burning

(1) Antique (Original)
(2) New Reproduction

Hexagram (CA) 1
London Venturers Company (MA) 1,2
Neri, C./Antiques (PA) 1
Nowell's, Inc. (CA) 1,2
Old Lamplighter Shop (NY) 1
Renovator's Supply (MA)
Roy Electric Co., Inc. (NY) 1,2
Victorian D'Light (CA) 2

Lighting Fixture Parts—Glass

(1) Globes
(2) Shades
(3) Prisms
(4) Other (Specify)

Alcon Lightcraft Co. (TX)
Angelo Brothers Co. (PA) 1,2
Bienenfeld Ind. Inc. (NY) 2
Brass & Copper Shop (MO) 1
Campbell-Lamps (PA) 1,2
City Knickerbocker, Inc. (NY) 1,2
Cumberland General Store (TN) 1,2
Electric Glass Co. (VA) 2,3
Faire Harbour Ltd. (MA) 1,2
Gillinder Brothers, Inc. (NY) 2
Hexagram (CA) 2
Luigi Crystal (PA) 1,2,3
Lundberg Studios (CA) 2
Moriarty's Lamps (CA) 2
Nowell's, Inc. (CA) 1,2
Ocean View Lighting and Home Accessories (CA) 1
Old Lamplighter Shop (NY) 1,2,3
Paxton Hardware Co. (MD) 2,3
Pyfer, E.W. (IL) 1,2
Renovator's Supply (MA)
Roy Electric Co., Inc. (NY) 1,2
Victorian D'Light (CA) 2
Victorian Lightcrafters, Ltd. (NY) 2
Victorian Reproductions, Inc. (MN) 2
Yankee Craftsman (MA) 2

Lamp Wicks & Lamp Oil

Cumberland General Store (TN)
Lehman Hardware & Appliances (OH)

Light Bulbs, Carbon Filament

City Knickerbocker, Inc. (NY)

Lighting Fixture Parts—Metal

Barap Specialties (MI)
Campbell-Lamps (PA)
Cumberland General Store (TN)
Faire Harbour Ltd. (MA)
Kenneth Lynch & Sons, Inc. (CT)
Lundberg Studios (CA)
Moriarty's Lamps (CA)
Old Lamplighter Shop (NY)
Paxton Hardware Co. (MD)
Renovator's Supply (MA)
Roy Electric Co., Inc. (NY)
Squaw Alley, Inc. (IL)

Switches, Electric Push-Button

Mohawk Electric Supply Co., Inc. (NY)

See Company Directory for Addresses & Phone Numbers

Antique Street Lamps
1901 South Lamar
Austin, TX 78704
(512) 443-4540

TUDOR STYLE LEADED GLASS LAMP

No. 109R

COMPLETELY HAND CRAFTED FROM GENUINE HAND BLOWN GLASS
ABOUT 9" HIGH • WEIGHT - 7 1/2 LBS. • OPEN BOTTOM
PORCELAIN SOCKET • 12" BLACK CHAIN

**COLORS: CLEAR • AMBER TINT
BLUE TINT • GREEN TINT • PINK TINT**

PRICE $75.00

OHIO RESIDENTS ADD SALES TAX
SHIPPING CHARGES • OHIO $3.00 • EASTERN U.S. $4.50 • WESTERN U.S. $6.00

Ascherl Studios
869 CENTER ROAD   HINCKLEY, OHIO 44233
PHONE (216) 278-4964

PURE VICTORIAN.

Welsbach offers a cornucopia of original design in exquisitely crafted metal furniture and authentic lighting. All pure Victorian. Welsbach, 240 Sargent Drive, New Haven, CT 06511.

WELSBACH

Outdoors Welsbach stands unique. Indoors Welsbach forms environments.

Hand-Crafted Copper Lanterns

Catalogue two dollars, refundable with order

The Washington Copper Works
Washington, Connecticut 06793

Handcrafted in the old tradition

*Lanterns
Copper Sculpture
Weathervanes
Custom Metal Work*

Metals by Maurice
Copper Sculpture, Weathervanes
Custom Metal Work

73 Burnside St, Lowell, MA 01851
617 - 452-9339

Paints, Finishes, Removers & Supplies

Bleach, Wood

Behlen, H. & Bros. (NY)
Cabot Stains (MA)
Chem-Clean Furniture Restoration Center (VT)
Daly's Wood Finishing Products (WA)
Finishing Products (MO)
Janovic/Plaza, Inc. (NY)
Wolf Paints And Wallpapers (NY)

Brass Lacquer

Behlen, H. & Bros. (NY)
Crawford's Old House Store (WI)
Gaston Wood Finishes, Inc. (IN)
Illinois Bronze Paint Co. (IL)
Janovic/Plaza, Inc. (NY)
Wolf Paints And Wallpapers (NY)

Bronzing & Gilding Liquids

Behlen, H. & Bros. (NY)
Finishing Products (MO)
Gold Leaf & Metallic Powders, Inc. (NY)
Janovic/Plaza, Inc. (NY)
Wolf Paints And Wallpapers (NY)

Cleaners & Polishes, Metal

(1) Brass & Copper
(2) Silver
(3) Stove Polish

Bradford-Park Corp. (NY)
Butcher Polish Co. (MA) 3
Competition Chemicals, Inc. (IA) 1,2
Cumberland General Store (TN) 3
Easy Time Wood Refinishing Products (IL)
Goddard & Sons (WI)
Hope Co., Inc. (MO) 3
Howard Products, Inc. (CA) 1,2
Renovator's Supply (MA)
Woodcare Corporation (NJ) 1

Finish Revivers

Behlen, H. & Bros. (NY)
Broadnax Refinishing Products (GA)
Cornucopia, Inc. (MA)
Crawford's Old House Store (WI)
Daly's Wood Finishing Products (WA)
Easy Time Wood Refinishing Products (IL)
Finish Feeder Company (MD)
Finishing Products (MO)
Formby's Refinishing Prod., Inc. (MS)
Furniture Revival and Co. (OR)
Hope Co., Inc. (MO)
Howard Products, Inc. (CA)
O'Sullivan Co. (MI)
Renovator's Supply (MA)
Sutherland Welles Ltd. (NC)
Woodcare Corporation (NJ)

Flatting Oils

Behlen, H. & Bros. (NY)
Janovic/Plaza, Inc. (NY)

Glass Cleaners

Butcher Polish Co. (MA)
Skrocki, Ed (OH)

Glazing Stains & Liquids

Behlen, H. & Bros. (NY)
Benjamin Moore Co. (NJ)
Daly's Wood Finishing Products (WA)
Gaston Wood Finishes, Inc. (IN)
Illinois Bronze Paint Co. (IL)
Janovic/Plaza, Inc. (NY)
Johnson Paint Co. (MA)
Wolf Paints And Wallpapers (NY)

GOLD LEAF

In the 19th century architectural details were often embellished with gold leaf. The elegance of Greek Revival houses was enriched by gilded column capitals and mouldings in formal rooms. Many Victorian revival styles—Renaissance, Rococo and neo-Grec—boasted as much gilding as their owners could afford. Fine American houses of the 1890's modelled the most important rooms after those of their French and English counterparts where the ornate architectural details were intended to be gilded. In addition, much 19th century furniture, mirror and picture frames were gilded for a sumptuous effect.

Gold Leaf

Behlen, H. & Bros. (NY)
Gold Leaf & Metallic Powders, Inc. (NY)
Illinois Bronze Paint Co. (IL)
Janovic/Plaza, Inc. (NY)
Swift & Sons, Inc. (CT)
Wolf Paints And Wallpapers (NY)

Lacquers, Clear & Colored

Barap Specialties (MI)
Behlen, H. & Bros. (NY)
Finishing Products (MO)
Gaston Wood Finishes, Inc. (IN)
Illinois Bronze Paint Co. (IL)
Janovic/Plaza, Inc. (NY)
Wolf Paints And Wallpapers (NY)

Marble Cleaners, Sealers & Polishes

Barap Specialties (MI)
Goddard & Sons (WI)
ProSoCo, Inc. (KS)
Sculpture Associates, Ltd. (NY)
Talas (NY)
Wolf Paints And Wallpapers (NY)

Oil Finishes, Natural

Barap Specialties (MI)
Behlen, H. & Bros. (NY)
Bix Process Systems, Inc. (CT)
Broadnax Refinishing Products (GA)
Cabot Stains (MA)
Cohasset Colonials (MA)
Daly's Wood Finishing Products (WA)
Deft Wood Finish Products (OH)
Easy Time Wood Refinishing Products (IL)
Formby's Refinishing Prod., Inc. (MS)
Gaston Wood Finishes, Inc. (IN)
McCloskey Varnish Co. (PA)
Minwax Company, Inc. (NJ)
Renovator's Supply (MA)
Watco - Dennis Corporation (CA)
Woodworkers' Store, The (MN)

HOPE'S GRILL and STOVE BLACK

Heat Resistant to 1200°F
Just wipe on! No Brushes Needed!

Retards Rust

Restores Beauty & Lustre to Pot Bellied Stoves, Bar B Q Grills, Iron Grill Work, Fireplace Equipment, Lite Posts & Iron Fences. **16 oz. $5.95 retail**

The Hope Co., Inc.
P.O. Box 28431 • St. Louis, MO 63141

M. SWIFT & SONS, INC.
GOLD-LEAF
MANUFACTURERS SINCE 1887

QUALITY GOLD LEAF IN ALL COLORS
WRITE FOR SAMPLES AND INFORMATION

M. SWIFT & SONS, INC.
Ten Love Lane, Hartford, CT 06101

See Company Directory for Addresses & Phone Numbers

WOODCARE CORPORATION
ONE STEP RESTORATION OF WOODS & METALS

DO IT YOURSELF
EASY, PLEASANT TO USE
NO HARSH FUMES
NO ACIDS
NO WASH

NO SCRAPING OR SANDING
DOES NOT BLEACH OUT PATINA
SAFE FOR GLUES, VENEERS AND INLAY
SOLUTION CAN BE REUSED
USE TO FINISH AND NEUTRALIZE AFTER HARSH STRIPPERS HAVE BEEN USED

INTRODUCTION TO WOODCARE:

WOODCARE Corporation manufactures WOOD CARE & METAL CARE products for the restoration of woods and metals. For the wood products we are distinct from the stripping method in that our products are formulated for one-step restoration. We eliminate the conventional steps of sanding, scraping, washing down and then staining after a finish has been removed. As our WOODCARE PAINT & VARNISH REMOVER contains no acid or lye it does not raise the grain of wood. It is also completely safe for wood inlay and veneers. It does not dissolve glue around joints. It restores wood without bleaching out the patina that aged wood acquires (and which differentiates it from new wood).

DESCRIPTION OF PRODUCT LINE & SERVICE:

1) WOODCARE PAINT & VARNISH REMOVER dissolves oil based enamel, varnish, shellac and lacquer. This product can be reused and is highly recommended for the complete restoration of vintage homes. It will not bleach out wood as it contains no acid. Examples: Wood doors, panelling, wainscotting, parquet floors, antiqued wide board flooring, kitchen cabinetry, old furniture, antiques, etc. This product is also recommended for clean-up and a hand-rubbed finish after use of OLD-HOUSE JOURNAL Heat Gun on heavy enamels. (See advertisement).

2) TUNG OIL FINISH is a penetrating sealer applied over restored patina or a stained surface. Not only does it bring out the natural color of wood but it also is a good wood preservative and a durable finish which can be used even on floors. The method described in the WOODCARE RESTORATION GUIDE allows a high gloss or a hand-rubbed natural finish.

3) WOODCARE COPPER & BRASS CLEANER is recommended for all metals (excluding silver and pewter) and neatly removes the heaviest of tarnish, corrosion, rust and oxidation.

4) METAL CARE CLEAR FILM is a barrier against oxidation and when used on interior metals guarantees a natural metal finish or soft patina for 4-5 years. It does not yellow with age and the finish can be removed easily with detergent and hot water.

5) PROMPT UNITED PARCEL POST DELIVERY. Woodcare Corporation guarantees fast, same day shipment on all orders of any size when THE OLD-HOUSE JOURNAL CATALOG is mentioned. Delivery time 2-4 days.

6) FREE RESTORATION GUIDE and WHOLESALE PRICE LIST available upon request from WOODCARE CORPORATION, P.O. Box 92H, Butler, NJ 07405.

7) Our retail pricing is substantially lower than the nationally advertised FORMBY product. In addition Woodcare offers 25% quantity discounts on case lots. Woodcare wholesale prices run 40% off retail and are available to any business or House Restoration Cooperative either using or retailing large volume. Dealers are wanted for the distribution and sales of Woodcare Products. (Antique shows, Flea Markets or retail stores). Contact Woodcare Sales, P.O. Box 92H, Butler, NJ 07405.

8) Upon written request Woodcare Technical Sales Service Department offers free written consultation on home restoration problems involving the removal of interior or exterior finishes. Woodcare has over 20 years experience in restoration of woods and metals. All products are *unconditionally guaranteed* to give professional results or your money will be refunded without return of product.

1 Qt.	Woodcare Paint & Varnish Remover	6.95ea.
1 Gal.	Woodcare Paint & Varnish Remover	21.95ea.
1 Case	(4 Gal.) Woodcare Paint & Varnish Remover	66.00ea.
1 8 oz.	TUNG OIL Natural Finish	2.79ea.
1 Case	(12-8oz.) TUNG OIL Natural Finish	27.00ea.
1 8 oz.	Metal Care Brass & Copper Cleaner	2.99ea.
1 Case	(12-8oz.) Metal Care Brass & Copper Cleaner	27.00ea.
1 8oz.	Metal Care Clear Film	2.99ea.
1 Case	(12-8oz.) Metal Care Clear Film	27.00ea.
1 Kit	Woodcare Finishing Kit (contains: 2-Qt. Woodcare Paint & Varnish Remover, 8 oz. Woodcare TUNG OIL Natural Finish, Dip Jar and steel wool)	16.49ea.
	Shipping & Handling (any size order)	2.50ea.
	Total Amount Enclosed	

Please send order to:

Woodcare Corporation
Sales & Technical Sales Service
P.O. Box 92H
Butler, NJ 07405
(201) 838-9536

or

Woodcare Corporation
P.O. Box 345H
New Castle, VA 24128
(703) 864-5178

PAYMENT

Send Check, Ship C.O.D., or use Master Card, Visa or American Express (on charge cards indicate account number and expiration date) — Next day shipment U.P.S. — Delivery 2-4 Days.

ACCOUNT# (ALL DIGITS)

EXPIRATION DATE _____ -to- _____ INTER BANK NUMBER SIGNATURE _____
(REQUIRED IF USING CREDIT CARD)

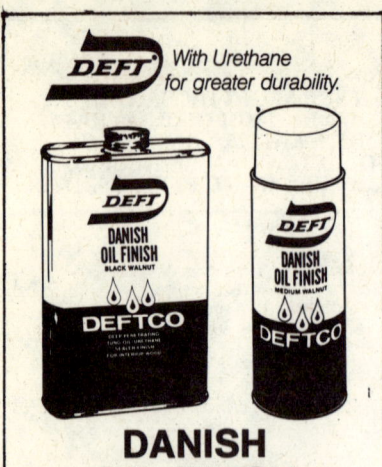

DANISH OIL FINISH
Seals and finishes wood.

DEFT With Urethane for greater durability.

Deep penetrating DEFTCO tung-oil urethane beautifies and hardens interior wood. Gives a rich lustrous finish that won't chip, peel, check, or wear away. Now in fast, clean, easy-to-use spray cans of Natural (Clear), Medium Walnut, Dark Walnut, or Black Walnut.

See Company Directory for Addresses & Phone Numbers

Finish Wood Like An Expert!
WATCO DANISH OIL
"Five-In-One" WOOD FINISH

One easy application primes, seals, hardens, protects, beautifies!

With Watco you just WET-WAIT-WIPE, and you have an elegant, extremely durable finish that would please the most critical professional.

Watco penetrates deeply — creates a tough finish INSIDE the wood — makes wood up to 25 percent harder. Can't chip, peel or wear away like a surface coating. Stains, scratches or minor burns usually are spot repairable.

For complete information fill in and mail the coupon.

WATCO DENNIS CORPORATION
1756 - 22nd St., Dept. OH-82
Santa Monica, California 90404

☐ Send name of nearest Watco Dealer
☐ Send Free booklet "How to Finish Beautiful Wood."

Name _____
Street _____
City _____
State _____ Zip _____

Paints—Period Colors
(1) Exterior
(2) Interior

Allentown Paint Mfg. Co. (PA)	1
Benjamin Moore Co. (NJ)	1,2
Cohasset Colonials (MA)	2
Craft House, Colonial Williamsburg (VA)	1,2
Devoe & Raynold Co. (KY)	1
Finnaren & Haley, Inc. (PA)	
Fuller O'Brien Paints (GA)	1,2
Janovic/Plaza, Inc. (NY)	1,2
Munsell Color (MD)	
Muralo Company (NJ)	1
Sherwin-Williams Co. (OH)	1
Stulb Paint & Chemical Co., Inc. (PA)	1,2
Sutherland Welles Ltd. (NC)	1,2
Wolf Paints And Wallpapers (NY)	1,2

OLD VILLAGE PAINT COLOURS

Authentic 18th and 19th Century Paint Colours for all manner of Reftoration and Decorating— Furniture, Walls, Woodwork, Infide and Outfide, Oil Bafe and Lead Free, Soft Low Sheen.
Exceptional durability, eafy to ufe.
Exclufive makers of Colours from Old Sturbridge Village.
COLOU'RS - Colonial White, Britifh Red, New England Red, Colonial Green, Cabinetmakers Blue, Pearwood, Antique Pewter, Salem Brick Colour, Antique Yellow, Soldier Blue, Old Gold, Golden Muftard, Wild Bayberry, Forest Green.
Send 1.00 for Colour Cards, Literature, and Name of Neareft Dealer.

Stulb's Colour Craftfmen
P.O. BOX 297 • 810 E. MAIN ST.
NORRISTOWN, PENNSYLVANIA 19404

When you decide to restore an old home...
Do it right!

Refinishing wood work and paneling in an older home, or the antique furniture you put in it, requires careful, meticulous work. To do the job right, please ask us first. This kind of work is a big part of our business. For interior finishing or refinishing you won't find a better product than Daly's Ben Matte Tung-Oil Stain, just one of many expertly prepared stains and wood product finishes we make ourselves to help people like you.

Write to: Jim Daly, Daly's Wood Finishing Products, 1121 N. 36th, Seattle, WA 98103, (206) 633-4204.

DALY'S
Wood Finishing Products

Authentic American colors look fresh & natural today

Quality finishes in historically-inspired colors from Benjamin Moore Paints.

Inside: Choose authentic historical colors for walls, trim and accents that reflect the dignity and warmth of past generations. Use them naturally, in traditional or colonial settings, or as inspiration for your own style. **Outside:** You'll find documented 18th & 19th century color combinations that restore the charm of yesterday, with finishes formulated to provide maximum protection today.

See your Benjamin Moore dealer for courteous service & expert advice, to help you create a personal look that is historically correct.

Benjamin Moore PAINTS

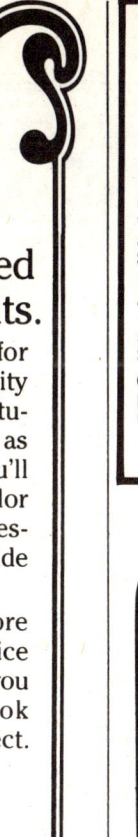

STOP STRIPPING

Try New INSTANT BRUSHLESS REFINISHING

Hope's **REFINISHER** rubbed on with steel wool—melts away old finish and restores original beauty. $6.95 qt.

Hope's **TUNG OIL VARNISH**, a rub-on finish. After old finish has been restored (or removed)—apply TUNG OIL, for a hard, fast drying, satin finish. (Just rub on, no brushes needed.) $4.65 pt.

(100% PURE TUNG OIL, still available at $6.50 pint.) And now Tung Oil Varnish in an easy to use aerosol. $4.95/can.

Post Paid from **THE HOPE CO.**
P. O. Box 28431 (OHJ) ST. LOUIS, MO. 63141

Like working with wood and furniture?

BIX, the #1 organization in its field, has 25 years experience putting people like you into their own profitable, enjoyable BIX FURNITURE STRIPPING / REFINISHING / COUNSELING / PRODUCT SALES & SERVICE CENTERS. More than 500 shops coast to coast. Write or call for your BIX Business Kit today.

BIX, Box 3011 Bethel, Conn. 06801
or call collect 203-743-3263

Join the Restoration Generation
with the Heritage Color Collection.

Fuller-O'Brien Paints has the colors to match the imagination and sense of history of this exciting Restoration Generation. We call them our Heritage Color Collection. For both interiors and exteriors, Heritage Colors bring back the charm and warmth of yesterday in a distinctive selection of traditional shades. Consider, too, our elegant Whisper White Collection—a gathering of subtle whites that wake up a room with a whisper. All made with the quality and muscle that Fuller-O'Brien puts in to keep them beautiful year after year.

So, if your restoration projects demand quality paints in authentic colors, be sure the paint you're buyin' is Fuller-O'Brien.

The Heritage Collection Color Card is available from Fuller-O'Brien Paint dealers or by writing to:

Fuller-O'Brien Paints
P.O. Box 864/Brunswick, Georgia 31521

18th Century Pilaster Capital in hand-carved pine courtesy of The Wrecking Bar, Atlanta, Georgia.

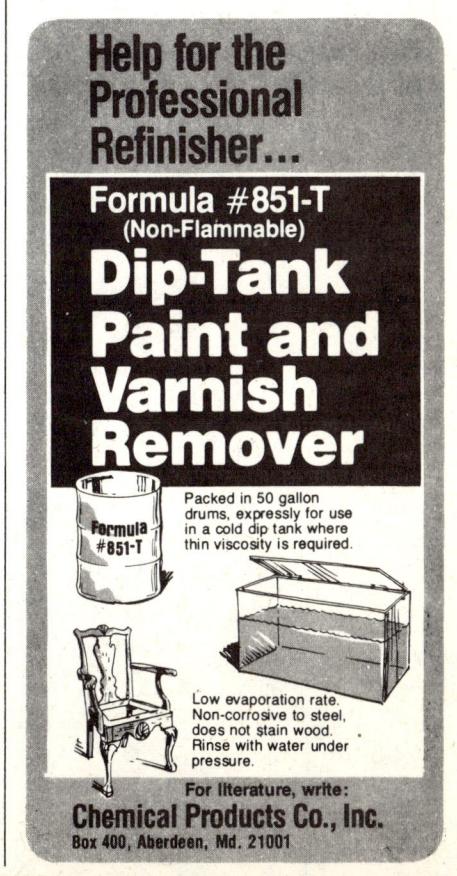

Help for the Professional Refinisher...

Formula #851-T
(Non-Flammable)

Dip-Tank Paint and Varnish Remover

Packed in 50 gallon drums, expressly for use in a cold dip tank where thin viscosity is required.

Low evaporation rate. Non-corrosive to steel, does not stain wood. Rinse with water under pressure.

For literature, write:
Chemical Products Co., Inc.
Box 400, Aberdeen, Md. 21001

Heritage Colors

Authentic Exterior Colors
for American Buildings · 1820/1920

Restore classic beauty to your home with forty historic 19th Century hues
Available in:
- SuperPaint™ Exterior Latex House & Trim
- SWP® Gloss Oil Base House & Trim

Sherwin Williams

Check your Yellow Pages for the store nearest you.

Paint Stripping Chemicals, Interior

Behlen, H. & Bros. (NY)
Bix Process Systems, Inc. (CT)
Chem-Clean Furniture Restoration Center (VT)
Chemical Products Co., Inc. (MD)
Easy Time Wood Refinishing Products (IL)
North Coast Chemical Co. (WA)
ProSoCo, Inc. (KS)
Savogran Co. (MA)
United Gilsonite Laboratories (PA)
Woodcare Corporation (NJ)
Woodworkers' Store, The (MN)

Pigments & Tinting Colors

Behlen, H. & Bros. (NY)
Benjamin Moore Co. (NJ)
Finishing Products (MO)
Janovic/Plaza, Inc. (NY)
Johnson Paint Co. (MA)

Porcelain Refinishing Materials

Janovic/Plaza, Inc. (NY)
Zynolyte Products Co. (CA)

Putty, Colored

Behlen, H. & Bros. (NY)
Daly's Wood Finishing Products (WA)

Rot Patching & Restoring Materials

Abatron, Inc. (IL)
BoatLIFE, Inc. (NY)
Defender Industries (NY)
E & B Marine Supply (NJ)

Rust & Corrosion Removers

Bradford-Park Corp. (NY)
North Coast Chemical Co. (WA)
Renovator's Supply (MA)

Sealers, Wood

Behlen, H. & Bros. (NY)
Benjamin Moore Co. (NJ)
Broadnax Refinishing Products (GA)
Daly's Wood Finishing Products (WA)
Garrett Wade Company (NY)
Gaston Wood Finishes, Inc. (IN)
Renovator's Supply (MA)
Sutherland Welles Ltd. (NC)
Sutherland Welles Ltd. (NC)
U.S. Gypsum Company (IL)
Watco - Dennis Corporation (CA)

Specialty Paints & Finishes

(1) Calcimine
(2) Casein
(3) Whitewash
(4) Texture Paints
(5) Milk Paint

Barnard Chemical Co. (CA)
Cohasset Colonials (MA) 5
Illinois Bronze Paint Co. (IL)
Janovic/Plaza, Inc. (NY) 2,3,4
Johnson Paint Co. (MA) 1,5
Muralo Company (NJ) 1,4
Old-Fashioned Milk Paint Co. (MA) 5
Sutherland Welles Ltd. (NC)
U.S. Gypsum Company (IL) 4
Wolf Paints And Wallpapers (NY) 2

ABATRON, INC.
141 Center Drive
Gilberts, IL 60136
312/426-2200

EPOXY SPECIALISTS
for over 20 years

The toughest, most versatile and permanent RESURFACING, CASTING & PATCHING COMPOUNDS, for floors, stairs, windows, decks, terrazzos, driveways, basements, structures.

STRUCTURAL RESINS for damaged walls & floors, to rebuild doors, frames, tanks, functional and decorative elements, furniture.

ADHESIVES, WOOD CONSOLIDANTS & FILLERS, MARINE COATINGS, LAMINATING & PATCHING RESINS, STRIPPERS, CHEMICAL SPECIALTIES, KITS, PRIVATE LABEL.

Send for free brochure

Stains, Wood

Behlen, H. & Bros. (NY)
Bix Process Systems, Inc. (CT)
Cabot Stains (MA)
Cohasset Colonials (MA)
Daly's Wood Finishing Products (WA)
Deft Wood Finish Products (OH)
Formby's Refinishing Prod., Inc. (MS)
Furniture Revival and Co. (OR)
Garrett Wade Company (NY)
Gaston Wood Finishes, Inc. (IN)
Illinois Bronze Paint Co. (IL)
Minwax Company, Inc. (NJ)
Sutherland Welles Ltd. (NC)
U.S. Gypsum Company (IL)
United Gilsonite Laboratories (PA)
Watco - Dennis Corporation (CA)

Textile Cleaners

Talas (NY)

Tung Oil

Behlen, H. & Bros. (NY)
Bix Process Systems, Inc. (CT)
Broadnax Refinishing Products (GA)
Crawford's Old House Store (WI)
Daly's Wood Finishing Products (WA)
Formby's Refinishing Prod., Inc. (MS)
Furniture Revival and Co. (OR)
Garrett Wade Company (NY)
Hope Co., Inc. (MO)
Renovator's Supply (MA)
Sutherland Welles Ltd. (NC)
Wolf Paints And Wallpapers (NY)
Woodcare Corporation (NJ)

FOR ALL YOUR PAINTING, RESTORATION, AND FINISHING NEEDS

Heavy Duty Paint Removers, • Graining Tools • Glazes • Minwax Stains • Period Paints and Wallpapers • Gold and Imitation Leafs • Bronze Powders • Garnet Papers • Aluminum Oxide Papers • Wet or Dry Tri-M-Ite • Emery Cloth • Pumice Powders • Rotten Stone • Aniline Stains • Penetrating Wood Stains • Non Grain Raising Stains • Pigmented Stains • Behlen Wood Finishing Products • Hope's 100% Tung Oil • Hope's Stove Black • Goddard's Waxes • Paraffin Wax • Bees Wax • Finishing Brushes • Stencil Brushes • Dry Pigments • Casein Colors • And More • Color Cards Available on Request

Mail and Phone Orders — Masterchage and Visa

FOR EXPERT ADVICE ON YOUR PAINT AND WALLPAPER PROBLEMS — CALL OR WRITE STEVE WOLF AT:

WOLF paints and wallpapers
Founded 1869
9th Avenue at 52nd Street, New York, NY 10019
1-212-245-7777

The Old-House Journal 1982 Catalog

Varnishes

Barnard Chemical Co. (CA)
Behlen, H. & Bros. (NY)
Benjamin Moore Co. (NJ)
Bix Process Systems, Inc. (CT)
Daly's Wood Finishing Products (WA)
Deft Wood Finish Products (OH)
Furniture Revival and Co. (OR)
Garrett Wade Company (NY)
Hughes Lumber & Building Supply Co. (SC)
Illinois Bronze Paint Co. (IL)
McCloskey Varnish Co. (PA)
Minwax Company, Inc. (NJ)
North Coast Chemical Co. (WA)
Pierce & Stevens Chemical Corp. (NY)
Sutherland Welles Ltd. (NC)
U.S. Gypsum Company (IL)
United Gilsonite Laboratories (PA)

Wallpaper Cleaners

Savogran Co. (MA)
Talas (NY)

Waxes, Microcrystalline & Other Specialty

Behlen, H. & Bros. (NY)
Black Wax — Pacific Engineering (CT)
Butcher Polish Co. (MA)
Finish Feeder Company (MD)
Janovic/Plaza, Inc. (NY)
Marshall Imports (OH)
O'Sullivan Co. (MI)
Renovator's Supply (MA)
Wolf Paints And Wallpapers (NY)

Wood Fillers & Patching Materials

Abatron, Inc. (IL)
Renovator's Supply (MA)

Wood Grain Fillers

Barap Specialties (MI)
Behlen, H. & Bros. (NY)
Benjamin Moore Co. (NJ)
Daly's Wood Finishing Products (WA)
Garrett Wade Company (NY)
Gaston Wood Finishes, Inc. (IN)
Janovic/Plaza, Inc. (NY)
Wolf Paints And Wallpapers (NY)

Other Finishes & Supplies

Behlen, H. & Bros. (NY)
BoatLIFE, Inc. (NY)
Butcher Polish Co. (MA)
Garrett Wade Company (NY)
Hope Co., Inc. (MO)
Renovator's Supply (MA)
Savogran Co. (MA)
Sutherland Welles Ltd. (NC)

See Company Directory for Addresses & Phone Numbers

For fine furniture and antiques...

Antiquax

A superb wax from England that feeds and protects wood – does not fingerprint.

200 gram tin **$8.95** incl. mailing

Marshall Imports
713 South Main, Dept. 15
Mansfield, Ohio 44907

BLACK WAX
A Shining Trio

BLACK WAX
Superior furniture cleaner which restores new lustre and gloss to the dullest of wood finishes....$4.00

CRYSTAL PASTE WAX
Top quality carnauba paste wax that provides the highest gloss and protection for fine furniture, leaving a beautiful crystal-like finish...$4.00

NEW — SIENNA PASTE WAX — NEW
Specialized blend of high quality paste wax, adding brown pigment to prevent the white chalky effect left by other paste wax....$4.00

Send listed amount + $1.50 postage & handling for each ½-lb. can to:
PACIFIC ENGINEERING CO., Box 145
Dept. OHJ, Farmington, CT 06032.
—Dealer Inquiries Invited—

MOISTURE IS THE PROBLEM

It robs building materials of strength; causes staining and pealing of finishes; promotes rot and efflorescence; and provides the perfect environment for termites, beetles and other pests.

We have the moisture meters to suit your needs. Call or write us today.

PRG
5619 Southampton Drive
Springfield, VA 22151
Tel: (703) 323-1407

GAZEBO

- Shady place for a cool drink
- Buffet place for your yard parties
- Change-house or bar at poolside
- Winter storage for lawn furniture

ARCHITECTS BLUEPRINTS AVAILABLE

Wood construction approx. 8 ft. diameter and 7'4" inside height. These drawings are ideal for contractor's estimate and construction. If you're handy and can read blueprints, build it yourself. $10 includes 3 drawings 17"x22" plus material list, postage and handling.

A.S.L. ASSOCIATES, Dept. OHJ
P.O. Box 6296 (3021 Hacienda St.)
San Mateo, Calif. 94403

FURNITURE REVIVAL & CO.

Solid brass furniture hardware, ice box hardware, roll top desk locks and replacement tambours, old office desk hardware, swivel mirror hinges, caning supplies, leather chair seat replacements, curved china cabinet glass and finishing supplies.

Catalog - $1.50

Furniture Revival & Co.
Dept. OHJ, Box 994
Corvallis, OR 97330

Tools & Other Supplies

Adzes, Froes & Hand Hewing Tools

Avalon Forge (MD)
Chicago Academy Tools (IL)
Cumberland General Store (TN)
Frog Tool Co., Ltd. (IL)
Kayne, Steve — Hand-Forged Hardware (NY)
Ricker Blacksmith Shop (ME)

Canvas for Walls

Janovic/Plaza, Inc. (NY)
Wolf Paints And Wallpapers (NY)

Chair Seat Repair

(1) Caning, Wicker, Etc.
(2) Chair Tapes
(3) Pressed Fiber Replacement Seats
(4) Leather Seats
(5) Other Chair Repair Supplies

Barap Specialties (MI) 1
Boseman Veneer & Supply Co. (TX) 1
Cane & Basket Supply Company (CA) 1
Dover Furniture Stripping (DE) 1
Finishing Products (MO) 1,3
Frank's Cane and Rush Supply (CA) 1,2,5
Furniture Revival and Co. (OR) 1,3,4
Guild of Shaker Crafts (MI) 2
Morgan Woodworking Supplies (KY) 1
Newell Workshop (IL) 1,5
Pat's Etcetera Company (TX) 3
Poor Richards Furniture Co. (NJ) 1
Pyfer, E.W. (IL) 1
Renovator's Supply (MA) 4
Shaker Workshops (MA) 2
Squaw Alley, Inc. (IL) 3

Conservator's Tools

(1) Contour Gauges
(2) Magnifiers, Portable
(3) Measuring Instruments
(4) Moisture Meters
(5) Telltales

PRG (VA) 1,2,4

Gazebo & Outbuilding Plans

A.S.L. Associates (CA)
Bow House, Inc. (MA)
Native Wood Products, Inc. (CT)
Sun Designs (WI)

GRAINING

Graining is a painted imitation of the grain of wood done in three stages—applying the background coat, making the wood grain, and varnishing. It is an authentic, economical and durable finish for hallways, old kitchen cabinets, exterior doors, old interior doors, furniture, woodwork and floors. In Colonial times plain pine doors and panelling were often grained to imitate the elegance of cedar, mahogany, oak or maple. In the 19th century tastemakers recommended grained imitations of ash, maple, birch and oak.

Graining Tools

Janovic/Plaza, Inc. (NY)
Johnson Paint Co. (MA)
Wolf Paints And Wallpapers (NY)

House Plans, Period Designs

(1) Early American
(2) Victorian
(3) Turn-of-Century

Bow House, Inc. (MA) 1
House Carpenters (MA) 1
Howard, David, Inc. (NH) 1
Pollitt, E., AIA (CT) 1
The Whistle Stop (GA) 2

Leaded & Stained Glass Supplies & Kits

(1) Tools & Supplies
(2) Lamp Shade Kits

Coran — Sholes Industries (MA) 1,2
Glassmasters Guild (NY) 1
Studio Design, Inc. t/a Rainbow Art Glass (NJ) 1,2
Whittemore-Durgin Glass Co. (MA) 1,2

Supplies For Moulds And Casts

(1) Mould-Making Materials
(2) Casting Plastics & Related Materials
(3) Casting Plaster

Abatron, Inc. (IL) 1,2
Industrial Plastic Supply Co. (NY) 1,2
Sculpture House (NY) 3
U.S. Gypsum Company (IL) 3

Bridges

Book consists of original designs for 22 foot bridges, 8 covered bridges, 36 cupolas and some history of each. Study Plan Book of Bridges and Cupolas $8.50 PPD. Complete plans available for each design.

Cupolas

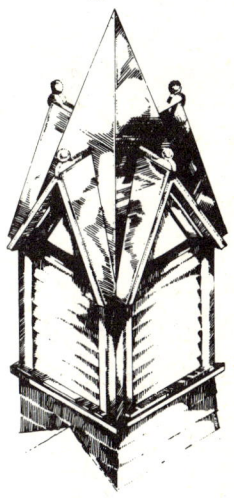

Study Plan Books FROM SUN DESIGNS
P.O. Box 206 Dept. OHJ, Delafield, WI 53186
(414) 567-4255

Gazebo

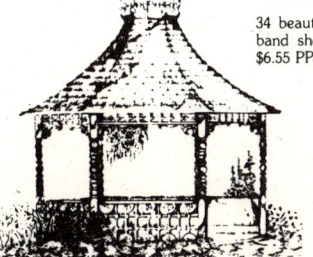

34 beautiful designs in 5 classic styles from band shell size to gazebos for small yards. $6.55 PPD. Complete plans also available.

Privy

The Classic Outhouse Book - 25 unique designs with conversions to playhouse, tool shed, sauna, etc., and humorous history. $7.95 PPD. Complete plans also available.

The Old-House Journal 1982 Catalog

Nails, Hand-Made

Cohasset Colonials (MA)
Kayne, Steve — Hand-Forged Hardware (NY)
Millham, Newton — Blacksmith (MA)
Renovator's Supply (MA)
Tremont Nail Company (MA)

Paint Stripping Tools

(1) Hot Air Guns
(2) Mechanical Scrapers
(3) Rotary Tools

Crawford's Old House Store (WI) 1,2,3
Easy Time Wood Refinishing Products (IL) . 1
Goldblatt Tool Co. (KS) 3
Hyde Manufacturing Company (MA)
Old-House Journal (NY) 1
Wolf Paints And Wallpapers (NY) 2

Planes, Wood-Moulding

Cumberland General Store (TN)
Fine Tool Shop, Inc. (CT)
Frog Tool Co., Ltd. (IL)
Garrett Wade Company (NY)
Iron Horse Antiques, Inc. (VT)
Williams & Hussey Machine Corp. (NH)

Plastering & Masonry Tools

Crawford's Old House Store (WI)
Goldblatt Tool Co. (KS)
Hyde Manufacturing Company (MA)
Marshalltown Trowel Co. (IA)
Mittermeir, Frank Inc. (NY)
Sculpture Associates, Ltd. (NY)
Sculpture House (NY)
Trow & Holden Co. (VT)
Wolf Paints And Wallpapers (NY)

Plaster Patching Materials

Muralo Company (NJ)
Sculpture Associates, Ltd. (NY)
Synkoloid Co. (CA)
U.S. Gypsum Company (IL)
Wolf Paints And Wallpapers (NY)

Plaster Washers & Anchors

Charles St. Supply Co. (MA)

Slate Roofing Tools

Evergreen Slate Co. (NY)

Specialty Power Tools

Garrett Wade Company (NY)
Goldblatt Tool Co. (KS)
Sculpture Associates, Ltd. (NY)
Trow & Holden Co. (VT)
U.S. General Supply Corp. (NY)

See Company Directory for Addresses & Phone Numbers

THIS IS THE BEST DOWELING JIG EVER MADE

Now, we're looking for craftsmen to support this contention—and we'll pay for testimonials we use in our ads.

The world doesn't always beat a path to your doorway when you invent a better mousetrap. For example, we're convinced this West-German invention is far superior to anything that's ever been available before. But so far we've been unable to communicate its ease and convenience, the magical way it lets you produce perfectly aligned and absolutely true dowel holes.

$20 WORTH OF EXTRAS— AT NO EXTRA COST!

Therefore, we're looking for testimonials—simple explanations of how it works, edge-to-end, edge-to-surface . . . and examples of situations in which doweling is the preferred and superior joining method. And we'll pay $100 for any testimonials we use.

In the meanwhile, we'll give you 300 fluted dowels, in assorted sizes, absolutely free. And, to add to the bargain, you'll also receive three FTS bits and a depth-stop collar to fit each bit at no extra cost. In all, a $20.00 bonus package that more than covers your cost!

NO RISK OR OBLIGATION

Dowel Magic consists of three separate jigs and guides. One each for ¼", 5/16" and ⅜" bits. For lightness and ease of handling, the jigs, guides and handles are made of high-impact plastic; for added strength, each jig has a hardened steel center to insure the bit stays vertical while you drill. For use with power or hand drills with stock up to 2" wide.

The three-piece ensemble is just **$19.95**. And you can return the ensemble to us *(you keep the dowels)* within 30 days for a complete refund if it's not as easy to work with as we say and an extremely valuable addition to your shop.

You have nothing to lose. And a chance to pick up a nice few dollars (with your name in print). You'll also be performing a real service for your fellow woodworkers. Order today. For quick service with your charge card use our toll free number.

CALL TOLL FREE
24 Hours—7 Days
800-243-1037
(In Connecticut 203-797-0772)

NO-RISK ORDER FORM

The Fine Tool Shops Inc.
20-28 Backus Ave.
Danbury, CT 06810 Dept. OHJ81

YES, please send me the three-piece Dowel Magic Ensemble (#101-0045) plus the 300 free fluted dowels *(mine to keep)* plus the three FTS bits and depth stop collars. I can get a complete refund by returning my order within 30 days. You also agree to pay me $100 if you use a testimonial I submit in one of your ads.

☐ Check or money order enclosed. (Include $1.50 for shipping and handling.)*
CHARGE my ☐ VISA ☐ Am.Ex. ☐ Master Charge ☐ Diners
Signature _____
Account No. _____ Exp. Date _____
☐ No, I'm not ordering, but please send me your 132-page Fine Tool catalog, for which I remit (charge or check) $5.00 to be refunded with my first order.

PLEASE PRINT

NAME
ADDRESS
CITY   STATE   ZIP
*Connecticut residents include sales tax.

FREE $5 CATALOG WITH EVERY ORDER

The Old-House Journal 1982 Catalog

Crawford's Old House Store

Those Hard-To-Find Tools...

...aren't so hard to find anymore! We proudly offer a great selection of the tools you really need to improve your old house!

Send $1.50, refundable, for our complete catalog. We have what you're looking for!

301 McCall Waukesha, Wisconsin 53186

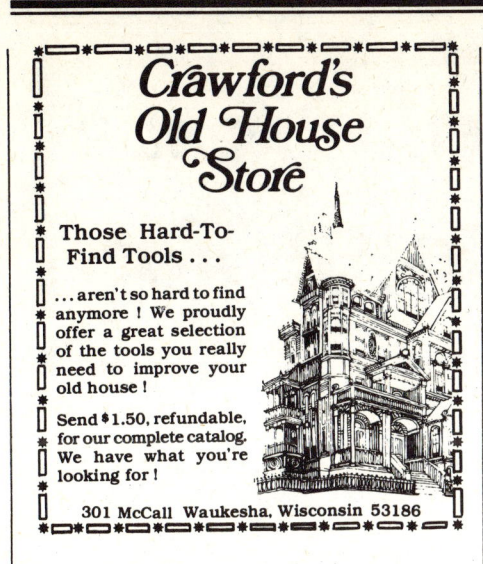

NOW—Restore your plaster ceilings and walls with plaster ceiling washers as seen and described in the October 1980 edition, The Old-House Journal.

Available now at

Charles St. Supply Co.
54 Charles Street
Boston, MA 02114

$1.25 per dozen (3 doz. min. prepaid)

EARLY AMERICAN PATTERNS & DESIGNS

This 25 page book from the famous series by Peg Hall allows you to become your own decorator. Contains 47 paintings and stencilling patterns. Designs for lace edge trays, chairs, deed boxes, bureau and tinsel pictures. 25 pages of tracing patterns, color suggestions and easy instructions.

THE DECORATOR'S HANDBOOK VOL. 4 with the yellow cover

Postpaid, $2.50; 1st Class Mail, $3.00. Brochure of design books, pattern sheets and supplies, $.25.

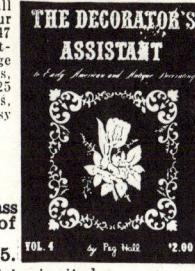

Dealer inquiries invited

THE PEG HALL STUDIOS
111 Clapp Rd., Scituate, Mass. 02066
Mass. residents add 3% tax

STENCILS STENCILS STENCILS

Catalog has over 300 reduced stencil patterns with simple instructions for application on walls, floors, furniture, fabric, glass, tile, tin...using latex or oil base paint. Durable plastic stencils are easily cut and are reusable!

PATTERNS INCLUDE
* Reproductions   * Classic * Contemporary
* Colonial Virginia * Victorian * Zodiac
* Dramatic Accent and Recreation * Classic
* Pennsylvania Dutch
  Stencil Paper   Doll House Stencil Kits

Complimentary workshop available to qualified retailers Distributors Inquiries Welcome

ITINERANT ARTIST
Box 222, Falls Church VA 22046
(703) 241-8371

THE HOUSE CARPENTERS
Box 217
Shutesbury, Ma 01072

The House Carpenters build traditional timber frames of carefully selected oak and pine. This Cape has an exposed frame. Its joints are mortised, tenoned, dovetailed and pegged. All members are hand planed, embellished with chamfers and stops.

Full architectural services are available and frames may be designed for individual plans.

Literature, including detailed drawings of five traditional houses with their floor plans, is available for a covering cost of four dollars.

STENCILLING

Stencilling is a fairly simple technique that requires few tools. Paint, stencils, cutting tools and paint brushes are about all that is necessary.

Much of the warmth and charm of Colonial rooms was due to stencilled walls—a substitute for expensive imported wallpaper. A variety of geometric, floral, foliage and symbolic motifs were used. Many frieze borders had swags, festoons and tassels reminiscent of French drapery. Weeping willows, the Federal eagle, sunbursts, woven baskets and vases filled with flowers were popular for the larger decorations, particularly over the mantelpiece. Blacks, greens, yellows, pinks and reds with some red-browns and blues are the predominating colors. For background color, either the original plaster or yellow and red ochres were most common.

For the Victorian house, stencilling can add elegance and enhance architectural detail. The great eclecticism of the period makes it easy to choose patterns and colors since Victorians used decorative motifs from the Roman, Egyptian, Gothic, Moorish, and Pompeian periods. Stencilling in conjunction with painted walls can be used to create a frieze—the decorative band at the top of a wall; to decorate the cove—the large concave moulding between ceiling and cornice of a room; to provide the richness of detail on a ceiling that doesn't have decorative plasterwork; as a wipeline—the beginning of the wall directly over the wainscotting or dado, so called because the housekeeper would eventually get a dirty smear on plain walls from dusting the top of the panelling.

Stencilling Supplies

(1) Brushes
(2) Stencil Paper
(3) Pre-Cut Stencils
(4) Stencil Kits

Behlen, H. & Bros. (NY) 1
Bishop, Adele, Inc. (VT) 4
Hand-Stenciled Interiors (MA) 3
Itinerant Artist (VA) 2,4
Janovic/Plaza, Inc. (NY) 1,2
Johnson Paint Co. (MA) 1
Stencilsmith (MA) 3,4
Timeless Patterns (MA) 3
Toby House (GA) 3
Wolf Paints And Wallpapers (NY) 1

Upholstery Tools & Supplies

(1) Upholstery Supplies, Webbing, Batting, Etc.
(2) Upholstery Tools

Barap Specialties (MI)
Dover Furniture Stripping (DE)
Osborne, C. S. & Co. (NJ) 2

Wallpapering & Decorating Tools

Crawford's Old House Store (WI)
Hyde Manufacturing Company (MA)
Peg Hall Studios (MA)
Rollerwall, Inc. (MD)
Wolf Paints And Wallpapers (NY)

Woodworking Tools, Hand

Brookstone Company (NH)
Chicago Academy Tools (IL)
Constantine, Albert and Son, Inc. (NY)
Crawford's Old House Store (WI)
Cumberland General Store (TN)
Fine Tool Shop, Inc. (CT)
Frog Tool Co., Ltd. (IL)
Garrett Wade Company (NY)
Iron Horse Antiques, Inc. (VT)
Leichtung, Inc. (OH)
Mittermeir, Frank Inc. (NY)
Princeton Co. (MA)
Sculpture Associates, Ltd. (NY)
Sculpture House (NY)
U.S. General Supply Corp. (NY)
Universal Clamp Corp. (CA)
Wikkmann House (CA)

Other Restoration Tools & Supplies

Wikkmann House (CA)

ALL YOUR STENCIL NEEDS from Adele Bishop

- Adele Bishop has everything you need for stenciling
- Complete stencil line for furniture, walls, floors, wooden or tin objects, fabrics and floorcloths
- Introducing **STENCIL-FAB**® the new, exclusive Adele Bishop stencil fabric paint
- **NATIONAL WORKSHOPS & SEMINARS**

® Registered trademark of Adele Bishop, Inc.

Send $2.00 for catalogue to:
Adele Bishop Inc., P.O. Box 557, Dept. OHJ1, Manchester, VT 05254
Tel: (802) 362-3537 or (802) 362-3538

STENCILS

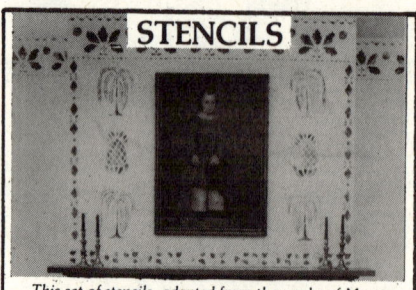

This set of stencils, adapted from the works of Moses Eaton, were designed for Historic Bulloch Hall's Antique Decorator's Show House. The 7 stencils are made of clear, flexible, reusable vinyl and are suitable for walls, floors, fabrics, and floor clothes. $35.00, VISA/MC/AE Brochure $2.50 patterns, supplies
Designer—Joanne Pirkle
The Toby House, 517 E. Paces Ferry Rd. N.E.
Atlanta, Georgia 30305

FROG® SUPER CATALOG

Send $2.00 for our big, complete 1982 catalog. Our low prices will surprise you.

FROG has everything you need in tools for renovation and fine woodworking. We feature unusual and hard-to-find tools, including:
- the largest selection of carving and wood turning tools
- over 200 different sizes and styles of German-made carving chisels
- a full line of wood and metal planes
- all sizes and pts./in. of quality Pax saws.

FROG TOOL CO., LTD. 700 W. JACKSON, DEPT. HJ1, CHICAGO, ILLINOIS 60606

DO-IT-YOURSELF
Redecorate • Restore

Remove and hang wallpaper, patch walls, do masonry projects, remove paint, etc., 32 pages of drawings and easy to follow instructions. Write today for your copy.

ENJOY AND SAVE MONEY TOO!

HYDE TOOLS HOW-TO-BOOK
SEND $1.00 TODAY. HYDE TOOLS, SOUTHBRIDGE, MA 01550

Name
Street
City _____ State _____ Zip

Antique & Recycled House Parts

Antique & Recycled House Parts

1874 House (OR)
Addco Architectural Antiques (LA)
Architectural Antique Warehouse, The (CAN)
Architectural Antiques (CAN)
Architectural Antiques Exchange (PA)
Architectural Emporium (IN)
Architectural Heritage (CAN)
Architectural Salvage of Santa Barbara (CA)
Art Directions (MO)
Artifacts, Inc. (VA)
Baker, A.W. Restorations, Inc. (MA)
Bank Architectural Antiques (LA)
Bare Wood Inc. (NY)
Bedlam Brass Beds (NJ)
Bill's Beauts (MS)
ByGone Era (GA)
Canal Co. (DC)
Canal Works (OH)
Castle Burlingame (NJ)
Cosmopolitan International Antiques (NY)
Croton, Evelyn — Architectural Antiques (NY)
Destin's Designs (WI)
Dovetail, Inc. (MA)
Farm Builders, Inc. (MD)
Gargoyles, Ltd. (PA)
Golden Movement Emporium (CA)
Great American Salvage (VT)
Housewreckers, N.B. & Salvage Co. (NJ)
Inglenook (NY)
Kensington Historical Co. (NH)
Ley, Joe/Antiques (KY)
Neri, C./Antiques (PA)
New Boston Building-Wrecking Co., Inc. (MA)
Old House Supplies (PA)
Olde Bostonian Architectural Antiques (MA)
Olde Theatre Architectural Salvage Co. (MO)
Pelnik Wrecking Co., Inc. (NY)
Red Baron's Antiques (GA)
Rejuvenation House Parts Co. (OR)
Renovation Source, Inc., The (IL)
Salvage One (IL)
Second Chance (GA)
Southern Accents Architectural Antiques (AL)
Spiess, Greg (IL)
Strip Shop (LA)
Structural Antiques (OK)
Sullivan's Antiques (CA)
Sunrise Salvage (CA)
United House Wrecking Corp. (CT)
Walker, Dennis C. (OH)
Wigen Restorations (NY)
Wilson, H. Weber, Antiquarian (MD)
Wrecking Bar of Atlanta (GA)
Wrecking Bar, Inc. (TX)

BYGONE ERA Architectural Antiques

20,000 sq. ft. of Architectural Antiques on two levels

Stained & Beveled Glass Windows,
Doors & Entry Sets
Back & Front Bars
Wooden, Brass, Copper & Wrought Iron
Doors & Gates
Carved Wooden, Stone & Marble Mantels
Restaurant & Home Decor Items
Reproduction Gingerbread, Porch & Gazebo
Components
Re-Sawn Heart Pine Flooring
Decorative Accessories & Collectables

BYGONE ERA
4783 Peachtree Road
Atlanta, GA 30341
(404) 458-3016 (404) 458-6883

STRIP SHOP

ANTIQUE FIREPLACE MANTELS
DOORS AND STAIRCASES

Quality Stripped Antique Victorian & Earlier Mantels

2201 Tchoupitoulas St. at Jackson Avenue
New Orleans, LA 70130
Hours 10 am - 4 pm Daily - Closed Sunday
504-522-7524

RENOVATE WITH ORIGINAL ARCHITECTURAL MATERIALS

• Stained Glass • Beveled Glass
• Antique Doors and Millwork • Old Pine Flooring
• Fine Brass and Other Hardware • Mantels
• Plumbing Fixtures • Ornamental Plaster

2601 Chartres St., New Orleans, La. 70117
(504) 945-4879 • 945-4890

Addco Architectural Antiques

For More Information About Restoration Supply Stores, See RENOVATOR'S SUPPLY Ad Inside Front Cover

See Company Directory for Addresses & Phone Numbers

Art Directions

Custom Built Front and Back Bars
for Residential and Commercial Installation

An Established Merchant of
Authentic Architectural Antiques

- 20,000 Sq. Ft. Showroom
- Stained and Beveled Glass Windows and Entrance Sets
- Antique Lighting Fixtures, Residential and Commercial Scale
- Saloon Front and Back Bars
- Architectural Bronze
- Complete Carved Rooms
- Millwork • Mantles
- Doors and Entrance Ways
- Columns, Cornices and Brackets
- Unusual Decorative Items

Send for free color brochure

6120 Delmar Blvd.
St. Louis, Mo. 63112

314·863·1895

ARCHITECTURAL ANTIQUES EXCHANGE
709-15 N. 2nd Street, Philadelphia, PA (215) 922-3669

28,000 sq. ft. warehouse of Victorian Salvage:
Doors, fretwork, ironwork, entryways, built-in wardrobes, mantels, lighting, stained glass, etc.
Also: Bars, backbars, and other commercial interiors

OLDE BOSTONIAN
Architectural Antiques

Newel Posts • Mouldings
Fireplace Mantels
Brackets • Brass Work
Unusual Doors
Old Bathtubs • Balasters
Wainscoting
Columns • Floor Registers
Stained Glass

135 Buttonwood Street
Dorchester, MA | (617) 282-9300

Antique Heart Pine Flooring and Paneling

Period Pine

since 1974

P. O. Box 77052 • Atlanta, Georgia 30309
404 876-4740

See Company Directory
for
Addresses & Phone Numbers

The Old-House Journal 1982 Catalog

The Canal Co.
ARCHITECTURAL ANTIQUES

- Doors • Door Hardware • Chandeliers
- Stained Glass • Fireplace Mantels
- Stair Handrails, Spindles & Newel Posts
- Fretwork • Sinks • Iron Fences & Gates

1612 14th Street N.W.
Washington, D.C. 20009
(202) 234-6637

Open Tuesday thru Saturday 10am-6pm • Sunday 1pm-5pm

Architectural Antiques

18,000 square feet of antique building elements! Doors and entries, columns, stained and beveled glass, balusters, corbels, chandeliers, mantels, paneling, iron gates and spiral staircases, Victorian fretwork, 17th through 19th Century; European, Oriental, and American.

The Wrecking Bar, Inc.
2601 McKinney • Dallas, Texas 75204
(214) 826-1717
We crate and ship anywhere

Joe Ley Antiques

620-632 East Market
Louisville, KY 40202
502-583-4014

"Memorabilia of a Bygone Era"

Six buildings within one block full of fine antiques and irreplaceable architectural items.

Wednesday through Saturday
9:00 a.m. to 5 p.m.
Closed all legal holidays

RENOVATION CONCEPTS INC.
SAVING THE PAST FOR THE FUTURE

Your Source for Period Reproductions

We represent over 40 manufacturers of:

Millwork	Doors & Windows
Brass Hardware	Decorative Glass
Metal Ceilings	Plumbing Fixtures
Lighting Fixtures	Brass Rail

and much more.

Architectural salvage items available on request.

Contact us for designers/contractors catalog, homeowners discount catalog or free brochure.

RENOVATION CONCEPTS INC.
P.O. Box 3720
Minneapolis, Minnesota 55403
Phone (612) 377-9526

Recycled Houses, Barns & Other Structures

Architectural Antique Warehouse, The (CAN)
Art Directions (MO)
Baker, A.W. Restorations, Inc. (MA)
Barn People, The (VT)
Belcher, Robert W. (GA)
Farm Builders, Inc. (MD)
Gest, Douglas Co. (VT)
Kensington Historical Co. (NH)
Mountain Lumber Company (VA)
Myers Restorations (KY)
Vintage Lumber Co. (MD)
Wigen Restorations (NY)

Renovation & Restoration Supply Stores

(1) Walk-In Stores
(2) Mail-Order Suppliers

Addco Architectural Antiques (LA) 2
Antique Reproduction Co. (TX) 1
Architectural Antique Warehouse, The (CAN) 2
Architectural Emporium (IN) 1
Ball and Ball (PA) 2
Bedlam Brass Beds — Denver (CO) 1
Conservatory, The (MI) 1
Crawford's Old House Store (WI) 2
Golden Movement Emporium (CA) 1,2
Hood, R. and Co. (NH) 2
Inner Harbor Lumber & Hardware (MD) 1
Keystone Furniture Stripping (CA) 1
Rejuvenation House Parts Co. (OR) 1,2
Remodelers' & Renovators' Supply (ID) .. 1,2
Renovation Concepts, Inc. (MN) 2
Renovation Products (TX) 1
Renovation Source, Inc., The (IL) 1
Renovator's Supply (MA) 2
Restoration Hardware (CA) 1
Restoration Works, Inc. (NY) 1,2
Squaw Alley, Inc. (IL) 1
Victorian Reproductions, Inc. (MN) 2
Weaver, W. T. & Sons, Inc. (DC) 2
Worthington Trading Company (MO)

See Remodeler's & Renovator's Supply ad on page 101

---

the Dennis C. Walker Company

Write for Our Brochure!

ARCHITECTURAL ANTIQUES
HISTORIC BUILDING MATERIALS

P.O. Box 309   Tallmadge, OH   44278   (216) 633-1081

Crawford's Old House Store

...for whatever you need!

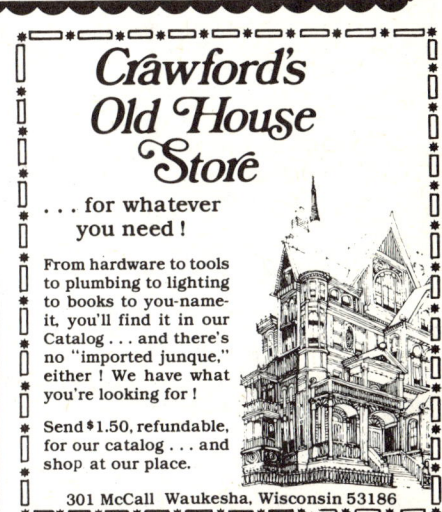

From hardware to tools to plumbing to lighting to books to you-name-it, you'll find it in our Catalog...and there's no "imported junque," either! We have what you're looking for!

Send $1.50, refundable, for our catalog...and shop at our place.

301 McCall Waukesha, Wisconsin 53186

Our showroom is listed in The National Register of Historic Places.

Just imagine what's inside.

At The Wrecking Bar of Atlanta, you'll discover why individuals and professionals from across the nation and around the world visit us: 18,000 square feet on three levels, showcasing a constantly maintained, 2 million dollar inventory of faithfully restored architectural antiques including many museum-quality pieces, representing up to 400 years of history and two continents.

THE WRECKING BAR of Atlanta

292 Moreland Ave. N.E./Atlanta, GA 30307/(404) 525-0468

The Old-House Journal 1982 Catalog

Restoration Services

Antique Shops

1874 House (OR)
Bare Wood Inc. (NY)
Barta, J.L. — Antiques (AL)
Berry, J.W. & Son (MD)
Brass & Copper Shop (MO)
Carriage Trade Antiques & Art Gallery (NC)
Conservatory, The (MI)
Cosmopolitan International Antiques (NY)
Ed's Antiques, Inc. (PA)
Grandpa Snazzy's Hardware (CO)
Iron Horse Antiques, Inc. (VT)
Morton's Auction Exchange (LA)
Sullivan's Antiques (CA)

Antique Repair & Restoration

Alexandria Wood Joinery (NH)
All-Tek Finishing Co. (NJ)
Antique Quilt Repair (CA)
Bare Wood Inc. (NY)
Barta, J.L. — Antiques (AL)
Beck, Nelson of Wash. Inc. (DC)
Berry, J.W. & Son (MD)
Billard's Old Telephones (CA)
Boston Cabinet-Making Inc. (MA)
Boulder Art Glass Co., Inc. (CO)
Brass Fan Ceiling Fan Co. (TX)
Bryant Steel Works (ME)
Cambridge Smithy (VT)
Cambridge Textiles (NY)
Carriage Trade Antiques & Art Gallery (NC)
Country Roads, Inc. (MI)
Dermit X. Corcoran Antique Services (NY)
Dotzel, Michael & Son (NY)
Dovetail, Inc. (MA)
Dura Strip of San Mateo (CA)
Ed's Antiques, Inc. (PA)
Gaudio Custom Furniture (NY)
Golden Fleece (NJ)
Hedrick Furniture Stripping & Refinishing (IN)

Hess Repairs (NY)
Inglenook (NY)
Keystone Furniture Stripping (CA)
Lost Arts, The (OH)
Master Wood Carver (NJ)
Matchmakers, Inc. (CA)
Mathis Fine Furniture Restoration (WV)
Ogren & Trigg Clock Service (MN)
Poor Richards Furniture Co. (NJ)
Porcelain Doctor (IL)
Restorations (NY)
Sawdust Room (MI)
Thomas Antique Services (NC)
Victorian Glass Works (CA)
Whitley Studios (PA)

Archeological Surveys & Investigations

Archeological Research Associates, Inc. (OK)
Archeological Research Consultants, Inc. (NJ)
Historic Preservation Alternatives, Inc. (NJ)
Preservation/Design Group, The (NY)

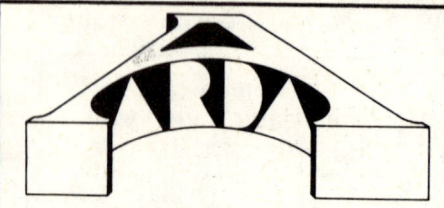

ARDA
ARCHITECTURAL RESTORATION & DESIGN ASSOCIATES
INCORPORATED

We offer a full range of restoration services for old buildings: research, design and construction.

ARDA, Incorporated
3320 Arch Street
Philadelphia, PA 19104
215-349-6758

ARCHITECTURAL SERVICES for historic preservation, restoration and rehabilitation of period buildings. Small town and village planning studies. Compatible design of additions, new and replica buildings. No literature.
Murrel Dee Hobt, Architect
P.O. Box 322, Williamsburg, VA 23185
(804) 220-0767

MATTHEW J. MOSCA

HISTORIC PAINT RESEARCH
INTERIOR DESIGN

✽

P.O. Box 960
BOWLING GREEN STATION
NEW YORK, NEW YORK 10274
(212) 375-9430

See Company Directory
for
Addresses & Phone Numbers

HISTORIC PRESERVATION ALTERNATIVES

15 SUSSEX STREET

NEWTON, NEW JERSEY 07860

(201) 383-1283

HISTORIC RESEARCH — NATIONAL REGISTER NOMINATIONS — PRESERVATION PLANNING — HISTORIC SITES SURVEYS — ADAPTIVE REUSE AND RESTORATION PROJECTS — GRANT PROPOSALS — HISTORIC DISTRICT ORDINANCES — SITE INTERPRETATION

AN ARCHITECT'S HELP

If your house needs extensive changes and complicated preservation work, hiring an architect may well be necessary. An architect's complete services will cost from 10% to 20% of the project's total costs. These services are:

1. Design and Development— Measuring and making an accurate plan of existing conditions; developing a list of the client's needs; designing and drawing new plans, layouts and elevations.

2. Construction documents— Providing working drawings (accurate, fully scaled detail drawings) and bid specifications: Written descriptions of the work to be done and the materials and methods to be used.

3. Supervision of contractors— Organizing (with the advice and consent of the owner) the bidding for the job; evaluating bids and selecting contractors: drawing up the construction contract; acting as the owner's agent in making payments and ordering changes; on site inspection of work in progress; quality control.

If your house doesn't require all of these services you can select from them and hire the architect on an hourly basis. Fees are usually in the $35—$55 range. A good method if you have more time and energy than cash is to have the architect design a master plan enabling you to do the work in stages...one project leading smoothly to the next.

Architectural Design & Consulting Services

(1) Architectural Design—Restoration
(2) Consulting Services
(3) Historical Research
(4) Paint & Materials Analysis
(5) Lectures & Seminars

Aachen Designers (FL) 1,2
Acquisition and Restoration Corp. (IN) 1,2
Arch Associates/ Steve Guerrant AIA (IL) ... 1
Archeological Research Consultants, Inc. (NJ) 3
Architectural Restoration & Design Assoc. (PA) 1
Architectural Woodworking (CT) 2
Baker, A.W. Restorations, Inc. (MA) 2
Barn People, The (VT) 2
Belcher, Robert W. (GA) 2
Berger/Spiers (PA) 1,2,3
Bierman & Associates (VA) 2
Blades/La Penta Construction Co. (PA) 1
Breakfast Woodworks Louis Mackall & Co. (CT) 1
Brooklyn Restorers (NY) 1
Brown, T. Robins (NY) 2,3
Brownstone Information Center (NY) 2
Building Conservation Technology (DC) . 2,3,4
CasaBlanca Glass, Ltd. (GA) 2
Clio Group, Inc. (PA) 2,3
Community Services Collaborative (CO) 1,2,3,4
Conservatory, The (MI) 1
Conti, John (PA) 3
Dierickx, Mary B. (NY) 3
Dovetail, Inc. (MA)
Downstate Restorations (IL) 2
Elmore, Chris/ Architectural Design (FL) ... 1
Ferris, R.D., Architect (CA) 1,2
Hart, Brian G./Architect (CAN) 1,3
Hasbrouck, W.R., Architect Historic Resources (IL) 1,2,3
Henderson, Zachary, AIA, Inc. (GA) 1
Hill, Allen Charles AIA (MA) 1,2,3,5
Historic Boulevard Services (IL) 5
Historic Interiors, Ltd. (MI) 5
Historic Preservation Alternatives, Inc. (NJ) 1,2,3,5
Hobt, Murrel Dee, Architect (VA) 1,2,3
Holm, Alvin Architect AIA (PA) 1,2
Image Group, The (OH) 1
Interior Decorations (NH) 5
International Architecture (TX) 2
International Consultants, Inc. (PA) 2
Jennings, Gottfried, Cheek/ Preservationists (IA) 2,3
Kaplan, Matthew L./Architect (NY) 1
Kensington Historical Co. (NH) 1,2
Kruger Kruger Albenberg (MA) 1,2
Moose Creek Restoration, Ltd. (VT) 1
Mosca, Matthew (NY) 4
Munsell Color (MD) 4
Myers Restorations (KY) 1
Northeast American Heritage Co. (MA) 1
Office For Metropolitan History (NY) 2,3
Old House Supplies (PA) 3
Olivo, Stephen A., Jr. (MA) 2
Pedersen, Arthur Hall — Design & Consulting Engineers (MO) 2
Preservation Associates, Inc. (MD) 2,3
Preservation Development Group (CT) 1
Preservation Partnership (MA) 1,2,3
Preservation Resource Center of New Orleans (LA) 3
Preservation Resource Group (VA) 2,3,5
Preservation/Design Group, The (NY) .. 1,2,3,5
Renovation Concepts, Inc. (MN)
Renovation Source, Inc., The (IL) 1,2
Resources in Housing Rehabilitation (NJ) ... 2
Restoration Workshop Nat Trust For Historic Preservation (NY) 2
Restoration-Preservation Architecture (IN) 1,2
Restorations (NY) 5
River City Restorations (MO) 2
San Francisco Renaissance (CA) 1
Silberman, Allen (NY) 5
Spigel, Herman, & Chapman Ltd., Architects (VA) 1,2,5
Stencilworks (GA) 5
Stevens, John R., Associates (NY) 1
Swofford, Don A., AIA (VA) 1,2
Szabo & Carrick, Architects, Inc. (CA) 1,3
T.A.G. Preservation Consultation (NY) 2
The Johnsons/Historic Preservation Consultants (NC) 2
Tindall, Susan M. (IL) 2
Townscape (OH) 2
Troyer, Le Roy and Associates (IN) 1
Welsh, Frank S. (PA) 4
Wilson, H. Weber, Antiquarian (MD) 2,5
Winans, Paul/Designer — Builder (CA) 1
Wm. Ward Bucher & Associates — Architects (DC) 1
Wollon, James Thomas, Jr., A.I.A. (MD) 1,2,5
Zillman, Marcus P., & Associates (IL) 2,5

ALLEN CHARLES HILL AIA

HISTORIC PRESERVATION AND ARCHITECTURE
25 ENGLEWOOD ROAD
WINCHESTER, MASSACHUSETTS 01890
617-729-0748

Old House INSPECTION COMPANY INC.

140 BERKELEY PLACE
BROOKLYN, N.Y. 11217

(212) 857-3647

Brownstones and other old houses our specialty.

ALVIN HOLM A.I.A.
ARCHITECT

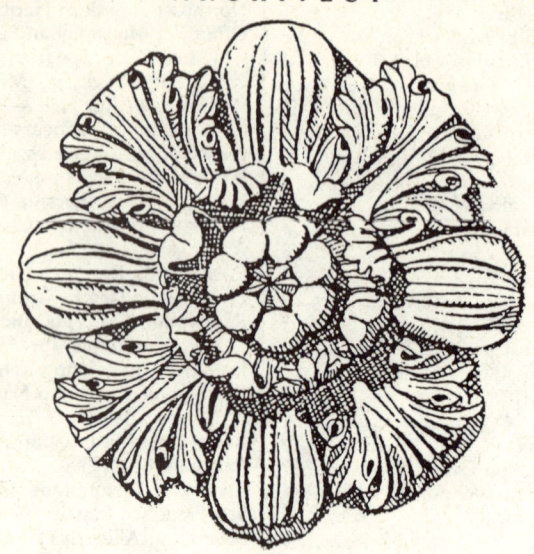

2014 SANSOM STREET, PHILA., PA 19103

ORIGINAL PAINT COLOR

WHAT WERE THE ORIGINAL PAINT COLORS OF YOUR HOUSE?

Don't guess! Let our modern microscopic techniques tell you.

SAVE by ordering our specially designed **PAINTPAMPHLET**. *It will carefully instruct you how to find, obtain and prepare your own paint samples for professional laboratory analysis.* **We will tell you the precise type, age and color of your paint and match it to the color system of a major paint company.**

Send $3.00 for each **PAINTPAMPHLET** to:

Frank S. Welsh
Historic Paint Color Consultant
859 Lancaster Avenue
Bryn Mawr, Pennsylvania 19010
Phone: 215-525-3564

Cabinetmaking & Fine Woodworking

Amherst Woodworking & Supply (MA)
Art Directions (MO)
Bare Wood Inc. (NY)
Boston Cabinet-Making Inc. (MA)
Campbell, Douglas Co. (RI)
Campbell, Marion (PA)
Chesapeake Restorations, Inc. (KY)
Congdon, Johns/Cabinetmaker (VT)
Crowfoot's Inc. (AZ)
Curvoflite (NH)
Custom Woodworking (CT)
D. Diehl Victorian Interior Restoration (OH)
Dixon Bros. Woodworking (MA)
Floors By Juell (IL)
Gest, Douglas Co. (VT)
Haas Wood & Ivory Works (CA)
Industrial Woodworking, Inc. (IL)
Lea, James — Cabinetmaker (ME)
Maurer & Shepherd, Joyners (CT)
Mead Associates Woodworking, Inc. (NY)
Millbranth, D.R. (NH)
Millworks Inc. (VT)
Nutt, Craig, Fine Wood Works (AL)
Olivo, Stephen A., Jr. (MA)
Pyramid Woodcraft Corp. (TX)
Restorations Unlimited, Inc. (PA)
Robillard, Dennis Paul, Inc. (ME)
S H M Restorations (MN)
Schmidt, Edward P. — Cabinetmaker (PA)
The Restoration Fraternity (PA)
Up Country Enterprise Corp. (NH)

Carpentry

Acquisition and Restoration Corp. (IN)
Anderson Reconstruction (MA)
Architectural Restoration (NY)
Beaumier Carpentry, Inc. (MD)
Castle Home Maintenance Co. (MA)
Kensington Historical Co. (NH)
Moose Creek Restoration, Ltd. (VT)
Olivo, Stephen A., Jr. (MA)
Ross, Douglas — Woodworker (NY)
S H M Restorations (MN)
Seitz, Robert/Fine Woodworking (MA)
Victorian Building & Repair (IL)
Whitehead & Roberts, Inc. (NJ)

D. Diehl
VICTORIAN INTERIOR RESTORATION & CABINETRY

Complete design and restoration service for residences, museums, and small businesses.

Individual and museum references available.

6374 Waterloo Road
Atwater, OH 44201
(216) 947-3385

DIXON BROS. WOODWORKING

CUSTOM MILLWORK

CABINETS
For the old house
Design & Duplication
617-445-9884

**Hand Turning
Custom Cabinetry**

For Restoration or
New Construction

Let Haas Give You a Hand

HAAS
Wood & Ivory

Artistry in Wood Since 1887

64 Clementina • San Francisco, CA 94105
415—421-8273

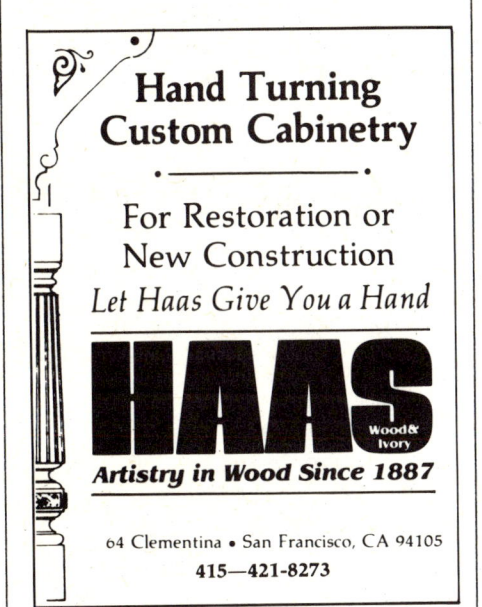

Contracting Services—Restoration

Acquisition and Restoration Corp. (IN)
Anderson Building Restoration (OH)
Architectural Restoration & Design Assoc. (PA)
Associated Construction Coordinators (TX)
Baker, A.W. Restorations, Inc. (MA)
Barn People, The (VT)
Beaumier Carpentry, Inc. (MD)
Blades/La Penta Construction Co. (PA)
Brandt Bros. General Contractors (IN)
Chesapeake Restorations, Inc. (KY)
Conti, John (PA)
D. Diehl Victorian Interior Restoration (OH)
Downstate Restorations (IL)
Elmore, Chris/ Architectural Design (FL)
Evergreene Painting Studios, Inc. (NY)
Gest, Douglas Co. (VT)
Great Northern Woodworks, Inc. (VT)
Historic Boulevard Services (IL)
House Carpenters (MA)
Huseman, Richard J. Co. (OH)
Kensington Historical Co. (NH)

Klinke & Lew Contractors (CO)
Lamb, J & R Studios (NY)
Lesco Restorations, Inc. (GA)
Moose Creek Restoration, Ltd. (VT)
Myers Restorations (KY)
Natural Wood Floors - Inlaid Wood Mosaic Div. (IL)
Navarre Builders, Inc. (NY)
Northern Design Builders (VT)
Odyssey Building & Maintenance Co. (MI)
Piazza, Michael Architectural Crafts (NY)
Preservation Associates, Inc. (MD)
Rambusch (NY)
Restoration A Specialty (OR)
Restoration Specialties (MD)
Restoration Workshop Nat Trust For Historic Preservation (NY)
Restorations Unlimited, Inc. (PA)
Richards, R.E., Inc. (CT)
River City Restorations (MO)
S H M Restorations (MN)
San Francisco Renaissance (CA)
San Francisco Restorations (CA)
Skyline Engineers, Inc. (MA)
Smolinsky, Ltd. (PA)
Stevens, John R., Associates (NY)
Stryker, Donald Restorations (NJ)
The Restoration Fraternity (PA)
Timberpeg (NH)
Up Country Enterprise Corp. (NH)
Victorian Building & Repair (IL)
Warren, William J. & Son, Inc. (CO)
Whitehead & Roberts, Inc. (NJ)
Wigen Restorations (NY)
Winans, Paul/Designer — Builder (CA)
Witt & Co. (CA)

Strawberry Hill & favorite delights:

RICK SCHAEFER

Festive Plaster, Trim and Ceilings

from the books and pictures you've collected. All affordably made to order by a craftsman who delights in making the fine corners and infills that are a hallmark of such work.

415 824-4672

Inquire direct or have your plaster work completed and color-matched as part of a room-set at Bradbury & Bradbury Wallpapers.

Remodelers' & Renovators' Supply

Recapture & Improve Upon the Past

with our period brass bath and kitchen faucets & fittings, Victorian mouldings & wood products, gas/electric light fixtures, brass door hardware, fancy screen doors, columns & porch posts, mantles, stained & beveled glass, architectural antiques & a host of old-style & reproduction products for your preservation, building, remodeling & decorating needs.

WRITE FOR OUR FREE, 24-PAGE CATALOG
611 E. 44th ST., #5, BOISE, ID 83704

Decorating Services

Fancy Painting—Gilding, Glazing, Lacquering, Etc.

Buecherl, Helmut (NY)
Craftsmen Decorators (NY)
Evergreene Painting Studios, Inc. (NY)
Floess, Stefan (NY)
Golden Fleece (NJ)
Hendershot, Judith (IL)
Holzman, S. (NY)
Rambusch (NY)
Reynolds, R. Wayne Restoration (MD)
Schmitt, Conrad Studios, Inc. (WI)
Silberman, Allen (NY)
The Grammar of Ornament (CO)
Zetlin, Lorenz — Muralist (NY)

Fireplace & Chimney Restoration

Acquisition and Restoration Corp. (IN)
Durvin, Tom & Sons (VA)
Gest, Douglas Co. (VT)
Haines Complete Building Service (IN)
Huskisson Masonry & Exterior Building Restoration Co. (KY)
Kensington Historical Co. (NH)
Olde New England Masonry (CT)
Restoration Masonry (CO)
Welles Fireplace Company (NY)

Graining

Buecherl, Helmut (NY)
Craftsmen Decorators (NY)
Evergreene Painting Studios, Inc. (NY)
Floess, Stefan (NY)
Holzman, S. (NY)
Mantia, Philip (PA)
Rambusch (NY)
Schmitt, Conrad Studios, Inc. (WI)
The Grammar of Ornament (CO)
The Johnsons/Historic Preservation Consultants (NC)
Willems Painting & Decorating (WI)

House Inspection Services

AMC Housemaster Home Inspection Svc. (NJ)
Acquisition and Restoration Corp. (IN)
Arch Associates/ Steve Guerrant AIA (IL)
Baker, A.W. Restorations, Inc. (MA)
Building Inspection Services, Inc. (MD)
Carson, Dunlop & Associates, Ltd. (CAN)
Claxton Walker & Associates (MD)
Gest, Douglas Co. (VT)
Guardian National House Inspection and Warranty Corp. (MA)
Haines Complete Building Service (IN)
Hart, Brian G./Architect (CAN)
Hill, Allen Charles AIA (MA)
Historic Preservation Alternatives, Inc. (NJ)
Kensington Historical Co. (NH)
Lieberman, Howard, P.E. (NY)
National Home Inspection Service of New England, Inc. (MA)
Oberndorfer & Assoc. (PA)
Old House Inspection Co., Inc. (NY)
Preservation Associates, Inc. (MD)
Preservation Partnership (MA)
Warren, William J. & Son, Inc. (CO)

House Moving

Baker, A.W. Restorations, Inc. (MA)
Barn People, The (VT)
Gest, Douglas Co. (VT)
Kensington Historical Co. (NH)
Myers Restorations (KY)
Wigen Restorations (NY)

Interior Design & Decorating—Period

Ambiance Interiors (NC)
Barta, J.L. — Antiques (AL)
Carriage Trade Antiques & Art Gallery (NC)
Castle Home Maintenance Co. (MA)
Cosmopolitan International Antiques (NY)
Dijon Galleries (CA)
Evergreene Painting Studios, Inc. (NY)
Grilk Interiors (IA)
Harris, Pat/Architectural Interiors (GA)
Historic Interiors, Ltd. (MI)
Hood, R. and Co. (NH)
Image Group, The (OH)
Interior Decorations (NH)
Jones Interior Design (TX)
Museum Enterprises, Inc. (WA)
Restoration A Specialty (OR)
Restorations Unlimited, Inc. (PA)
Schmitt, Conrad Studios, Inc. (WI)
Stencilworks (GA)

Landscape Gardening—Period Design

Blessing Historical Foundation (TX)
Gibbs, James W. — Landscape Architect (NY)
Renovator's Supply (MA)
White Nurseries, Inc. (NY)

Lighting Fixture Restoration & Wiring

Aladdin Lamp Mounting Co. (NJ)
Bernard Plating Works (MA)
Dermit X. Corcoran Antique Services (NY)
Dotzel, Michael & Son (NY)
Ed's Antiques, Inc. (PA)
Greene's Lighting Fixtures (NY)
Hexagram (CA)
Illustrious Lighting (CA)
Jennings Lights of Yesterday (CA)
Kayne, Steve — Hand-Forged Hardware (NY)
Mattia, Louis (NY)
Moriarty's Lamps (CA)
Old Lamplighter Shop (NY)
Pyfer, E.W. (IL)
Roy Electric Co., Inc. (NY)
Sarah Bustle Antiques (IL)
Squaw Alley, Inc. (IL)
Stanley Galleries (IL)
Victorian Reproductions, Inc. (MN)
Village Lantern (MA)
Yankee Craftsman (MA)

MARBLEIZING

The technique of using paint to simulate marble was a neo-classical fashion popular in 18th century France and England. Craftsmen came to the large cities of the Eastern seaboard from Europe to work in the more elaborate houses. They followed the French and English traditions and used marbleizing chiefly on doors and wall panelling. In simpler homes of the Colonial period marbleizing was less of an architectural trompe l'oeil and more of an attempt to suggest the color and texture of marble. It was used on floors, baseboards, stairs, the overmantel, doors and panelling.

American homes continued to be decorated with marbleizing through the Victorian period, when it was especially popular for mantels.

Marbleizing

Buecherl, Helmut (NY)
Dee, John W./Painting & Decorating (MA)
Evergreene Painting Studios, Inc. (NY)
Floess, Stefan (NY)
Holzman, S. (NY)
Rambusch (NY)
Schmitt, Conrad Studios, Inc. (WI)
The Grammar of Ornament (CO)
The Johnsons/Historic Preservation Consultants (NC)
Zetlin, Lorenz — Muralist (NY)

Helmut Buecherl
MASTER CRAFTSMAN

Specializing in painted decoration of all kinds— murals, marbleizing, graining, stencilling.

Located in N.Y.C. but will travel anywhere.
Call for appointment.
(212) 242-6558

See Company Directory for Addresses & Phone Numbers

Masonry Repair & Cleaning

Acquisition and Restoration Corp. (IN)
American Building Restoration (WI)
Anderson Building Restoration (OH)
Arndt Construction (MN)
Downstate Restorations (IL)
Durvin, Tom & Sons (VA)
Evergreene Painting Studios, Inc. (NY)
Haines Complete Building Service (IN)
Hayes and Associates Restoration (AL)
Huskisson Masonry & Exterior Building Restoration Co. (KY)
Lesco Restorations, Inc. (GA)
Navarre Builders, Inc. (NY)
Olde New England Masonry (CT)
Parsons, W.H., Jr. & Associates (NY)
Restoration Masonry (CO)
Skyline Engineers, Inc. (MA)

Metal Replating

Bernard Plating Works (MA)
Chandler — Royce (NY)
Estes-Simmons Silver Plating, Ltd. (GA)
Poor Richards Furniture Co. (NJ)
Pyfer, E.W. (IL)

Metalwork Repairs

Aladdin Lamp Mounting Co. (NJ)
Authentic Designs (NY)
Bernard Plating Works (MA)
Cambridge Smithy (VT)
Dermit X. Corcoran Antique Services (NY)
Dotzel, Michael & Son (NY)
Dura Strip of San Mateo (CA)
Experi-Metals (WI)
Flaharty, David — Sculptor (PA)
Flam Sheetmetal Specialty Co. (NY)
Howland, John — Metalsmith (CT)
Kayne, Steve — Hand-Forged Hardware (NY)
Moriarty's Lamps (CA)
Orthographic Engraving Co. (NY)
Retinning & Copper Repair (NY)

Mirror Resilvering

Atlantic Glass & Mirror Works (PA)
Keystone Furniture Stripping (CA)
Mirror Re-Silvering (MA)
Squaw Alley, Inc. (IL)

Musical Instrument Restoration

A Second Wind for Harmoniums (NY)

Paint Stripping Services

Addco Architectural Antiques (LA)
Alexandria Wood Joinery (NH)
American Building Restoration (WI)
Anderson Building Restoration (OH)
Architectural Restoration (NY)
Balzamo, Joseph (NJ)
Bare Wood Inc. (NY)
Bix Service Center (CO)
Cosmetic Restorations (NY)
Dover Furniture Stripping (DE)
Downstate Restorations (IL)
Dura Strip of San Mateo (CA)
Great American Salvage (VT)
Haines Complete Building Service (IN)
Hedrick Furniture Stripping & Refinishing (IN)
Keystone Furniture Stripping (CA)
Poor Richards Furniture Co. (NJ)

Painting & Decorating

Architectural Restoration (NY)
Buecherl, Helmut (NY)
Castle Home Maintenance Co. (MA)
Dee, John W./Painting & Decorating (MA)
Evergreene Painting Studios, Inc. (NY)
Floess, Stefan (NY)
Greenhalgh & Sons (MA)
Mantia, Philip (PA)
Rambusch (NY)
San Francisco Renaissance (CA)
Schaefer, Rick — Plasterer (CA)
Schmitt, Conrad Studios, Inc. (WI)
Wiggins, D.B. (NH)
Willems Painting & Decorating (WI)

Parquet Repair & Installation

Floors By Juell (IL)
Nassau Flooring Corp. (NY)
Natural Wood Floors - Inlaid Wood Mosaic Div. (IL)
Sutherland Welles Ltd. (NC)

Photography, Architectural

Byrd Mill Studio (VA)

Plastering, Ornamental

Acquisition and Restoration Corp. (IN)
Addco Architectural Antiques (LA)
Biagiotti, L. (NY)
Byrom's Plastering, Inc. (AL)
Casey Architectural Specialties (WI)
Castle Home Maintenance Co. (MA)
Felber, Inc. (PA)
Flaharty, David — Sculptor (PA)
Form and Texture (CO)
Giannetti Studios (MD)
Luczak Brothers, Inc. (IL)
Mangione Plaster and Tile and Stucco (NY)
Mantia, Philip (PA)
Olde New England Masonry (CT)
Ornamental Plaster-Works (NY)
Piazza, Michael Architectural Crafts (NY)
Saldarini & Pucci, Inc. (NY)
Schaefer, Rick — Plasterer (CA)
Schmitt, Conrad Studios, Inc. (WI)

Porcelain Refinishing

Perma Ceram Enterprises, Inc. (NY)
Porcelain Doctor (IL)
Porcelain Restoration (NC)
Tennessee Tub (TN)

Roofers, Specialty

Alte, Jeff Roofing, Inc. (NJ)
Arndt Construction (MN)
Haines Complete Building Service (IN)
Millen Roofing Co. (WI)
Skyline Engineers, Inc. (MA)
Wagner, Albert J., & Son (IL)

Sandstone (Brownstone) Repair

Brooklyn Stone Renovating (NY)
Evergreene Painting Studios, Inc. (NY)
Keuning, George (NY)
Navarre Builders, Inc. (NY)
Parsons, W.H., Jr. & Associates (NY)

Stencilling

Buecherl, Helmut (NY)
Castle Home Maintenance Co. (MA)
Craftsmen Decorators (NY)
Floess, Stefan (NY)
Greenhalgh & Sons (MA)
Hand-Stenciled Interiors (MA)
Hendershot, Judith (IL)
Hopkins, Sara — Restoration Stencilling (OR)
Itinerant Reproductions, Inc. (CT)
Rambusch (NY)
Schaefer, Rick — Plasterer (CA)
Schmitt, Conrad Studios, Inc. (WI)
Stencilworks (GA)
The Grammar of Ornament (CO)
The Johnsons/Historic Preservation Consultants (NC)
The Stenciller's Touch (OH)
Wiggins, D.B. (NH)

Wallpaper Hanging

Schaefer, Rick — Plasterer (CA)
Willems Painting & Decorating (WI)

Turnings, Custom

American Wood Column (NY)
Authentic Designs (NY)
Bare Wood Inc. (NY)
Craftsman Lumber Co. (MA)
Cumberland Woodcraft Co., Inc. (PA)
Dixon Bros. Woodworking (MA)
Industrial Woodworking, Inc. (IL)
Keystone Furniture Stripping (CA)
Michael's Fine Colonial Products (NY)
Nutt, Craig, Fine Wood Works (AL)
Period Productions, Limited (VA)
Robillard, Dennis Paul, Inc. (ME)
Sawdust Room (MI)
Woodstone Co. (VT)

Wood Carving

Able/Stanley Wood Carving Co. (NY)
Bare Wood Inc. (NY)
Dixon Bros. Woodworking (MA)
Jonathan Studios, Inc. (MN)
Lea, James — Cabinetmaker (ME)
Lost Arts, The (OH)
Master Wood Carver (NJ)
Nutt, Craig, Fine Wood Works (AL)
Shelley Signs (NY)
Whitley Studios (PA)

The Old-House Journal 1982 Catalog

THE COMPANY DIRECTORY

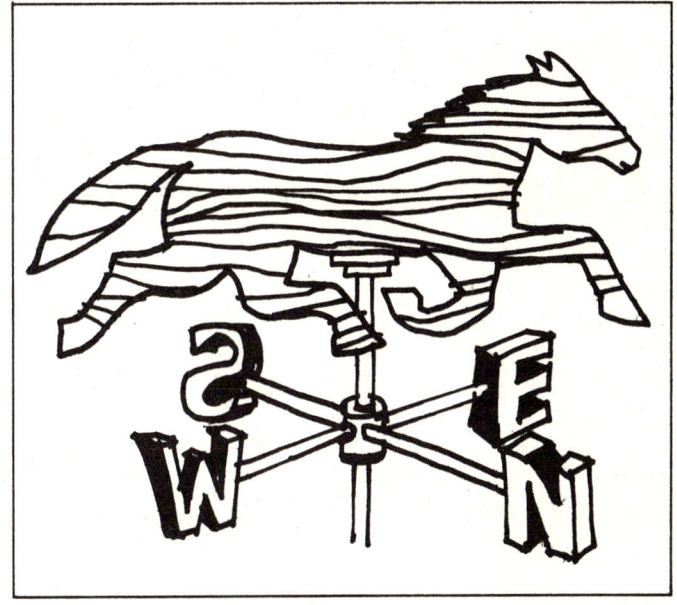

COMPANY DIRECTORY

1874 House
8070 S.E. 13th Ave.   Dept. OHJ
Portland, OR 97202
(503) 233-1874
RS/O
Specialists in architectural fragments, antique hardware for doors, cabinets, furniture, antique Victorian lighting fixtures, antique plumbing fixtures, antique sinks, replacements parts and pieces for almost everything. Walk-in shopping only. No literature.

1890 Iron Fence Co.
P.O. Box 467   Dept. OHJ
Auburn, IN 46706
(219) 925-4264
MO
Manufacturers of an historic style of iron fence, compatible with any style home built from the Civil War through the 1920s. Installation directions are geared to the handyman homeowner. Free descriptive brochure available.

18th Century Hardware Co.
131 East 3rd St.   Dept. OHJ
Derry, PA 15627
(412) 537-0645
RS/O MO
Reproduction Early American and Victorian brass hardware; furniture pulls, hooks, door knockers. Also decorative porcelain knobs and casters. Catalog, $2.50.

19th Century Company
P.O. Box 599   Dept. OHJ
Rough & Ready, CA 95975
(916) 273-6370
DIST RS/O MO
Manufacturer and distributor of hard-to-find parts and hardware for antique furniture and vintage homes. They carry a complete line of cast brass including Victorian and Chippendale period items through Art Deco and English hardware of the early 20th century. They also offer desk hardware, oak and walnut dowels and knobs, and much more. Wholesale and retail. Illustrated Catalog, $1.50.

A

• **AA-Abbingdon**
2149 Utica Ave.   Dept. OHJ
Brooklyn, NY 11234
(212) 236-3251
RS/O MO
24 patterns of hard-to-find embossed tin panels, and tin cornices in 8 patterns for metal ceiling installation. Popular 50-100 years ago, metal ceilings are an economical way to decorate in period style. Free illustrated brochure.

A.A. Used Boiler Supply Co.
8720 Ditmas Avenue   Dept. OHJ
Brooklyn, NY 11236
(212) 385-2111
RS/O
Offering reconditioned gas and oil cast iron boilers and sections. All types and sizes of cast iron steam and hot water radiators. Many choices of reconditioned gas and oil burners, controls, coils, and oil tanks. All products are tested and ready for immediate use. No literature; visit office or call.

• **A-Ball Plumbing Supply**
1703 W. Burnside St.   Dept. OHJ
Portland, OR 97209
(503) 228-0026
RS/O MO
Various plumbing supplies and hardware, including: Shower set-ups (brass or chrome), high-tank toilets, faucets, waste & overflow in brass, metal and tile cleaners, and epoxy tub-resurfacing kit, cast aluminum reproduction grates, and old-fashioned soap dishes that hang on footed tubs. Dealer inquiries welcome. Free brochure. Mail orders arranged.

• **A.E.S. Firebacks**
Grindstone Hill Road   Dept. OHJ
Stonington, CT 06359
(203) 536-0295
MO RS/O
Reproduction firebacks taken from original designs. Placed in the rear of the fireplace, the fireback protects masonry and radiates heat. Send SASE for brochure.

A.J.P. Coppersmith
34 Broadway   Dept. OHJ
Wakefield, MA 01880
(617) 245-1216
MO DIST RS/O
Long es Long-established company offers a complete line of authentic Colonial lighting fixtures. Chandeliers, sconces, post or wall lanterns are hand-crafted with a choice of finishes: Copper (antique or verdigris), Brass, Pewter-type (lead-coated copper or terne). A distinctive collection by three generations of craftsmen — send $2.00 for catalog.

AMC Housemaster Home Inspection Svc.
18 Hamilton St.   Dept. OHJ
Bound Brook, NJ 08805
(201) 469-6050
RS/O
House inspections and warranty service working in New York, New Jersey, Connecticut, and Philadelphia. Free brochure.

A.R.D.
1 Fourth Place   Dept. OHJ
Brooklyn, NY 11231
(212) 624-5688
RS/O MO
Purchasing service that supplies complete fixture packages to renovators at wholesale prices. Tin ceilings, hardware, mouldings and ornaments, tile, bathroom fixtures and accessories, custom kitchen cabinets, lighting, blinds and shutters, marble products, etc. Period or contemporary. Full design, fabrication and consultation services available. Ships anywhere in U.S. Handles over 500 product lines. Open by appointment only.

• **A.S.L. Associates**
P.O. Box 6296   Dept. OHJ
San Mateo, CA 94403
(415) 344-5044
MO
Plans for building a gazebo. The set consists of three 17" x 22" sheets, and includes full construction details and a materials list. The finished gazebo is 8 ft. in diameter and has an inside height of 7 ft. 4 in. clear. Price — $10. No literature.

Aachen Designers
308 NE Fifth Ave.   Dept. OHJ
Gainesville, FL 32601
(904) 372-5056
RS/O
Residential adaptive use and restoration: comprehensive design services (schematic through construction completion). Measured drawings, programming, consulting. Special expertise in kitchen design. Serving Southeast and Indiana. No literature; will respond to specific inquiries.

• **Abatron, Inc.**
141 Center Drive   Dept. OHJ
Gilberts, IL 60136
(312) 426-2200
MO
Chemical company specializing in epoxies (for patching, wood consolidation, adhesive uses, waterproofing, etc.) Also casting resins, structural coatings and sealants; other chemical specialties and custom formulations. Mostly a wholesale supplier (no dealers) — but will sell retail through the mail. Free product sheet.

• **Able/Stanley Wood Carving Co.**
368 Atlantic Ave.   Dept. OHJ
Brooklyn, NY 11217
(212) 834-9679
RS/O
Replaces parts and will custom make brackets, capitals, cornices, statues, mouldings, rosettes and much more. Send legal size envelope for free brochure.

• **Abraxas International, Inc.**
P.O. Box 4126   Dept. OHJ
Glendale, CA 91202
MO
Ornate brass/bronze keys for cabinets and skeleton keys for doors. Complete sets of solid brass cast door knobs; levers with plates. Ornamental door knockers. Decorative old style cast brass coat and hat hooks. Cabinet hardware. Catalog $3.00.

Ace Wire Brush Co.
30 Henry St.   Dept. OHJ
Brooklyn, NY 11201
(212) 624-8032
MO DIST
All types of chimney brushes: wire, fibre, nylon. Free catalog.

Acme Bent Glass
4821 rue de Roven   Dept. OHJ
Montreal, PQ, CN H1V1H6
(514) 255-7222
RS/O
Glass bending on custom orders for restoration. Walk-in service only.

Acme Stove Company
1011-7th St. N.W.   Dept. OHJ
Washington, DC 20001
(202) 628-8952
RS/O MO
Major supplier of pre-fab fireplaces, wood-stoves, and woodburning accessories in the Mid-Atlantic area. Also chimney systems, efficient heat-circulating systems, replicas of antique fireplace accessories. Professional counselors available to design complementary systems in townhouses and multifamily restorations. 9 locations; literature available free, please specify.

Acquisition and Restoration Corp.
1226 Broadway   Dept. OHJ
Indianapolis, IN 46202
(317) 637-1266
MO   RS/O
Experienced general contractors, construction mgrs., consultants, and interior designers in architectural restoration. House inspection, historical research, financing and property-tax abatement consultation. 417 residential and commercial projects completed. No fee for initial correspondence. Restoration, renovation, and preservation projects undertaken throughout continental U.S. Write for further information.

Adams Company
100 E. 4th St.   Dept. OHJ
Dubuque, IA 52001
(319) 583-3591
DIST
Manufactures a line of fireplace furnishings of heavy-gauge steel, solid brass, and cast iron. Sold through distributors, but a free descriptive brochure is available with list of distributors.

● **Addco Architectural Antiques**
2601 Chartres St.   Dept. OHJ
New Orleans, LA 70117
(504) 945-4879
RS/O   MO
Architectural antiques, architectural salvage retailers — leaded, beveled, stained glass windows, doors & entrance ways. Antique or reproduction old doors of all types; matched sets available in quantity. Old shutters restored, and authentic reproductions of old shutters to customers spec's. Beautiful ornamental plaster — medallions & moulding — stock designs and custom made. Antique hardware. Paint removal. Solid brass beds, hall trees. Back bars. Mantels. Old pine flooring. No literature.

Adirondack Hudson Arms
60 Kallen Ave.   Dept. OHJ
Schenectady, NY 12304
(518) 374-7200
RS/O   MO
Reproduction Shaker stoves, and museum-quality Shaker clocks. Pewter Spoon Molds and Pewter Casting. Further information to serious buyers.

● **Agape Antiques**
Box 43   Dept. OHJ
Saxtons River, VT 05154
(802) 869-2273
RS/O
Period cast iron kitchen ranges and parlor stoves for sale. Restored to original condition and ready to use. Excellent selection of stoves dating from late 1700's to 1920's. Illustrated brochure available.

Ainsworth Development Corp.
Beckford   Dept. OHJ
Princess Anne, MD 21853
(301) 651-3219
MO
Manufactures turnbuckle stars for reinforcing masonry walls. Will design & supply tension member for determining tension being applied by turnbuckle. For literature, send stamped self-addressed envelope.

● = Consult ad for more details. See Advertisers' Index on the last page of this Catalog.

Air-Flo Window Contracting Corp.
21 East 9th St.   Dept. OHJ
New York, NY 10003
(212) 254-0315
RS/O
Fabricates wood and metal storm and prime windows in 10 colors. Double-hung and casements available. Styles to suit old houses: windows conform to Landmark Commission standards. Can be glazed with Thermopane, Lexan, or Solar-Cool as well as single-pane glass. Free literature available on request, or call for more information.

Aladdin Industries, Inc.
P.O. Box 100255   Dept. OHJ
Nashville, TN 37210
(615) 748-3425
MO   DIST   RS/O
Manufacturers of a collection of authentic handcrafted Aladdin Kerosene (oil) and kerosene/electric table, shelf, hanging and wall lamps. These lighting products are handcrafted in solid brass, solid aluminum, and hand blown glass. A variety of shades and bases are available, and electric converter is UL listed. Dealers are located across the U.S. and catalog is available upon request.

Aladdin Lamp Mounting Co.
118 Monticello Ave.   Dept. OHJ
Jersey City, NJ 07304
(201) HE4-2869
MO   RS/O
Reproduction and restoration of all types of lighting fixtures. Services include fixture cleaning, rewiring, mounting of lamps, polishing. Also metal polishing for beds, tables, fixtures, etc. Crystal in stock. Reproduction sconces and fixtures at resonable prices. No literature; please call or write with specific request.

● **Alcon Lightcraft Co.**
1424 W. Alabama   Dept. OHJ
Houston, TX 77006
(713) 526-0680
RS/O   MO
Antique and reproduction early electric, gas and combination fixtures. Antique and reproduction lighting glassware replacements. Flyer available with stamped, self-addressed envelope.

Alexandria Wood Joinery
Plumer Hill Road   Dept. OHJ
Alexandria, NH 03222
(603) 744-8243
RS/O
Antique repair and restoration, furniture stripping and chair seating. Serving central New Hampshire. No literature.

Allentown Paint Mfg. Co.
P.O. Box 597   Dept. OHJ
Allentown, PA 18105
(215) 433-4273
RS/O   DIST   MO
Oldest ready-made paint company in U.S. (established 1855); offers a line of oil-based or latex exterior paints in colors appropriate for Colonial era houses. Many colors and formulations date from the 1860s, with the exception of additives for easy application and color fastness. Literature available through local paint stores, or contact Allentown office for name of distributor.

Allstate Flooring
837 E. 52nd St.   Dept. OHJ
Brooklyn, NY 11203
(212) 451-1818
RS/O
Sells strip oak and colored hardwoods that can be used for patching parquet floors. No literature; walk-in shop only.

All-Tek Finishing Co.
355 Bernard St.   Dept. OHJ
Trenton, NJ 08618
(609) 695-3644
RS/O
They specialize in wood, metal, and glass antique restoration. No literature.

Alte, Jeff Roofing, Inc.
PO Box 639   Dept. OHJ
Somerville, NJ 08876
(201) 526-2111
RS/O
General roofing contractors and roofing consultants serving Central and Northern New Jersey. Repair and reroofing of churches and older houses, including slate and cedar shingle work. Expertise and equipment to handle copper gutters, leaders, built-in gutters: their metal shop can fabricate gutters, ridge caps, etc. No literature; please call for appointment.

Ambiance Interiors
27 Broadway   Dept. OHJ
Asheville, NC 28801
(704) 253-9403
RS/O
Interior designers serving western North Carolina. Residential and commercial restoration and adaptive re-use. Carries Brunschwig & Fils, Scalamandre, etc., featuring historic fabrics and wall coverings. Specialists in kitchen remodeling. No literature.

Amerian Woodworking
1729 Little Orchard St.   Dept. OHJ
San Jose, CA 95125
(408) 294-2968
RS/O
Period-style wood mantels of oak, mahogany, cherry, or softwood. Prefabricated wainscotting. Mantel literature available.

American Building Restoration
9720 So. 60th St.   Dept. OHJ
Franklin, WI 53132
(414) 761-2440
RS/O
Restoration contractor specializing in chemical stripping and cleaning of historic buildings. Works throughout United States — system available through American Building Restoration. Free brochure.

● **American Delft Blue, Inc.**
P.O. Box 103   Dept. OHJ
Ellicott City, MD 21043
(301) 465-4220
MO   DIST   RS/O
Delft Blue tiles handpainted in 74 traditional designs. Custom orders for fireplaces, kitchens, bathrooms, etc. An illustrated catalog is available for $1.

KEY TO ABBREVIATIONS

MO	=	sells by Mail Order
RS/O	=	sells through Retail Store or Office
DIST	=	sells through Distributors
ID	=	sells only through Interior Designers or Architects

The Old-House Journal 1982 Catalog

American General Products
1735 Holmes Road   Dept. OHJ
Ypsilanti, MI 48197
(313) 483-1833
MO DIST
Spiral and circular stairs. Spiral stairs are available in both all wood, and wood and steel designs. Both are available in a variety of styles, diameters and in any floor to floor height. Circular stairs are for interior use and are shipped assembled. Spirals are shipped knocked down. Literature available; $1.00

American Olean Tile Company
1000 Cannon Avenue   Dept. OHJ
Lansdale, PA 19446
(215) 855-1111
DIST
A major tile manufacturer, makes the 1-inch square white ceramic mosaic floor tile and Bright White and Gloss Black glazed wall tiles used in early 20th century bathrooms. A terra-cotta quarry tile and a rough-textured tile are appropriate for rustic kitchens. Decorating Ideas Brochure No. 489 — $.50. Primitive Sheet 1329 — Free; Ceramic Mosaics Sheet 1352 — Free; Quarry Tile Sheet 1332 — Free; Primitive Encore Sheet 1381 — Free; Bright and Matte Sheet 1386 — Free.

American Ornamental Corporation
5013 Kelley St.   Dept. OHJ
Houston, TX 77026
(713) 635-2385
MO DIST RS/O
Manufacturers of steel spiral stairways. Free brochure.

American Wood Column
913 Grand Street   Dept. OHJ
Brooklyn, NY 11211
(212) 782-3163
RS/O
Produces custom wooden exterior and interior columns, capitals, and bases. Also wood turnings of any description and ornamental work. Brochure available.

Amherst Woodworking & Supply
Box 575, Hubbard Avenue   Dept. OHJ
Northampton, MA 01060
(413) 584-3004
RS/O
Contract millwork and reproduction furniture to order. Sells hardwood lumber. No literature.

Anderson Building Restoration
923 Marion Avenue   Dept. OHJ
Cincinnati, OH 45229
(513) 281-5258
RS/O
Exterior restoration contractors specializing in chemical paint removal and chemical cleaning of historic masonry structures. They provide expert tuck-pointing, caulking, epoxy consolidation, and painting. A member of The Association for Preservation Technology, the company takes great pride in using only the safest, most gentle methods. They work in the Ohio, Kentucky, and Southeastern Indiana areas. Free literature available.

Anderson Reconstruction
42 Boardman St.   Dept. OHJ
Newburyport, MA 01950
(617) 465-9622
RS/O
Works on houses built before 1850. White pine clapboards with graduated spacing, wooden downspouts, exterior and interior work. Replaces rotted corner posts, beams and sills with new or old wood. Wide pine floors and beaded sheathing. No literature.

Angelo Brothers Co.
10981 Decatur Rd.   Dept. OHJ
Philadelphia, PA 19154
(215) 632-9600
DIST
Primarily a wholesaler, this company has the largest selection of glass shades and globes for replacements on 19th century lighting fixtures. Angelo Master Catalog is $10. It can also be viewed at your local dealer.

Anglo-American Brass Co.
4146 Mitzi Drive Box 9792   Dept. OHJ
San Jose, CA 95157
(408) 246-0203
MO RS/O
Authentic solid cast and stamped brass reproduction hardware for the restoration of furniture, built-in cupboards, etc. Included are bails, handle sets, knobs, drops, hinges, catches, lock sets, ice box; kitchen hardware, coat hooks, etc. Since they are manufacturers, they can also custom-produce articles (in quantity) for builders, wholesalers or manufacturers. Catalog 113, $1.00.

Antares Forge and Metalworks
501 Eleventh St.   Dept. OHJ
Brooklyn, NY 11215
(212) 499-5299
RS/O
Design and forging of architectural ironwork, domestic implements, fireplace equipment, etc. Some period and restoration work; but almost all work is custom. No literature.

Antiquary, The
40 W. Ferry Street   Dept. OHJ
New Hope, PA 18938
(215) 862-5955
RS/O
Antique shop specializing in gas and gas/electric lighting fixtures. A photo is available on request of a specific item.

Antique Hardware Co.
PO Box 877   Dept. OHJ
Redondo Beach, CA 90277
(213) 378-5990
MO
Manufactures a collection of authentic handcrafted reproduction antique hardware. Drawer pulls, Armoire pulls, tear drop pulls, knobs, hooks and cabinet locks, etc. Catalog, $1.00.

Antique Quilt Repair
550 35th St.   Dept. OHJ
Manhattan Beach, CA 90266
(213) 545-0522
RS/O MO
Only old fabric or 100% cotton used for repairs — older and antique quilt repairs by HAND. Applique a specialty. Send photo or description & size of damage for price estimate. No brochure: This is not a company; please call before coming by. SASE, please.

Antique Reproduction Co.
6967 Blanco Rd.   Dept. OHJ
San Antonio, TX 78216
(512) 340-1606
MO RS/O
An old-house supply store dealing in architectural reproduction products. One of the Southwest's largest suppliers of period gingerbread, street lampposts, brass and copper accent pieces, and a complete nautical inventory. Also sells and installs metal ceilings, and stained, leaded and bevelled glass. Shipping can be arranged. No literature.

Antique Stove Imports
2111 Phillips Rd.   Dept. OHJ
Granville, OH 43023
(614) 587-3825
RS/O MO
Original antique stoves. All outside castings original and in good condition. Stoves assembled in Denmark from original manufacturers' catalogues to assure authenticity and accuracy of detail. In some cases several stoves were collected for their parts in order to complete one stove in its original state. Purchases on a first-come, first-served basis. Catalogs, $5.00.

Antique Street Lamps
1901 S. Lamar   Dept. OHJ
Austin, TX 78704
(512) 443-4540
ID
Manufactures old-fashioned street lamps for parkways, fairways, malls, etc. The lamps are constructed of high strength fiberglass and are available in a variety of styles and colors. Free flyer and price list.

Antique Trunk Supply Co.
3706 W. 169th St.   Dept. OHJ
Cleveland, OH 44111
MO
Trunk repair parts, handles, nails, rivets, corners, etc. Catalog, $.25. Instruction and repair manual, $3. postpaid. Price and identification guide to antique trunks, $4. postpaid.

Appropriate Technology Corp.
P.O. Box 975, Old Ferry Rd.   Dept. OHJ
Brattleboro, VT 05301
(802) 257-4501
DIST
Manufactures Window Quilt, a five-layered, quilted insulating window shade that can cut household heat loss by as much as 79%. The product is available through a national network of over 1100 dealers. Window Quilt, including all hardware, costs about $60 for the standard 2 1/2 x 4 window. Sizes available to fit any window and sliding glass door. Available in four decorator colors. Complete information package, including dealer list, available on request.

Arch Associates/ Steve Guerrant AIA
566 Chestnut Street, Suite 7   Dept. OHJ
Winnetka, IL 60093
(312) 446-7810
RS/O
Chicago-area firm that specializes in restoration and rehabilitation. Will provide measured drawings and building surveys as well as full architectural services. Maintains extensive materials resource catalog file. Will also inspect old houses on a fixed fee basis. No literature.

Archeological Research Associates, Inc.
P.O. Box 52827   Dept. OHJ
Tulsa, OK 74152
RS/O
Archeological Research Associates, Inc., is a non-profit research organization specializing in historic sites archeology and interpretation. Services cover all phases of archeological research and analysis, including site survey, excavation and interpretation. Services are available anywhere in the continental United States. Free personnel profile.

MO	= sells by Mail Order
RS/O	= sells through Retail Store or Office
DIST	= sells through Distributors
ID	= sells only through Interior Designers or Architects

Archeological Research Consultants, Inc.
179 Park Avenue   Dept. OHJ
Midland Park, NJ 07432
(201) 652-3785
RS/O
Archeological and historical interpretation services, including title examination, excavation and artifact analysis. Services available anywhere in the New York metropolitan area. No literature.

Architectural Antique Warehouse, The
P. O. Box 3065 Stn 'D'   Dept. OHJ
Ottawa, OT, Canada K1P6H6
(613) 526-1818
MO   RS/O
Antique architectural accessories, interior and exterior. Period decor in restaurants, etc. Design consultations. They also supply reproduction house parts, such as embossed metal ceilings, cast iron fencing, Colonial staircases, metal spiral stairs. Free literature — please specify your interest.

Architectural Antiques
410 St. Pierre St.   Dept. OHJ
Montreal, Quebec, Canada H2Y2M2
(514) 849-3344
RS/O
A comprehensive selection of antique architectural details from Montreal's fine old buildings. Doors, stained and beveled glass, mantels, staircase parts, window frames, shutters, columns, iron pieces, and other fixtures available. All items one-of-a-kind: no catalog available. Specific request can be answered with a photo.

• Architectural Antiques Exchange
715 N. 2nd Street   Dept. OHJ
Philadelphia, PA 19123
(215) 922-3669
RS/O   MO
Antique and recycled saloon fixtures and restaurant decor including bars, backbars, fretwork, ironwork doors, cabinets, counters and carved wall units. Also antique and recycled house parts; interior and exterior doors, fences and gates, iron railings and window grills, wall panelling, mantels, ceiling and wall fixtures, and stained, bevelled, and etched glass. No literature; call or drop in.

Architectural Arts
20 Waterfall Rd.   Dept. OHJ
Richmond, IN 47374
(317) 962-0930
MO   RS/O
Fine interior golden oak fretwork. Hand-crafted original designs, custom-made for any size opening. Brochure, $1.00.

Architectural Components
PO Box 246   Dept. OHJ
Leverett, MA 01054
(413) 549-1094
MO
Produces and supplies 18th and 19th century architectural millwork. Interior and exterior doors; small pane window sashes; plank window frames and a variety of reproduction mouldings patterned after Connecticut Valley architecture. Also custom work: panelled fireplace walls, pediments, shutters, fan lights etc. Send $2.00 for brochure or call.

> • = Consult ad for more details. See Advertisers' Index on the last page of this Catalog.

Architectural Emphasis
5701 Hollis St.   Dept. OHJ
Emeryville, CA 94608
(415) 654-9520
RS/O   MO
Importers of bevelled glass window and door panels, bevelled glass entryway sets, and glass accent pieces. Brochure $1.00. Please state whether wholesale or retail.

Architectural Emporium
1521 South Ninth Street   Dept. OHJ
Lafayette, IN 47905
(317) 742-7731
RS/O
Antique building supplies, and authentic reproductions. Mantels, doors, posts and pillars, light fixtures, bathroom and kitchen fixtures. Supplies for restoration, preservation, remodeling or new construction. The warehouse has a constantly changing supply of salvaged building parts, including some entire rooms. Photos sent on specific request. Design service available.

Architectural Heritage
1804 Merizale Road   Dept. OHJ
Ottawa, OT, Canada K2G1E6
(613) 226-2979
RS/O
Antique and recycled house parts including stained glass doors, sidelights, gingerbread, mantels, newel posts, shutters and antique bathroom fixtures. Free flyer.

• Architectural Iron Company
Box 674   Dept. OHJ
Milford, PA 18337
(717) 296-6371
RS/O
A full service restoration company specializing in 19th-century cast and wrought iron work. They make their own castings in their own foundry and fabricate wrought work with historically accurate techniques. They will also make custom castings and fabrications for individuals or other firms. Free brochure available.

• Architectural Paneling, Inc.
979 Third Avenue, Suite 1518   Dept. OHJ
New York, NY 10022
(212) 371-9632
RS/O   MO
Reproduces in carved wood English and French paneling and mantels and built-in cabinets and ceilings. Installations throughout the western hemisphere. Fireplace carvings and mouldings are also available. $5 for color brochure, refundable upon first order.

Architectural Restoration
1 Cottage Place   Dept. OHJ
New Rochelle, NY 10801
RS/O
Restoration of interiors for townhouses, brownstones, and private homes. Services include woodstripping and repairs, varnishing and staining, carpentry and decorative painting. Send $1 for brochure.

Architectural Restoration & Design Assoc.
3320 Arch St.   Dept. OHJ
Philadelphia, PA 19104
(215) 349-6758
RS/O   MO
Company offers a full range of restoration services for old buildings: Research, design and construction. They also do new design work. Serves New York — Philadelphia — Washington, D.C. area.

Architectural Salvage of Santa Barbara
726 Anacapa St.   Dept. OHJ
Santa Barbara, CA 93101
(805) 965-2446
RS/O
Antique and recycled house parts and fixtures. Specializing in old, unique, dissimilar and unusual elements (such as 200-year-old Mexican doors). Doors, windows, fixtures. Walk-in shop — no literature.

Architectural Sculpture
242 Lafayette Street   Dept. OHJ
New York, NY 10012
(212) 431-5873
RS/O   MO
Custom-order cast plaster ornament - medallions, mouldings, brackets, capitals, etc. Specializing in cast fiberglass ornament for exterior restorations. They have replicated ornament for cast-iron facades in NYC. Showroom hours M-F, 10-6. Catalog is $2.00.

• Architectural Terra Cotta and Tile, Ltd.
727 S. Dearborn, Ste. 1012   Dept. OHJ
Chicago, IL 60605
(312) 786-0229
RS/O   MO
Custom manufactures and designs architectural ceramics: Terra cotta, encaustic tiles and chimney pots. Specializes in preservation and restoration. Write or call for more information. No literature.

Architectural Woodworking
347 Flax Hill Rd.   Dept. OHJ
Norwalk, CT 06854
(203) 866-0943
RS/O   MO
Fine architectural woodwork. Cost estimates provided upon receipt of detailed material specifications. Consultation services available. No literature.

Armor Products
Box 290   Dept. OHJ
Deer Park, NY 11729
(516) 667-3328
MO   RS/O
Sells clock movements for restoring grandfather, mantel and banjo clocks. Also sells plans for those who wish to make their own. Other items include lamp parts, specialty hardware and butler tray hinges. Catalog $1.00.

Arndt Construction
2924 Farwell Ave.   Dept. OHJ
No. Minneapolis, MN 55411
(612) 529-6494
RS/O
Complete exterior restoration services for masonry buildings; tuckpointing, cleaning, cupola additions and repair, building additions & alterations in sympathetic style. Also traditional roofing, including copper valleys and gutters, and clay, slate, and stone roof work. Large and small jobs. Crews work around the country. No literature; Please call or write with specific queries.

• Arriaga, Nelson
418 Grand Avenue   Dept. OHJ
Brooklyn, NY 11238
(212) 783-1221
MO   RS/O
Men's period accessories — Victorian shirts, collars and ties. Also Victorian and Edwardian coats, suits, dresses, complete ensembles for men and women — stock and custom made. Catalog $3.00.

Arrowhead Forge
RFD 2   Dept. OHJ
Lincolnville, ME 04849
(207) 789-5243
MO   RS/O
The blacksmiths will reproduce traditional ironwork, restore antique iron pieces or create a new design for your specific need. Latches, hinges, door knockers, gates, railings, boot scrapers, weathervanes, fire screens, chandeliers and lamps are just some of the pieces of ironwork made or restored at Arrowhead Forge.

• **Art Directions**
6120 Delmar   Dept. OHJ
St. Louis, MO 63112
(314) 863-1895
RS/O
22,000 sq. ft. of architectural antiques — stained and beveled glass windows and entrance ways; hundreds of light fixtures including large-and small-scale bronze, brass, crystal, gas, and electric; front and back bars; custom-built millwork; paneled rooms, columns, bronze work bank cages, architectural woodwork, mantels, trim, corbels, Victorian porch trim. Large-scale bank clocks, kiosks, even elevators. Comprehensive catalog, $3.

Artifacts, Inc.
702 Mt. Vernon Ave.   Dept. OHJ
Alexandria, VA 22301
(703) 548-6555
MO   RS/O
Select items from demolished buildings. Photographs supplied for specific request. No literature.

Artistry in Veneers, Inc.
633 Montauk Ave.   Dept. OHJ
Brooklyn, NY 11208
MO
More than 80 architectural grade species in lots as small as a single leaf. Also: Fancy Butts, burls, crotches and swirls. Also tools, cements, glues, instructional books. Catalog, $.75.

• **Ascherl Studios**
869 Center Rd.   Dept. OHJ
Hinckley, OH 44233
(216) 278-4964
MO
Leaded glass lamps in Tudor style for $75. plus shipping charges. Call for further information.

A Second Wind for Harmoniums
45 Sidney Place   Dept. OHJ
Brooklyn Hgts., NY 11201
(212) 852-1437
RS/O
Restoration, voicing, tuning, & general rehabilitation of old reed organs, melodeons, and harmoniums. In-home service available. Greater NY area, unless the job is extensive & merits travel. Monograph on reed organs available for $1.00. Prefers telephone consultation (a.m. & eves) — not all mail inquiries can be answered.

Associated Construction Coordinators
P.O. Box 14348   Dept. OHJ
Austin, TX 78761
(512) 479-8979
RS/O
Complete renovation/restoration services for old houses: Design, woodworking, electrical and mechanical systems, painting, and interior work. Please call; no literature.

Astrup Company
2937 W. 25th St.   Dept. OHJ
Cleveland, OH 44113
(216) 696-2800
DIST
This 100 year old company makes fine fabric and the hardware for awnings. Window awnings not only keep a room cooler and save on air conditioning costs, but add an appropriate decorative feature to late 19th and turn-of-the-century houses. Write for free information.

Atlantic Glass & Mirror Works
439 North 63rd St.   Dept. OHJ
Philadelphia, PA 19151
(215) 747-6866
RS/O   MO
They resilver and restore old and antique mirrors. Resilvering cost: $18 per square foot, plus freight costs. ($20 minimum charge on small mirrored objet d'arts.) Costs for all other products and services will be given upon request. (All costs subject to change with the price of silver.) They cater to architects, interior decorators, antique and furniture dealers and private customers. Also re-gilding of antique frames with commercial gold. No literature.

Authentic Designs
330 East 75th St.   Dept. OHJ
New York, NY 10021
(212) 535-9590
RS/O   MO   DIST
Hand-crafted reproductions and custom adaptations of Early American lighting fixtures. A large selection of solid brass, wood and tin chandeliers, sconces and candelabras. Full sheet metal & spinning custom shop. Wood turning shop. Up to 10-ft. turnings. Illustrated catalog — $3.

Auto Hoe, Inc.
Lost Dauphin Dr. PO Box W121OH
    Dept. OHJ
De Pere, WI 54115
(414) 336-4753
MO
Besides the Auto Hoe, a tilling & hoeing machine invented by the company's founder, they manufacture and sell a no-nonsense set of wood stove and fireplace tools. The tools are attractive in their functional simplicity. Reasonable retail cost: $21.95 for the full set, which includes a brush. (Canada add $3. shipping.) Free flyer.

Avalon Forge
409 Gun Road   Dept. OHJ
Baltimore, MD 21227
(301) 242-8431
MO
Authentic replicas of 18th century goods for living history and restorations. Emphasis on military and primitive goods. Examples - Hornware: snuffboxes, dippers, cups, combs. Tinware: cups, canteens, plates. Leather: cartridge boxes, handmade shoes, buckets. Tools: Pitchforks, axes, bill hooks, tomahawks. Woodware: bowls, trenchers, spoons. Cookware: cast iron pots, spiders. Printed matter: maps, cards, books. Illustrated catalog $1.00.

• = Consult ad for more details. See Advertisers' Index on the last page of this Catalog.

B

BWH Stamping, Inc.
P.O. Box 32, Rt. 522   Dept. OHJ
Ft. Littleton, PA 17223
(717) 987-3640
MO   DIST
Manufacturers and suppliers of contemporary sliding and folding door hardware. An alternate source for replacement parts when reproduction hardware and fittings are unavailable. Free "Kennaframe" catalog.

Baker, A.W. Restorations, Inc.
670 Drift Rd.   Dept. OHJ
Westport, MA 02790
(617) 636-8765
RS/O
Restoration consultants, contractors, and documenters of 17th, 18th, 19th century structures, they specialize in southern New England historic architectural forms. Services include moving, dismantling, re-construction and on-site repairs, recycling and restoring. Available are a variety of structural, decorative, and utility house parts, and often very special whole houses. Free brochure available; please call for appointment.

Baldwin Hardware Mfg. Corp.
841 Wyomissing Blvd. PO Box 82   Dept. OHJ
Reading, PA 19603
(215) 777-7811
DIST
Solid brass exterior locks suitable for Early American houses. Interior latches, knobsets and turn pieces appropriate for period houses. Some lighting fixtures and accessories adapted from Early American designs. Quality candlesticks, etc. Rim Lock Brochure, Mortise Lock Brochure, and Lever Lock Brochure available at $.75 each. Brochure about lamps and accessories $.75 each. When writing for information, please specify the brochure you require.

• **Ball and Ball**
463 W. Lincoln Hwy.   Dept. OHJ
Exton, PA 19341
(215) 363-7330
RS/O   MO
Vast selection of reproduction hardware for 18th and 19th century houses. In addition to all types of hardware for doors, windows and shutters, the company also supplies security locks with a period appearance, lighting fixtures, and will also repair locks and repair or reproduce any item of metal hardware. Catalog — $4 by first class mail - 108 pages of reproductions from 1680 through 1900. More than 1500 items of quality reproductions.

Balmer Architectural Art Limited
69 Pape Avenue   Dept. OHJ
Toronto, OT, Canada M4M2V5
(416) 466-6306
RS/O   MO
Quality fibrous plaster and gypsum composition ornament. Cornices, ceiling centers, columns, pilasters, niches, domes, mantel and mantel ornament, restoration, sand sculpture, rib wall, panel mouldings and corners. Brochure free; full catalog $14.00; ceiling center brochure and cornice brochure, each $1.00.

Balzamo, Joseph
103 N. Edward St.   Dept. OHJ
Sayreville, NJ 08872
(201) 721-2651
RS/O
Will strip paint from woodwork in the house; no need for dismantling. No literature.

110   The Old-House Journal 1982 Catalog

Bangkok Industries, Inc.
Gillingham & Worth Streets   Dept. OHJ
Philadelphia, PA 19124
(215) 537-5800
RS/O   MO   DIST
A wide variety of exotic hardwood flooring in pre-finished and unfinished plank, strip and parquet patterns—many of which can be used in period houses. Of special interest are 2 ornamental border patterns. Custom colored pre-finished parquet. Can be completely installed in one day. Free consultation available. Architectural grade paneling historically correct for period dens, formal drawing rooms, etc. Free illustrated brochures.

Bank Architectural Antiques
1824 Felicity St.   Dept. OHJ
New Orleans, LA 70113
(504) 523-6055
RS/O
They offer a wide variety of original and reproduction building materials. Always in stock are bevelled and stained glass, brass hardware, mantels, millwork, doors, shutters, brackets, and columns. In addition they offer wood stripping and carry reproduction shutters, French doors, stair railings, interior and exterior spindles, and newels. No literature.

Barap Specialties
835 Bellows Ave.   Dept. OHJ
Frankfort, MI 49635
(616) 352-9863
MO
Mail-order catalog supplies cane, reed, rush; tools; brass hardware; lamp parts; finishing materials; other do-it-yourself supplies. Catalog is $.50.

● **Barclay Products Co.**
P.O. Box 12257   Dept. OHJ
Chicago, IL 60612
(312) 243-1444
MO
Full line of quality Victorian and turn-of-century reproduction bathroom accessories. Includes faucet sets, towel racks, and soap dishes. Retail distributor of the Sterline shower conversions. Also special size shower curtains. Free catalog.

Bare Wood Inc.
141 Atlantic Ave.   Dept. OHJ
Brooklyn, NY 11201
(212) 875-3833
RS/O   MO
Antique architectural accessories, both residential and commercial, interior and exterior, are sold as is or restored. Specializing in Victorian period elements and furnishings. Their London-trained craftsmen are hand-carvers, turners, and cabinetmakers, and will repair or replace any item in your choice of wood (from a knob to a four-poster bed). Consulting services available. No catalog — all inquiries must be specific please.

Baren, Joan
P. O. Box 12   Dept. OHJ
Sag Harbor, NY 11963
(516) 725-0372
RS/O   MO
Pen-and-ink and watercolor drawings of historic homes and interiors, farms, factories, and neighborhoods, available for private commission or as innovative tools for preservation fundraising. Sizes range from small drawings to wall murals. She will work on location, at the site, or from suitable photographs. Studio visits welcome by appointment. Illustrated brochure, $1.

Barn People, The
P.O. Box 4   Dept. OHJ
South Woodstock, VT 05071
(802) 457-3943
RS/O   MO
Offer 18th and 19th century Vermont barns, and frames of post and beam construction which have been dismantled, repaired/restored, shipped to any new site, and reassembled. Stock of salvaged building materials. Barn moving. Also related consulting services, such as feasibility and cost studies for restoration or relocation of barns in the Northeast. Portfolio (inventory, photo, etc.) is $10.00.

Barnard Chemical Co.
P.O. Box 1105   Dept. OHJ
Covina, CA 91722
(213) 331-1223
DIST
Manufactures fire retardant paints, coatings and varnishes. Coatings, for example, can add fire resistance to fine interior wood panel or exterior shakes and shingles. Will direct inquirers to nearest distributor or will fill orders direct from their warehouse when necessary. Free brochures.

Barnett, D. James — Blacksmith
710 W. Main St.   Dept. OHJ
Plano, IL 60545
(312) 552-3675
MO
A blacksmith who makes items in the style of the early smiths: hardware, hinges, door latches, shutter hardware, fireplace equipment, trivets, toasters, andirons, nails. Catalog, $1.

Barta, J.L. — Antiques
Rt. 1, Box 381-B   Dept. OHJ
Talladega, AL 35160
(205) 362-1406
RS/O   MO
Provides period American antiques for homes and offices. Repair and restoration of wooden antique furniture. Interior decorating consultant for proper period furnishings and techniques. No literature.

The Bartley Collection, Ltd.
121 Schelter Road   Dept. OHJ
Prairie View, IL 60069
(312) 634-9510
RS/O   MO
The Bartley Collection offers thirty authentic Queen Anne and Chippendale style furniture reproductions available either hand made or in kit form. Many of these pieces are exact reproductions of originals from the American furniture collection at the Henry Ford Museum at Greenfield Village in Dearborn, Michigan. The furniture is hand-crafted from solid Honduras mahogany and cherry. Kits include instructions and wipe-on finishing materials. Price range: $65.00 to $1600.00. Catalog cost $1.00.

● **Beall, Barbara Vantrease Studio**
23727 Hawthorne Blvd.   Dept. OHJ
Torrance, CA 90505
(213) 378-1233
RS/O   MO   DIST
Custom-designed and handpainted ceramic tile for residential and commercial projects. Can also copy any existing tile for restoration projects and match custom colors. Designs for exteriors, walkways, signs, kitchens, baths, staircases, pools, fireplaces, murals, entry floors...Custom tile is a unique and everlasting alternative. For more information or free consultation call or write.

Beaumier Carpentry, Inc.
5511 - 43rd Avenue   Dept. OHJ
Hyattsville, MD 20781
(301) 277-8594
RS/O
Designs, coordinates and executes the restoration and/or renovation of period rowhouses and single homes, in conjunction with the owner(s) and local authorities. Carpentry only, or a full spectrum of general contracting services is available in Washington, DC and Maryland. No literature.

● **Beauti-home**
3088F Winkle Ave.   Dept. OHJ
Santa Cruz, CA 95065
(408) 462-6452
RS/O   MO
Hand-made shutters and blinds, produced on order to any specifications. Any size, design, style, species of wood; flat or raised solid panels; interior or exterior. Quotes made on detailed drawings, or from samples. Serious inquiries are promptly answered.

Beck, Nelson of Wash. Inc.
1048 Potomac NW   Dept. OHJ
Washington, DC 20007
(202) 333-4437
ID
Upholstered furniture restored and reupholstered. Period draperies - various types of poles, wood and metal. Custom finials for poles. Tab curtains, Austrian shades. Will supply fabrics or will use client's fabrics. Trade shop only - no literature.

Bedlam Brass Beds
19-21 Fair Lawn Avenue   Dept. OH
Fair Lawn, NJ 07410
(201) 796-7200
RS/O   MO   DIST
Solid-brass furniture: Custom and authentic reproductions of antique designs, but in today's sizes. Beds, tables, etageres, wall and cheval mirrors, coat racks. Complete bar rail systems for commercial or residential use. Some antique fixtures, glass, etc. Bed & accessories catalog $3.00. Data sheet of parts for repairing antique brass or cast-iron beds $1.00. (Stores in Boston, San Francisco, San Antonio, Denver, Camden ME, Old Saybrook CT, Houston.)

Bedlam Brass Beds — Denver
3rd Ave. at Fillmore St.   Dept. OHJ
Denver, CO 80206
(303) 393-0333
RS/O   MO
In addition to an extensive line of brass beds, this store also stocks many restoration products: bar rails, handrails, ceiling fans, hardware (restoration), Victorian lighting fixtures, weathervanes, and quilts. Literature available on railing products.

KEY TO ABBREVIATIONS

MO	=	sells by Mail Order
RS/O	=	sells through Retail Store or Office
DIST	=	sells through Distributors
ID	=	sells only through Interior Designers or Architects

Behlen, H. & Bros.
Rt. 30 North   Dept. OHJ
Amsterdam, NY 12010
(518) 843-1380
MO
The largest stock of traditional and old world finishing supplies and products for hardwood finishing and paintings. Among the 90-year-old company's specialities: bronze powder and paste, lacquer tinting colors, wood fillers and glue, various lacquers, stains (including dry aniline) specialty waxes, hard-to-find brushes and tools, and varnish. Complete line of gilding supplies. $25 minimum order. $2.50 for general catalog, brush catalog and "Art Of Wood Finishing".

Beirs, John
45 So. Third St.   Dept. OHJ
Philadelphia, PA 19106
(215) 923-8122
RS/O
A small, personalized studio that designs and makes leaded glass windows. Designs often incorporate a good deal of clear glass as well as beveled insets. Average prices are in the range of $45 to $65 per square foot. No literature.

Bel-Air Door Co.
P.O. Box 829   Dept. OHJ
Alhambra, CA 91802
(213) 283-3731
MO DIST
Well-made carved exterior wood doors, several suitable for Victorian, turn-of-century, Tudor-style, and Chippendale influenced houses. New line of handcrafted doors in mahogany and tanguile with paneled designs and openings. Standard size: 30-in., 32-in., 36-in. x 80-in. x 1-3/4-in. Special sizes available upon request. Bevelled, etched, and leaded glass available in many styles. Free illustrated brochures.

Belcher, Robert W.
1753 Pleasant Grove Dr., NE   Dept. OHJ
Dalton, GA 30720
(404) 259-3482
RS/O
Has a supply of old weathered chestnut rails for zig-zag stacked rail fences. Supplies old barnboards, 55-gal. oak barrels and old yellow poplar and oak beams. Also has old hand hewn log houses, and consults on log house restoration. No literature; call for prices.

Bench Manufacturing Co.
PO Box 66, Essex St. Sta.   Dept. OHJ
Boston, MA 02112
(617) 436-3080
MO
Promenade benches in many styles, and planters, trash receptacles, gazebos, and custom-built small buildings. Please specify your interest for a free brochure.

Bendheim, S.A. Co., Inc.
122 Hudson St.   Dept. OHJ
New York, NY 10013
(212) 226-6370
RS/O
Supplier for replacement antique-type window glass. Also imported stained glass, bullseye glass, rondells, etc. No literature available.

KEY TO ABBREVIATIONS	
MO	= sells by Mail Order
RS/O	= sells through Retail Store or Office
DIST	= sells through Distributors
ID	= sells only through Interior Designers or Architects

Bendix Mouldings, Inc.
235 Pegasus Ave.   Dept. OHJ
Northvale, NJ 07647
(201) 767-8888
MO DIST
Supplies a diversified assortment of unfinished decorative wood mouldings, metal and plastic mouldings plus an extensive stock of pre-finished, authentic and carefully crafted picture frame mouldings. Also carved wood ornaments, pearl beadings, open fretwork, dentils, rosettes, crowns, cornices, functional hardware and scalloped plywood moulding. Illustrated catalog and price lists $1.00. Specify unfinished or pre-finished mouldings.

• **Benjamin Moore Co.**
51 Chestnut Ridge Road   Dept. OHJ
Montvale, NJ 07645
(201) 573-9600
RS/O DIST
This major paint manufacturer has exterior and interior paints for early American houses — Historical Color Collection and Cameo Collection. There are free leaflets about these lines as well as these useful booklets — "Interior Wood Finishing", "Painting Walls, Ceilings and Trim" and "How To Paint The Outside of Your House."

Berea College Student Craft Industries
CP0 No. 2347   Dept. OHJ
Berea, KY 40404
(606) 986-9341
RS/O MO
Reproductions of simple, classic period furniture - Empire armchairs, rope leg dining table, ladder back chairs, goose neck rocker. Also handcrafted decorative accessories and custom wrought iron work. Furniture catalog — $1.50. Gift catalog — $1.00.

Berger/Spiers
P.O. Box 3742   Dept. OHJ
Harrisburg, PA 17105
(717) 763-7396
RS/O
Architectural/Engineering firm specializing in preservation consultation and professional services including restoration rehabilitation and adaptive use, preparation of historic structure reports, condition surveys, research, state and national register nominations and grant-in-aid applications, in Pennsylvania and surrounding states. No literature.

Berkshire Porcelain Studios
Deerfield Ave.   Dept. OHJ
Shelburne Falls, MA 01370
(413) 625-9447
MO
Original paintings and designs on ceramic tile for custom bathrooms, kitchens, and murals. Glazes are applied to both imported bisque and standard glazed tile; they can decorate with a specialty tile of your choice or your own creation. Paintings and designs are permanent and are resistant to weather, fire, fading, and graffiti. Feel free to call for consultation. Flyer available.

Berman, B.K. Victorian Millshop
446 Acoma Street   Dept. OHJ
Denver, CO 80204
(303) 733-5569
MO DIST RS/O
Company will custom-duplicate historic millwork, making special knives when necessary. Installations available. They have worked on National Trust and National Register properties. Rosettes, doors, and brackets made. Catalog, $2.

Bernard Plating Works
660 Riverside Dr.   Dept. OHJ
Northampton, MA 01060
(413) 584-0659
RS/O MO
Silver, gold, copper, nickel replating. Silver and pewter items cleaned and repaired. All types of brass and copper cleaned and polished; lamps rewired and refinished. Old fashioned hand-wiped tinning on copper and brass cookware (excluding teakettles). No literature; please write or call with specific inquiry.

• **Berridge Manufacturing Co.**
1720 Maury   Dept. OHJ
Houston, TX 77026
(713) 223-4971
RS/O MO DIST
Manufactures metal roofing products, including Victorian classic and fish-scale metal shingles. Standing seam and batten seam metal roof systems are offered. These products are available in pre-finished galvanized steel, Galvalume, copper, and terne-coated stainless. Catalog free.

Berry, J.W. & Son
222 W. Read St.   Dept. OHJ
Baltimore, MD 21201
(301) 727-4687
RS/O
Restoration of antique furniture; also retail shop. In business since 1899. No literature.

Bevel Right Mfg.
34-34 Route 9   Dept. OHJ
Freehold, NJ 07728
(201) 462-8462
RS/O
Can make bevelled tempered glass for front doors in the wide 1 in. and 1-1/4 in. bevels. No literature; call for latest prices.

Beveled Glass Industries
900 N. La Cienega Blvd.   Dept. OHJ
Los Angeles, CA 90069
(213) 657-1462
DIST
Leaded and beveled glass panel inserts for doors and windows. Sold through distributors but you can get a complete catalog for $3.00.

Beveling Studio
15507 NE 90th   Dept. OHJ
Redmond, WA 98052
(206) 885-7274
MO RS/O
They manufacture bevelled windows and panels; also bevelled mirrors, to any size or shape. Windows and panels are reproduced to any designs for any period house or commercial building. All windows and panels are weather-proof. They also reproduce cut bevelled pieces and glue-chip bevelled glass. No literature available.

Biagiotti, L.
229 7th Ave.   Dept. OHJ
New York, NY 10011
(212) 924-5088
RS/O MO
Manufactures mouldings for ceilings and walls, centers for chandeliers, columns, pilasters, capitals. Does sets for motion pictures and Broadway shows. Restored mouldings in City Hall. Restores frames and antiques. Can reproduce and ship mouldings from samples. No literature

Bienenfeld Ind. Inc.
22 Harbor Park Dr., Box 22   Dept. OHJ
Roslyn, NY 11576
(516) 621-0888
DIST
Sells mouth-blown antique, Colonial, Cordele, Opalescent antique glass. Also other types in over 700 shades and colors. Sold only through distributors. For information about nearest distributor, call in NY (516) 621-0888; in Chicago, IL (312) 523-8400; in Houston, TX (713) 864-0193; in Wilmington, CA (213) 549-4324; in Mississauga OT, Canada (416) 677-8600. For free brochure on history of glass, send SASE.

Bierman & Associates
101 S. Whiting St., Suite 303   Dept. OHJ
Alexandria, VA 22304
(703) 751-2333
RS/O
Consulting services on the recreation, preservation and valuation of historic properties. Experience includes public and private preservation projects, court testimony, lectures, publishing, and professional valuations for resale and financing. Resume of qualifications upon request.

• **Biggs Company**
105 E. Grace St.   Dept. OHJ
Richmond, VA 23219
(804) 644-2891
RS/O   MO
Reproductions of 18th century furniture. Several expensive lines are authentic historic reproductions licensed by Old Sturbridge Village, Independence National Historic Park and the Thomas Jefferson Memorial Foundation, Inc. 82 pg. catalog and price list — $6.

Bill's Beauts
P.O. Box 2311, 1415 Main St.   Dept. OHJ
Columbus, MS 39701
(601) 329-1254
MO   RS/O
Architectural antiques, from panelled doors to entire soda fountain. Also custom-made stained glass windows — your pattern scaled up or down. Glass etching too. No literature available.

Billard's Old Telephones
21710C Regnart Rd.   Dept. OHJ
Cupertino, CA 95014
(408) 252-2104
MO
Old telephones and parts. Brass and oak sets. Old phones converted to modern use — nothing removed. Do-it-yourself kits available. Their private museum also buys unusual telephones. Complete restoration parts catalog, $1., refundable on purchase.

Bird — X
325 W. Huron St.   Dept. OHJ
Chicago, IL 60610
(312) 642-6871
MO
Supplier of complete line of bird-repelling products. Products include electronic ultrasonic bird repellers, bird lites, and chemical and steel needle roost inhibitors. Free brochures and consultation service available.

• **Bishop, Adele, Inc.**
Box 557   Dept. OHJ-1
Manchester, VT 05254
(802) 362-3537
MO   DIST   RS/O
Stencil kits for walls, floorcloths, and fabrics, and a full line of supplies: instant-drying japan colors, textile paint for fabrics, etc. Specific directions supplied for all designs; they also sell the definitive book about stenciling. Complete catalog, $2.00.

• **Bix Process Systems, Inc.**
PO Box 3011   Dept. OHJ
Bethel, CT 06801
(203) 743-3263
MO
Manufactures paint and varnish remover for woodwork and furniture. Can design special systems for stripping old houses. Also manufactures tung oil stains and varnishes for refinishing wood and woodwork. Markets complete furniture and wood stripping systems. An established business for 20 years. Brochure available free.

Bix Service Center
5212 East Colfax Avenue   Dept. OHJ
Denver, CO 80220
(303) 320-0889
RS/O
Working in the Denver metropolitan area, Bix removes old paint and finishes from furniture, mantels, doors, moulding, metal etc. Member of nation's oldest network of trained specialists. No hot lye dip tanks or caustics. Wood restoration center; natural finishes, supplies and counseling. No literature.

• **Black Wax — Pacific Engineering**
P.O. Box 145   Dept. OHJ
Farmington, CT 06032
(203) 677-0795
MO
Black wax can often save stripping and refinishing of dirty, cracked and crazed wood surfaces. Company also manufactures Crystal Wax, a top-quality carnauba paste wax providing gloss and protection for fine furniture. Sienna paste wax is a blend of quality paste wax and brown pigment which prevents chalky effect left by some paste waxes. Free flyer.

Blacksmith Shop, Inc.
P.O. Box 15   Dept. OHJ
Mount Holly, VT 05758
(802) 259-2452
RS/O   MO
Hand forged, standing or hanging fireplace and wood stove tool sets. Cooking andirons and reproduction type hearth accessories. A wide variety of hooks, plant and wall hangers. The Ashaway for storing hot and glowing ashes from a stove or fireplace. Complete illustrated catalog $1.00.

Blades/La Penta Construction Co.
157 North Third St.   Dept. OHJ
Philadelphia, PA 19106
(215) 627-2782
RS/O
Architectural and general contracting services for the renovation and restoration of old residential and recycled buildings in the Philadelphia area. No literature.

Blaine Window Hardware, Inc.
1919 Blaine Dr.   Dept. J
Hagerstown, MD 21740
(301) 797-6500
MO
A large selection of contemporary replacement hardware for doors and windows. Mechanical devices and rolling hardware that will fit old sliding doors and all types of old windows. Will also custom-duplicate interior hardware. 16 pg. catalog — $1.00.

● = Consult ad for more details. See Advertisers' Index on the last page of this Catalog.

Blessing Historical Foundation
Box 517   Dept. OHJ
Blessing, TX 77419
(512) 588-6332
MO
For fiber craftsmen and planters of ancient dye gardens: A "baker's dozen" of madder seeds will be sent for a $5 tax-deductible donation to the Foundation. Madder, rare in this country, is used in textile printing and craftsmen's yarns, both handspun and commercial. Directions for growing available.

BoatLIFE, Inc.
205 Sweet Hollow Road   Dept. OHJ
Old Bethpage, NY 11804
(516) 454-0055
DIST
Manufactures "Life Calk", a polysulphide sealant that resists water and weather, and "Git-Rot", a cure for rot that restores the strength of rotted wood. Available through marine-supply dealers. Free literature.

• **Bona Decorative Hardware**
2227 Beechmont Ave.   Dept. OHJ
Cincinnati, OH 45230
(513) 232-4300
RS/O   MO
Decorative hardware — mostly formal French and English in style. Bathroom fittings and accessories- several designs are appropriate for period houses. Also black iron door & cabinet hardware, brass rim locks, porcelain door knobs, carved and embossed wood moulding. Free illustrated catalog and price list. Also of interest are their brass bar rail hardware and brass sliding door pulls; faucets for footed tubs.

• **Boseman Veneer & Supply Co.**
403 Laurel   Dept. OHJ
Friendswood, TX 77546
(713) 482-5730
MO   RS/O
Stocks and distributes quality veneers and related supplies. Good selection of crotches, burls and quarter sawn veneer. Will accomodate specific size requirements. Free catalog available.

Boston Cabinet-Making Inc.
27 Kingston St.   Dept. OHJ
Boston, MA 02111
(617) 338-8356
RS/O   MO
A custom furniture manufacturing and antiques restoration shop. They specialize in one-of-a-kind reproductions of antiques in every style; modern and contemporary pieces, and also architectural detailing. No literature.

Boulder Art Glass Co., Inc.
1920 Arapahoe   Dept. OHJ
Boulder, CO 80302
(303) 449-9030
MO   RS/O   DIST
Stained and leaded glass installations, commercial and residential. They do leading, foiling, painting, staining, bending, beveling, slumping of any glass. Leading manufacturer of authentic glue-chip glass in the U.S. Specialists in reproducing sand-blasted design work. Also appraisals and repair of antique windows and lampshades. Literature — $1.00.

• **Bow & Arrow Stove Co.**
11 Hurley St.   Dept. OHJ
Cambridge, MA 02141
(617) 492-1411
MO   RS/O
Manufacturers of the "Vitroliner" enamel coated metal chimney liner and other stove related products. They also distribute Viking Magnetite interior storm windows. Company also carries ceiling fans and floor registers. Free literature.

The Old-House Journal 1982 Catalog
113

Bow House, Inc.
Randall Rd.   Dept. OHJ
Bolton, MA 01740
(617) 779-6464
MO
An architect-designed package that offers the buyer an authentic reproduction of a bow-roof Cape Cod house. The package supplies to the builder those items necessary for the period character of the house: roof and siding materials, trim, windows, doors, hardware, stairs, glass, etc; specifications working drawings, manual and detail book. Illustrated brochure — $4.00. Also — a belvedere or gazebo of classic and generous proportions is available in kit form. Illustrated brochure $1.00.

• **Bradbury & Bradbury Wallpapers**
PO Box 155   Dept. OHJ
Benicia, CA 94510
(707) 644-0724
MO   DIST
Fine quality hand-printed wallpapers after the style of the leading designers of the Victorian Era in England and America; Morris, Dresser, Pugin, Wight, etc. and reproductions from interiors of 19th century American historic houses, available direct by mail order. Ceiling papers, borders, friezes, and dadoes also available. They design and manufacture exclusively for the 19th century interior. Illustrated brochure, $1.00.

Bradford-Park Corp.
Box 151   Dept. OHJ
Clifton Park, NY 12065
(518) 371-5420
MO
B.P. Metal Cleaner: a biodegradable, non-corrosive rust and oxide remover that does not harm metal, finishes or normal skin. Liquid or paste formulas. Also B-P No. 1 Brightner — a metal cleaner for quick, economical removal of heat stains, discoloration and tarnish from stainless steel, chrome, nickel, copper or brass. Free literature.

Braid-Aid
466 Washington St.   Dept. OHJ
Pembroke, MA 02359
(617) 826-6091
RS/O   MO   DIST
A complete catalog of rug braiding and hooking materials and accessories, as well as quilting, shirret and weaving. Kits, patterns, instructions, wool by the yard or pound. Illustrated catalog with color and ''how-to-do-it'' tips, $1.50 (U.S. Funds) ppd.

Brandt Bros. General Contractors
2210 E. Southport Rd.   Dept. OHJ
Indianapolis, IN 46227
(317) 783-6633
RS/O
Primarily carpentry contractor but full complement of sub-contractors available if desired. Interior and exterior work. List of renovation projects in Indianapolis area can be furnished. No literature.

Brass & Copper Shop
2220 Cherokee   Dept. OHJ
St. Louis, MO 63118
(314) 776-8363
RS/O
Antique shop specializing in brass and copper fixtures. Lighting, bath fixtures, door hardware, glass globes, etc. Walk-in shop. No literature.

Brass Fan Ceiling Fan Co.
1144 W. Main   Dept. OHJ
Lewisville, TX 75067
(214) 436-3052
RS/O   MO
Repair and restoration of antique ceiling fans. Company also carries Hunter ceiling fans and parts. No literature.

Brass Lion
P. O. Box 1135   Dept. OHJ
Tyler, TX 75710
(214) 561-1111
MO   RS/O
Quality handmade reproduction of 17th and 18th century brass chandeliers and sconces. The brass is antiqued and hand polished. A complete illustrated catalog is available for $3.

Brass Menagerie
524 St. Louis Street   Dept. OHJ
New Orleans, LA 70130
(504) 524-0921
RS/O
Solid brass hardware & locks of all periods, antique & reproduction. Porcelain & wrought iron hardware, rim locks, unusual hardware: bar rails, solid brass drapery & curtain hardware, fireplace hooks, chandeliers, wall brackets and sconces. Bathroom fixtures & accessories of American and European design, including period toilets, with wall hung tanks, decorated sink bowls and turn-of- century pedestal type sinks. Send for free brochure.

Brasslight
90 Main Street   Dept. OHJ
Nyack, NY 10960
(914) 353-0567
RS/O   MO
Solid brass desk lamps, wall sconces, and ceiling fixtures. A variety of interchangeable glass shades in green, brown, white, frosted, etc. Stylings include Edwardian and late Victorian. All lamps and fixtures are polished and lacquered. Brochure, $.50.

Brasslight Antique Lighting
719 S. 5th St.   Dept. OHJ
Milwaukee, WI 53204
(414) 383-0675
RS/O
Restores and sells Victorian, Mission, and early 20th century brass lighting fixtures. Walk-in shop only. Call for appointment. All original antique fixtures; no reproductions. No literature, but photos will be supplied if you call with specific requests.

Brauer, Sandra
235 Dean Street   Dept. OHJ
Brooklyn, NY 11217
(212) 855-0656
RS/O
Custom design or reproduction of leaded and stained glass windows and lampshades. Also repairs and restores stained and leaded glass windows and panels. Literature available upon request.

Breakfast Woodworks Louis Mackall & Co.
50 Maple St.   Dept. OHJ
Branford, CT 06405
(203) 488-8364
RS/O
Louis Mackall & Co., and Breakfast Woodworks are two companies that work together to provide extensive architectural design and woodworking services. Almost any wooden element can be reproduced. Design expertise allows for complete restoration or renovation services. No literature available.

• **Broad-Axe Beam Co.**
RD 2, Box 181-J   Dept. OHJ
West Brattleboro, VT 05301
(802) 257-0064
MO
Authentically produced hand-hewn beams of white pine. Two types — structural and decorative — in standard 8, 12, 14 and 16 ft. lengths. Structural beams (7 1/2 in. square) $4.25 per linear ft.; decorative beams (3 1/2 x 7 1/2 in.), $3. per linear ft. Custom hewing done. Illustrated brochure and price list, $1.

Broadnax Refinishing Products
P.O. Box 196   Dept. OHJ
Ila, GA 30647
(404) 789-3346
MO   DIST
A method of reviving old wood finishes without chemical or mechanical stripping. The products can be bought separately or in kit form for $10.00. $1.50 shipping. Free pamphlets and price lists — send stamped envelope. Also a 56 page book on refinishing furniture, ''Good News'' — $3.50 & $1.50 shipping.

• **Broadway Collection**
601 W. 103rd   Dept. OHJ
Kansas City, MO 64114
(800) 255-6365
DIST   MO   RS/O
The Broadway collection includes solid brass, porcelain, crystal, and wood bathroom fixtures and fittings, featuring standing lavatories; door hardware (including rim locks), cabinet hardware, and switch plates for Colonial and Victorian style architecture. Complete lines of decorative hardware of formal French and English derivation. Also mail boxes, house letters, door knockers, hooks, etc. 90 page illustrated color catalog: $5.00.

Brooklyn Restorers
646 2nd Street   Dept. OHJ
Brooklyn, NY 11215
(212) 788-3671
RS/O
Historic preservation specialists. Services include restoration of wooden windows and doors with weather-stripping. They will examine your structure and match its texture and detail to original condition. No literature.

Brooklyn Stone Renovating
458 Baltic St.   Dept. OHJ
Brooklyn, NY 11217
(212) 875-8232
RS/O
Has expert masons who specialize in restoring brownstone stoops and facades. Will recreate carved ornament in brownstone stucco. Their services are in great demand, so you have to be persistent and prepared to wait awhile. No literature; call for appointment.

Brooklyn Tile Supply
184 4th Ave.   Dept. OHJ
Brooklyn, NY 11217
(212) 875-1789
RS/O
Carries small white hexagonal bathroom tiles, 6 x 3 white tile, American Olean tiles. No literature. Sells through store only.

Brookstone Company
569 Vose Farm Road   Dept. OHJ
Peterborough, NH 03458
(603) 924-7181
RS/O   MO
High-quality, hard-to-find tools such as a wooden smoothing plane, a chamfer spokeshave, a flexible sole plane, extra-long drill bits. Free illustrated catalog.

Brown, Carol
Dept. OHJ
Putney, VT 05346
(802) 387-5875
RS/O MO
Simple, natural white wool single and double spreads from Ireland, suitable for curtains. Woolen bedspreads and throws in colors and patterns. Cotton spreads. Wall hangings, including a Bayeux Tapestry panel. Irish tweeds for upholstery. Fine cottons, handkerchief linen. Osnaburg, Liberty, Khadi, many other natural fiber fabrics. Individual, personal attention. Color brochure on receipt of $.50 and a business-size self-addressed stamped envelope.

Brown, T. Robins
12 First Avenue   Dept. OHJ
Nyack, NY 10960
(914) 358-5229
RS/O
Consultant in architectural history and historic preservatio Services available in the Middle Atlantic states and Connecticut. Assistance with National Register applications. Historic sites survey work. Consultation for restoration or renovation of historic architecture. Research on history and significance of building. Preparation of walking tours and other publications about an area's architecture. No literature.

Brownstone Information Center
93 Prospect Place   Dept. OHJ
Brooklyn, NY 11217
(212) 643-4293
RS/O
A free service of Brooklyn Union Gas, the Center offers a three-hour workshop which discusses brownstone neighborhoods and the steps, procedures and programs pertaining to home buying. Renovation information is also provided. Reference books and publications, brochures, flyers and listings of craftsmen are available. By appointment only.

Brunschwig & Fils, Inc.
979 Third Ave.   Dept. OHJ
New York, NY 10022
(212) 838-7878
ID
Museums, restoration and historical agencies use the fine reproductions of 18th and 19th century fabric, trimming and wallpaper made by this firm. A new collection inspired by the Brighton Pavillion, coordinates chintzes and wallpapers in the French chinoiserie tradition. Their products are sold only through interior designers.

Bryant Steel Works
R.F.D. 2, Box 109   Dept. OHJ
Thorndike, ME 04986
(207) 568-3663
RS/O MO
Family-owned business restores and then sells antique cast-iron cookstoves and parlor heaters. They specialize in old kitchen ranges. Search service finds rare stoves for museums and historic restorations. Large stock of antique parts. Also — The Bryant Stove Museum is a collection of rare ornate stoves, many one-of-a-kind. Shipping can be arranged anywhere. Free literature.

You'll get better service when contacting companies if you mention The Old-House Journal Catalog

---

Wm. Ward Bucher & Associates — Architects
1638 R St., NW   Dept. OHJ
Washington, DC 20009
(202) 387-0061
RS/O
Architectural and interior design for renovations and restorations of houses and commercial buildings. Serving the Washington/Baltimore metropolitan area. Specialists in economic feasibility studies for adaptive re-use. Their Conn. Ave.—P St. Report is available for $3.50: It includes information on how to do an economic feasibility study yourself.

Buck Creek Bellows
PO Box 412   Dept. OHJ
Lovingston, VA 22949
MO
Company restores antique fireplace bellows for owners. They also make new bellows of hardwood, goatskin, and brass. Free brochure.

Buckingham Slate Co.
4110 Fitzhugh Avenue   Dept. OHJ
Richmond, VA 23230
(804) 355-4351
DIST
Excellent quality VA-region slate. Roofing slate available. Out-of-state shipping possible on orders. Samples and literature available upon request.

Buecherl, Helmut
548 Hudson St.   Dept. OHJ
New York, NY 10014
(212) 242-6558
RS/O
Master craftsman can re-create or duplicate any painted decoration from 18th or 19th century. Has executed work for several museums and many fine houses. Painted work includes: Marbleizing, graining, gilding, stencilling, glazing, striping, lacquered wall, murals. No literature; phone for appointment — evenings.

Building Conservation Technology
1555 Connecticut Ave., N.W.   Dept. OHJ
Washington, DC 20036
(202) 387-8040
RS/O
Consultant providing technical preservation services including restoration/rehabilitation planning and design, historical research, architectural description and analysis, masonry, wood, and metals cleaning and repair, paint and decorative finishes analysis, maintenance programming, specification writing and specialized construction supervision. Staff includes architects, architectural historians, and architectural conservators. Offices are located in Washington, DC, New York, and Nashville, TN. Brochure available, free.

Building Inspection Services, Inc.
12813 Prestwick Drive   Dept. OHJ
Oxon Hill, MD 20022
(301) 292-1299
RS/O
Prepurchase home inspections; renovating consultants. Serving Washington, D.C., and the metropolitan area. Members of the American Society of Home Inspectors. Please call for further information, prices, and brochure.

● = Consult ad for more details. See Advertisers' Index on the last page of this Catalog.

Burdoch Silk Lampshade Co.
3283 Loma Riviera Drive   Dept. OHJ
San Diego, CA 92110
(714) 223-5834
MO
Embroidered, hand-sewn fabric shades in Victorian and turn-of-the-century, Art Deco styles. These highly decorative shades come in many colors including burgundy, light brown, peach, and dark green. Can be used on table or floor-lamp bases. Send stamped, self-addressed envelope plus $1. for free color flyer.

Butcher Polish Co.
120 Bartlett St.   Dept. OHJ
Marlborough, MA 01752
(617) 481-5700
MO DIST
Manufacturers of paste wax for wood floors and furniture since 1880. In addition they make black stove polish, metal cleaner, brick and hearth cleaner, and fireplace/stove glass cleaner. Free brochure and price list. Booklet available: 'More Handy Tips on Wood Care'' $.50.

● **ByGone Era**
4783 Peachtree Rd.   Dept. OHJ
Atlanta, GA 30341
(404) 458-3016
RS/O MO
20,000 square feet of architectural antiques, including stained and bevelled glass, staircases, doors, mantels, columns. Specializing in bars/office/ restaurant furnishings. Always on hand: 50 stained glass windows, hundreds of doors and mantels, footed tubs, pedestal sinks, along with original fretwork and paneling. Stock constantly changing. Company will crate and ship. No literature; visit shop.

Byrd Mill Studio
Rt. 5 Box 192   Dept. OHJ
Louisa, VA 23093
(703) 967-0516
MO RS/O
Architectural photography - interior and exteriors. Photography of antique furniture & jewelry for insurance purposes or catalogues. No literature.

Byrom's Plastering, Inc.
P.O. Box 143   Dept. OHJ
Guntersville, AL 35976
(205) 582-6643
RS/O
Experienced in historical renovations of plastering and stucco. Please call; no literature.

KEY TO ABBREVIATIONS

MO = sells by Mail Order

RS/O = sells through Retail Store or Office

DIST = sells through Distributors

ID = sells only through Interior Designers or Architects

The Old-House Journal 1982 Catalog

C

C—E Morgan
601 Oregon St.   Dept. OHJ
Oshkosh, WI 54901
(414) 235-7170
DIST
A major manufacturer of millwork, some of which can be adapted to period houses. Staircases and stair parts of birch and red oak, or hemlock. Pine and fir, panel and sash doors, stair systems, entrance systems, patio doors. Specify interest, send $.10 for each brochure.

CW Design, Inc.
5155 Bloomington Ave., S.   Dept. OHJ
Minneapolis, MN 55417
(612) 721-3271
MO   RS/O
Custom silkscreening service. Capabilities include acid-etching of glass from your design or theirs, and custom wallpapers, borders, and murals. Residential and restaurant work a specialty. Free flyer on etched glass.

Cabot Stains
1 Union Street   Dept. OHJ
Boston, MA 02108
(617) 723-7740
DIST
The first company to manufacture wood stains, they make products primarily for exterior & interior wood surfaces . . . paneling, siding, clapboard, shingles and shakes. Free brochures and color cards.

California Heritage Wood Products, Ltd.
4206 Sorrento Valley Blvd-Rm D   Dept. OHJ
San Diego, CA 92121
(714) 453-1400
RS/O
Furnish, manufacture, finish and install period moldings; including crown, chair rail, base, as well as fancy door and window heads. No literature.

Cambridge Smithy
   Dept. OHJ
Cambridge, VT 05444
(802) 644-5358
RS/O
Metal antique restoration; handwrought stock items and custom designs; weathervanes. No literature.

Cambridge Textiles
   Dept. OHJ
Cambridge, NY 12816
(518) 677-2624
RS/O   MO
Professional conservation and restoration of textile artifacts, American, Oriental, pre-Columbian, Coptic . . . including tapestries, samplers, quilts, clothing, rugs. Services to antique-textile dealers and private collectors. Safe rural studio. Shipping insured parcel post or UPS. Collections surveyed; written condition reports available. Free estimates, latest protocol flyer.

KEY TO ABBREVIATIONS	
MO	= sells by Mail Order
RS/O	= sells through Retail Store or Office
DIST	= sells through Distributors
ID	= sells only through Interior Designers or Architects

Campbell-Lamps
1108 Pottstown Pike, Dept. 25   Dept. OHJ
West Chester, PA 19380
(215) 696-8070
RS/O   MO
New gas and electric shades from original molds. Lamp chimneys, lantern globes, and misc. glass lamp parts. Wholesale and retail. Cased glass shades including Emeralite desk shades — student shades and gas and electric. Solid cast brass parts for gas and electric lights. Distributor of Aladdin kerosene lamps and heaters; full line of replacement parts. Catalog, $1.; Aladdin catalog, $.75.

Campbell, Douglas Co.
31 Bridge St.   Dept. OHJ
Newport, RI 02840
(401) 846-4711
RS/O   MO
Custom-made reproductions of 17th and 18th century American furniture. Also exterior and interior millwork of the same period. Illustrated catalog and price list — $2.

Campbell, Marion
39 Wall St.   Dept. OHJ
Bethlehem, PA 18018
(215) 865-2522
RS/O
Architectural woodwork and furniture in American period styles designed and built to order. Authentic details and finest materials are used to match or recreate old work. Projects include, but are not limited to, mantels, paneling, cornices, valances, doors and door ways, shutters, built-in cabinets, chests, desks, tables, stands, bookcases., etc. Finishing and installation. Appointment necessary. Brochure $.25.

● **Campbellsville Industries**
P. O. Box 278   Dept. OHJ
Campbellsville, KY 42718
(502) 465-8135
MO
Manufacturers of aluminum cupolas, domes, steeples, weathervanes, cornices, louvers, balustrades, and columns for exterior ornamental use. (Columns are load-bearing.) Aluminum balustrades and railings have been reproduced in exact detail for historic buildings — also a selection of standard components. (Balustrades are primarily for roofs.) Free brochure available — please specify your interest.

● **Canal Co.**
1612 14th St., N.W.   Dept. OHJ
Washington, DC 20009
(202) 234-6637
RS/O
Architectural antiques including fully restored lighting fixtures from the 1860's thru the 1930's; fireplace mantels; stained and leaded glass; interior and exterior doors; medicine cabinets; handrails, newel posts, and balusters; columns; brass door hardware; pedestal sinks; iron fencing & window guards. No literature.

Canal Works
28 North Patterson Blvd.   Dept. OHJ
Dayton, OH 45402
(513) 223-0278
RS/O
Architectural salvage for the Dayton area. Large stock of interior parts, from ornate mantels to utilitarian doors. Specializing in fancy woodwork; also carries saloon/restaurant fittings, wrought iron and lighting fixtures. Contracting services offered for interior/exterior design and custom woodwork. Bevelled and stained glass windows. No literature.

Cane & Basket Supply Company
1283 South Cochran Avenue   Dept. OHJ
Los Angeles, CA 90019
(213) 939-9644
RS/O   MO
Every supply necessary to re-cane, re-rush and re-splint chair seats. Related tools and supplies. Also furniture kits for a side chair and 3 stools. Illustrated catalog with price list — $1.

Canterbury Designs, Inc.
PO Box 5730   Dept. OHJ
Sherman Oaks, CA 91413
(213) 936-7111
RS/O   MO
Company has a line of streetscape and mall equipment — some pieces in period style. Of special interest are 4-faced outdoor clocks, oak and iron promenade benches, an 1890 hexagonal bench, and cast aluminum or cast iron tree grates. Equipment is high-quality and costly. (17-ft. 4-faced Victorian steet clock is $18,000.00) Color catalog — free. Prices on specific request.

Cape Cod Cupola Co., Inc.
78 State Road   Dept. OHJ
North Dartmouth, MA 02747
(617) 994-2119
RS/O   MO   DIST
Wooden cupolas in a variety of sizes and styles. Over 200 weathervane designs in a choice of finishes and sizes. Illustrated catalog and price list — $1.00.

Capitol Victorian Furniture
P.O. Box 60   Dept. OHJ
Montgomery, AL 36101
(205) 262-0381
DIST
Solid mahogany reproduction Victorian furniture. Sold through interior designers and retail outlets including Magnolia Hall and Martha M. House. For dealer nearest you write or call the above address.

● **Carlisle Restoration Lumber**
Rt. No. 123   Dept. OHJ
Stoddard, NH 03464
(603) 446-3937
RS/O   MO
Restoration lumber dealer selling wide pine or oak boards, ship-lapped boards, feather-edge clapboards, and natural weathered (grey) board. Also supplies cedar shingles, custom-made wide-board batten doors, and custom-made raised panels & wainscot. Free brochure — please specify your needs for a price quote.

Carolina Leather House, Inc.
P.O. Box 5195   Dept. OH-1
Hickory, NC 28601
(704) 322-4478
RS/O   MO
Fine hand-made leather furniture. Styles from camel-back Queen Anne sofas and authentic tufted Chesterfields, to comfortable club chairs, and their Safari collection in suede. Top-grain leather (50 colors), brass appointments, solid mahogany legs and stretchers. A domestic source for well-made leather furniture at reasonable cost. Catalog $2.00.

● = Consult ad for more details. See Advertisers' Index on the last page of this Catalog.

Carpenter Assoc., Inc.
40 Timber Swamp Rd.   Dept. OHJ
Hampton, NH 03801
(603) 926-3801
RS/O   MO
They produce custom designs as well as reproduction pieces of any wood product with an historic architectural reference. Any type custom millwork including stairways, turnings, windows, doors and entrances, mantels, all types of period wall paneling, and much more. Forward your specific needs for price quotations. Call for more information. Brochure available, $1.

Carriage Trade Antiques & Art Gallery
406 W. Lenoir Ave.   Dept. OHJ
Kinston, NC 28501
(919) 523-2946
MO   RS/O
Unique services for the collector: customer can buy direct from the shop, or they will search for you on a cost-plus basis. Their refinishing department does all work by hand; also custom restoration and relining of antique trunks. Interior design consultation. Please call for appointment. No literature.

Carson, Dunlop & Associates, Ltd.
130 Winchester St.   Dept. OHJ
Toronto, ON, Canada M4X1B4
929-0820
RS/O
Prepurchase home inspection services available in the greater Toronto area. Written report includes analyses of structure, heating, plumbing, wiring, insulation, interior and exterior finishes. Budget figures are also offered for recommended improvements. Purchasers are invited to attend inspection. Brochure available on request.

CasaBlanca Fan Co.
1350 Manufacturing St.   Dept. OHJ
Dallas, TX 75207
(214) 651-7256
DIST
Manufacturers of a full line of quality ceiling fans. Sold through distributors nationwide..Write for name of nearest retailer.

CasaBlanca Glass, Ltd.
1935 Delk Industrial Court   Dept. OHJ
Marietta, GA 30067
(404) 952-1281
RS/O   MO
A design consulting service, also offering beveled glass work that has been used in restaurants, hotels, and fast food chains in the U.S. and abroad. They can match existing pieces, copy from photos, and design new concepts. Beveled windows, $70, per sq. ft.; beveled mirrors, $80. Frosted panels also available. Write for free brochure.

• **Cascade Mill & Glass Works**
21 Parkway, Hwy. 23   Dept. OHJ
Ouray County, CO 81427
(303) 325-4780
MO
Collection of high-quality handcrafted entry, interior, and screen doors. Available in a selection of woods and styles. Custom orders accepted. Catalog $2.50

Casey Architectural Specialties
1124 East Lyon Street   Dept. OHJ
Milwaukee, WI 53202
(414) 765-9531
RS/O
Ornamental plasterer does stock and custom mouldings; restoration, residential or commercial work. Operates primarily in the Wisconsin area, but can travel. Free flyer available.

Castle Burlingame
R.D. 1, Box 352   Dept. OHJ
Basking Ridge, NJ 07920
(201) 647-3885
RS/O
Antique building materials of all types, but specializes in antique wide-board flooring, including installation, sanding & finishing. Three booklets available: "Where to find and how to select antique flooring"; "How to install antique flooring — step by step"; "How to sand and finish antique flooring." $3.99 each or all three for $9.99.

Castle Home Maintenance Co.
47 Cypress   Dept. OHJ
Brookline, MA 02146
(617) 731-1229
RS/O
Company carries on ordinary building construction services; however, they specialize in antique and Victorian restorations, coloring and rehabilitation of Victorian exteriors, and interior design of period rooms and ornamental artistry (stencilling, plastering, etc.) Free brochure.

• **Cedar Gazebos, Inc.**
10432 Lyndale Avenue   Dept. OHJ
Melrose Park, IL 60164
(312) 455-0928
MO
Pre-fabricated gazebo kits. Modular units are made of heartwood cedar; each wall and roof panel is handcrafted and comes pre-assembled. Three styles available: Pagoda (either 6- or 8-sided), South Seas Classic, and Midwestern Classic (both 6-, 8-, and 10-sided). Optional features: counter ledges, double entry door, and full lattice panels. Write for free brochure and price list.

• **Ceiling Fan Company, Inc.**
4220 S. W. 75th Avenue   Dept. OHJ
Miami, FL 33155
(305) 266-5899
MO   RS/O   DIST
In addition to carrying new fans manufactured by Hunter, Homestead, they manufacture a line of decorative components adaptable to the Hunter and other fans. Fans are available in a number of standard colors & in brass, copper or chrome-plated finishes. Lights are available on most units. They manufacture replacement parts for antique fans & carry a stock of fully restored antique fans. They make paddles from solid oak, walnut, mahogany etc. Also offer complete restoration service for antique fans. Color brochure, $2. Old fan parts catalog, $2.

Ceilings, Walls & More, Inc.
Box 494, 124 Walnut St. Dept O   Dept. OHJ
Jefferson, TX 75657
(214) 665-2221
RS/O   MO   DIST
Old tin ceiling panels reproduced in light-weight, hi-impact polymer materials. The 24 by 24 in. panels are easily installed in a suspended grid system or glued directly onto sheetrock or plaster ceilings. The decorative patterns are appropriate to any decor and especially to rooms of the Victorian period. Free literature and price list on request. Sample kits $5.50.

Center Lumber Company
85 Fulton Street, Box 2242   Dept. OHJ
Paterson, NJ 07509
(201) 742-8300
RS/O
Stock hardwoods at reasonable prices. Most architectural millwork, including custom hardwood mouldings. No literature.

Century Glass Inc. of Dallas
1417 N. Washington   Dept. OHJ
Dallas, TX 75204
(214) 823-7773
RS/O   MO
They will bevel 1/4", 3/8", 1/2" and 3/4" thick clear or colored plate glass. Widths of bevels range from 1/4" to 1-1/2". All bevels custom. Also offer glue chip design for mirrors, and leaded-beveled installations. Price list available for bevel work, including OG and double bevels.

Chandler — Royce
185 E. 122 St.   Dept. OHJ
New York, NY 10035
(212) 876-1242
RS/O   MO
Electro-plating shop. Will take small jobs. No literature.

• **Charles St. Supply Co.**
54 Charles St.   Dept. OHJ
Boston, MA 02114
(617) 367-9046
MO
This retail store has agreed to ship plaster washers to OHJ readers who can't find them locally. Price is $1.25 per dozen (ppd.), minimum order 3 dozen. No billing, no literature.

Charolette Ford Trunks
Box 536, Dept. OH   Dept. OHJ
Spearman, TX 79081
MO
Antique trunk hardware and supplies. 32 pg. catalog, $.50.

Chelsea Decorative Metal Co.
6115 Cheena Drive   Dept. O
Houston, TX 77096
(713) 721-9200
MO   RS/O
Embossed metal for ceilings are stamped with the original dies that date back as far as the Civil War. There are eighteen designs and they come in 2' x 8' sheets. They are 26 gauge and have a silvery tin finish. Metal cornice comes in 4 ft. lengths, but the widths vary. Catalog free.

Chem-Clean Furniture Restoration Center
Rt. 7   Dept. OHJ
Arlington, VT 05250
(802) 375-2743
RS/O   MO
Wood finishing products for floors, stairs, fine furniture — paint and varnish removers, bleach, brush cleaner, satin finish polyurethane varnish. Brochure and price list — $.25.

• **Chemical Products Co., Inc.**
P.O. Box 400   Dept. OHJ
Aberdeen, MD 21001
(301) 272-0100
DIST
Supplies chemicals in commercial quantities for professional vat strippers. Write for literature.

Cherry Creek Ent. Inc.
937 Santa Fe Drive   Dept. OHJ
Denver, CO 80204
(303) 892-1819
MO   RS/O   DIST
Specializes in the making of beveled glass for interior and exterior doors, windows and cabinets. They carry a large variety of sizes and shapes in beveled blanks, but will produce any size and shape needed. Panels can also be made with cut or etched glass designs. Free catalog.

Chesapeake Restorations, Inc.
1103 Bank Lick Street   Dept. OHJ
Covington, KY 41011
(606) 261-5493
RS/O
Complete restoration services including paint removal and woodwork duplication. No literature.

Chicago Academy Tools
1633 W. Fullerton   Dept. OHJ
Chicago, IL 60614
(312) 871-6666
MO
Extensive selection of high-quality hand tools for woodworkers. Over 1,500 items shown in full-color 130-page catalog. Special monthly sales to current catalog holders. Also gives classes in fine woodworking. Send $5 for catalog.

Chilstone Garden Ornament
Sprivers Estate   Dept. OHJ
Horsmonden, Kent, UK
(089) 272-3553
RS/O   MO   DIST
Handsome garden ornaments — exact copies of 16th, 17th, and 18th century models — in cast stone. Urns, planters, benches, statuary, obelisks, pedestals, balls and bases, columns, balustrades — all by noted designers. Catalog — $6.00.

• **City Barn Antiques**
362 Atlantic Ave.   Dept. OHJ
Brooklyn, NY 11217
(212) 855-8566
MO   RS/O
A large selection of restored brass antique gas lighting fixtures with original etched glass shades. 1860 — 1910. No literature.

City Knickerbocker, Inc.
781 Eighth Ave.   Dept. OHJ
New York, NY 10036
(212) 586-3939
RS/O
A large selection of 19th century lighting fixtures and lamps. Reproduction cased glass Emeralite Shades. Restores, rewires, adds antique or reproduction glass shades. Also, the "Tee" series — seven reproduction variations in the green glass shade type of fixture. "Tee" series brochure free.

• **City Lights**
2226 Massachusetts Ave.   Dept. OHJ
Cambridge, MA 02140
(617) 547-1490
RS/O   MO
Dealer in fully restored antique lighting. Fixtures are repaired, rewired, cleaned, polished, and lacquered and have all antique glass shades. Fixtures displayed at shop. Photo sheet of typical fixtures available for $2. Will respond to specific requests with Polaroids, $1. each, refundable with purchase.

Clarence House Imports, Ltd.
40 East 57th St.   Dept. OHJ
New York, NY 10022
(212) 752-2890
ID
Re-creation of antique textile designs in fine fabrics and wallcoverings. Used by museums, including the Frick and Metropolitan museums in New York. Specializing in 18th and 19th century hand printed cottons and wallpaper as well as fine silks, leathers, horsehair, mohair and woven textures. Through interior designers only.

Clarksville Foundry & Machine Works
P.O. Box 786   Dept. OHJ
Clarksville, TN 37040
(615) 647-1538
RS/O
Gray iron foundry and machine shop in operation since 1854. They produce a wide range of rough and finished castings in volumes of one piece to several hundred. They have many old patterns, and can produce quality castings using a customer's sample as a pattern. Custom and jobbing work a specialty. No literature.

• **Classic Illumination**
431 Grove St.   Dept. OHJ
Oakland, CA 94607
(415) 465-7786
DIST   ID
Manufacturers of authentic handcrafted solid brass Victorian and Turn-of-the-century lighting including the bronze griffin collection. These U.L. listed, all-electric chandeliers, wall sconces and table lamps are available in a variety of shades, lengths and finishes (Custom variations available). Also: plaster ceiling medallions in 7 different patterns. Free brochure upon request. Wholesale inquiries invited. Write for illustrated catalogue ($3.00) and nearest dealers.

Claxton Walker & Associates
10000 Falls Road   Dept. OHJ
Potomac, MD 20854
(301) 299-2755
RS/O
House inspection services in Washington, D.C., and surrounding Virginia and Maryland. Newly expanded service to Annapolis and Norfolk. Free brochure and price list of books and articles on home inspection and maintenance.

Claymont Forge
P.O. Box 112   Dept. OHJ
Charles Town, WV 25414
(304) 725-9573
RS/O   MO
The Claymont Forge produces a line of hand-wrought iron home furnishings and fireplace tools. They accept commissions for unique pieces ranging from letter openers to large architectural works such as gates, railings, and chandeliers. They work in traditional or contemporary styles. Please send drawings or description of work for an estimate. Catalog, $1.; current price list, free.

Clio Group, Inc.
3961 Baltimore Ave.   Dept. OHJ
Philadelphia, PA 19104
(215) 386-6276
RS/O
Consultants in architectural and land use history providing a full range of restoration and preservation services. Preparation of National Register Nomination forms; applications for Tax Certification; counseling for adaptive re-use projects. Specialists in archival, demographic and property research; interpretation of historic structures. Survey drawings. Free brochure.

Cohasset Colonials
40 Parker Ave.   Dept. OHJ
Cohasset, MA 02025
(617) 383-0110
MO
Knocked-down furniture kits that are copies of museum originals or reproductions of outstanding pieces in private collections. Cohasset Colonial stain and paints; Colonial accessories & lighting fixtures. Also Colonial reproduction fabric and curtains. Color catalog $1.

Cole, Diane Jackson
9 Grove Street   Dept. OHJ
Kennebunk, ME 04043
(207) 985-7387
RS/O   MO
Handwoven 100% virgin wool coverlet for all size beds, in traditional blooming leaf design. Available in range of color-blends. Sample of fabric with color choices — $2.00. Handwoven wool strip rug with sturdy Irish linen warp, braided ends. Any size: widths more than 5 ft. are joined in traditional manner. Rug woven in any color blend to match interior. Rug sample — $2.00. Large throws and lap robes in mohair/wool blend available in 6 colors. Color sample and information, $2.

Colonial Brick Co.
3344 W. Cermak Road   Dept. OHJ
Chicago, IL 60623
(312) 927-0700
RS/O
Company specializing in Chicago used common brick and antique street pavers. For samples and further information, please call. No literature.

Colonial Casting Co.
443 South Colony St.   Dept. OHJ
Meriden, CT 06450
(203) 235-5189
MO   DIST
Handcrafted pewter candlesticks and sconces in Early American and Queen Anne styles. Also; Plates, mugs, ash trays & goblets. Catalog and price list — $.50.

• **Colonial Lock Company**
172 Main St.   Dept. OHJ
Terryville, CT 06786
(203) 584-0311
MO
Box type rim locks based on the old-fashioned style but with modern engineering. A maximum dead bolt security lock. Send $.25 for catalog.

Colonial Tin Craft
7805 Railroad Ave.   Dept. OHJ
Cincinnati, OH 45243
(513) 561-3942
RS/O   MO   DIST
An array of folk art creations, plus Early American, 18th century and Colonial lighting. Chandeliers, lanterns, sconces, candleholders and lamps. 40-page catalog available: $2.00

Colonial Weavers
   Dept. OHJ
Phippsburg Center, ME 04562
(207) 389-2033
MO   RS/O
Handwoven reproductions of antique coverlets in Colonial Overshot or summer & winter techniques. Coverlets are woven to order in a wide choice of traditional patterns and colors. Drapery fabric woven to match coverlets or tablecloths and runners. A reproduction of an antique Maine coverlet was purchased by the Renwick Gallery of the Smithsonian Institution for their 'Crafts Multiples' show. Also tablecloths, placemats. Brochure available on request.

• **Combination Door Co.**
P.O. Box 1076   Dept. JC
Fond du Lac, WI 54935
(414) 922-2050
DIST   MO
Manufacturers (since 1912) of wood combination storm and screen doors. Plain wood screen doors, wood combination doors in many styles, wood combination windows, wood basement and garage windows, and wood patio storm doors available through distributors and lumber dealers in 18 states, and direct to consumers in those states without distributors. Write for free brochures and name of your distributor.

Community Services Collaborative
1315 Broadway   Dept. OHJ
Boulder, CO 80302
(303) 442-3601
RS/O
Complete consulting and architectural services for historic preservation and restoration. Property surveys, interior/exterior design, specifications, construction management, and historic development research. Economic and adaptive use studies and plans. Consultant to National Park Services. Historic materials laboratory; including paint, mortar and plaster analysis. Literature available on request.

Competition Chemicals, Inc.
P.O. Box 820   Dept. OHJ
Iowa Falls, IA 50126
(515) 648-3683
DIST
Importers of SIMICHROME POLISH for all metals (brass, pewter, copper, etc.). Sold through distributors/dealers. Literature available from distributors/dealers or from main office at above address.

● **Condon Studios — Stained Glass**
33 Richdale Ave. (Porter Sq.)   Dept. OHJ
Cambridge, MA 02140
(617) 661-5776
RS/O   MO
Fine antique leaded-glass windows, lamps, and firescreens, c. 1860-1930; original commissioned leaded-glass design in contemporary and classic motifs on residential or architectural scale; restoration services — repair, releading, structural resupporting, framing, plexi-protection and installation; curved panel bending for antique lamps and glass etching. Appointment suggested; phone inquiries welcome. Brochure and color sampler of available windows, $1.

Congdon, Johns/Cabinetmaker
RFD 1   Dept. OHJ
Moretown, VT 05660
(802) 485-8927
RS/O   MO
Fine cabinetwork in period styles. Authentic reproductions, or original designs in appropriate period fashion. All work done by hand; all solid woods; fine brass hardware. Custom design service built on a sound knowledge of 18th century furniture. Prefers personal consultation with customers, but will work through mail or by phone if necessary. Photos and references to serious inquiries — no catalog.

Conklin Tin Plate & Metal Co.
P.O. Box 2662   Dept. OHJ
Atlanta, GA 30301
(404) 688-4510
RS/O   MO
Manufactures metal roofing shingles, including one pattern typical of late 19th century houses. Available in galvanized steel, copper, aluminum microzinc or terne. Also supplies galvanized roofing sheets, gutters and leaders. Flyer 'Metal Shingles'', $1.00.

KEY TO ABBREVIATIONS

MO = sells by Mail Order

RS/O = sells through Retail Store or Office

DIST = sells through Distributors

ID = sells only through Interior Designers or Architects

Conservatory, The
209 W. Michigan Ave.   Dept. OHJ
Marshall, MI 49068
(616) 781-4790
RS/O
Shop offers old and new products for the older home, including selected architectural artifacts, lighting fixtures, hardware, and window furnishings. Of special interest is the catalog center, featuring the catalogs and brochures of numerous fine companies. Old-house design consultation is also available. No literature.

● **Constance Carol, Inc.**
PO Box 899   Dept. OHJ
Plymouth, MA 02360
1-800-343-5921
RS/O   MO
Fine curtains from Plymouth, Massachusetts. Colonial tab curtains a specialty. Large variety of styles and fabrics, including Waverly and Schumacher. Standard and custom sizes available. Wooden rods and brackets. Color catalog free. Call toll free. Mass. residents call 1-800-242-5815. Collection of over 150 fabric and trim samples, $4.00.

Constantine, Albert and Son, Inc.
2050 Eastchester Rd.   Dept. OHJ
Bronx, NY 10461
(212) 792-1600
RS/O   MO
Carries extensive selection of hardwoods and veneers, tools, kits, furniture hardware, craft books, and finishing materials. Catalog, $1.

Conti, John
Box 189, Martins Corner Rd.   Dept. OHJ
Wagontown, PA 19376
(215) 384-0553
RS/O
Building restorations by craftsmen skilled in the use of 18th & 19th Century methods and materials. Research work, restoration of existing structures, design and building of appropriate period-style additions, and supplying of authentic hardware are among their services. No literature; call or write with specific inquiry.

Cooper Stair Co.
1331 Leithton Road   Dept. OHJ
Mundelein, IL 60060
(312) 362-8900
DIST   RS/O
Manufacturers of wood stairs: straight, circular, and spiral. Custom fitted with stock parts; or handrails, balusters, and newel posts may be manufactured to your architect's specifications in any wood. Installation instructions available. Available knocked-down, pre-assembled,, or for professional installation. Also sculptured wood paneling. Brochures, $.25 each.

Copper House
RFD 1, Rt. 4   Dept. OHJ
Epsom, NH 03234
(603) 736-9798
MO   RS/O
Handmade copper weathervanes and lanterns, for post, wall, or hanging. Authentic reproductions. A variety of styles and sizes are available. Flagpole balls and weathervane parts. Catalog $1.00.

● = Consult ad for more details. See Advertisers' Index on the last page of this Catalog.

Coran — Sholes Industries
509 East 2nd Street
South Boston, MA 02127
(617) 268-3780
RS/O   MO
Manufactures and distributes lead, glass, tools, equipment, pattern books to the stained glass artisan. A very complete line of Tiffany-style lamp kits. Illustrated catalog with price list — $3.00.

Dermit X. Corcoran Antique Services
Box 568 Montauk Hgwy.   Dept. OHJ
East Moriches, NY 11940
(516) 878-4988
RS/O
Specializing in the repair and restoration of ornamental and decorative metal items — lighting fixtures, brass beds, statuary, cast iron architectural features, weather vanes, American and European antiques. Custom work done on request. Inquiries welcomed. Flyer available.

Corner Legacy
P.O. Box 102, 17 Hilton St.   Dept. OHJ
Eureka Springs, AR 72632
(501) 253-7416
RS/O   MO
This small, family business specializes in fine corner cabinetry in limited production. They have a line of hand-crafted oak corner medicine chests, plus corner curio cabinets in various native hardwoods. Distribution is primarily through mail-order. Literature available, free.

Cornucopia, Inc.
PO Box 44-J Westcott Road   Dept. OHJ
Harvard, MA 01451
(617) 456-3201
MO
Handmade and factory-built country primitive and Early American furniture A nice variety of settees and rockers. The company also sells a furniture dressing for restoration of old pieces. Catalog, $2.

Cosmetic Restorations
21 Lebkamp Avenue   Dept. OHJ
Huntington, NY 11743
(516) 673-6327
RS/O
Large scale paint stripping services to restore wood and masonry buildings to their original surface. Specializes in old houses and churches. Literature free.

Cosmopolitan International Antiques
Box 314   Dept. OHJ
Larchmont, NY 10538
(914) 698-1586
MO   RS/O
Antique lighting fixtures, Victorian furniture & accessories, and turn-of-the-century furnishings. Interior design services available for the owners of turn-of-the-century or late Victorian homes. Please write or call with specific request.

Country Braid House
Clark Road   Dept. OHJ
Tilton, NH 03276
(603) 286-4511
RS/O   MO
Traditional New England Colonial braided rugs. Hand-laced all-wool rugs are made to order. They'll also make up custom kits for you to lace yourself. Free company brochure. Prices quoted on your requested size and style — or phone ahead to visit the shop.

The Old-House Journal 1982 Catalog

Country Catalog
265 Petaluma Ave., Box 339   Dept. OHJ
Sebastopol, CA 95472
(707) 823-6557
MO   RS/O
This catalog displays a large and varied selection of wood stoves. 250 domestic and imported models offered. Specialized information makes catalog function as a wood-heating guide. Available for $2.95, and $2.50 is refunded with first $20.00 order.

● **Country Curtains**
At The Red Lion Inn   Dept. OHJ
Stockbridge, MA 01262
(413) 298-5565
RS/O   MO
Curtains in cotton muslin, permanent-press and other fabrics, some with ruffles, others with fringe, braid or lace trim. Also bedspreads, dust ruffles, canopy covers and tablecloths. Tab curtains and wooden rods. Retail shops in Stockbridge, Salem and Braintree, Mass. Free catalog includes illustrations and color photographs.

● **Country Floors, Inc.**
300 East 61st St.   Dept. OHJ
New York, NY 10021
(212) 758-7414
RS/O   MO   DIST
Handmade tiles for floors and walls, from Holland, France, Spain, Portugal, Italy, Israel, Mexico, & Finland. 60 page color catalog, $5. Regional representatives' names, and installation instructions available on request.

Country Loft
South Shore Park   Dept. OHJ
Hingham, MA 02043
(617) 749-7766
MO
Furnishings and decorative accessories with an Early American flavor. Many attractive housewares appropriate for the country or Colonial home. Lifetime subscription to The Country Loft 48-page color catalog, with a minimum of 3 issues per year for just $5. (refundable with your first order).

Country Roads, Inc.
1122 South Bridge St.   Dept. OHJ
Belding, MI 48809
(616) 794-3550
MO   DIST   RS/O
This company restores old theater seats. Repair and refinishing of wood parts, metal refinishing, and reupholstering done on-site or in their shop. Their "Mobile Plant" — a renovation facility on wheels — goes anywhere to provide quick service for public buildings. No literature — please call or write for consultation.

Cowtan & Tout, Inc.
979 Third Avenue   Dept. OHJ
New York, NY 10022
ID
Domestic and imported glazed chintzes, wovens and silks; fine, handblocked wallpapers; wallcoverings with coordinating fabrics. Custom colorings available. Specialists in 18th and 19th century patterns. Many William Morris wallpapers. Literature available on some items; please write on your letterhead.

● = Consult ad for more details.   See Advertisers' Index on the last page of this Catalog.

Craft House, Colonial Williamsburg
Box CH   Dept. OHJ
Williamsburg, VA 23185
(804) 229-1000
RS/O   MO
Fine reproductions and adaptations of the English Georgian style furniture, lighting, fabrics, wall coverings and accessories approved by the Colonial Williamsburg Foundation. The handsome 286 pg. full-color illustrated catalog and price list at $4.95 is a must for those interested in the Georgian period.

Craftsman Lumber Co.
Main St.   Dept. OHJ
Groton, MA 01450
(617) 448-6336
RS/O   MO
Specializing in wide pine boards, 12" to 24" wide. Clear pine clapboards. All new wood. Also custom made wainscotting, panelling, flooring, moldings, doors. Leaflet and price list $.30. Stamps ok.

Craftsmen Decorators
2611 Ocean Avenue   Dept. OHJ
Brooklyn, NY 11229
(212) 769-1024
RS/O
Specializes in graining, glazing, gilding, antiquing, stencilling and traditional decorating techniques. Restorations a particular specialty. No literature.

● **Crawford's Old House Store**
301 McCall   Dept. OHJ
Waukesha, WI 53186
(414) 542-0134
MO
A wide variety of old-house items, including unusual reproduction door and window hardware, lighting and plumbing supplies, reproduction marble fireplace mantels, custom made wood storm, screen and replacement sash, all shapes in kits. Wood corner blocks, finials, fancy cut shingles, and corner beads. Specialty tools. Wood and brass refinishing kits. Reference books and furniture kits. Illustrated catalog, $1.50, refundable with purchase.

● **Creative Openings**
1013 Holly Street   Dept. OHJ
Bellingham, WA 98225
(206) 671-7435
RS/O   MO
Hand-crafted hardwood screen doors, for Victorian or other style houses. Solid brass mesh screen. Your choice of oak, mahogany, ash. Bent laminations, hand-turned spindles. Brochure sent upon request; send $3 for design booklet.

Creatus
P.O. Box 6124   Dept. OHJ
Lancaster, PA 17603
MO
Personalized "House Blessing" Frakturs to record births, marriages, family tree, and special events. Creatus Frakturs are authentic designs all printed in color on 9 x 12 natural parchment. Each is handlettered with your information. Handcrafted frames in Fraktur style are available. Catalog showing Frakturs and folkart is available for $1.00.

You'll get better service when contacting companies if you mention The Old-House Journal Catalog

---

Croton, Evelyn — Architectural Antiques
51 Eastwood Lane   Dept. OHJ
Valley Steam, NY 11581
(516) 791-4703
MO   RS/O
Antique architectural items such as marble and terra-cotta keystones, ornate iron registers and fence panels, iron and wood newel posts, balusters, door carvings, door surroundings, pilasters, fretwork, etc. Specializing in hand-carved corbels. Selling to dealers, architects, designers, and consultants only. Specific inquiries made on letterhead answered with photos, dimensions, prices.

Crowfoot's Inc.
3831 No. Oracle Rd.   Dept. OHJ
Tucson, AZ 85705
(602) 888-4493
RS/O   MO
Fine woodworking, cabinetmaking, turnings, furniture reproduction, Victorian and Early American. Works mainly in Southwest area. Will supply photos of work done to serious inquirers.

● **Cumberland General Store**
Route 3   Dept. OH-82
Crossville, TN 38555
(615) 484-8481
RS/O   MO
"Complete outfitters for your journey back to basics." From chamber pots to covered wagons — over 10,000 items, many available only here & all new goods. Of particular interest are the period kitchen utensils and implements, and wood-burning cookstoves. The interesting, illustrated 250 pg. catalog makes fascinating browsing for $3.00 plus $.75 postage & handling.

● **Cumberland Woodcraft Co., Inc.**
2500 Walnut Bottom Rd Dept 40   Dept. OHJ
Carlisle, PA 17013
(717) 243-0063
RS/O   MO
Specializes in solid wood reproductions of all types of Victorian millwork. Using catalogs, drawings, photographs or even fragments of original pieces, they have developed a complete line of Victorian appointments to create an atmosphere of nostalgia and quiet beauty. You can select from a standard full line of grilles, fretwork, panels, brackets and turnings. Literature — $3.50.

Curry, Gerald — Cabinetmaker
Pound Hill Road   Dept. OHJ
Union, ME 04862
(207) 785-4633
MO
Small shop specializing 18th-century furniture reproductions. Design, construction, and materials are faithfully copied from the originals. Fine craftsmanship combined with years of study results in the museum-quality reproductions. An illustrated brochure is available for $2.

Curvoflite
RFD 2, Box 145AC   Dept. OHJ
Kingston, NH 03848
(603) 642-3425
RS/O   MO
Solid oak spiral staircases and circular staircases custom made to your specifications. Two basic circular styles (Colonial and Contemporary) with custom options. Also custom architectural millwork: cabinetwork, raised panelling, hand-turned balusters. Curvoflite staircase color brochure — $1.00.

Cushwa, Victor & Sons Brick Co.
MD RT 68   Dept. OHJ
Williamsport, MD 21795
(301) 223-7700
RS/O   DIST
Manufacturers and distributors of distinctive "Calvert" machine-molded and custom handmade old brick. Specialize in matching old brick and special brick designs for color, texture, and size. Complete line of brick available in numerous colors. Restoration work includes Independence Hall and Betsy Ross House. Catalog, $2.00.

Cusson Sash Company
128 Addison Road   Dept. OHJ
Glastonbury, CT 06033
(203) 633-4759
RS/O   MO
Manufactures a combination storm-screen window with wooden sash. Double-hung, picture windows, oriel-style. Storm/screen inserts are interchangeable. Sized to order. Flyer and price list, free.

Custom House
South Shore Drive   Dept. OHJ
Owl's Head, ME 04854
(207) 236-4444
MO
Manufacturers of 3 reproduction lines: (1) Cast brass or bronze door knockers, hooks, ornaments. (2) Victorian lace lampshades and tablecloths from $5 to $150. (3) Bronze toys, banks, doorstops, paperweights. All items made by New England Craftsmen. Send SASE for price sheets.

Custom Woodworking
RFD 1, Box 84, Wood Creek Rd.   Dept. OHJ
Bethlehem, CT 06751
(203) 266-7619
RS/O
Specializes in working with customers to build cabinets, furniture, and paneling, etc. to fit both the period of their house and their own personal taste. Work is done with complete modern machinery and by old hand methods for historic accuracy. No literature.

Cyrus Clark Co., Inc.
267 Fifth Avenue   Dept. OHJ
New York, NY 10016
(212) 684-5312
DIST
Their line of "Everglaze" chintzes features some early 19th century European patterns in an old-fashioned glazed finish. Chintz is excellent for wall covering, upholstery and draperies. Sold at department stores and fabric shops, or write for name of distributor nearest you. An instruction booklet, "Everglaze Chintz Makes A Beautiful Wallcovering" is free.

KEY TO ABBREVIATIONS

MO	=	sells by Mail Order
RS/O	=	sells through Retail Store or Office
DIST	=	sells through Distributors
ID	=	sells only through Interior Designers or Architects

D

• **Daly's Wood Finishing Products**
1121 North 36th St.   Dept. OHJ
Seattle, WA 98103
(206) 633-4204
RS/O   MO   DIST
Manufacturing and marketing of wood finishing products including brasswire brushes and a wooden scraping tool; bleaches and stain removers; BenMatte Danish finishing oil, clear and stain; Floor Fin treatment. A complete guide to wood finishing: 'Class Notes,' $2. Free descriptive literature; free guidance in solving wood finishing problems.

Davis Cabinet Co.
Box 60444   Dept. OHJ
Nashville, TN 37206
(615) 244-7100
DIST
Solid wood bedroom, dining room, and occasional items. Booklet available for $2.00 that illustrates manufacturer's production method and displays several collections — Victorian, Early American, English, French, and Oriental. The Lillian Russell Victorian Collection is the oldest collection in continuous manufacture in the United States.

• **Dean, James R.**
15 Delaware Street   Dept. OHJ
Cooperstown, NY 13326
(607) 547-2262
RS/O   MO
Provides professional, individualized counselling and custom stair and handrail work. All phases of common, intricate, straight curved, new and alteration work. Stair and railwork matched or copied. All woods, all work special order only. Material shipped anywhere F.O.B. Cooperstown, N.Y. Planning, layout design and consulting services available. Repair assistance information available via phone/mail. $15.00 minimum fee for services. Phone calls returned collect only. No literature.

• **Decorators Supply Corp.**
3610 So. Morgan St., rear bldg   Dept. OHJ
Chicago, IL 60609
(312) 847-6300
RS/O   MO
Thousands of composition and wood fibre ornaments for woodwork, furniture and architectural trim; hundreds of plaster ornaments, composition capitals and brackets; 15 wood mantels in Colonial, French and English styles. 4 illustrated catalogs and price lists. Plaster Ornaments — $2.00, Capitals & Brackets — $2.00 Mantels — $1.00, Wood Fibre Carvings — $1.00, Woodwork-Furniture Ornaments — $13.00.

Dee, John W./Painting & Decorating
41 Blossom St.   Dept. OHJ
Bradford, MA 01830
(617) 373-6607
RS/O
Specializing in the restoration of finer old homes. Interior/exterior. Wallcoverings, stencilling. Serving greater Boston and Southern N.H. No literature; please call.

Defender Industries
255 Main Street   Dept. OHJ
New Rochelle, NY 10801
(914) 632-3001
MO
Marine supplies, including epoxy consolidants for rotted wood, fiberglass and resins, and high-performance caulks. Catalog, $1.00.

• **Deft Wood Finish Products**
411 E. Keystone   Dept. OHJ
Alliance, OH 44601
(216) 821-5500
MO   DIST   RS/O
Products for wood staining and finishing. Free brochures.

Delaware Quarries, Inc.
River Rd.   Dept. OHJ
Lumberville, PA 18933
(215) 297-5647
DIST   RS/O
Producers of an extensive line of building stone. Specialists in the matching of stone from old, unavailable sources. Custom fabrication of slate, limestone, granite, marble and sandstone for a variety of uses in the home. Genuine soapstone warming plates for your wood stove. Building stone brochure available at no cost.

Dentro Plumbing Specialties
63-42 Woodhaven Blvd.   Dept. OHJ
Rego Park, NY 11374
(212) 672-6882
RS/O   MO
Supplies modern or obsolete faucet & shower stems only. Cannot supply porcelain faucet handles or complete faucets. Only stems or spindles. But must have the old one for a sample. No diagrams or sketches. Complete line of case parts for tanks. No catalogs or other literature available.

• **Deseret Industries Manufacturing**
1680 So. Industrial Rd.
Salt Lake City, UT 84104
(801) 531-4094
RS/O
Pioneer woven rag rugs. Multi colors or made to order. Free literature.

Destin's Designs
422 S. 2nd St.   Dept. OHJ
Milwaukee, WI 53204
(414) 276-6177
RS/O
Lighting, hardware, paneling, doors, stained glass, and wrought iron from old buildings. No literature.

• **Devenco Louver Products**
Box 700   Dept. OHJ
Decatur, GA 30030
(404) 378-4598
RS/O   MO
Traditional wood-slat Venetian blinds, all custom-made to individual window's specifications. Fine-quality, available stained or painted. Mail orders accepted and shipment arranged. Interior shutters also available. Please telephone for specific information. Send for free color brochure.

Devoe & Raynold Co.
400 Dupont Circle   Dept. OHJ
Louisville, KY 40207
(502) 897-9861
DIST
Several years ago, Devoe was the first company to issue a line of reproduction Victorian paints for exteriors. Their "Traditions" line includes 48 exact reproductions of Devoe's line of 1885. Acrylic-latex only. Contact office above if your local paint store doesn't carry Devoe paints.

The Old-House Journal 1982 Catalog

• DeWeese Woodworking
P.O. Box 576   Dept. OHJ
Philadelphia, MS 39350
(601) 656-4951
MO

Company manufactures a line of solid oak commode seats. Mail order seats are $50.00 ppd. Available in dark walnut or natural finish. All seats have either brass or chrome plated brass hinges. Brochure available free.

• Diedrich Chemicals-Restoration Technologies, Inc.
300 A East Oak Street   Dept. OHJ
Oak Creek, WI 53154
(414) 761-2591
DIST   MO

Professional restoration chemicals for building exteriors: masonry, restorer-cleaner, water-repellent preservative sealers. Paint removers for both wood and masonry. Chemicals sold ONLY to dealer/contractors around the country. Film demonstrating products is available. Write for free brochure and name of your nearest dealer or contractor.

• D. Diehl Victorian Interior Restoration
6374 Waterloo Rd.   Dept. OHJ
Atwater, OH 44201
(216) 947-3385
RS/O   MO

Design services for period-home interiors and small commercial buildings as well as museums. Also execution of all finish work: woodwork replacement and refinishing, wallpapering, custom cabinetwork, and restoration of decorative painting and plasterwork. Brochure free with SASE. References on request.

Dierickx, Mary B.
125 Cedar Street   Dept. OHJ
New York, NY 10006
(212) 227-1271
RS/O

Architectural preservation consultant providing such preservation services as: restoration, preservation & rehabilitation programs and planning; maintenance programs; materials conservation; architectural and historical research and analysis; architectural surveys; feasibility studies; photographic documentation; & assistance with National Register nominations, local landmark status & 1976 Tax Reform Act certification. Free brochure.

Dijon Galleries
3130 Turk Blvd.   Dept. OHJ
San Francisco, CA 94118
(415) 387-5600
RS/O

Dijon Galleries - Interior furnishings, appointments, antiques and objets d'art. Period interior design. Consultations throughout U.S. No literature.

Dimension Lumber Co.
517 Stagg   Dept. OHJ
Brooklyn, NY 11237
(212) 497-7585
RS/O

Custom mouldings and millwork for wholesale customers. Minimum order of 200 feet to individuals, walk-in cash business only. No literature.

You'll get better service when contacting companies if you mention The Old-House Journal Catalog

---

• Dixon Bros. Woodworking
72 Northampton St.   Dept. OHJ
Boston, MA 02118
(617) 445-9884
RS/O   MO

This custom millwork and cabinet shop can produce most pieces required in the restoration of old houses. They specialize in period entry doors, paneling, interior shutters, mouldings, turnings, and carving. Also kitchen cabinetry; straight and curved handrailing and complete staircases. Furniture specialties include an all-hardwood rolltop desk. Literature in preparation — please call or write with your specific requests.

Doll Depot
103 N. 5th St.   Dept. OHJ
Middletown, IN 47356
(317) 354-4885
MO   RS/O

Hand-made porcelain dolls, dressed in appropriate period fashions. Prices range from $5.00 to $150.00 plus freight. Will ship UPS. Lady fashion dolls, baby dolls, & children dolls. Send SASE plus $.25 for catalog.

Domestic Environmental Alternatives
495 Main St., Box 1020   Dept. OHJ
Murphys, CA 95247
(209) 728-3860
RS/O   MO

Plumbing for Victorian decor: Brass & porcelain fixtures, pull-chain toilets, clawfoot roll-rim tubs, oak accessories. Walk-in shop — smaller items can be ordered and sent by mail. Also: antique faucets repaired; brass cleaning and polishing. Descriptive literature available.

• Dorothy's Ruffled Originals
6721 Market Street   Dept. OHJ
Wilmington, NC 28405
(919) 791-1296
MO

Handmade ruffled curtains, specializing in perma-press country curtain with a 7 in. ruffle. Also complete line of ruffled accessories: dust ruffles, pillow sham, coverlets, and lampshades. Curtains can be made in any length. $4.00 for color brochure & samples.

Dorz Mfg. Co.
P.O. Box 456   Dept. OHJ
Bellevue, WA 98009
(206) 454-5472
MO   DIST

Manufacturer of built-in cabinet ironing boards. Board swivels to save space. Doors to fit are made of pine with raised panels, alder with raised panels or flat birch plywood panels. Also available are pads and covers that fit older home's built-in ironing boards. Free literature.

Dotzel, Michael & Son
402 East 63rd Street   Dept. OHJ
New York, NY 10021
(212) 838-2890
RS/O

Restores, repairs, cleans brass, copper, pewter, iron, lead, tole. Restores antiques to original condition. Wires chandeliers and lamps. Retinning; polishing and lacquering. No literature.

KEY TO ABBREVIATIONS

MO	=	sells by Mail Order
RS/O	=	sells through Retail Store or Office
DIST	=	sells through Distributors
ID	=	sells only through Interior Designers or Architects

Dover Furniture Stripping
505 S. Governors Ave.   Dept. OHJ
Dover, DE 19901
(302) 674-0220
RS/O   MO

A professional paint stripping service using dip tanks - also offering supplies for restoring and refinishing furniture, a full line of furniture parts and solid brass hardware - also carries trunk hardware, veneer, embossed wood, upholstery supplies, caning tools. They also have a gift shop that carries reproduction Early American and Victorian furniture. Retail catalog $1.75 includes tips on selecting hardware. Free booklets: "How to Apply Veneer," "Use of Stick Shellac" and "Machine Woven Caning." Wholesale catalog available to the trade.

• Dovetail, Inc.
P.O. Box 1569-102   Dept. OHJ
Lowell, MA 01853
(617) 454-2944
RS/O   MO

Specialist in custom duplication of plaster ornament, making new molds and new castings in plaster. Company has extensive experience on restoration projects nationwide. Design and consultation services offered. Illustrated catalogue is available for $1.00. Offered in the catalogue are a unique complete ceiling for the homeowner to install, medallion collection all obtained from old homes and custom order department for drawn plaster.

Downstate Restorations
P.O. Box 276   Dept. OHJ
Macomb, IL 61455
(312) 929-5588
RS/O

Building restoration firm specializing in exterior masonry cleaning and chemical paint removal. Ornamental cornice repairs — metal and plaster. Consulting and research services. Extensive painting expertise. Serving Illinois and the Midwest. Free company literature and Diedrich Chemicals specifications on request.

Driwood Moulding Company
P.O. Box 1729   Dept. OHJ
Florence, SC 29503
(803) 669-2478
RS/O   MO

They have been fabricating embossed hardwood period mouldings for over 50 years. Hundreds of historically authentic designs suitable for cornices, chair rails, door and window casings, bases, etc. They custom manufacture mantels, doors, and architectural millwork. Custom-made curved wood stairs. Two catalogs of mouldings and millwork, $6 (cost credited against orders of $100 or more).

Drums Sash & Door Co., Inc.
P. O. Box 207   Dept. OHJ
Drums, PA 18222
(717) 788-1145
RS/O   MO

Architectural woodwork company supplying clear white pine custom window sash; stair treads, risers and mouldings; stock hardwood trim (casing, base, cove); wood screen/storm doors, custom interior & exterior doors. Also cabinet fronts in oak, birch, cherry, or poplar. Will supply window glass and other window parts. Catalog/price list: $2.00.

● = Consult ad for more details. See Advertisers' Index on the last page of this Catalog.

Dura Strip of San Mateo
726 S. Amphlett Blvd.   Dept. OHJ
San Mateo, CA 94402
(415) 343-3672
RS/O
Professional paint-stripping company using immersion process on all types of interior/exterior wood and metalwork: stained-glass windows, mouldings, registers, railings, gingerbread, doors, mantels, and pillars. Also metal de-rusting and etching. Specializing in antique repair-restoration-refinishing; and chair caning. Also reproduction oak tables and chairs. No literature.

Durvin, Tom & Sons
Rt. 6, Box 307   Dept. OHJ
Mechanicsville, VA 23111
(804) 746-3845
RS/O
Family-owned and operated brick contracting business. Services include fireplace and chimney restoration. Small, quality-oriented company with old-house experience. Greater Richmond area. Please phone for free estimate.

● **Dutch Products & Supply Co.**
14 South Main St.   Dept. OHJ
Yardley, PA 19067
(215) 493-4873
MO   DIST
The complete line — 26 patterns — of Royal Delft Tiles. Colonial chandeliers in solid brass and brass with Delft or Limoges parts. Also hanging brass oil lamps; wall sconces in brass/pewter. Brochure, $1.

Duvinage Corporation
P.O. Box 828   Dept. OHJ
Hagerstown, MD 21740
(301) 733-8255
MO
Manufactures complete lines of spiral and circular stairway systems for residential, commercial, and industrial applications; interior and exterior use. Circular and spiral stairs are custom built to specifications. Steel, aluminum, grating, cast iron, cast aluminum, and stainless steel. Treads covered in wood, carpet, rubber, terrazzo, marble, concrete or tile. Continuous rails of aluminum, steel or wood. Free brochure.

E

E & B Marine Supply
PO Box 747   Dept. OHJ
Edison, NJ 08817
(201) 442-3940
MO
High performance marine supplies — caulks, exterior finishes, rot-patching materials, epoxy fillers — are useful for first-rate restoration projects. If you have no source nearby, this company will fill mail orders. Call for current stock and prices, and to charge an order.

Easy Time Wood Refinishing Products
PO Box 686   Dept. OHJ
Glen Ellyn, IL 60137
(312) 858-9630
MO   DIST
Company sells a wood refinisher that removes varnish, lacquer, shellac, and light coats of paint (no methylene chloride). Also tung oil penetrating sealer, lemon oil, and a lightweight electric heat gun for removing paint. Products distributed through antiques and hardware stores, but they will also sell direct. Free brochures.

Ed's Antiques, Inc.
422 South Street   Dept. OHJ
Philadelphia, PA 19147
(215) 923-4120
RS/O
Antique shop specializing in repair and rewiring of lighting fixtures, recaning, wood furniture refinishing, and reframing of antique stained glass. Walk-in shop; no literature.

Electric Glass Co.
1 E. Mellen St.   Dept. OHJ
Hampton, VA 23663
(804) 722-6200
RS/O   MO
They offer new beveled glass door and window inserts, stained glass panels, new and old art glass and Tiffany style shades. Beveled Glass Catalog — $3.00.

Elegant Accents Incorporated
23012 Del Lago Dr.   Dept. OHJ
Laguna Hills, CA 92653
(714) 768-9492
RS/O   MO
Specialist in bevelled glass. Fully bevelled panels (door and window inserts); bevelling with stained glass; stained glass windows; and etched glass. Stock and custom work. Delivery in the Orange Cty./San Diego areas; shipping can be arranged by customer elsewhere. Brochure and price list $2.00.

Elk Valley Woodworking Company
Rt. 1, Box 23   Dept. OHJ
Carter, OK 73627
(405) 486-3337
MO   RS/O
They specialize in redwood and cedar porch columns and white pine, ash, poplar, oak, mahogany, walnut, and white cedar room columns and balusters. They will also turn to your pattern or duplicate columns for partial replacements. 8 decorative brackets are also available. Free brochure.

Elliott Millwork Co.
640 E. Fairchild St.   Dept. OHJ
Danville, IL 61832
(217) 446-8443
RS/O
Manufacturers of architectural woodwork and custom hardwood mouldings. A large line of stock items, including wainscotting, chair rails, and crown mouldings. Also manufactures "Enduro" stile and rail 6-panel solid red oak prefinished doors. Standard moulding for all inside and outside mouldings. All of these mouldings are custom manufactured. Free literature.

Elmore, Chris/ Architectural Design
707 Simonton St.   Dept. OHJ
Key West, FL 33040
(305) 294-2014
RS/O
Restoration of old structures — both design and execution. Working primarily in FL Keys, but will travel for selected jobs throughout South. Extensive background in the American Arts & Crafts Movement: Will travel anywhere in U.S. to work on Stickley, Wright, etc. houses. Complete attention given to one job at a time. No literature: call or write for referrals.

Elon, Inc.
642 Sawmill River Rd.   Dept. OHJ
Ardsley, NY 10502
(914) 592-3323
DIST   RS/O
Source for Elon Carillo handmade glazed and unglazed terra cotta tiles and accessories from Mexico. Also ceramic tiles from Portugal and Italy; Palace Collection of hand-painted English delft tile and trim. Catalog, $3.

Empire Stove & Furnace Co.
793-797 Broadway   Dept. OHJ
Albany, NY 12207
(518) 449-5189
RS/O   MO
In addition to many wood and coal-burning stoves, this shop (in business since 1901) carries an extensive inventory of old stove parts and accessories. There are also patterns for many parts that aren't in stock. No literature. For best results — phone number above or 449-2590.

Energy Marketing Corporation
PO Box 636   Dept. OHJ
Bennington, VT 05201
(802) 442-8513
MO   DIST
Manufacturers of Home Heater Coal and Wood-heating systems. Copper-coil domestic hot water systems available for use with Home Heater. Also hot air add on bonnet available. Home Heater Coal/Wood Boiler also available. Free brochure.

Englewood Hardware Co.
25 No. Dean St.   Dept. OHJ
Englewood, NJ 07631
(201) 568-1937
RS/O
A restoration supply/hardware store, well-stocked with reproduction faucets, door and furniture hardware, fine brass fittings, ceiling and ornament and cornice mouldings, etc. Walk-in sales only; mail-order buyers contact Renaissance Decorative Hardware, their subsidiary.

Envirostyle Direct
2785 N. Fairview Ave.   Dept. OHJ
St. Paul, MN 55164
(612) 633-1376
MO
A tubular fireplace grate that takes advantage of the natural convection heat transfer principle to increase the net heat output from an open woodburning fireplace. When combined with a glass door enclosure, heat loss is cut and output is greatly increased. All units can be supplemented with blowers. Literature offered.

Ephraim Forge
RR 3, Box 215   Dept. OHJ
Frankfort, IL 60423
(815) 469-3201
MO
Hand-forged ironwork. Specialist in reproduction items. Work is done on an individual commissioned basis. Fireplace screens, cranes and tools, kitchen implements, pot racks, door knockers, hinges and latches, brackets, hooks, trammels, etc. No literature. Price quotes on specific items. Please write.

Ephraim Marsh Co.
PO Box 266, Dept. 760   Dept. OHJ
Concord, NC 28025
(704) 782-0814
MO
Adaptions and reproductions of 18th century furniture with some 19th century pieces. Mostly moderate in price. Catalog with price list — $1.

Essex Forge
15 Old Dennison Rd.   Dept. OHJ
Essex, CT 06426
(203) 767-1808
MO   RS/O
Authentic hand-forged reproductions of early American fireplace accessories; terne, copper and iron chandeliers and sconces, copper and brass exterior lanterns. Illustrated catalog — $2 (refunded with purchase).

The Old-House Journal 1982 Catalog   123

Estes-Simmons Silver Plating, Ltd.
1168 Howell Mill Rd.   Dept. OHJ
Atlanta, GA 30318
(404) 875-9581
RS/O
Plating and restoration. Walk-in shop — no literature.

Evergreen Slate Co.
34 North Street   Dept. OHJ
Granville, NY 12832
(518) 642-2530
MO   RS/O
Producers of roofing slate in all colors and thicknesses: Semi-Weathering Gray-Green, VT Black & Gray-Black, Unfading Green, Red, Royal Purple, Unfading Mottled Green & Purple, and Rustics. Also, floor tile, flagstone. Company also sells 'ESCO' Slate Cutters, Slate Rippers, Slate Hammers, and Slate Hooks for slate repairs. Write or call for free brochure.

Evergreene Painting Studios, Inc.
365 West 36th St.   Dept. OHJ
New York, NY 10018
(212) 239-1322
RS/O
Architectural construction and decorative painting services. Int./ext. paint contracting. Interior & exterior services include mural painting, trompe l'oeil, frescoes, woodgraining & marbleizing, gold leafing. Designed treatment of walls, ceilings, floors. Free flyer.

Experi-Metals
524 W. Greenfield Avenue   Dept. OHJ
Milwaukee, WI 53204
(414) 384-7910
RS/O   MO
Individual craftsman does high-quality custom castings in brass, bronze and related alloys. Excellent reproduction work. Has done custom duplication of hardware through the mail. No literature — you must call.

F

• **F M P**
327 S. Edgefield   Dept. OHJ
Dallas, TX 75208
(214) 942-8316
RS/O
Architectural mouldings and millwork: Baseboards, door and window facings, rosettes, corner blocks. No literature. Please write or call.

Facemakers, Inc.
140 Fifth St.   Dept. OHJ
Savanna, IL 61074
(815) 273-3944
RS/O   MO
Creates original paintings done to customer specifications. Specializes in period portraits that are done from clients' photographs. Customer can have portrait done in almost any style and in the appropriate costume of the period selected. Paintings done in oils on stretched canvas. Prices start at $750. Send $5.00 for brochure.

KEY TO ABBREVIATIONS	
MO =	sells by Mail Order
RS/O =	sells through Retail Store or Office
DIST =	sells through Distributors
ID =	sells only through Interior Designers or Architects

Faire Harbour Ltd.
44 Captain Peirce Rd.   Dept. OHJ
Scituate, MA 02066
(617) 545-2465
RS/O   MO
Distributors of Aladdin kerosene mantle lamps and manufacturers of several old-style kerosene table and bracket lamps. These well-made brass and brass-finish lamps with glass shades and chimneys give a steady light equal to a 75 watt bulb. Optional electric converter. Replacement parts and supplies. Illustrated catalog and price list — $1.00 by 1st class mail — refunded on purchase.

• **Fan — Attic, Inc.**
P.O. Box 628   Dept. OHJ
Delaware, OH 43015
(614) 369-2626
RS/O   MO
Retail store sells both Homestead and Hunter Old Tyme ceiling fans. Will ship via UPS anywhere in the U.S.A. Fans are available in two sizes and a variety of motor-case finishes. Free illustrated catalog with prices.

• **Farm Builders, Inc.**
4708 Roland Ave.   Dept. OHJ
Baltimore, MD 21210
(301) 235-4260
MO   RS/O
Restoration lumber suppliers, selling salvage from weathered boards to entire restored log houses. Specializing in barn siding; timbers; old, new, or resawn tongue-and-groove flooring; reclaimed architectural woodwork. (Fire code coatings available.) Also supply stained and bevelled glass; hardware. Free brochure.

• **Feather River Wood and Glass Co.**
PO Box 444, 1632 Midway   Dept. OHJ
Durham, CA 95938
(916) 895-0752
Doors with glass panels — singles, transoms, sidelights, entryways. Wood panels with custom mouldings. Bars, mantels, mirrors. Free color brochure and illustrated catalog.

• **Felber, Inc.**
110 Ardmore Ave.   Dept. OHJ
Ardmore, PA 19003
(215) 642-4710
MO   RS/O
Felber Studios maintains a collection of 8,000 plus architectural ornamental enrichments. In addition to stock service, they have a custom department that can replace and/or renew period plaster mouldings to private homes and commercial institutions. They have completed jobs at the White House in Washington, D.C., and at the Molly Brown House in Denver, Colorado. Custom architectual planning consultation service also available. Inquire about their new fiberglass-reinforced plaster ornament. Catalog available, $2.00.

Fenton Art Glass Company
Caroline Ave.   Dept. OHJ
Williamstown, WV 26187
(304) 375-6122
RS/O   MO   DIST
Early American, handmade glassware and lamps, many of which are handpainted and signed by the artist. Also baskets, bells, vases, and figurines. Send $4. for 80-page color catalog.

FerGene Studio
4320 Washington Street   Dept. OHJ
Gary, IN 46408
(219) 884-1119
MO
Reproduction turn-of-century fireplace tiles. Face tiles 6 x 6. Hearth tile 6 x6, 6 x 3, 6 x 1-1/2 with some special sizes on request. Can color tiles, using modern commercial glazes, to complement other tiles, wallpaper or fabric. Patterns include: vine pattern, morning glory, scrolls, and medieval lady and knight. Free flyer (large self-addressed, stamped envelope please.)

Ferris, R.D., Architect
3776 Front St.   Dept. OHJ
San Diego, CA 92103
(714) 297-4659
RS/O
Architectural design services for interior and exterior restoration and rehabilitation of all types of buildings, including public buildings, commercial and residential. All types of construction, including adobe; adaptive re-use studies, feasibility reports and planning. Southern California and Hawaii. No literature.

Fiebiger, Inc.
462 10th Ave.   Dept. OHJ
New York, NY 10018
(212) 563-5818
RS/O
Artists in wrought iron. Create original designs to customer specifications. Have done work for restorations such as the U.S. Capitol & Bow Bridge in NYC's Central Park. No literature.

• **Fine Tool Shop, Inc.**
20-28 Backus Avenue   Dept. OHJ-81
Danbury, CT 06810
(203) 797-0772
MO   RS/O
Importers and retailers of high-quality woodworking tools including "Primus" wood planes, gouges, chisels, wood carving sets, power tools, tool chests, saws, vises and much more. Send $5.00 for 132 page color catalog.

Finish Feeder Company
P.O. Box 60   Dept. OHJ
Boyds, MD 20720
(301) 972-1474
RS/O   MO   DIST
A furniture polish based on an 18th century cabinetmakers' formula. For furniture, wood panelling and floors. Free literature.

Finishing Products
4611 Macklind Ave.   Dept. OHJ
St. Louis, MO 63109
(314) 481-0700
MO
Mail-order source for furniture finishing products, including: lacquers, paint removers, sanding belts and paper, bleaches, dye stains, burn-in sticks and tools, respirators and dust masks, paint and varnish removers, caning supplies, fiber replacement seats, Makita power tools, veneers, vinyl and furniture repair kits, antique brass drawer pulls.

Finnaren & Haley, Inc.
2320 Haverford Road   Dept. OHJ
Ardmore, PA 19003
(215) 649-5000
RS/O   DIST
Interior and exterior paints in 31 colors of historic Philadelphia, 10 of which were authenticated through the cooperation of the National Park Service as used in historic Philadelphia buildings. F&H Color Card available upon request; send $.28 in stamps.

Fireplaces by Martin
P.O. Box 128   Dept. OHJ
Florence, AL 35630
(205) 767-0330
DIST
Full line of zero-clearance and freestanding fireplaces, including the Martin QUADRA-THERM II, an efficient, heat-circulating fireplace that features outside air for combustion. Full color brochures available on request. Catalogs, $.25.

Flaharty, David — Sculptor
79 Magazine Rd., R.D. 1   Dept. OHJ
Green Lane, PA 18054
(215) 234-8242
RS/O   MO
Specializes in the reproduction and restoration of architectural details and ornaments, especially in plaster and fiberglass. Among his clients are the State Department, the White House, the U.S. Capitol, the University of Virginia, Georgetown University, Metropolitan Museum of Art. No literature. Photos of work supplied for serious inquiries.

Flam Sheetmetal Specialty Co.
330 East 75th St.   Dept. OHJ
New York, NY 10021
(212) 427-5853
RS/O
Custom fabrication in sheet metal: liners, pans, flower trays and boxes, etc. Also reproductions of colonial lanterns and tinware. Walk-in shop only; no literature.

Flexi-Wall Systems
P.O. Box 88   Dept. OHJ
Liberty, SC 29657
(803) 855-0500
MO
They offer a patented, gypsum-impregnated flexible wallcovering, designed for problem wall surfaces (especially masonry). They have passed the rigid fire and toxicity tests required for use in New York City. An ideal finish for the thermal mass walls in the field of passive solar energy. "Scotland Weave" decorative finish. Complete test data, catalog information, and prices are available.

Floess, Stefan
R.D. 3, Rt. 416   Dept. OHJ
Montgomery, NY 12549
(914) 457-5676
MO
Interior restoration — painter specializing in historical places. Wood graining, marbleizing, stencilling and other intricate decorative skills. Please call for appointment. No literature.

Floorcloths Incorporated
P.O. Box 812   Dept. OHJ
Severna Park, MD 21146
(301) 798-6850
RS/O   MO
Reproductions of 18th and 19th century painted canvas floorcoverings. Patterns are documented or adapted from original sources. Finest hand-painting and stencilling techniques. Their trained designers also work from designs supplied by the client. Prices start at $10.00 per square foot. Design portfolios available at $2.00 to cover postage and handling.

● = Consult ad for more details. See Advertisers' Index on the last page of this Catalog.

Floors By Juell
642 Greenbay Rd.   Dept. OHJ
Kenilworth, IL 60043
(312) 251-6500
RS/O
Hardwood floor specialists, supplying a variety of creative and technical capabilities. Services include: custom designs; installation; refinishing; restoration; cleaning and waxing; antiquing; inlaid borders; custom tables; paneling; cabinetry. No literature available.

● **Focal Point, Inc.**
2005 Marietta Rd., N.W.   Dept. Y2-2a
Atlanta, GA 30318
(404) 351-0820
MO   DIST
Manufactures a handsome line of architecturally accurate ceiling medallions, cornice mouldings, niche caps, mantels, overdoor pieces, and more. Made of polymers, the product is resilient and lightweight. Factory-primed to receive paint or stain and is indistinguishable from wood or plaster. Easy to install with usual carpentry tools. Styles are appropriate for 18th & 19th century houses. Color catalog — $1.50.

● **Folger Adam Co.**
Box 688   Dept. OHJ
Joliet, IL 60434
(815) 723-3438
MO   DIST   RS/O
Cast brass rimlock and hinge reproductions approved and licensed by the Colonial Williamsburg Foundation. These are authentic replicas of locks, hinges, and trim found in the original Colonial buildings at Williamsburg, VA. Modern lock cylinders available for exterior doors. Free brochure.

Follansbee Steel
State St.   Dept. OHJ
Follansbee, WV 26037
(304) 527-1260
DIST
Manufactures terne roofing and terne-coated stainless for standing-seam metal roofs. One of the oldest types of metal roofing, terne is used on many historic buildings such as Monticello and the Smithsonian Institution. It's a a premium-quality long-lasting material. Free brochures: "Terne Roofing" and "Terne-Coated-Stainless Roofing."

Form and Texture
12 So. Albion St.   Dept. OHJ
Denver, CO 80222
(303) 388-1324
RS/O
Restoration of ornamental plasterwork, interior and exterior. Also original designs for desired period. Sculptor and designer Leo Middleman works primarily in Colorado, but will travel for larger projects. Please write for references. Specific inquiries will be answered.

Formby's Refinishing Prod., Inc.
P.O. Box 667   Dept. OHJ
Olive Branch, MS 38654
(601) 895-5594
DIST
Manufactures and distributes wood refinishing products, tung oil varnish and stains. Free Furniture Fact Books on furniture restoration and finishing.

Fourth Avenue Stove & Appliance Corp.
59 Fourth Ave.   Dept. OHJ
Brooklyn, NY 11217
(212) 638-2477
RS/O   MO
Coal and wood-burning stoves, including Franklin and pot-belly; parts for old stoves. Also sell ranges and heaters; parts for ranges and heaters, gas and electric. No literature; primarily a walk-in store, but special shipments can be arranged.

Frank's Cane and Rush Supply
16442 Gothard St., Unit D   Dept. OHJ
Huntington Beach, CA 92647
(714) 847-0707
MO   RS/O
Caning and various weaving supplies, basketry materials, wicker repair materials, oak parts for chairs, instruction books. Also, oak mouldings, roll-top desk locks, cane cabinet doors. Catalog, $.75.

● **Frog Tool Co., Ltd.**
700 W. Jackson Blvd.   Dept. HJ1
Chicago, IL 60606
(312) 648-1270
MO   RS/O
Store has extensive collection of traditional and old-fashioned woodworking tools, including imported tools. Adzes, froes, broad axes, myford lathes, wood moulding planes, wood finishing materials and wood carving chisels. Books, furniture plans, and many other unusual items. Mail order catalog available — $2.00.

● **Fuller O'Brien Paints**
P.O. Box 864   Dept. OHJ
Brunswick, GA 31520
(912) 265-7650
DIST
Has a handsome collection of Early American and Traditional colors for both interior and exterior use. Free color chips include "Heritage" Color Collection, Whisper Whites and their Decorating Guide which has 136 different colors to choose from.

● **Furniture Revival and Co.**
P.O. Box 994H   Dept. OHJ
Corvallis, OR 97330
(503) 754-6323
RS/O   MO   DIST
Wholesale/retail sales of unusual restoration hardware: solid brass; ice box and Hoosier cabinet hardware; roll top desk locks and replacement tambours; swivel mirror hinges; leather, wood, and fiber chair seats; curved china-cabinet glass; porcelain and brass castors. Catalog, $1.50.

Fypon, Inc.
Box 365, 108 Hill St.   Dept. OHJ
Stewartstown, PA 17363
(717) 993-2593
DIST
FYPON is a high density polyurethane that can be nailed, drilled and sawn with carpenter tools. The company's exclusive millwork includes pediments, pilasters, cross heads, specialty millwork and mouldings suitable for Colonial and Victorian entranceways and windows. Free brochures upon request.

You'll get better service when contacting companies if you mention The Old-House Journal Catalog

G

Garbe's
4137 S. 72nd East Avenue   Dept. OHJ
Tulsa, OK 74145
(918) 627-0284
RS/O   MO
Selection of genuine porcelain knobs and pulls. Rim-lock sets with black or white porcelain knobs; cast aluminum case and strike with wrought steel trim. Free illustrated sheet. Also "Deco-Ceil" cold-cast ceiling mouldings and fixture medallions. Can be shipped direct, available in 4-ft. lengths. Illustrated brochures available — please specify.

Gargoyles — New York
38 East 21st St.   Dept. OHJ
New York, NY 10010
(212) 228-8887
MO   DIST   RS/O
Fine reproductions of mirrors, architectural detail, gargoyles, and other objects. Many styles represented. Composition hydrastone is hand-finished in simulation of appropriate material, (porcelain — walnut — bronze- stone — etc.) Complete illustrated catalog is $2.

Gargoyles, Ltd.
512 South Third Street   Dept. OHJ
Philadelphia, PA 19147
(215) 629-1700
RS/O   MO
Architectural antique & reproductions, ironwork, fretwork, ceiling fans, tin ceilings, bars & backbars, leaded glass, mantels, Victorian wall units, complete store interiors, chandeliers, brackets, and anything we can find. Your best bet will be a visit to their warehouse/ showroom, but please call & make an appointment if you come from out of town. Weekend hours by special appt.

Garrett Wade Company
161 Avenue of the Americas   Dept. OHJ
New York, NY 10013
(212) 695-3358
RS/O   MO
A comprehensive selection of quality hand woodworking tools, many imported from Western Europe and Japan. Also a complete line of wood-working benches and a complete line of finishing supplies, including dyes and stains. Power tools include INCA Swiss circular saws, handsaws, jointer/planers, English lathes. Extensive book list on working with wood. Illustrated catalog with price list, $1.

Gaston Wood Finishes, Inc.
3630 E. 10th St., PO Box 1246   Dept. OHJ
Bloomington, IN 47402
(812) 339-9111
MO
An excellent selection of traditional wood finishing supplies, reproduction furniture hardware, and veneer. Catalog $1.25.

● **Gates Moore**
River Road, Silvermine   Dept. OHJ
Norwalk, CT 06850
(203) 847-3231
RS/O   MO
Handmade reproductions of early American lighting fixtures in a variety of finishes: old paint effect, distressed tin, pewter, flat black. Will make anything from drawings or sketch with complete dimensions. Illustrated 29 pg. catalog with price list — $2.

Gaudio Custom Furniture
21 Harrison Ave.   Dept. OHJ
Rockville Centre, NY 11570
(516) 766-1237
RS/O
Specializing in creations constructed with fine veneer inlays of floral marquetry and geometric parquetry. Also: antique reproduction and restoration, bronze ormolu mounts, architectural paneling. No literature.

G. Brittain M. Co. Stained Glass Studios
P.O. Box 537   Dept. OHJ
Haleiwa, HI 96712
(808) 531-2933
RS/O   MO
Leaded stained glass windows by a designer/fabricator with experience remodelling Victorian houses. Has handled commissions from Guam to New York. As President of the Stained Glass Assn. of Hawaii, he can help clients contact other stained-glass artists. No literature; please write.

Georgia Lighting
530 14th Street, NW   Dept. OHJ
Atlanta, GA 30318
(404) 875-4754
RS/O   MO
Extensive line of lanterns and lighting fixtures, some of which are period-inspired. Send $3.00 for full-color catalog.

Gest, Douglas Co.
R.R. No. 2   Dept. OHJ
Randolph,, VT 05060
(802) 728-9286
RS/O
Complete restoration services, specializing in interior restoration — fine woodworking and cabinetmaking. From time to time they have antique houses available for purchase and reconstruction on clients property. They also offer a "locating service" for those interested in acquiring an antique house suitable for reconstruction on their property. No literature.

Giannetti Studios
3806 38th Street   Dept. OHJ
Brentwood, MD 20722
(301) 927-0033
RS/O   MO
Primarily engaged in the design, manufacture and installation of ornamental plaster in the Washington, DC metropolitan area. Some restoration/preservation services. Brochure $3.00 (refundable on purchase).

Gibbons, John — Cabinetmaker
2070 Helena St.   Dept. OHJ
Madison, WI 53704
(608) 241-5364
RS/O   MO
Cabinetmaker specializing in doors and windows. Late Victorian and early 20th century panel doors in 1-3/4-inch red oak with safety glass. Jambs available. Sash in cherry, pine, or mahogany; jambs and storm sash also. Custom sash and door work for restorations welcomed. Free quotes given from drawings or photos. Literature and price list $1.00.

Gibbs, James W. — Landscape Architect
340 E. 93rd St., No.14C   Dept. OHJ
New York, NY 10028
(212) 722-7508
MO
Restoration of gardens; period garden designs. Landscape architect (Purdue '77) specializes in rooftop and townhouse designs, small gardens, and courtyards. Garden design and consultation can be arranged throughout the country. References and portfolio available upon request.

Gifford, D.K.
230 Windshadow Ct.   Dept. OHJ
Roswell, GA 30075
(404) 993-3281
MO   RS/O
Architectural paintings, commissioned works by a painter who has had numerous shows all over the East. Average price is $4,000. Paintings are large panels done in Gifford's "Stereo-Line Realism". Also limited-edition prints, $75.00, of depots, Victorian houses, gazebos, etc. Free brochure.

Giles & Kendall, Inc.
P.O. Box 188   Dept. OHJ
Huntsville, AL 35804
(205) 776-2979
DIST
4 x 8 ft. aromatic cedar closet panels to line existing closets or for construction of free-standing closets, entry hall and under-the-stair closets. Cedar closet plans booklet — $.25

Gill Imports
P.O. Box 73   Dept. OHJ
Ridgefield, CT 06877
(203) 438-7409
MO
Hand-made crewel fabric for upholstery, curtains, bedspreads. Made in India of 100% wool embroidery on natural cotton. From $13/yd. ppd. Send $1.00 for swatch and catalog.

Gillinder Brothers, Inc.
Erie & Liberty Sts.   Dept. OHJ
Port Jervis, NY 12771
(914) 856-5375
DIST
Manufacturers of glass parts for the lamp and lighting industry. Products include cased glass shades, clear & colored, gas shades, electric shades, lamp bodies...Thousands of molds date back to the 1800's. Sales are wholesale only. Their catalog can be seen at many retail lighting fixture stores. No literature available to retail customers.

Gladding, McBean & Co.
PO Box 97   Dept. OHJ
Lincoln, CA 95648
(916) 645-3341
ID
Produces architectural terra cotta: trim and all decorative pieces for restorations. This company, established in 1875, has supplied the terra cotta for many extensive projects, such as the Hotel Utah in Salt Lake City and the Prospect Park Boat House in Brooklyn. Also, a full line of durable clay roofing tiles, distributed nationally. Company works through architects and other preservation professionals only. Write or phone for more information. Free roofing tile brochure.

Glass Etch Designs
1 Chase Court   Dept. OHJ
Fort Worth, TX 76110
(817) 927-7385
RS/O
Studio creates quality acid-etched art on glass with a wide selection of designs, or you may provide one of your own. Design ideas for windows, mirrors, lamps, or restorational etchings are offered. Designs can be etched on regular, tempered, or laminated safety glass up to an inch thick. Wholesale and retail services. A brochure may be obtained for $.50.

● = Consult ad for more details. See Advertisers' Index on the last page of this Catalog.

126   The Old-House Journal 1982 Catalog

Glass Menagerie Designs Ltd.
2070 Tulare Way   Dept. OHJ
Upland, CA 91786
(714) 985-7719
RS/O   MO
Designs and makes stained and leaded glass panels for doors, windows, and skylights. Corner pieces; etching. Antique glass used at no extra cost. Approx. cost $42.50 per sq. ft. (shipped) — regardless of design or glass used. They will also do installation within 100 miles of Upland. Free literature.

Glassmasters Guild
621 Avenue of the Americas   Dept. OHJ
New York, NY 10011
(212) 924-2868
RS/O   MO
A stained glass craft center, with a gallery of blown and leaded glass, which carries an extensive selection of domestic and imported glass, tools, supplies and books for hobbyist and professional. Beginner's copperfoil kit with step by step instructions, $49.95. Demonstrations held every Saturday beginning at 11:00 A.M. Catalog costs $1.00, which can be applied to any subsequent order of $5.00 or more.

Glen — Gery Corporation
Draw S, Route 61   Dept. OHJ
Shoemakersville, PA 19555
(215) 562-3076
DIST
Manufacturers of a large array of molded colonial brick that looks just like old brick. Free brochure — "1776 Face Brick."

Goddard & Sons
P.O. Box 808   Dept. OHJ
Manitowoc, WI 54220
(414) 682-6153
DIST   MO
Manufactures a line of metal polishes and cleaning compounds. Brochure available.

Goldblatt Tool Co.
511 Osage   Dept. OHJ
Kansas City, KS 66110
(913) 621-3010
MO   DIST
Well-established company offers a full line of trowel trades tools, including power trowelers and all accessories. Great for anyone who is getting into serious masonry or plastering work. Their "glitter gun" can be used for sand painting. Extensive updated catalog is free.

Golden Fleece
127 Dunham's Corner Rd.   Dept. OHJ
East Brunswick, NJ 08816
(201) 254-9360
MO   RS/O
Antiques restoration including striping, stenciling and gilding of furniture. They can also restore picture frames, clock faces, and toleware; oil paintings, reverse glass painting. No literature.

KEY TO ABBREVIATIONS

MO	=	sells by Mail Order
RS/O	=	sells through Retail Store or Office
DIST	=	sells through Distributors
ID	=	sells only through Interior Designers or Architects

Golden Movement Emporium
417 Colorado Ave.   Dept. OHJ
Santa Monica, CA 90401
(213) 395-3289
MO   RS/O
Top-quality architectural antiques from around the world. Antique art glass, mantelpieces and inglenooks, stained glass windows, doors, ceilings, panelled rooms, and entire pub and shop interiors. Also a line of reproduction Victorian architectural pieces — street lamps, back bars, ceiling fans, etc. Catalog, $5.00.

Gold Leaf & Metallic Powders, Inc.
2 Barclay St.   Dept. OHJ
New York, NY 10007
(212) 267-4900
MO   RS/O
Distributes a complete line of Genuine and Imitation Gold Leaf and other Leaf products such as 22K XX Deep Gold, Patent Gold, Lemon Gold, White Gold, Composition Gold Leaf, Aluminum Leaf, Copper Leaf, Variegated Leaf. Manufactures metallic pigments in bronze, copper and aluminum with a wide range of shades available in mesh sizes suitable for many applications. Product list and color card available — $.50.

Good Stenciling
Box 387   Dept. OHJ
Dublin, NH 03444
(603) 563-8021
MO
Their floorcloths have hand-stencilled designs that have been inspired by Early American floorcloths and floor stencils. Heavy canvas and warm colonial colors are used. Sizes range from 2 ft. x 3 ft. up to large room sizes. Prices start at $22. Brochure, $1.

Gorsuch Foundry
120 E. Market St.   Dept. OHJ
Jeffersonville, IN 47130
(812) 283-3585
DIST   ID
Authentic exterior cast iron & cast bronze ornament. Castings can be made from photograph, sample or artist rendering. Foundry will arrange for a local ironworks to install custom castings. No literature.

Gould-Mesereau Co., Inc.
35 West 44th Street   Dept. OHJ
New York, NY 10036
(212) 575-0670
DIST
Manufactures a complete line of metal and real wood drapeware products, both utility and decorative in extensive variety of styles and finishes to complement every decor. "Sierra", Gould's all wood drapeware/ decorative products line, is available in traverse, pole sets and component parts. All accessories & installation aids. Consumer brochures for Sierra line available; catalogs available to the trade ONLY — both free.

The Grammar of Ornament
2626 Curtis Street   Dept. OHJ
Denver, CO 80205
(303) 433-9456
RS/O
Stencilers and interior ornamentists able to restore or re-create painted Victorian and other period interiors. Besides decorative painting, they can produce stencils and custom stencil kits from tracings found in old buildings or from pattern books. In addition, they offer woodgraining and marbleizing services. Free literature.

Grandpa Snazzy's Hardware
1832 S. Broadway   Dept. OHJ
Denver, CO 80210
(303) 935-3269
RS/O
An antique store which stocks reproduction hardware from 23 companies as well as antique hardware and parts for: furniture, telephones, lamps, stoves, barber chairs. Specializing in door hardware: plates, knobs, etc. Consultation assistance to customers completing restoration projects. No literature.

Grant Hardware Company
20 High St.   Dept. OHJ
West Nyack, NY 10994
(914) 358-4400
DIST
Manufactures a line of sliding and folding door hardware, including roller/sheaves suitable for replacements on old sliding doors. Condensed catalog available for $.25.

Great American Salvage
3 Main Street   Dept. OHJ
Montpelier, VT 05602
(802) 223-7711
MO   RS/O
An extensive collection of architectural components, fixtures, and ornamentation. 12,000 sq. ft. of quality antique building and restoration materials. Specializing in stained and leaded glass. Please call or write. Free flyer.

Great Northern Woodworks, Inc.
199 Church Street   Dept. OHJ
Burlington, VT 05401
(802) 862-1463
RS/O
This full service contracting firm specializes in quality restoration of 18th and 19th century buildings, both residential and commercial. Also available for home improvement, custom design/build, new construction additions, commercial establishment design and construction, custom case work: display and counters. All work includes one year free warranty inspection and a client list is available for references.

Greene's Lighting Fixtures
40 Withers St.   Dept. OHJ
Brooklyn, NY 11211
(212) 388-6800
MO   RS/O
Large stock of period-style chandeliers; reproduction styling at reasonable prices. Also restoration of antique fixtures. Catalog — $3.00.

Greenfield Village and Henry Ford Museum
20900 Oakwood Blvd.   Dept. OHJ
Dearborn, MI 48124
(313) 271-1620
RS/O   MO
Handsome reproductions of clocks, furniture, lamps, hooked rugs, wallpaper, fabrics and accessories from Greenfield Village and the Henry Ford Museum. The furniture, chiefly Queen Anne, comes in kit form at considerable savings. Catalog $2.50, postpaid.

Greenhalgh & Sons
Farwell Road   Dept. OHJ
Tyngsborough, MA 01879
(617) 649-7887
RS/O
Interior and exterior painting, wallpapering, stenciling. Serving Northern Mass. and Southern N.H. areas. In N.H., call (603) 880-7887. Free brochure.

The Old-House Journal 1982 Catalog

Greenland Studio, The
147 W. 22nd St.   Dept. OHJ
New York, NY 10011
(212) 255-2551
RS/O
New stained glass; restoration of antique leaded stained glass. Museum-quality conservation. Conservators for the stained glass of St. Ann's and the Holy Trinity in Brooklyn. All kinds of leaded and Tiffany lamp shade repair. No literature.

● **Greg's Antique Lighting**
12005 Wilshire Blvd.   Dept. OHJ
Los Angeles, CA 90025
(213) 478-5475
RS/O
Original antique lighting fixtures, 1850-1930. Stock includes floor and table lamps, wall sconces, and chandeliers. Specializes in high-quality gas fixtures from the Victorian period. Primarily supplying the Los Angeles area. No literature.

Grilk Interiors
2200 E. 11th St.   Dept. OHJ
Davenport, IA 52803
(319) 323-2735
RS/O
Custom interior design studio. Historically correct interiors or adaptive renovation. Dealers in reproduction wallpaper, furniture, lighting, carpets, Oriental rugs and all related items. Period designs in window treatments custom made. Drapery and upholstery fabrics. Complete workroom services. Consultation available. Staff of professional ASID Designers. Write for free brochure.

Guardian National House Inspection and Warranty Corp.
PO Box 115   Dept. OHJ
Orleans, MA 02653
(617) 255-6609
RS/O   DIST
Headquarters for the company. Services are currently offered in twenty-two states. Company provides in-depth engineering surveys of all structural and mechanical components of an old or newer house. A highly accepted guarantee is available to back up their survey. Also, a comprehensive program to train qualified representatives is available. Free introductory brochure.

● **Guerin, P.E. Inc.**
23 Jane Street   Dept. BD-1
New York, NY 10014
(212) 243-5270
RS/O   MO
Fabricators and importers of fine traditional brass decorative hardware since 1857. Some Early American and English designs, but the emphasis is on period French hardware. Among the splendid bathroom fittings, there are several suitable for 19th and turn-of-the-century houses. Over 50,000 models available for custom manufacture. Prices are not cheap. 64 pg. (16 in color) illustrated catalog and price list — $4.

Guild of Shaker Crafts
401 West Savidge St.   Dept. OHJ
Spring Lake, MI 49456
(616) 846-2870
RS/O   MO
A representative selection of Shaker furniture reproductions and accessories. Includes large case pieces, chairs, rockers, oval boxes, peg boards and accessories. Catalog and price list, $3.00.

Guild, The
2749 E. Anaheim St.   Dept. OHJ
Long Beach, CA 90804
(213) 434-1255
MO   RS/O
Roll top desk lock and key hole cover. Free brochure upon request.

Gurian's
276 Fifth Ave.   Dept. OHJ
New York, NY 10001
(212) 689-9696
MO   RS/O
Hand-embroidered crewel fabric from India. Multi-color wool on natural cotton. Also ready-made bedspreads and table covers. Send $1. for swatch and catalog.

H

● **Haas Wood & Ivory Works**
64 Clementina St.   Dept. OHJ
San Francisco, CA 94105
(415) 421-8273
RS/O   MO
They manufacture hand-turned ornamentation for both new construction and restoration projects. Items include newels, brackets, arches for windows and doors, scrolls, crestings, balusters, dormers, handrails, mouldings, columns, capitals, caps and hoods, finials. Custom cabinet shop builds a wide variety of hand-constructed and finished pieces for home or business. They work from your plans and specifications, in any type or combination of woods. Write for brochure.

Haines Complete Building Service
2747 N. Emerson Ave.   Dept. OHJ
Indianapolis, IN 46218
(317) 547-5531
RS/O
One of the oldest and largest masonry restoration companies in Indiana; since 1936. Specialties include building cleaning; tuckpointing, waterproofing, slate roofing, caulking, any and all types of masonry restoration. They also do some painting and remodeling, serving the complete state of Indiana. They will give free technical advice, inspections, and estimates. "Protection of Masonry Surfaces", $1.00.

● **Hallelujah Redwood Products**
Box 669   Dept. OHJ
Mendocino, CA 95460
(707) 937-4410
RS/O   MO
Many stock patterns of sawn wood ornaments and decorative parts for the house and porch: Applique and mouldings, porch brackets, corbels, porch railings, belt course brackets. Custom work also. Illustrated catalog with price list — $1.

Hand-Stenciled Interiors
590 King Street   Dept. OHJ
Hanover, MA 02339
(617) 878-7596
MO
Personal, specialized stencilling service with hundreds of unpublished patterns available and custom stencil designs. Pre-cut patterns individually suited to customer's needs are sent with complete instructions; or professional stenciller will come to your home/business to complete the work. For information, send $1.; no catalog.

Hanscom's Corner Shop
Depot Road   Dept. OHJ
North Lebanon, ME 04027
(207) 457-2164
MO
Traditional Chippendale reproductions — camelback sofas, wing chairs, ottomans. Built the old way, upholstered in your fabric with a plain seat or separate cushion. Custom designs available. For more information, send SASE.

Hardwood Craftsman, Ltd.
811 Morse Avenue   Dept. OHJ
Schaumburg, IL 60193
(312) 351-1979
MO
Furniture kits. Solid woods. Cherry, birch and oak. Easy to assemble. Instructions included. Free catalog.

Harmon, Ruth
710 So. Ross   Dept. OHJ
Santa Ana, CA 92701
(714) 543-1715
RS/O
A professional artist who captures old houses on canvas. Please call for more information.

Harris Manufacturing Company
P.O. Box 300   Dept. OHJ
Johnson City, TN 37601
(615) 928-3122
DIST
This 80 year old company makes hardwood flooring in 22 parquet and plank patterns — many of which are suitable for period houses. Available in red oak, white oak, yellow pine, walnut, angelique teak and maple. Plank available V-joint or square joint. Illustrated catalog and technical notes, $1.00 each.

Harris, Pat/Architectural Interiors
63 17th St., NE   Dept. OHJ
Atlanta, GA 30309
(404) 892-8114
RS/O
Renovation planning and design; specializing in image-building environments. Interior design services, residential and commercial. Mostly design and adaptive re-use of older buildings. Will travel throughout SE. No literature.

Hart, Brian G./Architect
4375 West River Road   Dept. OHJ
Delta, BC, Canada V4K1R9
(604) 946-8302
RS/O
Architectural services in the area of restoration, conservation, rehabilitation and adaptive re-use of historic buildings. Inspection services, feasibility studies, and building code analysis for existing buildings. Design Services for compatible additions to older buildings and sympathetic infill buildings for historic areas. Complete urban design services, historical research and inventories for heritage conservation areas. Primary involvement on the West Coast. No literature.

Hartco
PO Drawer A   Dept. OHJ
Oneida, TN 37841
(615) 569-8526
DIST
Prefinished solid-oak parquet flooring. Available in 4 finish colors. Easy installation. Company also sells all mouldings needed for finishing, and floor-care products. Free brochure.

● = Consult ad for more details. See Advertisers' Index on the last page of this Catalog.

Hartland Forge
250 Bank Street   Dept. OHJ
Lebanon, NH 03766
(603) 448-3326
MO   RS/O
Early American handforged hardware, including latches, hinges, shutter hardware, andirons, cranes and custom work. Examples of his restoration work at Old Sturbridge Village, Newport Restoration Foundation, and the Iron Hardware for the Restoration of Old Fort San Juan, San Juan, Puerto Rico. New expanded catalog $2.00.

Hartman — Sanders Company
4340 Bankers Circle   Dept. OHJ
Atlanta, GA 30360
(404) 449-1561
MO
Architectural columns of clear heart redwood, or clear poplar. Pilasters and square columns as well as round columns in the Greek orders. Also cornices, colonial entranceways, special woodwork. Composition capitals; fiberglass bases, caps, and plinths. Finest quality materials, construction, detail (entasis, fluting). Load-bearing. Free color catalog.

Hasbrouck, W.R., Architect Historic Resources
711 South Dearborn St.   Dept. OHJ
Chicago, IL 60605
(312) 922-7211
RS/O
Architectural firm specializing in historic restorations and adaptive reuse. They prepare feasibility studies, programming, and furnish complete architectural service; the firm has acted as a consultant on numerous National Register properties. No literature.

Hayes Equipment Corp.
PO Box 526, 150 New Britain Av   Dept. OHJ
Unionville, CT 06085
MO   DIST
Efficient wood-heating stoves of heavy gauge steel plate. Specialists in fireplace stoves, and they also make freestanding stoves. Better'n Ben's stoves have been manufactured for over 30 years. Wood-heating, energy saving accessories also available. Also stowaway folding trailers; garden carts. Booklet, "Making Sense Out of Wood Stoves", $1.00.

Hayes and Associates Restoration
Route 12, Box 48   Dept. OHJ
Dothan, AL 36303
(205) 794-7788
RS/O
Exterior restoration, especially of masonry bldgs; acrylic coating. They are mortar-matched experts, and do chemical stripping and cleaning, professional painting, replastering (exterior), and caulking. Also offer consultation services for alternatives and the most economical approach — incl. tax advantages. Free color brochure.

Hearth Shield/Berry Metal
Molasses Hill Road   Dept. OHJ
Lebanon, NJ 08833
(201) 735-8330
DIST   RS/O
Hearth Shield mats are installed on either walls or floors to prevent heat and fire damage caused by open hearth fireplaces and stoves. These UL-listed boards are made from decorative, heavy-gauge textured steel laminated to fire-resistant insulation core. Mat allows installation of fire-standing fireplace or stove anywhere in the home without fire hazard. Phone for free literature.

Hearthstone Tile Co.
2 West 31 Street/Rm. 403   Dept. OHJ
New York, NY 10001
(212) 594-9531
RS/O
Handmade ceramic wall, floor, and fireplace tiles; murals. Custom size, design, and color. Original designs and restoration work. Call or write for appointment. No literature.

Heckler Bros.
464 Steubenville Pike   Dept. OHJ
Pittsburgh, PA 15205
(412) 922-6811
MO   RS/O
They have acquired the original patterns for, and will repair/supply parts for the following: Williamson, Economy, Boomer, Leader, and Berger coal furnaces; and for Columbia and Economy coal boilers. Also supply and stock parts for thousands of coal furnaces, coal boilers, coal heating and coal cookstoves. Firebrick and grates for most coal furnaces. Please call or write with your specific request.

Hedrick Furniture Stripping & Refinishing
159 North Kentucky St.   Dept. OHJ
Danville, IN 46122
(317) 745-3386
RS/O
No-dip, flow-over stripping system. For furniture, interior woodwork, doors and frames. Antique repair, chair caning, pressed fiber replacement seats, and replacement hardware available. Walk-in shop. No literature available.

Heirloom Rugs
28 Harlem Street   Dept. OHJ
Rumford, RI 02916
(401) 438-5672
MO   DIST
Over 500 hand-drawn hooked rug patterns (on burlap base). Sizes range from chairseats to room-size. Company does not sell hooking materials or accessories. Illustrated catalog show 297 of the patterns — $1.50.

Hendershot, Judith
1408 Main Street   Dept. OHJ
Evanston, IL 60202
(312) 475-6411
RS/O
Decorative stencilling for ceilings, walls and floors. Custom designs created in all periods and styles for medallions, borders, dados, etc. Original Victorian stencilled ceilings restored or recreated. Decorations also designed to match wallpapers,, draperies and other patterns. On-premise custom work only; no stencils or stencil kits available. Illustrated brochure is free.

● **Henderson Black & Greene, Inc.**
PO Box 589   Dept. OHJ
Troy, AL 36081
(205) 566-5000
DIST
Manufactures stock millwork items as follows: Columns, turned posts, spindles, balusters, sidelights, mantels, and Colonial entrance features. Literature available on all items — except sidelights — please specify.

Henderson, Zachary, AIA, Inc.
1060 Old Canton St.   Dept. OHJ
Roswell, GA 30075
(404) 992-3308
RS/O
Architectural services including old house design concepts, authentic restoration designs, passive solar expertise. No literature.

Hendricks Tile Mfg. Co., Inc.
P.O. Box 34406   Dept. OHJ
Richmond, VA 23234
(804) 275-8926
RS/O   MO
Concrete and steel-reinforced roofing tiles in a variety of styles. Some styles resemble Colonial round butt and hand-split shakes, but are fire-proof and long lasting. Tiles are custom made in colors and textures selected for each specific job. Frost-proof and fireproof, Hendricks Tiles have been used in the Williamsburg and Old Salem restorations. Free color and application brochures.

Heritage Design
PO Box 103   Dept. OHJ
Monticello, IA 52310
(319) 465-3270
MO   DIST   RS/O
Manufactures a reproduction platform swing rocker kit. Available in walnut, cherry, or maple with either caned or upholstered style seat and backrest. Literature is free.

Heritage Lanterns
70A Main Street   Dept. OHJ
Yarmouth, ME 04096
(207) 846-3911
RS/O   MO   DIST
Wide selection of hand-crafted reproduction lanterns for interior or exterior use. Available in brass, copper or pewter. 52 page catalog - $2.00.

Heritage Rugs
P.O. Box 404, Lahaska   Dept. OHJ
Bucks County, PA 18931
(215) 794-7229
MO   RS/O
Heritage Rugs has preserved the old craft of weaving early American rag rugs on their antique looms. These all wool rugs are custom made in sizes up to 15' wide and 25' long. Just send the colors you would like included (by enclosing paint, fabric or wallpaper samples). Each rug is numbered and registered as a Heritage original. Brochure available for $.50.

Hess Repairs
200 Park Ave., So.   Dept. OHJ
New York, NY 10003
(212) 260-2255
RS/O   MO
All types of repairs on fine antiques. Specializes in silver, glass, crystal, porcelain. Supplies missing parts and restores old dresser sets. No literature.

Hexagram
418 2nd St.   Dept. OHJ
Eureka, CA 95501
(707) 443-8247
RS/O   MO
Specializing in antique lighting fixtures since 1968. Large selection of sconces and chandeliers, both gas and electric. They will completely restore, wire, and polish any lighting fixture. Also a big selection of antique glass shades. Free photographs; please call or write.

KEY TO ABBREVIATIONS	
MO	= sells by Mail Order
RS/O	= sells through Retail Store or Office
DIST	= sells through Distributors
ID	= sells only through Interior Designers or Architects

Hexter, S. M. Company
2800 Superior Ave.   Dept. OHJ
Cleveland, OH 44114
(216) 696-0146
DIST
This company manufactures Greenfield Village fabrics and wallcoverings: Designs are taken from documentary material found at the Henry Ford Museum, Greenfield Village in Dearborn, MI. Several of their books — including "Greenfield Village" and "The Countryside Collection" — are widely available at wallcovering distributors around the country. No literature.

Hi-Art East
6 N. Rhodes Center N.W.   Dept. OHJ
Atlanta, GA 30309
(404) 876-4740
MO   RS/O
Hi-Art East is the East Coast representative for the W.F. Norman Sheet Metal Manufacturing Co., makers of Hi-Art steel ceilings. A ceiling catalog is available for $3.00.

Hickory Chair Company
P.O. Box 2147   Dept. OHJ
Hickory, NC 28601
(704) 328-1801
DIST
Historical James River Plantation Collection - Reproductions and adaptations of 18th century furniture in mahogany. The collection features many upholstered and occasional pieces. 144 pg. catalog — $6.00.

● Hill, Allen Charles AIA
25 Englewood Road   Dept. OHJ
Winchester, MA 01890
(617) 729-0748
RS/O
Consulting firm offering services in preservation & architecture: Architectural services for conservation, restoration and adaptive use; Surveys, inventories and preservation planning; Historical & architectural analysis, bldg documentation, & historic structures reports; National Register nominations; Technical consulting Assistance with grant applications; Lectures & workshops. Services range from brief consultations to extended architectural & preservation projects. Brochure available; specific inquiries answered.

● Hilltop Slate Co.
Rt. 22A   Dept. OHJ
Middle Granville, NY 12849
(518) 642-2270
DIST   MO
NY—VT region slate in all colors and sizes. Specializing in roofing slate for restoration and new construction. Shipment arranged. Also structural slate and flagging. Free color brochure.

Historic Boulevard Services
1520 West Jackson Blvd.   Dept. OHJ
Chicago, IL 60607
(312) 829-5562
RS/O   MO
Restoration services, including space design, structural engineering consultation, and general contracting. Will travel, consult, and speak nationally. Also have re-issued book on Masonry, Carpentry, and Joinery methods c. 1899; $20 postpaid. No literature available.

MO	=	sells by Mail Order
RS/O	=	sells through Retail Store or Office
DIST	=	sells through Distributors
ID	=	sells only through Interior Designers or Architects

Historic Buildings Group
350 Fifth Avenue, Ste. 3308   Dept. OHJ
New York, NY 10001
MO
Sells customized bronze plaques for properties located in districts listed on the National Register of Historic Places. Other bronze plaques to customer's specifications. Historic Associations' inquiries invited; organization discounts available. Free literature.

Historic Charleston Reproductions
105 Broad Street   Dept. OHJ
Charleston, SC 29402
(803) 723-8292
MO
The sale of these reproductions of 18th — early 19th century pieces from historic Charleston generates royalties to further the preservation work of Historic Charleston Foundation. Charleston-made furniture, imported English pieces; porcelains; documentary fabrics; needlework; brass accessories; lamps, hand-made mirrors. Silver, glass, pewter; period paints by Devoe. 60-page color catalog and paint chart, $3.50.

Historic Interiors, Ltd.
122 Lodewyck Avenue   Dept. OHJ
Mount Clemens, MI 48043
(313) 468-3090
RS/O
Interior decorating firm specializes in period interiors. Handles Williamsburg, Sturbridge Village, Greenfield Village fabrics and wallcoverings, among others. Colonial and Victorian lighting fixtures. They also make custom floorcloths. Lectures, seminars, classes available. Serving Southern Michigan. No literature.

● Historic Preservation Alternatives, Inc.
15 Sussex Street   Dept. OHJ
Newton, NJ 07860
(201) 383-1283
RS/O
A multidisciplinary firm of planners, architects and historians specializing in preservation planning, historical research, National Register nominations, historic site surveys, adaptive reuse and restoration projects, grant proposals, building inspections, historic district ordinances and site interpretation. Brochure describing services provided free of charge on request.

Historic Windows
Box 1172   Dept. OHJ
Harrisonburg, VA 22801
(703) 434-5855
MO
Custom made Early American indoor shutters. Full or half in 3/4" solid hardwoods. An excellent insulator for drafty windows. Small sample is available for $12. (refundable). Send $.50 for color brochure.

Hitchcock Chair Co.
   Dept. OHJ
Riverton, CT 06065
(203) 379-8531
DIST
Manufacturers of high-quality American traditional designs, crafted in solid maple and cherry. Send $3.00 for the 32-page catalog of 'The Hitchcock Maple Collection' or send $2.00 for 'The Connecticut House Cherry Collection' catalog. Both are printed in full color.

Hobt, Murrel Dee, Architect
P.O. Box 322   Dept. OHJ
Williamsburg, VA 23185
(804) 220-0767
RS/O
Architectural services in the areas of historic restoration, conservation, rehabilitation and/or adaptive reuse of vintage buildings. Design of new buildings, structures or additions compatible with older buildings or historic districts. Designs for the reconstruction of period, replica buildings, commercial or residential. Historic surveys and inventories. No literature.

Holcomb, Tracy
147 Barbaree Way   Dept. OHJ
Tiburon, CA 94920
(415) 383-7826
ID
She makes lampshades for turn-of-century bases, using expensive laces, velvets, and Chinese silks. Glass bead fringe, hand-strung, is imported from Italy. Her styles range from Victorian to Art Deco. Her business is on a low-volume, custom, one-of-a-kind basis for interior designers only. She also distributes the Burdoch line. Send $.50 for 4-color flyer.

● Holm, Alvin Architect AIA
2014 Sansom St.   Dept. OHJ
Philadelphia, PA 19103
(215) 963-0747
RS/O
Architectural services for historic structures. Design and consultation, preservation, adaptive re-use, appropriate additions. Also historic structures reports, systems analysis, National Register nomination, etc. Registered in NJ, DE, and PA. Serving individuals as well as organizations. Resume on request.

Holzman, S.
30 W. 15th St.   Dept. OHJ
New York, NY 10011
(212) 255-4091
RS/O
Restoration of painted surfaces, architectural mouldings, ceilings. Wood graining, marbleizing, wood-staining. No literature; call for further information.

Homecraft Veneer
901 West Way   Dept. OHJ
Latrobe, PA 15650
(412) 537-8435
MO
Specialists in veneer and veneering supplies — domestic and imported veneers, tools, adhesives, wood finishes, brushes, sanding papers, saw blades, steel wood screws, dowels, dowel pins. 4 pg. illustrated instruction brochure, descriptive literature with price list — $.50.

Home Fabric Mills, Inc.
P.O. Box 662, Rte. 202   Dept. OHJ
Belchertown, MA 01007
(413) 323-6321
MO   RS/O
A complete collection of decorative home fabrics; including velvets, antique satins, prints, upholstery fabric, thermal fabrics, sheers. Also casements, linings, and accessories. Custom drapery and curtain work. Prices discounted. Inquiries for mail orders welcomed. Stores in Cheshire, CT; Scotia, NY; as well as Belchertown, MA. No literature.

● = Consult ad for more details. See Advertisers' Index on the last page of this Catalog.

Homespun Weavers
530 State Ave.   Dept. OHJ
Emmaus, PA 18049
(215) 967-4550
MO   RS/O
Cotton homespun fabric handwoven in authentic Pennsylvania Dutch patterns. Suitable for tablecloths, drapes, bedspreads. Available by-the-yard or in custom-made tablecloths. 7 colors. Also available, 100% Cotton Kitchen Towels in 10 colors. Free color brochure with swatches.

Hood, R. and Co.
RFD 3 College Rd.   Dept. OHJ
Meredith, NH 03253
(603) 279-8607
RS/O   MO
Early American decorating specialists, distributing Williamsburg line, Sturbridge reproductions, and other historic paints, wallpaper, fabrics, drapes, furniture, accessories, hardware, lighting fixtures, etc. Free brochure on Colonial hardware - send SASE.

Hooterville Manufacturing Co.
3507 Lawrenceville Highway   Dept. OHJ
Tucker, GA 30084
(404) 938-9324
MO   RS/O
Handcrafted solid brass beds. Also tables, doll beds, easels, hat racks, blanket racks, and many small items. Brochures available upon request.

● **Hope Co., Inc.**
P.O. Box 28431   Dept. OHJ
St. Louis, MO 63141
(314) 432-5697
MO   DIST
Manufactures furniture refinishing and care products. 100% Tung Oil — no thinners added; Instant Furniture Refinisher; Tung Oil Varnish; Furniture Cleaner; Lemon Oil contains no wax or polish to build up; and new Hope's grill and stove black, a high-heat black finish for BBQ grills, woodburners, etc. Free brochure & literature on request.

Hopkins, Sara — Restoration Stenciling
3319 SW Water Ave.   Dept. OHJ
Portland, OR 97201
(503) 222-2903
RS/O
Restoration of Victorian wall, floor, and ceiling stenciling (especially ca. 1890 - 1910). Professionally trained craftsperson, BFA, references. Personal service, including color matching, advice, original design consultation. Will travel. No literature.

● **Horton Brasses**
P.O. Box 95-OJ, Nooks Hill Rd.   Dept. OHJ
Cromwell, CT 06416
(203) 635-4400
RS/O   MO
Manufacturers of reproduction brass furniture hardware for over 50 years. Their hardware covers periods from 1680 to 1920. Send $1.50 for catalog showing over 475 items.

● **House Carpenters**
Box 217   Dept. OHJ
Shutesbury, MA 01072
MO   RS/O
Custom-fabrication of 18th century millwork, including doors, windows, paneling, and flooring. The House Carpenters build 18th century timber framed houses throughout the Eastern U.S. All work is custom. Information on millwork is free. A brochure of timber framed house designs is available for $4.00.

● **House of Webster**
P.O. Box 488-Hwy. 62N   Dept. OHJ
Rogers, AR 72756
(501) 636-4640
MO
This established family business has a mail-order gift catalog. Of interest is a line of electric kitchen appliances (wall stoves, ranges) that are replicas of old-fashioned wood burners. Catalog is $.25.

Housewreckers, N.B. & Salvage Co.
396 Somerset St.   Dept. OHJ
New Brunswick, NJ 08901
(201) 247-1071
RS/O
This company has been salvaging old house-parts for over 50 years. Always a good supply of doors, windows, plumbing fixtures, interior and exterior moulding, posts and spindles, radiators, old brick and lumber, mantels, and so on. No literature.

HowAll Products, Inc.
3999 Millersville Road   Dept. OHJ
Indianapolis, IN 46205
(317) 545-5363
RS/O   MO
Wooden storm window frames in easy to complete kit form with lower glass and screen inserts. Supplied without glazing and screen material. Literature $1.00.

Howard Products, Inc.
411 W. Maple Ave.   Dept. OHJ
Monrovia, CA 91016
(213) 357-9545
MO   DIST   RS/O
They sell Restor-A-Finish, which can be used to restore naturally finished (but not painted) wood; it cleans and reamalgamates, rather than strips, the old finish. They also sell stripping chemicals of varying strengths. Free brochure: "How To Use Howard Finish Restorers."

Howard, David, Inc.
P.O. Box 295   Dept. OHJ
Alstead, NH 03602
(603) 835-6356
RS/O   MO
Designs and builds old style braced post and beam houses in a variety of sizes and styles. Frame members are pre-fitted, numbered, and shipped to site. Their crew can erect the structure. Windows, doors, siding, roofing, hardware, cabinets and stairs can be supplied. Free introductory brochure. Detailed literature, $5.00.

Howland, John — Metalsmith
Elizabeth St.   Dept. OHJ
Kent, CT 06757
(203) 927-3064
MO   RS/O
Restoration and repair of metal antiques. He will reproduce or manufacture missing parts, either from original or a sketch. Works in wrought iron, brass, copper, bronze, etc. Restores hardware, andirons, lamps, hinges, locks, brassware, etc. Can be reached by phone or mail Monday through Saturday. Estimates for work can be given upon visual inspection of the job. No literature.

Hubbard Folding Wood Box Co., Ltd.
Box 36 Main St.   Dept. OHJ
Downing, WI 54734
(715) 265-4451
MO
Custom millwork, sash & doors, baseboard, casing, plinth blocks, wainscotting, coves. For quote: specific style (sample preferred), quantity in linear feet, and wood desired. Free literature available on wooden folding boxes.

Huber, S. & C. — Accoutrements
82 Plants Dam Rd.   Dept. OHJ
East Lyme, CT 06333
(203) 739-0772
RS/O   MO
Company produces hand crafted goods of 18th and early 19th century design on its small 1710 farm. They conduct lessons for such crafts as wool dyeing, soap making, candle dipping, paper making, rug braiding, etc. Among items for sale: Spinning wheels and fibers, handspun yarns and fabrics, weaving and textile tools, natural dyes, candles, candle making supplies, handmade soap, stencils and papermaking supplies. Craft books. Wooden treen ware. Charming catalog — $.75.

Hughes Lumber & Building Supply Co.
82 Mary Street   Dept. OHJ
Charleston, SC 29403
(803) 577-6671
MO
This company imports — and will handle mail orders for — a superior-quality exterior varnish. Sunshield Clear Architectural Finish is resistant to ultra-violet, rain, fungus, and detergents, and lasts 5-7 years. Price is approx. $20 per imperial quart. Literature available free.

Hunrath, Wm. Co., Inc.
153 E. 57th St.   Dept. OHJ
New York, NY 10022
(212) 758-0780
RS/O
Shop carries a full line of decorative hardware in brass, bronze, iron. Furniture hardware, bathroom accessories, etc. No literature.

Hunter Div. - Robbins & Myers
PO Box 14775   Dept. OHJ
Memphis, TN 38114
(901) 743-1360
DIST
Manufacturer of "Olde Tyme Ceiling Fan", little changed from models introduced in 1903. Hunter offers two sizes (36" and 52"), four motor finishes (brass, black, antique white, chestnut brown) and three choices of blades (pecan finish, antique white finish, cone insert). Blades are mounted on hardwood irons, available in colors to match motors, which allows a multitude of combinations. Illustrated catalog $1.00. Brochure free.

Hurley Patentee Lighting
R.D. 7 - Box 98A   Dept. OHJ
Kingston, NY 12401
(914) 331-5414
RS/O   MO
17th and 18th century lights reproduced by hand from fixtures in museums and private collections. These unusual lights are authentic in appearance thanks to a special aging process. Over 150 tin, iron and brass bettys, candleholders, sconces, lanterns and chandeliers. A few non-lighting items — a bootscraper, iron firescreen and candle extinguishers. Illustrated catalog and price list — $2.

Huseman, Richard J. Co.
2824 Stanton Avenue   Dept. OHJ
Cincinnati, OH 45206
(513) 861-7980
RS/O
Company has 45 years of experience in all phases of renovation and re-construction of some of the finest historical homes, churches and institutions in the Cincinnati area. They have their own cabinet shop for duplicating woodwork in every detail. No literature.

Huskisson Masonry & Exterior Building Restoration Co.
Box 949, 148 Jefferson St.   Dept. OHJ
Lexington, KY 40587
(606) 252-5011
RS/O
Contracting masonry restoration, renovation, reconstruction, and new masonry construction. Services available in Kentucky only. No literature.

• **Hyde Manufacturing Company**
54 Eastford Road, Dept N   Dept. OHJ
Southbridge, MA 01550
(617) 764-4344
DIST
A long established manufacturer of tools designed to prepare surfaces for painting, decorating and refinishing. Among the tools are — joint knives, paint, wood and wallpaper scrapers, putty knives, seam rollers, craft knives. Illustrated how-to book and catalog — $1.00.

Hydrozo Coatings Co.
855 W Street   Dept. OHJ
Lincoln, NE 68501
(402) 477-6981
MO   DIST
Established manufacturer of water-repellent exterior coatings. Masonry coatings, wood coatings protect surface without creating impermeable film. Also manufactures a sealer/preservative for wood that protects against rot and fungus, but contains safer zinc compounds — not mercury or chlorine compounds. Free literature.

I

Iberia Millwork
500 Jane Street   Dept. OHJ
New Iberia, LA 70560
(318) 365-5644
MO
New custom-made exterior wood rolling-slat shutter: hand stapled w/round crown copper coated staple. Shutters also appropriate for interior use as blinds. Standard fixed-slat shutters are available. Circle head shutters can also be fabricated. No literature; Photographs and scale drawings available free of charge for serious inquiries.

• **Ice Nine Glass Design**
1507 S. 6th St.   Dept. OHJ
Minneapolis, MN 55454
(612) 375-9669
MO   RS/O
The Ice Nine Collection includes glass designs from 18th, 19th and 20th century woodcuts and copper engravings. There are stock patterns in two sizes, but they can also etch any design to any size you wish. Catalog is $2.00, refundable with first order.

Illinois Bronze Paint Co.
300 East Main Street   Dept. OHJ
Lake Zurich, IL 60047
(312) 438-8201
DIST
All purpose high gloss spray paints, epoxy spray paints, brush-on latex enamels, anti-rust enamels. Free literature.

• **Illustrious Lighting**
1812 Divisadero St.   Dept. OHJ
San Francisco, CA 94115
(415) 922-3133
RS/O
Restoration of lighting fixtures — antique gas-electric chandeliers a specialty. Over 100 in shop restored & for sale. Reproductions also available. No literature, but letters will be answered with photos of available antique or reproduction fixtures.

Image Group, The
398 So. Grant Ave.   Dept. OHJ
Columbus, OH 43215
(614) 221-1016
RS/O
Architectural and interior design services in the area ob building rehabilitation and restoration as well as specializing in "Theme" restaurant design. Offices across the country. No literature.

Import Specialists, Inc.
82 Wall Street   Dept. OHJ
New York, NY 10005
(212) 248-1633
DIST
Importers and distributors of various kinds of natural fiber matting and rugs; i.e. sisal, coco, rice straw, seagrass, etc. An extensive selection of cotton rag rugs and dhurries. Distributed nationally to many large department stores and specialty stores like Bloomingdale's, Room & Board, Marshall Field's, etc. You can write for name of nearest retail store, but they do not sell outside of the trade.

Industrial Plastic Supply Co.
309 Canal Street   Dept. OHJ
New York, NY 10013
(212) 226-2010
RS/O   MO
Sells mould-making compounds and casting materials for modern casting process. Stock includes polyester resin, fiberglass reinforcing strands, RTV rubber. Primarily a distributor with walk-in business, but they'll quote prices and arrange mail- order if necessary. How-to book also available: Plastics for Craftsmen, $7.45 ppd. No other literature.

Industrial Woodworking, Inc.
1331 Leithton Rd.   Dept. OHJ
Mundelein, IL 60060
(312) 367-9080
MO
Industrial Woodworking, Inc., is a full service mill featuring stock as well as custom interior woodwork and mouldings. Detailed brochure available.

Inglenook
523 Hudson Street   Dept. OHJ
New York, NY 10014
(212) 675-0890
MO   RS/O
An antiques shop specializing in American furniture and decorations of the 19th century. Also sell architectural details such as stained glass windows, fretwork and mantel pieces. Since they do not deal in new manufactured merchandise, there is no catalogue; however, photographs furnished upon request. Extensive restoration experience.

● = Consult ad for more details. See Advertisers' Index on the last page of this Catalog.

Inner Harbor Lumber & Hardware
900 Fleet St.   Dept. OHJ
Baltimore, MD 21202
(301) 837-0202
RS/O
Renovation products center in downtown Baltimore. Stock includes structural as well as decorative materials. (Bricks, framing lumber, flooring, treated lumber, gutters, plumbing & electrical; also Fypon moulding, decorative hardware, ABR chemicals, shutters.) Custom orders on replacement window sash. No literature.

Interior Decorations
48-52 Lincoln Street   Dept. OHJ
Exeter, NH 03833
(603) 778-0406
RS/O
17th — 18th — 19th century interior restoration throughout New England by decorator Jane Kent Rockwell. Specializing in period draperies, documentary fabrics, wallcoverings and carpets. Lectures given. No literature.

International Architecture
1309 Montana Ave.   Dept. OHJ
El Paso, TX 79902
(915) 533-9735
RS/O
Suppliers of complete architectural packages, working through architects, designers, & contractors. Special connections to old-world artisans in stone carving, ceramics, iron mongery, other traditional crafts. Fountains, arches, stone columns; marble & terra-cotta flooring; park benches; ornamental iron all available. Call or write; literature free to the building trade.

International Building Components
Box 51   Dept. OHJ
Glenwood, NY 14069
(716) 592-2953
DIST
Cupolas, carved wooden mantels, china cabinets, ironing board cabinets, and spiral and circular stair components. Sold through distributors. Product literature is free — please specify your interest.

International Consultants, Inc.
227 South Ninth St.   Dept. OHJ
Philadelphia, PA 19107
(215) 923-8888
RS/O
Company is versed in project management, cost estimating and CPM scheduling. Has performed design and project management services for many historic restoration projects in the Mid-Atlantic and New England states. Brochure free.

Iron Horse Antiques, Inc.
R.D. No. 2   Dept. OHJ
Poultney, VT 05764
(802) 287-4050
RS/O   MO
Specializes in old and antique tools. Also carries books dealing with restoration, tools, crafts, etc. Antique tool and book catalog, illustrated and with price list, is published twice a year at $6 per year.

Iron-A-Way, Inc.
220 W. Jackson   Dept. OHJ
Morton, IL 61550
(309) 266-7232
MO   DIST
Manufacturers of built-in ironing centers. Several models; many safety features. Free literature.

Island City Wood Working Co.
1801 Avenue C   Dept. OHJ
Galveston, TX 77550
(713) 765-5727
MO   RS/O
Made-to-order cypress movable slat shutters, old oversize cypress doors, sash, sash doors, balusters, and walnut hand rail. Brass, hardware, restoration materials. Custom millwork since 1908. Wood mantels (old marble and slate also available.) No literature.

● **Itinerant Artist**
Box 222   Dept. OHJ
Falls Church, VA 22046
(703) 241-8371
DIST   RS/O
Over 300 durable plastic stencils for walls, floors, fabric, furniture, glass, tile, and tin. Patterns include New England Reproduction, Pennsylvania Dutch, Classic, Colonial Virginia, Victorian, and Contemporary. Accent and recreation stencil paper available; also doll house kits. Stencils are easily cut and applied using latex or oil house paint. Custom patterns also available. Catalog of reduced patterns with instructions, $4 plus $.50 postage.

Itinerant Reproductions, Inc.
261 Hinman Lane   Dept. OHJ
Southbury, CT 06488
(203) 264-8000
MO   DIST   RS/O
Wall and floor stencilling from Early American patterns. Also hand-stencilled fireboards, used in Colonial homes to close off firebox in the summer. They also do stencil restoration, consultation, research, and lectures. Brochure, $1.00.

J

● **JMR Products**
1335 Main St.   Dept. JC
St. Helena, CA 94574
(707) 963-2077
MO   DIST
Reproduction Victorian screen doors; four decorative styles available in stock or custom sizes. Free brochure.

Jacobsen, Charles W., Inc.
401 S. Salina St.   Dept. OHJ
Syracuse, NY 13202
(315) 471-6522
RS/O   MO
3000 or more handmade Oriental rugs - new, used, semi-antique and antique - in many sizes are in stock at all times. The company, whose president is a recognized authority in the field, keeps its prices below the market level by acting as direct importers or contractors on new rugs and by volume of retail and mail order sales. Free and very complete, helpful and informative literature and descriptive lists.

Janovic/Plaza, Inc.
1292 First Ave.   Dept. OHJ
New York, NY 10021
(212) 535-8960
RS/O   MO
Store has probably the largest stock of specialty painting and decorating supplies in the U.S. Will also service mail orders. No literature.

Jaxon Co., Inc.
PO Box 618, 118 N. Orange Ave.   Dept. OHJ
Eufaula, AL 36027
(205) 687-8031
MO   RS/O
Representatives of Jaxon Co. are available to assist customers plan and implement historical & civic markers, signage & monument programs. Range of products is from metal castings (bronze or aluminum) to sculpted marble and granite. Call or write for further information.

Jennifer House
Dept. OJ   Dept. OHJ
Great Barrington, MA 01230
(413) 528-1500
MO   RS/O
Their 96-page catalog offers fine gifts, decorative accessories, dinnerware, flatware, rugs, lamps, furniture, etc. Also Early American hardware and authentic reproduction of Early American furniture.

Jennings, Gottfried, Cheek/Preservationists
Box 1890   Dept. OHJ
Ames, IA 50010
(515) 292-7192
RS/O
Provides historic preservation services, including architectural, archeological, and historic surveys; cultural resource analysis; preservation planning; preservation implementation through public policy and private initiative; neighborhood conservation planning; public education including volunteer training; preparation of National Register forms and certification applications; rehabilitation guidelines; interior or exterior design consultation; townscape design. Send SASE for free literature.

● **Jennings Lights of Yesterday**
1523 San Pablo Ave.   Dept. OHJ
Berkeley, CA 94702
(415) 526-1008
RS/O   MO
Original restored chandeliers and wall sconces from the 1800's to 1920's. They also make reproduction brass chandeliers and wall sconces; brass towel bars and tissue holders. Also pull-chain toilets, oak seats, and brass plumbing fixtures. No literature available.

Jo-El Shop
7120 Hawkins Creamery Rd.   Dept. OHJ
Laytonsville, MD 20760
(301) 972-4100
RS/O
Specialists in restored electric and gas-electric lamps and light fixtures installed when a house was first electrified in 1890-1930's. Most are solid brass with glass shades, some with bulbs 50 to 75 years old. Call for information and/or appointment. No literature.

Johnson Paint Co.
355 Newbury St.   Dept. OHJ
Boston, MA 02115
(617) 536-4838
RS/O   MO
A specialty paint distributor catering to the Boston restoration market. They will ship hard-to-find calcimine paint on receipt of a written order and payment (no COD's). Minimum order 25 lbs. of powder (makes between 12-15 qts). Please call for current prices & shipping charges before ordering.

Johnson, R.L. Interiors
312 South Fifth East   Dept. OHJ
Missoula, MT 59801
(406) 549-2061
MO   RS/O
Competitively-priced suppliers for leading reproduction and quality wallcoverings, fabrics, trims, and carpets. Delivery 2-3 weeks from order date. Quotations given at no charge. Free cuttings available when customer sends color sample and indicates desired material. Call for prices; no literature available.

The Johnsons/Historic Preservation Consultants
831 N. Magnum St.   Dept. OHJ
Durham, NC 27701
(919) 682-1061
RS/O
Preservation-planning consultants. Also specialists in woodgraining, marbleizing, and stencilling. They will work anywhere in North America on a cost-plus basis — each job requires an individual estimate. (Estimates free except for travel expenses.) No literature, but all inquiries will be answered.

Jonathan Studios, Inc.
619 South 10th Street   Dept. OHJ
Minneapolis, MN 55404
(612) 338-0213
RS/O   MO
Custom ceramic tiles for fireplace mantels, kitchen backsplashes, and bathroom wainscoting; ceramic tile murals. Stained, leaded, and etched glass. Fireplace mantels. Brochures, $1.00.

Jones Interior Design
5617 Wonder Drive   Dept. OHJ
Ft. Worth, TX 76133
(817) 292-3964
RS/O
An interior design firm specializing in preserving the period feeling of old homes. They will match paints and restore wallpapers where possible. No literature.

Jotul U.S.A., Inc.
343 Forest Ave., PO Box 1157   Dept. OHJ
Portland, ME 04104
(207) 775-0757
DIST
United States subsidiary of A/S Jotul, Oslo, Norway, manufacturer of Jotul cast-iron wood and coal burning stoves and combi-fires. All models UL-listed and ICBO-approved. Enamelled stoves available in red and green. Free brochures and flyers on request.

KEY TO ABBREVIATIONS

MO = sells by Mail Order

RS/O = sells through Retail Store or Office

DIST = sells through Distributors

ID = sells only through Interior Designers or Architects

K

Kaplan, Matthew L./Architect
808 Union St.   Dept. OHJ
Brooklyn, NY 11215
(212) 789-8537
RS/O
Architectural firm specializing in brownstones, townhouses, restoration and adaptive re-use of old buildings and commercial interiors. Metropolitan NYC area. No literature.

• **Kayne, Steve — Hand-Forged Hardware**
17 Harmon Place   Dept. OHJ
Smithtown, NY 11787
(516) 724-3669
RS/O   MO
Custom blacksmith work, hardware, fireplace tools, cranes, andirons, dutch-oven doors, enclosures, hooks, brackets, candlesticks, wall & ceiling fixtures, drawer/door hardware, locks repaired/restored, gate & shutter hardware, boot scrapers, kitchen utensils. Sand cast brass & bronze interior/exterior hardware, hinges, thumb latches, ice box hardware, door knockers. Repairs & restorations. Fireplace tools; custom forged hardware; cast brass & bronze hardware catalog—$1 each. Please specify. Basics of blacksmithing booklet—$2. Packet of all catalogs—$3.50.

• **Kenneth Lynch & Sons, Inc.**
Box 488   Dept. OHJ
Wilton, CT 06897
(203) 762-8363
MO
Metal cornice parts, ornamental gutters & leaders, weathervanes...thousands of stamped metal designs made from original dies. Work done in copper, lead, zinc, etc. Also brass parts for chandeliers; cast stone garden ornament. Cast iron garden furniture, sun dials, park benches, & bldg. ornaments of all kinds. Custom hammerwork. Architectural Sheet Metal Ornament cat. 7474—$3.50. Garden Ornament book 2076—$7.50. Other architectural handbooks available. Free folder on roof snow guards; free flyer — Oriel Windows.

Kensington Historical Co.
RFD   Dept. OHJ
East Kingston, NH 03827
(603) 778-0686
RS/O   MO
All services provided for the authentic restoration of 18th century New England buildings. Structural inventory of antique house parts always includes hand-hewn beams, random-width floorboards, antique millwork (doors, entryways, etc.), beaded sheathing, wainscot and panelling, staircases. Also supply salvaged glass, brick, hardware. Custom blacksmithing and millwork. Consulting, dating, and design services. Dismantling and re-erection of 18th century homes throughout U.S. Free brochure.

Kentucky Wood Floors, Inc.
7761 National Turnpike   Dept. OHJ
Louisville, KY 40214
(502) 368-5836
DIST
Full line of wood flooring. Random-width planks in oak, ash, walnut and cherry. Specialists for new parquet floor installations. Also sell contrasting strip borders. Literature, $1.00.

Keuning, George
24 Fence Lane   Dept. OHJ
Levittown, NY 11756
(516) 735-2937
RS/O
Company specializes in the exterior restoration of masonry buildings, including brownstone repair, cleaning and waterproofing. No literature; call for appointment.

Keystone Furniture Stripping
3201 Adams Ave.   Dept. OHJ
San Diego, CA 92116
(714) 280-1337
RS/O
Restoration service for San Diego area. Stripping, repairing, and refinishing of furniture and architectural details, such as doors and mouldings, window frames, mantels. Some custom wood-turning work done. Also carry a line of restoration supplies including hardware, lighting fixtures, veneers, caning materials, and refinishing supplies. Booklet, 'A Guide to Furniture Restoration' is available by mail for $2.50.

Kimball Furniture Company
1549 Royal Street   Dept. OHJ
Jasper, IN 47546
(812) 482-1600
DIST
Manufacturers of authentic 19th century Victorian reproductions. Company uses hand-carved solid Honduras mahogany, Italian marble, and Belgian fabrics for detailed reproductions. Products include sofas, chairs, tables, complete dining room, and various accent pieces. A free color brochure is available.

• **King's Chandelier Co.**
Highway 14   Dept. OHJ
Eden, NC 27288
(919) 623-6188
RS/O   MO
A huge collection of chandeliers, sconces and candelabra — each assembled from imported and domestic parts that are designed and maintained by the company. There are Victorian styles, and elegant formal 18th century crystal ones, including Strass crystal. Also early American brass and pewter ones. 96 page illustrated catalogue — $1.50.

• **Kingsway**
4723 Chromium Drive   Dept. OHJ
Colorado Springs, CO 80918
(303) 599-4512
MO
They sell Victorian restoration materials: gingerbread brackets and fretwork, stair parts, door and window casings, brass hardware for doors and bathrooms, panelling, wainscotting, wood shingles, front doors, plaster and composition ornaments, mouldings, and wood fiber carvings. Catalog, $2.50.

Kittinger Company
1883 Elmwood Avenue   Dept. OHJ
Buffalo, NY 14207
(716) 876-1000
DIST   ID
Kittinger traditional furniture including Williamsburg and Historic Newport Furniture Reproductions may be seen at Kittinger showrooms, and is sold through accredited furniture dealers and interior designers. 180-page catalog: "Library of 18th-Century English and American Designs", $8.

Klinke & Lew Contractors
1304 Greene Street   Dept. OHJ
Silverton, CO 81433
(303) 387-5713
RS/O   MO
Specializing in Victorian construction and restoration. Distributors for W.F. Norman Co. pressed tin ceilings in Western Colorado. No literature.

Klise Manufacturing Company
601 Maryland Ave.   Dept. OHJ
Grand Rapids, MI 49505
(616) 459-4283
MO   DIST
Furniture and cabinet work. Manufactures decorative carved-wood mouldings and ornaments. Bamboo, ropes, dentils, classical patterns, carved and plain rosettes. Metal furniture grilles of formed or woven wire, brass plated and antiqued. Send two $.18 stamps for Accent Mouldings literature and prices: two $.18 stamps for metal-grille catalog.

• **Kohler Co.**
Dept. OH
Kohler, WI 53044
(414) 457-4441
DIST
Major plumbingware manufacturer offers complete line of period-style products — high-tank, pull-chain toilet with wooden seat; rolled-rim cast iron bathtub with ball-and-claw feet, and antique-style faucets for lavatory and bath installations. Send $1. for colorful brochures. (Also available — turn-of-the-century artwork reproduced from early Kohler Plumbingware Catalogs and printed in brown on beige stock, suitable for framing, $1.50 each, $5.00 for set of four.)

Kool-O-Matic Corp.
1831 Terminal Road   Dept. OHJ
Niles, MI 49120
(616) 683-2600
DIST
This manufacturer of residential ventilating equipment even makes an attic fan concealed in an Early American cupola. Also roof, gable and 'Energy Saving' whole house ventilators, complete with solid state speed controls and timer features. For complete information send $.25.

Koppers Co.
1900 Koppers Bldg.   Dept. OHJ
Pittsburgh, PA 15219
(412) 227-2000
DIST
Manufactures fire-retardant red cedar shakes and shingles. Also produces "Wolmanized" pressure-treated lumber for outdoor use. This process gives long-term termite and rot resistance to economical, plentiful types of wood. How to Build A Deck $1.00/How to Build a Fence $1.00.

Kraatz Hand Blown Glass
RFD 2   Dept. OHJ
Canaan, NH 03741
(603) 523-4289
MO   RS/O
Manufactures hand-blown, wavy bulls-eye window panes with pontil mark in center, appropriate for side lights and transoms in Early American restorations and reproductions. Panes are cut to customer's specifications; sizes from 5 in. x 5 in. to 10 in. x 12 in. Also makes diamond-pane leaded casement windows for 17th century buildings. Brochure, $.50.

G. Krug & Son
415 W. Saratoga St.   Dept. OHJ
Baltimore, MD 21201
(301) 752-3166
RS/O   MO
Specializing in custom restoration of ornamental ironwork such as gates, fences, tables, etc. Work done to customer's drawings or photographs. Fancy blacksmithing work also done. This is the oldest continuously operating iron shop in the country: since 1810. No catalog or regular mail-order procedure.

Kruger Kruger Albenberg
2 Central Square   Dept. OHJ
Cambridge, MA 02139
(617) 661-3812
RS/O
Architects, engineers, builders serving the New York Metropolitan area and New England. Office also at 24 Beverly Rd., West Orange, NJ 07052 (201) 325-8040. Services include determination of replacement cost of construction, investigation of construction problems, construction documents for and construction management of repairs and changes. No literature.

L

Lachin, Albert & Assoc., Inc.
2742 Perdido Street   Dept. OHJ
New Orleans, LA 70119
(504) 821-5404
MO   DIST   RS/O
Architectural sculptors specializing in ornamental plaster and cement work. Ceiling medallions (ornate, 18-60-in.), mouldings, columns and capitals, domes, finials, etc. Reinforced plaster or stone. Custom work. Cement products shop: Columns, finials, fountains, and balustrades. Free flyer.

Lake Shore Markers
P.O. Box 59   Dept. OHJ
Erie, PA 16512
(800) 458-0463
MO
Makes historical markers, date plates, and plaques out of cast aluminum. Also custom ornamental aluminum work. Weatherproof vinyl coatings in many colors can be applied to plaques. Catalog 178 free.

Lamb, J & R Studios
30 Joyce Drive   Dept. OHJ
Spring Valley, NY 10977
(914) 352-3777
RS/O   MO
Established in 1857, they do large-scale restoration, repair, and new work in leaded and stained glass, mosaic, stone, metal, wood, and general decoration. Also install protective covering on stained glass windows. Free brochures.

Lamplighter Shoppe
1507-B Richmond Rd.   Dept. OHJ
Williamsburg, VA 23185
(804) 220-1044
RS/O   MO
Distributes solid brass reproductions of early American & traditional lamps, chandeliers, lanterns and sconces, electric or for candles or oil. Indoor-outdoor lighting fixtures. Catalog, $2.

Landmark Doors
28 Marcy Ave.   Dept. OHJ
Brooklyn, NY 11211
(212) 834-8534
MO
Manufactures doors and wainscotting in Victorian and turn-of-century styles. There are 4 models of panel doors that can be made in any dimension in oak or poplar. Heavy exterior townhouse doors are available in 8/4 or 10/4 thicknesses — with 1-1/4 in. bevelled glass — in poplar or oak. Oak wainscot has matching cap and base. Send $1 for sample of oak wainscotting and cap.

● **Lavoie, John F.**
P.O. Box 15   Dept. OHJ
Springfield, VT 05156
(802) 886-8253
RS/O   MO
Manufacturers of historical windows: Rounds, ovals, fanlights, transoms. Frames are clear pine; double-strength glazing. Brochure $2.00.

Lea, James — Cabinetmaker
Harkness House   Dept. OHJ
Rockport, ME 04856
(207) 236-3632
MO   RS/O
Handcrafted reproductions of 18th century American master cabinetmakers' furniture. Prices compare favorably with commercial reproduction furniture. Illustrated catalog and price list — $1.50

Lee Woodwork Systems
466 Harvey's Bridge Rd.   Dept. OHJ
Unionville, PA 19375
(215) 486-0346
MO   RS/O
Colonial beaded tongue and groove wainscot system, including baseboard, 32 in. vertical beaded boards, chair rail. Hardwoods & clear poplar. Also random-width tongue and groove hardwood flooring: 13/16-inch, hardwoods, end-grain plugs or Tremont nails. Brochure not yet available, so send dimensions and accessory needs for fixed price quote and photo. Shipment anywhere.

Lehman Hardware & Appliances
PO Box 41   Dept. OHJ
Kidron, OH 44636
(216) 857-5441
MO   RS/O
Old-fashioned but still useful appliances from the Amish/Mennonite community. Includes wood-coal-electric stoves; quality tools. Catalog of ranges $1.00. Full catalog — $2.00.

Leichtung, Inc.
4944 Commerce Parkway   Dept. OHJ
Cleveland, OH 44128
(216) 831-6191
MO   RS/O
U.S. distributor of Lervad (Denmark) workbenches, Bracht (Germany) chisels, Sarjent (England) woodthreading tools plus a treasury of fine, difficult-to-find tools from all over the continent. 1979 catalog (64 pages) available for $1.00.

KEY TO ABBREVIATIONS	
MO	= sells by Mail Order
RS/O	= sells through Retail Store or Office
DIST	= sells through Distributors
ID	= sells only through Interior Designers or Architects

Lemee's Fireplace Equipment
815 Bedford St.   Dept. OHJ
Bridgewater, MA 02324
(617) 697-2672
RS/O   MO
Handmade bellows & fireplace accessories & equipment. Also: iron hardware, brass bowls, candlesticks & doorknocker, cast iron banks & doorstops, black doorknockers, cast iron firebacks, copper kettles & buckets, black bath accessories, black & brass eagles, lighting fixtures in brass, copper & black, post lanterns, fireplace cranes, andirons & screens. Plant hooks, black kettles, hooks & umbrella stands. Illustrated catalog & price list of fireplace equipment — $1. refundable with first order.

Leo, Brian
7344 Columbus Ave., S.   Dept. OHJ
Minneapolis, MN 55423
(612) 861-1473
MO
Reproduction 19th century door & window hardware of cast silicon bronze. Several models of hinges, including full exterior door, full-bearing hinges. Knobs, escutcheons, roses and lever handles. Custom reproduction of artifacts. Write for free specifications and complete prices.

Lesco Restorations, Inc.
PO Box 13313   Dept. OHJ
Atlanta, GA 30324
(404) 873-2156
RS/O
Exterior waterproofing and restoration contractor of masonry buildings. Services include stone and brick repointing, all types of caulking, concrete repair, shelf anglerepair, coatings, roof repairs, exterior building cleaning, brick replacement/repair, needle caulking, window replacement and other related waterproofing. Are prepared to submit written budget estimates and set up repair programs. No literature.

Levine Associates
9 Mountain Rd.   Dept. OHJ
Somers, CT 06071
(203) 729-3468
RS/O
Professional design services to the trade.

Lewis, John N.
156 Scarboro Drive   Dept. OHJ
York, PA 17403
MO   RS/O
Antique barometers bought and sold. Mechanical repair and complete restoration for those looking for professional craftsmanship. Unable to ship finished product by way of common carrier — barometers have to be picked up by owner due to the elusiveness of the mercury. No problem with shipping aneroid barometers. No literature.

● **Ley, Joe/Antiques**
620-632 E. Market St.   Dept. OHJ
Louisville, KY 40202
(502) 583-4014
RS/O
Six buildings stocked with architectural antiques. Hard-to-find items including mantels, columns, newels. Specializing in light fixtures, restaurant items, doors, garden ornament, brass hardware, and iron fences/gates. Literature available — $2.00.

● = Consult ad for more details. See Advertisers' Index on the last page of this Catalog.

Liberty of London
229 East 60th St.   Dept. OHJ
New York, NY 10022
(212) 888-1057
ID
Decorator fabrics, including English glazed chintz, all of which are imported from their famous parent store. Through decorators showrooms — no literature.

Lieberman, Howard, P.E.
434 White Plains Rd.   Dept. OHJ
Eastchester, NY 10709
(914) 779-3773
RS/O
Prepurchase building inspection and consulting, engineering services. No literature.

Lisa — Victoria Brass Beds
5747 Charles City Circle   Dept. OHJ
Richmond, VA 23231
(804) 226-9331
MO
Handcrafted solid brass beds, available in many plain-to-fancy Victorian styles. Prices are reasonable. This is a small company and their line of brass beds is available only by mail-order. Color catalog, $3. (refundable).

Litchfield House
Pocket Knife Square   Dept. OHJ
Lakeville, CT 06039
(203) 364-0236
MO   RS/O   DIST
Exclusive importer of English porcelain china door fixtures, cabinet and wardrobe knobs, and radiator humidifiers from Manchester, England. Door knobs, push plates and florets (keyhole covers) available individually or in complete sets in range of antique designs and colors. Complete fittings to U.S. specifications included for simple installations. Tra- ditional decorative china radiator humidifiers available in several designs and antique patterns. Exclusive importer and distributor of cast-iron fireplace grates for coal and wood. Send for free illustrated color brochure.

• **London Venturers Company**
2 Dock Square   Dept. OHJ
Rockport, MA 01966
(617) 546-7161
RS/O   MO
Specializing in original gas, oil, and early electric lighting fixtures: chandeliers, hall lights, wall sconces and table lamps. Also quality reproductions of gas, oil, and early electric lighting, as well as gas and early electric shades. Illustrated catalog, $2.00.

Loose, Thomas — Blacksmith/ Whitesmith
R.D. 2, Box 124   Dept. OHJ
Leesport, PA 19533
(215) 926-4849
MO   RS/O
Hand-wrought items for home and hearth, finely decorated with brass and copper inlay. Kitchen and fireplace utensils and lighting devices. Hardware and other items for old home restoration made to your specifications. Brochure available; please enclose a stamp with your request.

Lost Arts, The
4939 Glenway Avenue   Dept. OHJ
Cincinnati, OH 45238
(513) 471-2390
RS/O
Repair and refinishing of quality furniture — veneer service, inlay repair, custom carving for duplication, regluing. Also duplication of moulding, trim, window sash in the Cincinnati area. No literature.

Louisville Art Glass Studio
1110 Baxter Ave.   Dept. OHJ
Louisville, KY 40204
(502) 585-5421
MO   RS/O
Leaded glass designs and ornaments for home use, designed and manufactured by a 90-year-old company. Custom stained glass. "Creative Leaded Glass", a 32-pg. unbound catalog — $10.00.

Lovelia Enterprises, Inc.
Box 1845, J, Grand Central Sta   Dept. OHJ
New York, NY 10017
(212) 490-0930
MO   RS/O
Importers of machine woven tapestries from France, Belgium and Italy in sizes 10 inches to 10 feet. Gobelin and Aubusson tapestries are woven on old looms from original jacquards in either wool or 100% cotton. Some are copies of masterpieces with the signature of the original artist. 20-page color catalog, $2.

Luczak Brothers, Inc.
4052 N. Elston   Dept. OHJ
Chicago, IL 60618
(312) 478-3570
RS/O
This company does both plain and ornamental plastering in the greater Chicago area. No literature — please call.

Ludowici-Celadon Co.
P.O. Box 69   Dept. OHJ
New Lexington, OH 43764
(614) 342-1995
MO   RS/O   DIST
Manufactures wide range of handsome ceramic roofing tiles. Free product data sheets on each style, which include: Barrel mission style, Spanish and various interlocking roof tiles, also flat ceramic shingle tile.

Luigi Crystal
7332 Frankford Ave.   Dept. OHJ
Philadelphia, PA 19136
(215) 338-2978
MO
Painted glass Victorian table lamps, cut crystal chandeliers, hurricane lamps, sconces. Reasonably priced. Imported crystal prisms. Illustrated catalog & price list — $.50.

Lundberg Studios
P.O. Box 26   Dept. OHJ
Davenport, CA 95017
(408) 423-2532
MO   DIST
They offer a variety of art glass, including Tiffany-style surface decorated paper-weights and vases. They specialize in lamps and shades imitating Tiffany and Steuben shades. Over 20 different shades in Art Nouveau style available. Metal lamp bases and replacement parts also available. They will buy or trade for original Tiffany lamp bases. Quantity discounts offered to distributors. Individuals can order from $3 color catalog.

Lyemance International
P.O. Box 6651   Dept. OHJ
Louisville, KY 40206
(502) 896-2441
MO   DIST
Top-sealing fireplace damper saves energy; reduces heat loss by controlling down drafts when fireplace is not in use. Seals out birds and insects, keeps out rain, sleet and snow and saves on air conditioning costs. The damper is shut by means of a stainless-steel cable that extends down the flue to the firebox, where it is secured to a bracket on the side firebox wall. Installed on chimney tops. Brochure free.

M

• **Mad River Wood Works**
P.O. Box 163   Dept. OHJ
Arcata, CA 95521
(707) 826-0629
MO
Manufactures of ornate restoration house parts in redwood. Includes several Victorian patterns of ornamental shingles, mouldings, old-style screen door replicas. Custom work also. Free literature.

Magnolia Hall
726 Andover Dr., Dept. OH9   Dept. OHJ
Atlanta, GA 30327
(404) 256-4747
MO
Well-built, solid mahogany, hand-carved Victorian reproduction furniture. Some brass and oak pieces. Collection of highly-carved Louis XIV French sofas, chairs. Also lamps, clocks, mirrors, footstools. Large selection of whatnot stands and wall curio cabinets. 80-page illustrated catalog and fabric samples — $1.00.

Manchester Lite
P.O. Box 143   Dept. OHJ
Manchester, MA 01944
(617) 526-4706
MO
Reproduction millwork, specializing in custom window sash and frames. Fanlights, ovals, and round windows are available pre-hung or sash only — information and price list available on request. Custom work and design also accepted. Free flyer.

Mangione Plaster and Tile and Stucco
21 John St.   Dept. OHJ
Saugerties, NY 12477
(914) 246-9863
RS/O
Specializes in the restoration of ornamental plasterwork. Will also reproduce plaster domes and mouldings. Serving upstate New York area. No literature.

Manor Art Glass
20 Ridge Road   Dept. OHJ
Douglaston, NY 11363
(212) 631-8029
RS/O   MO
Professionally trained craftsmen will restore your antique stained glass windows to their original strength and beauty, either in your home or at their studio. Will create new windows to blend with the period architecture of your home. Slides available on specific request.

Mansion Industries, Inc.
14711 East Clark   Dept. OHJ
Industry, CA 91745
(213) 968-9501
DIST
Hemlock stairparts in traditional styles: newel posts, balusters, and railings. Installation instructions, architectural tracing details, reference wall charts, audio-visual training films — all available on request. Contact Customer Service Dept. for direct assistance.

Mantia, Philip
227 E. Ross St.   Dept. OHJ
Lancaster, PA 17602
(717) 291-9071
RS/O
Professional painter/decorator offers services in paperhanging, ornamental plasterwork, graining, and the repair of stucco. Free estimates; no literature.

Marble Technics Ltd.
40 E. 58th St.   Dept. OHJ
New York, NY 10022
(212) 750-9189
DIST   RS/O
Real Italian marble is available now at costs comparable to quality hardwood flooring, carpeting, or ceramic tile. Tiles are cut in easy-to-handle 6" x 6" x 1/4" size and can be used over any sound surface as flooring, wall covering, or fireplace facing. Available in 15 colors. Send $12.50 for designer's sample kit or write for free color brochure.

MarLe Company
170 Summer St.   Dept. OHJ
Stamford, CT 06904
(203) 348-2645
RS/O   MO
Individually fabricated lanterns of brass and copper - most for exterior use, but some suitable for interiors. Designs are taken from the 50 year old company's collection of antique lanterns. Primarily early American in style, there are 2 designs specifically for Victorian and turn-of-the-century houses. Also custom-made work. Catalog with photos of 18 lanterns and price list — $2.

● **Marshall Imports**
713 South Main   Dept. 15
Mansfield, OH 44907
(419) 756-3814
MO
Sole United States importer of Antiquax, the pure wax polish used by museums. Gives a soft mellow sheen, will not fingerprint, produces a deep patina on both antique and contemporary finishes. Ideal for kitchen cupboards. Sold through better stores or by mail. A brochure describing Antiquax products is available at no charge.

Marshalltown Trowel Co.
PO Box 738   Dept. OHJ
Marshalltown, IA 50158
(515) 754-6100
DIST
Trowels and other tools for working with cement, brick, concrete block, dry wall and plaster. Free illustrated catalog. A useful 24 pg. booklet "Troweling Tips and Techniques" is available for $1.00.

Martha M. House
1022 So. Decatur Street   Dept. OHJ
Montgomery, AL 36104
(205) 264-3558
RS/O   MO
A large mail-order source for Victorian reproduction furniture. Hand-carved solid mahogany pieces; tables with wood or Carrara marble tops. Sofas, chairs, bedroom and dining furniture. Large choice of covers and finishes. "Southern Heirlooms" catalog (includes a line of brass beds) — $1.00.

Mason & Sullivan Co.
39 Blossom Ave.   Dept. 4512
Osterville, MA 02655
(617) 428-5726
MO   RS/O
Heirloom-quality clock kits, movements, and dials. Also assembled clocks, specialty tools, and books. Catalog, $1..

● = Consult ad for more details. See Advertisers' Index on the last page of this Catalog.

Master Wood Carver
103 Corrine Dr.   Dept. OHJ
Pennington, NJ 08534
(609) 737-9364
MO   RS/O
Handcrafts authentic Colonial reproduction pieces in solid wood. Each item is signed and numbered. Antique restoration and repair expertly done. Custom pieces from drawings or pictures. Please call for appointment or send $.50 for introductory brochure.

Master's Stained and Etched Glass Studio
729 West 16th St., No. B-1   Dept. OHJ
Costa Mesa, CA 92627
(714) 548-4951
RS/O   MO
Painted, leaded, etched and bevelled glass. Residential and commercial commissions. Antique windows. No literature.

Matchmakers, Inc.
1718 Airport Ct.   Dept. OHJ
Placerville, CA 95667
(916) 626-5672
MO   RS/O
Can match missing pieces from old Haviland and Noritake china sets. Send them pattern name and number with a list of pieces needed. If name and/or number does not appear on backmark of china, send them a damaged piece you can spare. A $5 charge for identification of unknown patterns. No literature.

Mather's
31 E. Main Street   Dept. OHJ
Westminster, MD 21157
MO
Old-fashioned calico curtains. Full catalog with 50 swatches, $1.

Mathis Fine Furniture Restoration
1141 Washington St.   Dept. OHJ
Harpers Ferry, WV 25425
(304) 535-2385
RS/O
Specializes in the repair and restoration of antique furniture and antique clocks. Estimates provided. Pick-up and delivery arranged. Serving the greater Washington, D.C. area. No literature.

Mattia, Louis
980 2nd Ave.   Dept. OHJ
New York, NY 10022
(212) 753-2176
RS/O
This little store is full of Victorian and turn-of-century lighting fixtures. Mattia restores, rewires, adds antique or reproduction glass shades. Hundreds of wall sconces — wired or for candles. Cannot handle mail orders. No literature.

● **Maurer & Shepherd, Joyners**
122 Naubuc Ave.   Dept. OHJ
Glastonbury, CT 06033
(203) 633-2383
RS/O   MO
Handcrafted custom-made interior and exterior 18th century architectural trim. Finely-detailed Colonial doors and windows, shutters, wainscot and wall panelling, carved details, pediments, etc. Wide pine and oak flooring, half-lapped. Pegged mortise and tenon joints — authentic work. Free brochure.

Mazza Frame and Furniture Co., Inc.
35-10 Tenth Street   Dept. OHJ
Long Island City, NY 11106
(212) 721-9287
RS/O   MO
Manufacturers of hardwood furniture frames in period styles. Mail orders shipped throughout the U.S. and overseas. Firm sells primarily to decorators and upholstery shops. Can handle variations of standard designs, and custom work. Free brochure; prices and specific photos on request.

McAvoy Antique Lighting
1901 Lafayette Avenue   Dept. OHJ
St. Louis, MO 63104
(314) 773-9136
RS/O   MO
Large stock of restored antique lighting fixtures available. Ornate gas and electric fixtures, oil lights, circa 1910 chain fixtures, many wall sconces, as well as antique and reproduction ceiling fans. Design and rebuilding of fixtures on specific order. Shipping pre-arranged by customers request. Sample sheet — send SASE. Photos of specific items are $.50 each. Please: Always call for an appointment.

McCloskey Varnish Co.
7600 State Road   Dept. OHJ
Philadelphia, PA 19136
(215) 624-4400
DIST
Manufactures a complete line of wood finishing and refinishing products, stains, sealers, floor varnishes, rubbing varnishes, and polyurethanes. No literature.

McGivern, Barbara — Artist
8680 Market Place   Dept. OHJ
Oak Creek, WI 53154
(414) 762-0849
MO   RS/O
Will do renderings of old homes from your photo (returnable) for paintings/logos/stationery, etc. Full color or black & white — $10.00.

● **McNair Construction Co.**
Box 6414   Dept. OHJ
Baltimore, MD 21230
MO
Manufacturer and mail-order supplier for wooden inside- mounting storm windows. Poplar frames, acrylic glazing — they are invisible from outside and installation does not mar woodwork. Made to customer's specifications; shipped unfinished. Easy to install. For double-hung windows, and some casements. Send $.50 for brochure.

KEY TO ABBREVIATIONS

MO   = sells by Mail Order

RS/O = sells through Retail Store or Office

DIST = sells through Distributors

ID   = sells only through Interior Designers or Architects

Mead Associates Woodworking, Inc.
63 Tiffany Place   Dept. OHJ
Brooklyn, NY 11231
(212) 855-3884
RS/O
Fine custom cabinets and furniture, architectural woodworking, and millwork. Work from architectural drawings only. Cabinetmakers to The Old-House Journal. No literature; references available; call for appointment.

Meierjohan — Wengler, Inc.
10330 Wayne Ave.   Dept. OHJ
Cincinnati, OH 45215
(513) 771-6074
MO
Firm has been making cast tablets and markers for over 50 years. Available in a variety of stock shapes or special sizes. Emblems, symbols or crests can be incorporated to create a special one-of-a-kind design. Choice of material: Bronze, aluminum or silver-bronze. Can also do lost-wax casting. Catalog: $1.00.

Melotte-Morse Studios
3 Old State Capitol Plaza S.   Dept. OHJ
Springfield, IL 62701
(217) 789-9515
RS/O
Melotte-Morse Studios designs, fabricates and renovates stained glass art for ecclesiastical, commercial, and individual clients. A division of Melotte-Morse, Architects and Planners, the Studio also works extensively with existing antique glass works, performing corrective maintenance and restorative repairs or renovations. The studio has refurbished entire stained glass collections for churches as well as individual panels for residential reinstallation. Brochure is free.

Memphis Hardwood Flooring Co.
P.O. Box 7253   Dept. OHJ
Memphis, TN 38107
(901) 526-7306
DIST
Hardwood flooring available through distributors. Colorful 12-page catalog available $.50 postpaid.

Mercer Tile & Pottery Works
130 Mercer St.   Dept. OHJ
Jersey City, NJ 07302
(201) 432-0489
RS/O
Custom design, painting, and replication of ceramic tiles. Specializing in tiles for restoration work, including fireplace surrounds, kitchens. Will try to match old tiles or produce reasonable facsimiles. NY-NJ metropolitan area. Free estimate on receipt of a specific request.

Meredith Stained Glass Studio, Inc.
8472-C Tyco Road   Dept. OHJ
Tysons Corner, VA 22180
(703) 442-8322
RS/O   MO
Stained glass restoration and repair. Specialize in design and fabrication of stained and etched glass art pieces. Expert reproductions of period styles, notably Victorian, Nouveau, and deco. Full line of new and reproduction ornamental glass products, including stained, beveled, etched, and sandblasted glass in lead, copper, foil, or zinc. Clear antique glass for windows and furniture fronts. No literature; showroom open to public, inquiries welcome.

• **Metals by Maurice**
73 Burnside St.   Dept. OHJ
Lowell, MA 01851
(617) 452-9339
MO
Copper lanterns — Orleans, Tall and Stable, made in the old tradition of cutting the metal free-hand, and hammering and shaping all by hand. Prices range from $130 to $250. For more information, send SASE.

Mexico House
Box 970   Dept. OHJ
Del Mar, CA 92014
(714) 481-6099
MO   RS/O
A good source for chandeliers, candleabra and lighting fixtures suitable for Spanish Colonial houses. Also custom design work for Spanish Colonial fittings: Window grilles, rails, outdoor furniture, fireplace screens and tools. Catalog $2. (refundable with purchase).

Michael-Regan Wood Turnings
14711 E. Clark Avenue   Dept. OHJ
Industry, CA 91745
(213) 968-9501
DIST
Railings and turned balusters, post-tops and finials, stair parts; all stock items in machine-sanded clear hemlock. Some of this large standard stock could be appropriate for period houses. Available through distributors; free literature — please specify interest.

• **Michael's Fine Colonial Products**
Rte 44, RD1, Box 179A   Dept. OHJ
Salt Point, NY 12578
(914) 677-3960
MO
Custom-made millwork appropriate for 19th century as well as Colonial houses: Divided light sash; circle head sash; Gothic, triangle, and segment windows; raised panel blinds & shutters; stock and custom stair parts; doors. Mouldings to pattern. Free flyer.

Michels, Dale/Illustrator
1126 Avery Street   Dept. OHJ
Parkersburg, WV 26101
(304) 422-1147
MO
Offers a variety of artistic services, possibly as a fund raising tool. Limited edition prints & post cards for community and/or commercial restoration projects can be done for 50% of the revenues generated after costs. Will also do home portraits. Pen & ink prices range from $150. — $300., water color and other media available. Write for free samples.

KEY TO ABBREVIATIONS

MO = sells by Mail Order

RS/O = sells through Retail Store or Office

DIST = sells through Distributors

ID = sells only through Interior Designers or Architects

Midwest Spiral Stair Company
2153 W. Division Street   Dept. OHJ
Chicago, IL 60622
(312) 227-8461
MO   RS/O
A complete selection of spiral stairs in both metal and wood, shipped anywhere in the U.S. Flyer available.

Miles Lumber Co, Inc.
Railroad Avenue   Dept. OHJ
Arlington, VT 05250
(802) 375-2525
RS/O
Custom millwork from shop drawings or architect's drawings. No stock items; no literature.

Millbranth, D.R.
RR No. 2, Box 462   Dept. OHJ
Hillsboro, NH 03244
(603) 464-5244
RS/O   MO
18th century furniture reproductions and adaptations. No literature.

Millen Roofing Co.
2247 N. 31 St.   Dept. OHJ
Milwaukee, WI 53208
MO   RS/O
Tile and slate roofing. Large supply of old types of roofing tile and weathered slate for restoration work. Tools, equipment, copper nails, copper clips and fasteners, brass snow guards also available. Does consulting, design, specifications, and inspections. No literature.

Miller, Howard Clock Co.
860 E. Main   Dept. OHJ
Zeeland, MI 49464
(616) 772-9131
DIST   ID
Reproductions and adaptations of antique wall, mantel, and grandfather clocks using the finest of woods, movements, and craftsmanship. Sold through fine furniture distributors. Literature free to the trade.

• **Millham, Newton — Blacksmith**
672 Drift Road   Dept. OHJ
Westport, MA 02790
(617) 636-5437
RS/O   MO
Offers a wide selection of 17th, 18th and early 19th century architectural house hardware: latches, spring latches, H and strap hinges, bolts, shutter dogs. Household ironware includes: cooking utensils, hearth items, early candleholders, candlestands, rush lights pipe tongs, etc. Illustrated catalog and price list $1.00.

Millworks Inc.
403 Barre St.   Dept. OHJ
Montpelier, VT 05602
(802) 223-6210
RS/O   MO
Custom architectural millwork and cabinetry. They have 495 antique custom moulding knives, enabling duplication of almost any New England-area moulding. Servicing entire East Coast. No literature; please call about specifications and shipping.

Minwax Company, Inc.
102 Chestnut Ridge Rd.   Dept. HC
Montvale, NJ 07645
(201) 391-0253
DIST
Easy-to-use stains and woodfinishing products for durable, attractive finishes from a 75-year old company. Free literature & color card. Also free: "Tips on Wood Finishing", a 22 page booklet providing do-it-yourselfers with information ranging from how to apply a preservative stain to a house exterior to preparing antiques for refinishing.

Mirror Re-Silvering
Chipmunk Hollow   Dept. OHJ
Millbury, MA 01527
(617) 799-0760
MO   RS/O
Re-silvering, especially to preserve the beveling, etchings etc. of antique mirrors that are not replaceable. Formula dates back to 1700's, giving mirrors an original finish using 60 grams of silver imparting 98% reflectivity, as compared with 78% in today's mirrors. All steps of this traditional process are done by hand. Any size mirror. No literature.

Mittermeir, Frank Inc.
3577 E. Tremont Ave., POB 2   Dept. OHJ
Bronx, NY 10465
(212) 828-3843
MO
Imported and domestic quality tools for woodcarvers, sculptors, engravers, ceramists, and potters. Of special interest are their tools for ornamental plasterwork. They also sell a number of books on sculpture, wood carving, and related arts. Free catalog.

Mohawk Electric Supply Co., Inc.
36 Hudson Street   Dept. OHJ
New York, NY 10013
(212) 227-0466
MO   RS/O
Old-fashioned push-button electric light switches. No catalog. Can ship COD via UPS. Telephone for details and prices.

Moose Creek Restoration, Ltd.
12-22 North Street   Dept. OHJ
Burlington, VT 05401
(802) 862-6765
RS/O
Unique construction company offering design, development, contracting, millwork and cabinetry services. Residential and commercial work: restoration, new additions in appropriate character, and energy-efficient building. Please call; brochure with photos available on request.

Morgan & Company
443 Metropolitan Ave.   Dept. OHJ
Brooklyn, NY 11211
(212) 387-2196
RS/O
Company will bend glass. Can make bent glass to repair tops of leaded glass shades, curio cabinets and china closets. No literature; walk-in shop only.

You'll get better service
when contacting companies
if you mention
The Old-House Journal
Catalog

Morgan Bockius Studios, Inc.
1412 York Road   Dept. OHJ
Warminster, PA 18974
(215) 674-1930
RS/O   MO
Stained, painted, and leaded glass, period and custom designs. Their artists design and craft Victorian and contemporary adaptations for any architectural situation. Coats of arms, and other decorative work available including mirrors, beveled glass, etched and carved panels on clear and tinted glass. Custom designed lamps; repairs to old fixtures including glass bending and painting, and metal work. Call for more information or driving directions. Free brochure.

● **Morgan Woodworking Supplies**
1123 Bardstown Rd.   Dept. OO3K1
Louisville, KY 40204
(502) 456-2545
MO   RS/O
Hardwood lumber and a complete line of veneering supplies. Also embossed furniture mouldings, picture frame mouldings, chair cane, and furniture plans. Free illustrated catalog with simplified veneering instructions.

Moriarty's Lamps
512 Brinkerhoff Avenue   Dept. OHJ
Santa Barbara, CA 93101
(805) 966-1124
RS/O   MO
Sells old chandeliers, wall sconces, kerosene lights, old electric and gas-electric fixtures, old shades. Also metal refinishing and old lamp parts. Also refinishes old doorknobs, window latches, plumbing fixtures, etc. Inquiries answered; no literature.

Morton's Auction Exchange
643 Magazine St.   Dept. OHJ
New Orleans, LA 70190
(504) 561-1196
RS/O
One of the largest auction houses in the South. Specializing in 19th century furniture, clocks and decorations from Europe and America, Morton's usually conducts major estate auctions once a month throughout the year. Morton's also has a retail division specializing in English Antiques. Staff is available for appraisals. Call for price of current catalog.

● **Mosca, Matthew**
PO Box 960, Bowling Green Sta.   Dept. OHJ
New York, NY 10274
(212) 375-9430
RS/O
Historic paint specialist. Microscopic techniques and chemical testing are used to determine the original composition and color of paints and other architectural finishes. Has done work on Mt. Vernon and National Trust properties. Can analyze samples taken by architect or homeowner. Complete interior design capability available utilizing research for restorations and historically compatible rehabilitations. Before taking samples, write describing your needs and objectives.

Moser Brothers, Inc.
3rd & Green Sts.   Dept. OHJ
Bridgeport, PA 19405
(215) 272-1052
MO   RS/O
This company makes quality screen/storm doors and windows in wood. Old styles, choice of patterns and wood species, including Brazilian mahogany. Standard or custom designs, all sized on order. Removable screen or safety-glass panel is held in place by handsome bronze tabs. Also: fine kitchen cabinetwork. Raised-panel, hardwood, etc. Specialists in restoration. Mail orders accepted and shipment arranged. Please call; no literature.

Moultrie Manufacturing Company
PO Drawer 1179   Dept. OHJ
Moultrie, GA 31768
(912) 985-1312
MO   RS/O
Ornamental columns, gates, and fences of cast aluminum. Old South Reproductions catalog shows selection of period-style fence panels and gates; also aluminum furniture, fountains, urns, plaques, etc. Catalog is $1.00.

● **Mountain Lumber Company**
PO Box 285   1327 Carlton Ave.
Dept. OHJ
Charlottesville, VA 22902
(804) 295-1922
RS/O
Dealers in rare and special woods. Also random-width and wide-plank, heart pine flooring; wormy chestnut, old pine, and mahogany paneling. Handhewn and rough-sawn beams. Custom millwork. Brochure and price list available upon request. Also wood samples: $6.50 plus shipping, sent COD (will be refunded with order).

"Mr. Slate" Smid Incorporated
   Dept. OHJ
Sudbury, VT 05733
(802) 247-8809
RS/O
Quality salvaged roofing slate for repair work, resortations, and new construction. Inventory includes most common colors. Also available, new slate from the quarries of the East Coast, with personal service and competitive prices. Write for free literature.

Munsell Color
2441 North Calvert St.   Dept. OHJ
Baltimore, MD 21218
(301) 243-2171
MO   RS/O
The Munsell color notation system is a professional reference resource. In restoring an old house to its original appearance, color samples would be collected and checked against the Munsell Book of Colors. The painter or decorator would then be given the appropriate color codes and could mix the paints accurately. There are two basic books — glossy finish $499.00, and matte finish, $399.00. Free full-color brochure.

● = Consult ad for more details. See Advertisers' Index on the last page of this Catalog.

The Old-House Journal 1982 Catalog   139

Muralo Company
148 E. Fifth St.   Dept. OHJ
Bayonne, NJ 07002
(201) 437-0770
DIST
Besides being the inventor (and major manufacturer) of Spackle, this old company may be the only remaining maker of old-fashioned calcimine paint. Also makes a full line of latex paints, wallpaper adhesives, texture and sand finish, Georgetown colors in latex house paint, 100 percent pure linseed oil house paint, and fire-retardant paint. No literature — please write for name of distributor.

Museum Enterprises, Inc.
211 W. 21st Ave.   Dept. OHJ
Olympia, WA 98501
(206) 753-2580
RS/O   MO   DIST
Carries historic Tumwater Fancy chair with hand stencilled decoration, graining and rawhide seat, also drop leaf tables, nightstands, peg racks, decorated boxes and other decorative items. Victorian interior restoration and consultation by contract. Wholesale and retail. No literature.

Myers Restorations
Box 234   Dept. OHJ
Old Washington, KY 41096
(606) 759-7470
MO
Company will dismantle, transport, rebuild antique hewn log houses throughout United States (and other countries). All houses hand-hewn mixtures of ash, oak, walnut, poplar, chestnut. Range in size from 750 sq. ft. to 2500 sq. ft. Museum-quality restorations only. Write with specific needs. Inquiries answered individually. Serious inquiries only.

Mylen Spiral Stairs
650-I Washington St. Box 350   Dept. OHJ
Peekskill, NY 10566
(914) 739-8486
RS/O   MO   DIST
Spiral Stair Kits: Complete selection of models, options and sizes available in both stock adjustable and custom. made models. Diameters from 3 ft. 6 in. up to 8 ft. All kits include hardware and instructions. No extra tools needed. Open Riser Stair Kits: all kits include hardware and instructions. Free design services or job site planning. $.50 for brochures. Call 800-431-2155.

N

Nassau Flooring Corp.
P.O. 351, 242 Drexel Ave.   Dept. OHJ
Westbury, NY 11590
(516) 334-2327
RS/O   MO
Will reproduce old parquet patterns as well as install new flooring and repair worn floors. No literature.

● **Nast, Vivian**
49 Willow St., 3B   Dept. OHJ
Brooklyn, NY 11201
(212) 596-5280
RS/O
Expert designer and colorist does commission work in stained and leaded glass. Also works in etched glass, both sand blasting and acid-etched. Will reproduce work from existing originals, or will create original designs in period styles. Makes etched patterns in flashed glass. Also fine art portraits of your historic building. No literature; call for further details.

National Home Inspection Service of New England, Inc.
2 Calvin Rd.   Dept. OHJ
Watertown, MA 02172
(617) 923-2300
RS/O
Complete structural and mechanical pre-purchase home inspections anywhere in New England. After the inspection, a complete written report of the condition of the property is issued to you. Maintenance and restoration advice is also provided if desired. All inspectors are members of the American Society of Home Inspectors and subscribe to its Standards and Code of Ethical Conduct. No literature available.

National Shutters and Millwork
21-16 43rd Avenue   Dept. OHJ
Long Island City, NY 11101
(212) 729-0395
MO   DIST   RS/O
Specialists in the manufacture of custom shutters and in the reproduction and duplication of shutter styles for both interior and exterior. No literature.

Native Wood Products, Inc.
Drawer Box 469   Dept. OHJ
Brooklyn, CT 06234
(203) 774-7700
MO   RS/O
Blueprint, material list, and instruction sheet for building a post and beam carriage shed. $8.00. Also, complete lumber package to customers in New England, NY, and PA. Many sizes and styles of post and beam buildings available from storage buildings to barns. Information and prices available upon request. Also available, colonial reproduction wood products including beaded clapboard, wainscot paneling and post and beam materials.

Natural Wood Floors - Inlaid Wood Mosaic Div.
PO Box 25469   Dept. OHJ
Chicago, IL 60625
(312) 561-2203
RS/O   MO
Flooring contractor specializing in Victorian wood floors. Complete services for wood floor installation; custom staining and refinishing. Will reproduce any inlaid wood mosaic parquetry, center pieces or border designs, 1800-1920. Historical research services available on manufacturers of parquetry patterns c.1890. No literature — please call.

Navarre Builders, Inc.
10 Waterside Plaza, Ste. 18H   Dept. OHJ
New York, NY 10010
(212) 682-5409
RS/O
General contracting services, specializing in masonry restoration and exterior building cleaning. Brownstone experts. Please call for appointment.

Neri, C./Antiques
313 South Street   Dept. OHJ
Philadelphia, PA 19147
(215) 923-6669
RS/O
Fine antique mantels and backbars; one of the largest selections of American antique lighting fixtures in the country. Catalog, $5.

● = Consult ad for more details. See Advertisers' Index on the last page of this Catalog.

New Boston Building-Wrecking Co., Inc.
84 Arsenal Street   Dept. OHJ
Watertown, MA 02172
(617) 924-9090
RS/O
Dealers in original architectural finishwork for quality restoration or contemporary application in the home or commercial space. Inventory from 17th through 19th centuries includes millwork, mantels stained/bevelled glass, doors, plumbing/lighting fixtures, columns, corbels, wrought iron and decorative accessories. Call for appointment. No literature.

● **New England Brassworks**
220 Riverside Avenue   Dept. OHJ
Bristol, CT 06010
(203) 582-6100
MO   DIST
Manufactures and distributes solid brass hardware and decorative accessories including towel bars, toilet paper holders, shower curtain rods and a large assortment of candlesticks, wall sconces, & candelabras. Also produces a wide range of custom brass hardware for architects and designers. An illustrated brochure is available for $.50.

New York Marble Works
1399 Park Ave.   Dept. OHJ
New York, NY 10029
(212) 534-2242
MO   RS/O
Manufacturers of marble vanities, sinktops, fireplaces, hearthstones, pedestals, steps and saddles. They also repair, restore and repolish marble. No literature.

Newbury Carpets
22 Unicorn St., P.O. Box 609   Dept. OHJ
Newburyport, MA 01950
(617) 462-4734
MO   RS/O
Suppliers of high grade reproduction of Brussels and Wilton carpets for historical restorations, museums, etc. Wide selection of traditional designs, many documented, or special designs produced. All are custom made to required specifications. Current prices start at approx. $65.00 per yard. Complete service if required, including consultation, research, planning, installations. No catalog — please inquire.

Newburyport Stained Glass Studio
P.O. Box 683 2A Whites Ct.   Dept. OHJ
Newburyport, MA 01950
(617) 465-2989
RS/O   MO
Repair and restoration of stained and leaded glass, including windows, skylights, and lamps. Ecclesiastic and secular work. Sash repairs. Fabrication of protective coverings. Also design and manufacture of original stained glass windows. Written estimates given. Free brochure.

KEY TO ABBREVIATIONS

MO = sells by Mail Order

RS/O = sells through Retail Store or Office

DIST = sells through Distributors

ID = sells only through Interior Designers or Architects

Newby, Simon
P.O. Box C414   Dept. OHJ
Westport, MA 02790
(617) 636-5010
MO   RS/O
Offers a selected line of hand-produced architectural exterior and interior finish woodwork for the 17th and 18th century homes on a custom basis: entrance ways, raised panel doors, wainscotting, chimney breasts, shutters, etc. Also custom reproduction of 17th and 18th century furniture. Specific inquiries welcomed. Illustrated brochure, $1.

Newell Workshop
19 Blaine Ave.   Dept. OHJ
Hinsdale, IL 60521
(312) 323-7367
MO
Restoration materials for chairs — cane webbing, rush seating material, flat weaving material, hand caning kits. Free catalog with price list.

• **Newstamp Lighting Co.**
227 Bay Rd.   Dept. OH-82
North Easton, MA 02356
(617) 238-7071
RS/O   MO   DIST
Large selection of Early American lanterns, sconces and chandeliers. Catalog is $2.00, refundable. Also distributor of Hunter Olde Tyme Ceiling Fans; catalog is $.50.

Niland, Thomas M. Company
1309 Montana Ave.   Dept. OHJ
El Paso, TX 79902
(915) 533-9735
RS/O   MO
Authentic municipal light standards, sand cast of heavy aluminum alloy from original moulds. Six styles with complementary park benches. Globes and luminaires also available. Free brochure — phone inquiries welcome.

Nixalite of America
417 25th Street   Dept. OHJ
Moline, IL 61265
(309) 797-8771
MO   DIST
Nixalite is a stainless steel strip with protruding, needle-sharp points. Used to prevent pigeons and other birds from nesting on roofs, ledges, in eaves and gutters. Free flyer.

Nord, E.A. Company
P.O. Box 1187   Dept. OHJ
Everett, WA 98206
(206) 259-9292
DIST
The world's largest manufacturer of stile and rail doors produces stock wood columns, 8 spindle designs, turned posts, a lamp post, fancy stair parts, exterior louver blinds, spindle, louver, and panel bifold doors and entry doors, many of which are suitable for period houses. Standard line of hemlock screen doors sold through lumberyards, etc. Free brochures.

• **Norman, W.F., Corporation**
P.O. Box 323   Dept. OHJ
Nevada, MO 64772
(417) 667-5552
MO   DIST
This company is again producing an 81-year old line of metal ceiling, wainscotting, wall panels, cornices, mouldings and metal Spanish Tile roofing. Patterns come in many architectural styles: Greek, Gothic, Rococo, Colonial Revival. Unique patterns; made from original dies. Write for: Ceiling Catalog No. 350 — $3.00.

North American Solar Development Corp.
2800 Juniper St.   Dept. OHJ
Fairfax, VA 22031
(703) 241-8886
RS/O   DIST
A distributor of energy-conservation, solar, and waste-heat recovery products serving dealers in the mid-Atlantic states. Retail sales in the Washington, DC metropolitan area. Free literature.

North Coast Chemical Co.
6300 17th Ave. So.   Dept. OHJ
Seattle, WA 98108
(206) 763-1340
MO   DIST
Free data sheets available on: S-E-G professional paint remover, Durofilm gym finish and penetrating seal, Northco Masonry Cleaner, Rustphoil metal treatment compound, Northco rust remover, lemon oil & cleaners, Barnacle Milk additive to improve adhesion and workability of portland cement.

North Pacific Joinery
76 West Fourth Street   Dept. OHJ
Eureka, CA 95501
(707) 443-5788
MO   RS/O
Custom fabrication of millwork, turnings, and trim: Newels, balusters, handrails, mantels, windows, doors, wainscot, scrollwork. Design service available. Company brochure, $1.00, or call or write with your specific request.

Northeast American Heritage Co.
77 Washington St., N., Ste. 53   Dept. OHJ
Boston, MA 02114
MO
Custom design service for owners or builders who are considering restoration, remodelling or additions to old houses. Custom design pack $7.00. Free style guide.

Northern Design Builders
28 Elm Street   Dept. OHJ
Montpelier, VT 05602
(802) 223-3484
RS/O
Serves the state of Vermont, specializing in energy conservation oriented renovation and restoration of old buildings. Architectural services. No literature.

Nowell's, Inc.
Box 164   Dept. OHJ
Sausalito, CA 94965
(415) 332-4933
RS/O   MO   DIST
Victorian reproduction brass lighting fixtures, made by hand. Aladdin Lamps, parts and shades. Brass oil lamps both table and hanging. Complete line of Victorian glass shades and lamp parts. Fixture catalog $3.50, refundable with purchase.

Nutt, Craig, Fine Wood Works
2014 Fifth St.   Dept. OHJ
Northport, AL 35476
(205) 752-6535
RS/O   MO
Fine cabinet-making and joinery; wood carving. Museum-quality furniture: reproductions, adaptations, and custom designs. Southern American furniture is a specialty. Mostly custom work. Small showroom with ready-to-sell items. Send $.25 for brochure and current price list.

O

Oberndorfer & Assoc.
1979 Quarry Rd.   Dept. OHJ
Yardley, PA 19067
(215) 968-6463
RS/O
A house inspection company serving the Princeton-Bucks County and Philadelphia areas with complete structural, mechanical and electrical inspection of property. Free brochure.

• **Ocean View Lighting and Home Accessories**
1810 Fourth St.   Dept. OHJ
Berkeley, CA 94710
(415) 841-2937
RS/O   MO
Retail sellers of fine antique and reproduction lighting fixtures, & table lamps. Handle Classic Illumination products. Line of plaster ceiling medallions. Replacement glass shades. Brochures on Classic Illumination products and mail order price list available for $1.

Odyssey Building & Maintenance Co.
P.O. Box 7994   Dept. OHJ
Ann Arbor, MI 48107
(313) 665-9456
RS/O
Builders specializing in quality restoration, renovation & maintenance of historic & older homes in the Ann Arbor area; providing a full range of services. For information and appointments, please call number above. No literature.

Office For Metropolitan History
216 W. 89th St.   Dept. OHJ
New York, NY 10024
(212) 799-0520
RS/O   MO
Firm does research and consultation for any architectural/historical project. Specializes in New York City, but will work on projects anywhere in U.S. National Register work, search for architectural drawings and old photographs. Also will research date, architect, original owner, etc. for private homes. No literature.

Ogren & Trigg Clock Service
2616 Colfax Ave So.   Dept. OHJ
Minneapolis, MN 55408
(612) 377-2290
RS/O   MO
Company specializes in the repair and restoration of antique clocks. No literature.

Ohman, C.A.
455 Court Street   Dept. OHJ
Brooklyn, NY 11231
(212) 624-2772
RS/O   MO
Supplies and installs metal ceilings in the New York metropolitan area. Shipping and literature available.

You'll get better service
when contacting companies
if you mention
The Old-House Journal
Catalog

The Old-House Journal 1982 Catalog 141

Old Carolina Brick Co.
Rt. 9, Box 77 Majolica Rd.   Dept. OHJ
Salisbury, NC 28144
(704) 636-8850
RS/O   DIST
Company produces hand-moulded bricks, architectural brick shapes, and arches in 8 color ranges. A complete line of patio pavers is available including 8" x 8" Dutch pavers, 4" x 8" pavers, and hexagonal pavers. Can match existing handmade brick: send sample and indicate desired quantity. Illustrated brochure — $1.00.

Old English Brass, Ltd.
10778 Trenton Avenue   Dept. OHJ
St. Louis, MO 63132
(314) 423-3323
DIST
Major supplier of solid brass giftware and decorative hardware (residential). Full range of solid brass hardware for the home: cabinet, furniture, door, etc. Everything is imported from England. Catalogs available free to retail companies requesting information on letterhead. To individuals, Hardware catalog, $4.50; Giftware catalog, $1.50.

Old-Fashioned Milk Paint Co.
Box 222H   Dept. OHJ
Groton, MA 01450
(617) 448-6336
RS/O   MO   DIST
Genuine milk paint, homemade in the traditional way, gives an authentic look to period furniture, old houses, weathered signs, cupboards, and stencilling. In powdered form, it is available in 8 colors by pints, quarts or gallons. Distributors for Watco/Dennis products which include Watco Danish Oil for furniture, woodwork, floors and exterior use. Brochure and color card, $.60. (Stamps okay.)

Old Hickory Stained Glass Studio
221 S. 3rd St.   Dept. OHJ
LaCrosse, WI 54601
(608) 784-6463
RS/O
Tiffany style stained glass lamp and window construction and repair. Serving the Winona, Minnesota and LaCrosse, Wisconsin area. Studio has a lamp and window showroom and also specializes in custom work and restoration of lamps and windows. No literature.

• **Old House Inspection Co., Inc.**
140 Berkeley Place   Dept. OHJ
Brooklyn, NY 11217
(212) 857-3647
RS/O
House inspection service by licensed registered architect. Specializes in brownstones and other old houses in the New York City metropolitan area. Member of "American Society of Home Inspectors." No literature.

• **Old-House Journal**
69-A Seventh Ave.   Dept. OHJ
Brooklyn, NY 11217
(212) 636-4514
MO
Sells the Heavy-Duty Master Heat Gun. Ideal for stripping paint when large areas are involved. Saves mess and expense of chemical removers. Won't scorch wood or vaporize lead pigments as a propane torch will. Heat bubbles paint — which can then be lifted with a scraper. Minor cleanup with chemical remover usually required. Price of **$67** includes same-day shipping via United Parcel Service. Free flyer.

Old House Supplies
2014 Old Philadelphia Pike   Dept. OHJ
Lancaster, PA 17602
(717) 299-5305
RS/O
Has old shutters, latches, hinges, doors, gates, fences, stained glass, and other antique building pieces. Will also do your historic house research for tax and grant benefits to you through state or federal historic property designation. Will publish research, photos, maps, in limited edition book form also.

Old Lamplighter Shop
At the Musical Museum   Dept. OHJ
Deansboro, NY 13328
(315) 841-8774
RS/O   MO
Specialists in the restoration and repair of Victorian and turn-of-the-century lamps and lighting fixtures. In addition to antiques, they also make reproduction lamps and lighting fixtures of these periods. Also a small stock of working melodeons dating from 1850 — 1860. The Musical Museum workshop repairs melodeons, grind and pump organs, etc. Free brochure.

Old'N Ornate Wooden Reproductions
1121 Bailey Hill Rd.   Dept. OHJ
Eugene, OR 97402
(503) 344-6817
MO   RS/O
A small company dedicated to Victorian craftsmanship in custom woodwork. Specializing in ornate screen doors, porch parts, brackets, fretwork, exterior gingerbread. Also red cedar fancy-butt shingles. Free brochure.

Old Stone Mill Corp.
Route 8, PO Box 307   Dept. OHJ
Adams, MA 01220
DIST   RS/O
Wallpaper manufacturer, machine and hand print; Old Stone Mill lines. Also print on commission. Please write with specific request for more information.

Old World Moulding
115 Allen Boulevard   Dept. OHJ
Farmingdale, NY 11735
(516) 293-1789
RS/O   MO
Hardwood embossed mouldings, cornices, baseboards, mantels and a modular system of panelling suitable for a variety of period styles. Custom work also. Color catalog and price list $2.00.

Old World Stucchi Decor
1238 Lititz Pike   Dept. OHJ
Lancaster, PA 17601
(717) 397-1199
MO   RS/O
Reproduction, sales, & installation of plaster moulding and ornaments; also paint & wallpaper sales. Stock line of real plaster mouldings, spandrels, ceiling ornament, and medallions. Custom design & casting service for reproduction & duplication of plaster ornaments. Free brochure.

• **Olde Bostonian Architectural Antiques**
135 Buttonwood St.   Dept. OHJ
Dorchester, MA 02125
(617) 282-9300
RS/O
Has a wide collection of old doors, fireplace mantels, columns, floor registers, stained glass, brackets, newel posts, wainscotting, balusters, electric lighting and brass work. They specialize in mouldings. No literature; call or visit.

Olde New England Masonry
27 Hewitt Rd.   Dept. OHJ
Mystic, CT 06355
(203) 536-0295
RS/O
Company specializes in chimney repair, plastering, fireplaces, exterior stonework and bakeovens. No literature; call for appointment.

Olde Theatre Architectural Salvage Co.
1309 Westport Rd.   Dept. OHJ
Kansas City, MO 64111
(816) 931-0987
RS/O
Large selection of antique and recycled house parts. Free brochure.

Olde Timer Watch & Clock Shoppe
3401-C Mt. Diablo Blvd.   Dept. OHJ
Lafayette, CA 94549
(415) 284-4720
RS/O   MO
Restore, trade, buy and sell old and new clocks and watches. Nationwide clock locating service for specific antique timepieces. Photos available; please specify your wants or needs. Will ship anywhere. Brochures about new grandfather and wall clocks are available free upon request.

Olde Village Smithery
PO Box 1815 61 Finlay Rd.   Dept. OHJ
Orleans, MA 02653
(617) 255-4466
MO
Traditional crafted period lighting fixtures in brass, tin, and copper: primitive Colonial, 18th century, and Pennsylvania Dutch designs. They offer chandeliers, sconces, lanterns, postlights, candlesticks, and beeswax candles. Catalog available, $2.50.

Oliver, Bradley C.
Box 246   Dept. OHJ
Jim Thorpe, PA 18229
(717) 325-2859
RS/O   MO
Dealer in antique iron fences, urns, furniture, etc. Write with a description of what you require. No literature, but inquiries will be answered. They can ship anywhere.

Olivo, Stephen A., Jr.
East River Rd.   Dept. OHJ
North Chester, MA 01050
(413) 667-8835
RS/O
Colonial restoration and design consultant in the western Massachusetts region. All aspects of carpentry & finish work. No literature.

Ornamental Plaster-Works
1715 President Street   Dept. OHJ
Brooklyn, NY 11213
(213) 774-2695
RS/O
Restoration of mouldings and other plaster detail. Will design styles to meet individual needs. No literature.

Orr, J.F., & Sons
081 Village Green   Dept. OHJ
Sudbury, MA 01776
(617) 443-3650
RS/O   MO   DIST
Cupboards, dry sinks and tables, whose originals are in the possession of collectors, museums and early inns. Pieces are constructed of wide, hand planed New England pine and cut nails, with an antique pine finish. Interiors painted old red or slate blue. Send $2. for 32 pg. color catalog with a list of dealers.

Orthographic Engraving Co.
15 Seventh Ave. Dept. OHJ
Brooklyn, NY 11217
(212) 638-1640
RS/O
Custom brass engraving: Door plates, door knobs, house numbers, historical markers, desk plates, etc. Brass restoration. Cleaning, buffing, reworking where necessary, lacquering. Hand engraving of all types of metals. Call for more information, prices. No literature.

Osborne, C. S. & Co.
125 Jersey St. Dept. OHJ
Harrison, NJ 07029
(201) 483-3232
DIST
Manufactures a complete line of upholstering hand tools, including certain do-it-yourself kits with instruction books. Free brochure and name of nearest distributor available on receipt of self-addressed, stamped envelope.

Ostrom Studios
532 SE Belmont St. Dept. OHJ
Portland, OR 97214
(503) 233-6847
RS/O
Designs and produces period acid etched, sandblasted and gluechip glass, mirrors and signs. Reproduction of broken panels. Many old style patterns available. All work custom made, no premade panels in stock. No literature.

O'Sullivan Co.
156 S. Minges Road Dept. OHJ
Battle Creek, MI 49017
(616) 964-1226
MO DIST
Manufactures O'Sullivans Liquid Wax Furniture Polish - an 18th century formula that is designed for wood panelling, board floors, kitchen cabinets as well as furniture. Dries to a soft luster without buffing. Cleans and polishes. Erases light scratches and white rings. Free descriptive folder and mail order form.

Outer Banks Pine Products
Box 9003 Dept. OHJ
Lester, PA 19113
(215) 534-1234
MO
8 corner cabinets made of pine available knocked down or set up. Coat racks/chairs; oak, scrolled legs, curved arms, mirror with 4 metal coat hangers. Solid oak ladder-back chairs with woven seat. "Kennedy" oak rockers. Oak curved-glass curio cabinets. Brochure, $.50.

KEY TO ABBREVIATIONS

MO = sells by Mail Order

RS/O = sells through Retail Store or Office

DIST = sells through Distributors

ID = sells only through Interior Designers or Architects

P

● **P & G New and Used Plumbing Supply**
155 Harrison Ave. Dept. OHJ
Brooklyn, NY 11206
(212) 384-6310
RS/O
Shop has a selection of old-fashioned used bathroom and plumbing fixtures, radiators etc. No literature — walk-in shop only.

● **PRG**
5619 Southampton Drive Dept. OHJ
Springfield, VA 22151
(703) 323-1407
MO
They sell by mail specialized books, instruments and tools (moisture meters, pocket microscope, profile gauge, etc.), which are useful for the restoration and maintenance of old houses. Book list and descriptive material available free.

Pandora's Quilt Museum
2014 Old Philadelphia Pike Dept. OHJ
Lancaster, PA 17602
(717) 299-5305
RS/O MO
Museum quality antique quilts. Prices start at $150 and go up to $3500 for old Mennonite and Amish quilts. Will send Polaroid photo for $10, refundable with purchase. Other old textiles and fabrics also available.

Paramount Exterminating Co.
460 9th Avenue Dept. OHJ
New York, NY 10018
(212) 594-9230
RS/O
Exterminating company providing termite inspections, termite control treatment, and general pest control services in the New York Metropolitan area. Free brochure.

Parsons, W.H., Jr. & Associates
19 Eagle St. Dept. OHJ
Cooperstown, NY 13326
(607) 547-9639
RS/O
Restoration of masonry. Will resurface brownstone; repoint walls, bridges, steps as well as buildings; remove graffiti and paint. Consulting services available. Please call or write — no literature.

Past Patterns
2017 Eastern S.E. Dept. OHJ
Grand Rapids, MI 49507
(616) 245-9456
MO
Authentic patterns for Victorian and Edwardian fashions taken from museums and private costume collections. Each pattern includes: Historical notes, detailed instructions for sewing, scale drawings of the original trim, notes on original fabric and substitutions. Catalog, $10.

Pat's Etcetera Company
P.O. Box 777 Dept. OHJ
Smithville, TX 78957
(512) 237-3600
RS/O MO DIST
8 designs of fibre replacement seats for late 19th-century chairs. Curved china cabinet glass custom cut. Send SASE for free literature. They also include PECO Bevelled Glass: specializing in full bevelled-leaded glass doors, windows, entrance sets, and panels. Also custom glass bevelling for bevelled-leaded door panels, windows, transoms, and entrance sets. Bevelled glass catalog, $3.

Paxton Hardware Co.
Dept. OHJ
Upper Falls, MD 21156
(301) 592-8505
MO
Period furniture hardware, both brass and iron. Items include: Brass bandings, bed hardware, roll top desk locks, escutcheons, caning supplies, and decorated glass shades plus lamp parts. Catalog, $1.50.

Pedersen, Arthur Hall — Design & Consulting Engineers
34 North Gore Dept. OHJ
Webster Groves, MO 63119
(314) 962-4176
RS/O MO
Solar, structural, architectural, and mechanical engineers specializing in solar greenhouses and other passive and active solar system design services for retrofit, add-on, energy conservation, restoration, or new construction. No literature.

● **Peg Hall Studios**
111 Clapp Road Dept. OHJ
Scituate, MA 02066
(617) 545-3605
MO
Patterns and design books for decorating period furniture and accessories. Catalog and price list, $.25.

Pelnik Wrecking Co., Inc.
1749 Erie Blvd., E. Dept. OHJ
Syracuse, NY 13210
(315) 472-1031
RS/O
Wreckers with 50-years' experience in sensitive salvaging. Bevelled and stained glass a specialty. Mantels, newel posts, railings, entryways, corbels, tin ceilings, brass rails, cast iron elements, columns, marble sinks, old brick and timber, terra-cotta friezes. Further services for restaurant designers and architects. Photos on request.

Pendulum Shop
424 South Street Dept. OHJ
Philadelphia, PA 19147
(212) 925-4014
RS/O MO
Handmade Victorian, turn-of-the-century, and Art Nouveau chandeliers, sconces, and floor and table lamps. Not exact reproductions, but rather styled to the period. Will custom make and design fixtures to meet special needs. All fixtures are solid brass. Also reproduction pendulum clocks with one-year guarantee. Walk-in shop. Catalog for lighting only, $1.

Pennsylvania Firebacks
1011 E. Washington Lane Dept. OHJ
Philadelphia, PA 19138
(215) 843-9965
MO DIST
Manufactures an original line of cast iron firebacks for the fireplace. Seven designs currently available to accomodate any hearth size. Firebacks are sold through fireplace shops, hardware and home centers, architects, and designers; also available through mail order. Catalogue featuring a variety of fireplace accessories and period inspired home furnishings, $2.00.

● = Consult ad for more details. See Advertisers' Index on the last page of this Catalog.

The Old-House Journal 1982 Catalog

Period Furniture Hardware Co.
123 Charles St.   Dept. OHJ
Boston, MA 02114
(617) 227-0758
RS/O   MO
Reproduction ornamental brass hardware, bath sinks, brass and porcelain bath fittings, hand-crafted sconces, chandeliers and lanterns, fireplace accessories. Illustrated catalog — $2.

● **Period Lighting Fixtures**
1 West Main Street   Dept. OJ-2
Chester, CT 06412
(203) 526-3690
MO
Handmade 17th & 18th century early American lighting fixtures, chandeliers, wall sconces and lanterns. Finishes vary from hand rubbed pewter, naturally aged tin, and old glazed colors for interior fixtures, to exterior post and wall-mounted lanterns in oxidized copper. Their catalog is also a reference source on the origin, selection and installation of early lighting. Catalog & price list $2.50.

● **Period Pine**
P.O. Box 77052   Dept. OHJ
Atlanta, GA 30309
(404) 876-4740
RS/O   MO
They salvage Southern Yellow Heart Pine from the demolition of turn-of-the-century warehouses and cotton mills, and recycle the salvaged material into flooring, paneling, beams, and mouldings. Free brochure and moulding cut-sheet available.

Period Productions, Limited
1823 W. Main Street   Dept. OHJ
Richmond, VA 23220
(804) 353-5976
RS/O   MO   DIST
Interior and exterior architectural millwork & jointery; all work custom-manufactured on order. Price estimates from customer's drawings or specs. Consultation services & design work available.

Perkowitz Window Fashions
135 Green Bay Rd.   Dept. OHJ
Wilmette, IL 60091
(312) 251-7700
RS/O   MO
A major supplier of louvered shutters carries a full line of stock shutters and custom sizes. Shutters are pine and can be ordered unfinished or with standard colors or stains. Free price lists and catalog.

Perma Ceram Enterprises, Inc.
65 Smithtown Blvd.   Dept. OHJ
Smithtown, NY 11787
(516) 724-1205
DIST
Exclusive supplier of Porcelaincote: a unique, patented synthetic porcelain designed to resurface bathtubs, sinks, toilets and tiles. Offered in a variety of hues, Porcelaincote is claimed to restore antique and worn fixtures to their original beauty and shine in just hours, and without repositioning. Porcelaincote is available from Perma Ceram dealer in your area. Free brochure. Toll-free number: 800-645-5039.

You'll get better service when contacting companies if you mention The Old-House Journal Catalog

---

Peterson, Robert H., Co.
530 N. Baldwin Park Blvd.   Dept. OHJ
City of Industry, CA 91744
(213) 960-5085
DIST
A complete line of Real-Fyre radiant gas logs for woodburning fireplaces. Brochure and price list available. Also offer hallmark handcrafted fireplace accessories, including solid brass firesets, woodholder, hearth fenders, andirons, and standing screens. Catalog and price sheet, $1.

Pfanstiel Hardware Co.
Hust Road   Dept. OHJ
Jeffersonville, NY 12748
(914) 482-4445
MO   DIST
Manufactures and imports an extensive line of decorative hardware, primarily brass and bronze. Styles are French, Renaissance Revival, Rococo, and Georgian. Among their unusual items are decorative finials and finial-tipped hinges. Handsome 96 page catalog — $3.50 ($5.50 outside U.S.)

Piazza, Michael Architectural Crafts
540 80th Street   Dept. OHJ
Brooklyn, NY 11209
(212) 745-6111
RS/O
Craftsman skilled in restoration, reproduction and preservation. Work is performed on site following conventional procedures and using authentic materials. Consultation services provided on a general basis; restoration services are provided to the profession and to qualified individual homeowners and organizations. Serious inquiries invited.

Pierce & Stevens Chemical Corp.
710 Ohio St., Box 1092   Dept. OHJ
Buffalo, NY 14240
(716) 856-4910
DIST
The manufacturers of Fabulon wood finishing products have two useful booklets for $.50 each. 'A Short Course in Natural Wood Finishing'' and 'How To Finish Wood Floors.''

Plaskolite, Inc.
1770 Joyce Ave., P.O. Box 1497   Dept. OHJ
Columbus, OH 43216
(614) 294-3281
DIST
A clear rigid plastic storm window with vinyl mounting trim that can be cut to fit for the inside of the house. A do-it-yourself solution to the odd-shaped bay or oriel window that defies conventional storm window installation, or an additional energy saver with existing storm windows. Free brochure.

● **Pocahontas Hardware & Glass**
Box 127   Dept. OHJ
Pocahontas, IL 62275
(618) 669-2880
RS/O   MO
Etched glass especially suited for windows, doors, transoms and cabinets. Patterns are exact reproductions of old glass. They also produce three stock doors (five panel, oval, or three panel) of solid sugar pine. Wood carving is added on request. Doors have etched glass inserts. Custom made doors can be ordered. Illustrated brochure is $1.50.

Pollitt, E., AIA
Vista Drive   Dept. OHJ
Easton, CT 06612
(203) 268-5955
MO
A collection of Colonial period house plans, measured and drawn from originals. Exteriors are faithfully reproduced; interiors are updated. Specifications make use of stock building materials. Full plans are $62.00 each. Two portfolios available: Old Colonial Houses, 32 reproduction houses; Old Cape Cod Houses, 24 reproductions and adaptations. Each $5.00.

Pompei Stained Glass
455 High St. (Rt. 60)   Dept. OHJ
Medford, MA 02155
(617) 395-8867
RS/O   MO
Reproduction of period leaded and stained glass shades and window panels of all types, including fan lights, side lights, transoms, cabinet doors, mantel mirrors & signs & logos. Fabrication may incorporate beveled, etched and sand-blasted glass. Repair and restoration of leaded windows and shades. Glass slumping, resizing, "secularization", and installation services. Serves greater Boston and the six New England states. Free literature.

Poor Richards Furniture Co.
69 No. Willow St.   Dept. OHJ
Montclair, NJ 07042
(201) 783-5333
RS/O
Furniture stripping, refinishing and repair, metal polishing and plating; reupholstery work; cane and rush work and supplies. Walk-in shop only — no literature.

Porcelain Doctor
4131 Main St.   Dept. OHJ
Skokie, IL 60076
(312) 674-4766
RS/O   MO
Fine antiques repaired and restored. Specializing in porcelain, pottery, ivory, bisque, and jade. No dinnerware or furniture; quality items only. Also glass repair in consultation with Crystal Cave. No brochure; specific inquiries answered.

Porcelain Restoration
Box 278 Pleasant Ave.   Dept. OHJ
Stanfield, NC 28163
(704) 372-9039
RS/O   MO
Porcelain resurfacing in the home. Not an epoxy, but a curothane — polyvinyl butyral primer with multiple glaze coats. Specialists in pedestal sinks, footed tubs, original water closets. They make available original plumbing fixtures and reproduction brass hardware for sinks, tubs and showers. Also brass-plating available and oak washstands with marble lavatory bowls. Catalog, $3.50.

● **Porcelli, Ernest**
123 7th Ave.   Dept. OHJ
Brooklyn, NY 11215
(212) 857-6888
RS/O
Original creations in stained and leaded glass. Will also do custom work. Also will do stained & leaded glass repair. Free estimates with stamped self-addressed envelope. Send dimensions. No literature.

● = Consult ad for more details. See Advertisers' Index on the last page of this Catalog.

Portland Stove Foundry, Inc.
157 Kennebec St., Box 1156   Dept. OHJ
Portland, ME 04104
(207) 773-0256
DIST   RS/O   MO
They manufacture wood-and-coal-burning cast iron stoves for space heating. Also free-standing fireplaces; Franklin stove and kitchen ranges from original patterns and molds. Catalog, $.50.

Preservation Associates, Inc.
Box 202   Dept. OHJ
Sharpsburg, MD 21782
(301) 432-5466
RS/O
Nationwide building-restoration and research services to individuals, organizations, and agencies. Full consulting services; surveys and preparation of state and National Register nominations. Also specialists in restoration of old log houses. Introductory brochure available on request.

Preservation/Design Group, The
388 Broadway   Dept. OHJ
Albany, NY 12207
(518) 463-4077
RS/O
Highly-qualified group of individuals deals with a full range of preservation/architectural services. Extensive experience and capabilities. "A Primer of Historic Preservation Services", $2.00.

Preservation Development Group
200 Henry Street   Dept. OHJ
Stamford, CT 06902
(203) 324-9317
RS/O
The Preservation Development Group is a planning and design firm whose work focuses on the restoration of historic structures. Activities include preservation planning for governmental agencies, historic resource inventories, National Register nominations, and the design of historically compatible new construction. Please call or write for more information.

Preservation Partnership
7 Irving St.   Dept. OHJ
New Bedford, MA 01740
(617) 996-3383
RS/O
A preservation firm whose architectural and planning services include surveys, historic structures reports, and the inspection, conservation, rehabilitation, restoration, and adaptive reuse of existing buildings. Some 300 completed projects range from private homes to scores of house museums. Conservation of institutional and public cultural property is a specialty. Free brochure.

Preservation Resource Center of New Orleans
604 Julia Street   Dept. OHJ
New Orleans, LA 70130
(504) 581-7032
RS/O
They do house research, accept facade servitudes, sponsor tours, and publish "Preservation Press."

Preservation Resource Group
5619 Southampton Dr.   Dept. OHJ
Springfield, VA 22151
(703) 323-1407
RS/O
Assists agencies, organizations and individuals in development of their historic preservation programs and personnel. Lectures and workshops for owners of old houses are conducted for groups on request. No literature.

Preway, Inc.
1430 2nd Street, North   Dept. OHJ
Wisconsin Rapids, WI 54494
(715) 423-1100
DIST
Energy-efficient built-in and glass-enclosed fireplaces. Manufacturers of "Energy-Mizer" fireplaces. All units are rated zero-clearance to combustibles and are UL Listed. Choices of hearth opening sizes available, plus accessories. UL Listed chimney systems also available. Free 8-page color brochure illustrates fireplace units, dimensions, and fireplace installation procedures.

Princeton Co.
P.O. Box 276   Dept. OHJ
Princeton, MA 01541
(617) 464-5209
MO   RS/O
High quality woodworking tools including German bench chisels and gouges, drilling and boring tools, doweling and dovetailing jigs, Japanese woodworking tools, picture framing equipment, English tenon saws, Arkansas whetstones, carving tools, project supplies, books, etc. Catalog, $1.00.

ProSoCo, Inc.
P.O. Box 4040   Dept. OHJ
Kansas City, KS 66104
(913) 281-2700
DIST   RS/O
Manufacturers of Sure Klean masonry cleaning and sealing materials. For restoring brick, stone and other masonry surfaces. The solvent cleaner is less costly than sandblasting and does not harm the masonry surface. Free brochures.

• **Progress Lighting**
G St. & Erie Ave.   Dept. OHJ
Philadelphia, PA 19134
(215) 289-1200
DIST
A selection of document American Victorian lighting fixture reproductions: Classical Revival, Rococo Revival, Colonial Revival, Art Nouveau. Authenticated by Dr. Roger Moss. All electrified; most of solid brass. Also matching wall, hall, and streetlight adaptations. Quality production by the world's largest manufacturer of home lighting fixtures. Full color catalog $1.00.

Puget Sound Shake Brokers
12301 218th Pl. SE Suite 711   Dept. OHJ
Snohomish, WA 98290
(206) 568-6642
MO   RS/O
Fancy butt red cedar shingles 5" x 18", 9 cuts: octagonal, arrow, square, fish scale, diagonal, half cove, diamond, round, hexagonal. Shipped to customer direct from distributor. Prepayment required. Eastern time differential no problem; call and leave message. Sample shingle and literature $1.00. Refundable first order.

• **Purcell, Francis J., II**
88 North Main Street   Dept. OHJ
New Hope, PA 18938
(215) 862-9100
RS/O
Antique American fireplace mantels dating from 1750 to 1850. Large collection of formal and folk art mantels. 70 examples are cleaned of paint and have hand rubbed finishes. Majority of mantels priced between one and two thousand dollars. No literature — collection seen by appointment only.

• **Putnam Rolling Ladder Co., Inc.**
32 Howard St.   Dept. GNP
New York, NY 10013
(212) 226-5147
RS/O   MO
Of special interest is their rolling library ladder — made-to-order from oak and finished to customer's specifications. They make an oak pulpit ladder, "office ladders", stools and carts. Also full line of wooden and aluminum ladders, and aluminum scaffolds. Catalog No. 640 — free.

Pyfer, E.W.
218 North Foley Ave.   Dept. OHJ
Freeport, IL 61032
(815) 232-8968
MO   RS/O
Lamp repair and rewiring: chandeliers restored, oil and gas lamps converted, replacement of missing lamp parts. Brass plating service. Chair recaning (rush, reed, and splint). Also sells caning supplies and instruction books. Free description of services — please call for appointment before visiting.

Pyramid Woodcraft Corp.
280 Park Ave.   Dept. OHJ
League City, TX 77573
(713) 332-8577
RS/O
Manufacturer of custom cabinets and limited production of millwork: verge boards, cupolas, fretwork, brackets. Also distributes Castlegate steel-clad thermal entry doors in traditional designs. Send for free brochures.

Q

Quaker City Manufacturing Co.
701 Chester Pike   Dept. OHJ
Sharon Hill, PA 19079
(215) 727-5144
DIST
WINDOW FIXER Replacement Window Channels can be used with standard wood sash to give snug fit and prevent heat loss. Available through most lumber yards, home centers and major hardware stores. Free literature.

KEY TO ABBREVIATIONS

MO	=	sells by Mail Order
RS/O	=	sells through Retail Store or Office
DIST	=	sells through Distributors
ID	=	sells only through Interior Designers or Architects

R

Rambusch
40 West 13th St.   Dept. OHJ
New York, NY 10011
(212) 675-0400
ID
Company specializes in major restoration projects for museums, churches and public buildings. Has a large staff of skilled craftsmen in such areas as painting and decorating, lighting and stained glass. Free brochure: "Restorations By Rambusch." Through Interior Designers and Architects only.

RAM's Forge
2501 E. Mayberry Rd.   Dept. OHJ
Westminster, MD 21157
(301) 346-7873
MO   RS/O
Colonial and contemporary hand-forged wrought iron work. Specializing in fireplace equipment; also railings, gates, window grilles, lighting, hardware, boot scrapers, kitchen pot racks, and weather vanes in hand-wrought iron. Each piece custom forged for its particular application, using traditional designs and forging techniques. Write giving your specific need in colonial ironware. No literature.

Readybuilt Products, Co.
Box 4411, 1701 McHenry St.   Dept. OHJ
Baltimore, MD 21223
(301) 233-5833
MO   DIST
More than 25 different styles of hand-crafted ready to install wood mantels for built-in masonry fireplaces or factory-built metal units. Most mantels have wood openings 50" wide x 30" high and can be modified at additional cost. A Booklet, "Wood Mantel Pieces" shows styles and a diagram for taking measurements — $2.00.

Red Baron's Antiques
234 Hilderbrand Drive   Dept. OHJ
Atlanta, GA 30328
(404) 255-1074
RS/O
Always a large inventory of American architectural antiques and collectibles. Specializing in stained and bevelled glass windows and doors. Walk-in shop throughout the year, with periodic auctions. They also own the Peachtree Antique Emporium on 3264 Peachtree Road NE — (404) 237-9338. No literature.

Reflections
300 Kater Street   Dept. OHJ
Philadelphia, PA 19147
(215) 922-8538
RS/O
Reflections' Antique Stained Glass Showroom has a collection of quality bevelled, stained, clear and etched glass windows, doors, sidelights, and skylights. Also stained glass screens, room dividers, partitions, and lighting fixtures. Restoration, repairs, framing, and interior design services available. Specializing in antique leaded glass windows. No literature.

You'll get better service when contacting companies if you mention The Old-House Journal Catalog

---

• **Reggio Register Co.**
P.O. Box 511   Dept. OJ-2
Ayer, MA 01432
MO
Decorative cast iron floor register is designed for use with a wood burning stove. It allows the control of warm air to other rooms. It can also be used with a forced-air heating system. Can be used in any room that will accept a 10-1/2 in. x 12-1/2 in. opening above the heat source, and fits between joists 16 in. on center. Also — 16 in. x 20 in. cast iron floor grille is available — other sizes to choose from. Send $1 for catalogue.

Rejuvenation House Parts Co.
4543 North Albina Ave.   Dept. OHJ
Portland, OR 97217
(503) 282-3019
RS/O   MO
A restoration general store selling new and used architectural parts, including light fixtures, doors, hardware, millwork etc. Also manufactures authentic new solid brass Victorian light fixtures. All are U.L. listed. Light fixture and parts catalogue available for $2.00, refundable with purchase. Free brochures available on cast iron roof cresting and anaglypta wall covering.

• **Remodelers' & Renovators' Supply**
611 E. 44th Street, No. 5   Dept. OHJ
Boise, ID 83704
(208) 377-5465
MO   RS/O
Suppliers of quality bldg., finishing & decorating products for renovators, remodelers & preservationists. Old-style faucets, fittings, pedestal sinks in ceramic or wood, & brass sinks; Victorian mouldings, fretwork & millwork; reproduction gas/electric lighting; porch & garden furniture & accessories; fine tools; Victorian reproduction cast aluminum spiral staircase; brass door & cabinet hardware; tin ceiling; brass accessories; anaglypta wall covering; old-style entrance doors & screen doors; Large inventory hard-to-find items, incl. architectural antiques. Free cat.

• **Renaissance Decorative Hardware Co.**
PO Box 332   Dept. OHJ
Leonia, NJ 07605
(201) 568-1403
MO
Renaissance Decorative Hardware Co. is an importer of solid brass door, cabinet and furniture hardware. The door hardware includes pulls, knobs, and lever handles. The knobs and lever handles are intended for older homes utilizing mortise mechanisms. Catalog—$2.50.

• **Renovation Concepts, Inc.**
PO Box 3720   Dept. OHJ
Minneapolis, MN 55403
(612) 377-9526
RS/O   MO
Source for period building supplies in the Midwest. Unique and decorative materials for bars and restaurants, residential renovation, and commercial design. Products can be shipped to any job site in the nation. Trade catalog, $10; homeowners catalog, $5, refundable with purchase; free brochure.

● = Consult ad for more details.   See Advertisers' Index on the last page of this Catalog.

• **Renovation Products**
5302 Junius   Dept. OHJ
Dallas, TX 75214
(214) 827-5111
MO   RS/O
Restoration/renovation products source. Common items such as doors & mouldings, turnings in stock. Showroom and retail store with special-order service for a variety of other materials: custom made and stock screen doors, gingerbread, fretwork, Victorian design porch swings, park benches, lamp posts, bath accessories, gargoyles, cenotaphs, metal ceilings, much more. Stencil artist available. Design consultation available to customers. Catalog, $2.

Renovation Source, Inc., The
3512 N. Southport Ave.   Dept. OHJ
Chicago, IL 60657
(312) 327-1250
MO   RS/O
Firm provides both architectural consulting/design services, and restoration/renovation products. Architectural services from site consultation to a complete set of construction drawings. Supplier of salvaged architectural trim, newly reproduced decorative materials, and restoration aids. Also represent growing number of oldhouse products manufacturers. General catalog $1.50.

Renovators Co.
Box 284   Dept. OHJ
Patterson, NY 12563
(914) 279-3624
RS/O   MO
Individually crafted oak medicine cabinets available in two styles, with options. Offer custom sizing for slight additional charge. Mail order only. 4-6 weeks delivery. Free brochure.

• **Renovator's Supply**
71A Northfield Rd.   Dept. OHJ
Millers Falls, MA 01349
(413) 659-3542
MO
A wide selection of fine quality items for restoration, renovation and decoration of the antique home. A comprehensive full color catalog of quality old style hardware, specialty lighting, plumbing fixtures, fireplace equipment, decorative accessories, and other miscellaneous items in solid brass, porcelain, wrought iron, and oak. All items are manufactured for a life-time of use. Illustrated catalog $2.00 refundable with purchase.

Resources in Housing Rehabilitation
16 N. Newark Ave.   Dept. OHJ
Ventnor, NJ 08406
(609) 347-5775
MO
Service for organizations or individuals involved/planning to get involved in federally funded housing rehabilitation programs. Provides access to literature in the field: books, papers, rehab guides etc. on financial techniques, program implementation & operation; forms used in the rehab process, code enforcement and many others. Send $25 for complete material catalog, explaining where to buy material and how much suppliers charge.

Restoration A Specialty
6127 N.E. Rodney   Dept. OHJ
Portland, OR 97211
(503) 283-3945
RS/O   MO
Restoration contracting/interior design services for authentic individual home restoration. Individualized custom design for period homes. Serving Pacific NW. Literature available for individualized work.

● **Restoration Hardware**
438 Second St. Dept. OHJ
Eureka, CA 95501
(707) 443-3152
RS/O
A walk-in store for restoration materials: door hardware, bath fittings, lighting, millwork, cabinet hardware, etc. Specializing in Victorian and Period house parts. Manufacturers of authentic Victorian mouldings, wainscotting, mantels, etc. Complete catalog, $3.

Restoration Masonry
1141 Adams Street Dept. OHJ
Denver, CO 80206
(303) 377-6566
RS/O
All types of old house masonry restoration and repair: Tile work, stucco, ornamental brickwork, fireplaces, consultation. No literature.

Restoration-Preservation Architecture
51 South Ritter Dept. OHJ
Indianapolis, IN 46219
(317) 353-9808
RS/O
Architectural firm providing design, planning, and consulting services for historic buildings. Company synopsis sent on request.

Restoration Specialties
Box 2539 Dept. OHJ
Laurel, MD 20811
MO
Restoration of old houses and apartments, especially Victorian and post-Victorian era buildings. No literature available.

● **Restoration Works, Inc.**
412-1/2 Virginia Street Dept. OHJ
Buffalo, NY 14201
(716) 881-1159
MO RS/O
Hard-to-find hardware and specialty products for the restoration/rehab builder's or do-it-yourself market. Energy savers and security devices. Catalog, $2.00, refundable with first purchase.

Restoration Workshop Nat Trust For Historic Preservation
635 South Broadway Dept. OHJ
Tarrytown, NY 10591
(914) 631-6696
Preservation/restoration construction and maintenance services provided on a contractual basis to qualified organizations and individuals; for guidelines contact the Director, Restoration Workshop. If travel and living expenses are reimbursed they can serve nationwide. Also: paid apprenticeships available to those committed to a career in the preservation trades. Brochure available on request.

Restorations
382 Eleventh Street Dept. OHJ
Brooklyn, NY 11215
(212) 788-7909
RS/O MO
Quality restoration of antique lace curtains, hooked rugs, quilts, samplers and household textiles. Consulting services and lectures available on textile conservation, and American rugs and carpets from the 17th century to present. Textile restoration supplies available. Free price list on request.

Restorations Unlimited, Inc.
24 West Main St. Dept. OHJ
Elizabethville, PA 17023
(717) 362-3477
RS/O
Full restoration contracting and interior period design services, including: Analysis of remodeled old houses for reconstruction of original layout; Design and execution of period and creative interiors; Custom cabinets, furnishings, and woodwork; Procurement of architectural antiques. Authorized dealers of Rich Craft custom cabinets. Literature available on Rich Craft $1.00. Period & modern kitchen design and installation services. Company literature $.25.

Retinning & Copper Repair
525 West 26th St. Dept. OHJ
New York, NY 10001
(212) 244-4896
MO RS/O
Specializes in tin plating and finishing of copper cookware, bakery equipment and refrigerator racks. Repairs on all copper, brass and tin items. Cleaning and buffing included in services. Goods accepted at shop in person or via UPS. Estimates available by phone or mail. A selection of copperware available on sale at shop. No literature.

Reynolds, R. Wayne Restoration
PO Box 28 Dept. OHJ
Stevenson, MD 21153
(301) 484-1028
RS/O
The complete conservation and restoration of gessoed and gold leafed surfaces, including carved wood or cast plaster objects, furniture, mirror frames, picture frames and architectural gilding of interior or exterior ornamental mouldings. Design and construction of period reproduction frames and pier mirrors. Has done work for the National Gallery. Call or write for information.

● **Rheinschild, S. Chris**
2220 Carlton Way Dept. OHJ
Santa Barbara, CA 93109
(805) 962-8598
MO RS/O
This business specializes in quality reproductions for old house kitchens and bathrooms. They make reproductions of the oak pull chain toilets and of the oak tank low toilets. They make a reproduction of the old wood trimmed copper bath tub, and a copper kitchen sink. Also any period style faucet. They also do custom work. Brochure is $1.35.

Rich Craft Custom Kitchens, Inc.
141 West Penn Avenue Dept. OHJ
Robesonia, PA 19551
(215) 693-5871
RS/O DIST
Manufacturers of a variety of kitchen cabinet work. A few are period-inspired. There are 100 door styles, available in 8 different woods. Cabinets produced to buyer's specifications, so you may want to purchase them through Rich Craft distributors (designers, architects) who will help plan your kitchen. Send $1.00 for catalog.

Richards, R.E., Inc.
P.O. Box 285 Dept. OHJ
West Simsbury, CT 06092
(203) 658-4347
RS/O
Home design and restoration firm serving Connecticut. This small firm works closely with homeowners to solve the particular problems of individual houses. Please call for an appt — No literature.

Richardson, Matthew Coppersmith
Box 69 Dept. OHJ
Greenfield, MA 01302
(413) 773-9242
MO
Craftsman producing contemporary interpretations of the traditional metalsmith's art. Copper and brass windvanes, garden ornament, fountains, interior & exterior lighting, original wall art. Pieces can be compatible with a broad range of historical styles. Range hoods a specialty. Custom work is considered. Catalog, $2.

Ricker Blacksmith Shop
Campbell Hill Dept. OHJ
Cherryfield, ME 04622
(207) 546-7954
RS/O MO
This shop has been a family business since the late 1700's. All traditional blacksmith services; most work is custom. Reproduction and modern exterior ironwork, fireplace accessories, lighting fixtures, hardware, etc. Also ship and mooring hardware, edge tools, carriage fittings. Customers served by mail, phone, or in person. No literature; you give them an idea of your needs and they'll submit a drawing and price estimate.

Ring, J. Stained Glass, Inc.
618 North Washington Ave. Dept. OHJ
Minneapolis, MN 55401
(612) 332-1769
MO RS/O
Fine art-glass studio specializing in restoration/reproduction for major commissions (architects, government, etc.) Hand-bevelling and engraving, stained glass work, glass painting and bending; reproduction of quality antique pieces; mirror restoration. Also stock bevels. Some literature available: Please specify interest.

Rising & Nelson Slate Co.
Dept. OHJ
West Pawlet, VT 05775
(802) 645-0150
MO
Vermont Colored Roofing Slate available in all colors, sizes, thicknesses, designs to match and restore old roofs. Also slate flagstone. Brochure with descriptive and technical information available free.

KEY TO ABBREVIATIONS

MO = sells by Mail Order

RS/O = sells through Retail Store or Office

DIST = sells through Distributors

ID = sells only through Interior Designers or Architects

• **Ritter & Son Hardware**
46901 Fish Rock Rd., Dept. 911   Dept. OHJ
Gualala, CA 95445
(707) 884-3363
MO
Manufacturers of solid brass 19th century hardware. They carry a large selection of hathooks, binpulls, cast and stamped dresser pulls, keyholes, bailsets and icebox hardware. New to their line are cardholder pulls, library pulls, wash stand brackets, roll top locks and porcelain knobs. Also, they carry French door hardware. Exclusive mail order merchandiser for Cirecast, makers of an unusually good looking line of bronze hardware in late Victorian styles. Illustrated catalog $1., or call.

River City Restorations
200 South 7th   Dept. OHJ
Hannibal, MO 63401
(314) 248-0733
RS/O
Serves N.E. Missouri, West Central Illinois, and Southern Iowa. Specializing in non-abrasive cleaning, paintstripping, repointing. Other services include exterior/interior restoration and rehabilitation of private residences and commercial properties. Contracting business helps clients with design, estimates, and priorities. Answers to all inquiries. Free brochure available.

• **Robillard, Dennis Paul, Inc.**
Front Street   Dept. OHJ
South Berwick, ME 03908
(207) 384-9541
RS/O   MO
Established artisans located in historic New England. Production of custom millwork (mantels, paneled walls, doors, Palladian windows, etc.) and mouldings a specialty. Duplication of porch parts, balusters, doors, brackets, turnings, and window sash. Restoration services for the aging home, repair and reproduction of architectural antiques. No fee for prices supplied on request; literature available, $1.50.

• **Robin's Roost**
167 Maynard Ave.   Dept. OH
Newbury Park, CA 91320
(805) 498-6543
MO
Nostalgic brass table lamps, including a Victorian gooseneck, and electric "oil lamp", and a classic desk lamp with swivel shade. Reasonable prices. Write or call for more information.

• **Robinson Iron Corporation**
Robinson Road   Dept. OHJ
Alexander City, AL 35010
(205) 329-8484
RS/O   DIST
Authentic 19th century cast iron for the home and garden including: flowing fountains, urns and vases, planters, statuary, fence posts, hitching posts, street lamp standards, garden furniture, and traditional railroad benches. Historic restoration and custom casting services also available. Send $3.00 to receive complete brochure.

Rocker Shop
1421 White Circle NW, Box 12   Dept. OHJ
Marietta, GA 30061
(404) 427-2618
RS/O   MO
The Brumby rocker made of solid red oak with cane seat and back. A smaller, armless rocker is part of the line, as are a child's rocker and an oak slat porch swing (4, 5, and 6 feet lengths available). Also 2 country-style dining chairs, 2 stools, a lap desk, and small round and oval tables (coordinating). Free catalog and price list.

Rohlf's Stained & Leaded Glass
783 South 3rd Ave.   Dept. OHJ
Mount Vernon, NY 10550
(212) 823-4545
RS/O   MO
Since 1920 this company has been designing and making stained (i.e. painted not merely colored) and leaded glass windows for the religious community. They also provide an extensive leaded glass selection to the furniture industry. Not for the budget-minded home owner. A repair and restoration service for glass and windows. Free literature.

Rollerwall, Inc.
P.O. Box 757 (OHJ)   Dept. OHJ
Silver Springs, MD 20901
(301) 649-4422
MO
Sells the design paint roller. A wallpaper effect can be obtained by the use of a 6-in. rubber roller with a design embossed on its surface. Can also be used on fabric and furniture. Over 100 patterns including wood grain and marble. Illustrated brochure — free.

• **Roman Marble Co.**
120 W. Kinzie   Dept. OHJ
Chicago, IL 60610
(312) 337-2217
RS/O
Company sells imported antique marble mantels. Restoration and installation of marble mantels. Also — pedestals and statuary of marble, from Italy and France. Shipment can occasionally be arranged. No literature — please come in or telephone only.

Ross, Douglas — Woodworker
P.O. Box 480   Dept. OHJ
Brooklyn, NY 11215
(212) 499-5152
RS/O
Custom cabinetwork and furniture; restoration and finish carpentry. Free estimate; no literature.

• **Roy Electric Co., Inc.**
1054 Coney Island Avenue   Dept. OHJ
Brooklyn, NY 11230
(212) 339-6311
RS/O   MO
Large selection of gas and electric fixtures, sconces, brackets, pendants, table and pole lamps, Emeralites, bases and fixture parts, glass shades. Antique Victorian and turn-of-century brass beds and brass & iron beds. Also reproductions of gas and electric fixtures and lamps, custom brass beds and brass accessories. They restore, repair, cast, bend, plate, polish, lacquer, and extend old brass beds to Queen/King size. Catalog and price list, and pictures available for $3.00.

• **Royal Windyne Limited**
1316 W. Main Street   Dept. OH3
Richmond, VA 23220
(804) 358-1899
MO
Hand-built reproductions of 19th century ceiling fans. Nostalgic fans save energy by cooling in summer and circulating warm air in winter. Solid-brass appointments and hand-rubbed furniture-finish dark walnut or golden oak blades made of one-piece solid wood. Available with or without lights. Please allow 3-5 weeks for fabrication of your order. Illustrated catalog, $1.00.

S

S H M Restorations
887 Ashland Ave.   Dept. OHJ
St. Paul, MN 55104
(612) 291-7117
RS/O
Carpentry, general contracting, cabinetmaking, and fine woodworking. They specialize in restoration of Victorian houses and commercial structures. Design services for Victorian recreation and architecturally compatible remodeling. Reproduce mouldings, spindle work, etc. Dealers for many restoration products. No literature available.

S & W Framing Supplies, Inc.
120 Broadway   Dept. OHJ
Garden City Park, NY 11040
(800) 645-3399
MO   RS/O
Major distributor of framing supplies and machinery, serving the picture framing trade and art galleries. Their picture rail hangers, sold in gold with gold buttons and rope, were recommended by an OHJ subscriber. Free illustrated catalog.

• **St. Louis Antique Lighting Co.**
PO Box 8146   Dept. OHJ
St. Louis, MO 63156
(314) 535-2770
MO   RS/O
Antique and reproduction ceiling fixtures, sconces and lamps. Gas, electric and combination fixtures from 1880 to 1930. Catalog $3.00.

• **Saldarini & Pucci, Inc.**
156 Crosby St.   Dept. OHJ
New York, NY 10012
(212) 673-4390
RS/O   MO   DIST
Plaster and composition (fiberglass) ornaments: Ceiling medallions, ornaments for complete ceilings, niche shells, domes, capitals, cornices, mouldings, exterior fiberglass cornices. Also do restoration and custom plasterwork. Has thousands of molds for composition ornaments applicable on wood: Scrolls, wreaths, cornices, rosettes, beading, etc. No catalog available. Send drawing of what you wish and they will tell you what they have that is closest.

• **Saltbox**
2229 Marietta Pike   Dept. OHJ
Lancaster, PA 17603
(717) 392-5649
RS/O   MO   DIST
American period lighting fixtures: Extensive collection of lanterns and chandeliers handcrafted of tin, copper, brass and pewter. The Period Collection is designed for traditional, Early American and Colonial homes in primitive, country or formal styles. Stores also in Lexington, Ky, Green Bay, WI, and Greensboro, NC. Illustrated brochure showing 25 of over 250 pieces — $1.00.

Salvage One
1524 S. Peoria   Dept. OHJ
Chicago, IL 60608
(312) 733-0098
RS/O
Enormous selection of architectural artifacts, housed in a 7-storey warehouse. Can supply complete room interiors for restorations, or period decor in restaurants, etc. In-stock items available for prop rentals. Walk-in store only, open to the public. No literature.

San Francisco Renaissance
2501 Bryant Street   Dept. OHJ
San Francisco, CA 94110
(415) 826-0447
RS/O   MO
Architects — general contractors — painters well known for their historic facade restorations, color consultation, and fine painting. Also produce architectural ornaments & stenciling. Free assistance in placing historic buildings in the National Register. Free brochure.

San Francisco Restorations
2416 Pine St.   Dept. OHJ
San Francisco, CA 94115
(415) 282-9857
RS/O
Restoration contractor specializing in Victorian embellishments — especially the re-creation of ornate wooden facades and interiors. Extensive use of stock mouldings — avoiding the added expense of custom woodwork. Also provides design and consulting services. Works primarily in the Northern California area, but will do design and consulting work elsewhere. No literature; call for appointment.

San Francisco Victoriana
2245 Palou Avenue   Dept. OHJ
San Francisco, CA 94124
(415) 648-0313
RS/O   MO
Manufactures stock lines or reproduction Victorian and traditional wood mouldings, shingles, stair components; also reproductions of fire-place mantels; plaster ceiling centerpieces, cornices, and brackets. Supplies embossed anaglypta wallcoverings; embossed wall and frieze border papers; bronze door and window hardware in matched patterns; and cast iron spiral staircases. Custom duplications from plaster or wood samples. Write for free brochure and description of illustrated catalogs.

Sanders, David & Co.
115 Bowery   Dept. OHJ
New York, NY 10002
(212) 966-0838
RS/O
Large selection of brass & bronze hardware including wheels and tracks for sliding doors. No literature; walk-in store only.

● **Santa Cruz Foundry**
Courthouse Square   Dept. OHJ
Hanford, CA 93230
(209) 584-1541
RS/O   MO   DIST
Three attractive wood and wrought iron garden benches in a variety of sizes, a wrought iron 1842 English pub table and a Victorian table base. Free illustrated brochure and price list.

Sarah Bustle Antiques
1701 Central St.   Dept. OHJ
Evanston, IL 60201
(312) 869-7290
RS/O
They specialize in the restoration and sale of brass and copper ceiling lighting fixtures, dating from 1860 to 1920. All fixtures complete with antique light shades. Also old brass, copper, and bronze hardware in stock. No supplies or literature.

● = Consult ad for more details. See Advertisers' Index on the last page of this Catalog.

Savogran Co.
P.O. Box 130   Dept. OHJ
Norwood, MA 02062
(617) 762-5400
DIST
Manufactures a variety of house repair and maintenance products — paint strippers, tile grout, wood putty, wallpaper remover, floor leveler, vinyl spackle, water putty, deglosser, wood preservative, TSP cleaner and wood floor cleaner. $.25 for informative booklet "Home Upkeep Projects."

Savoy Studios
1228 C Street   Dept. OHJ
Eureka, CA 95501
(707) 442-7821
ID
Custom glass: stained, carved, deep-etched, sandblasted. Most of their work is in California, but they do work around the country. (They are currently working on panels for Maxwell's Plum and Tavern on the Green.) Restoration work done as well. No literature, but calls are welcome.

Sawdust Room
P.O. Box 327, 1856 S. Sierra   Dept. OHJ
Stevensville, MI 49127
(616) 429-5338
MO   RS/O
Early American wood products made and repaired: canopy beds, spinning wheels, custom wood products. Cylindrical lathe duplications. Light antique repair: chair rungs, rockers, spokes, Shaker clothes racks, etc. Will answer serious inquiries if you enclose a stamped, self-addressed envelope.

● **Scalamandre, Inc.**
950 Third Avenue   Dept. OHJ
New York, NY 10022
(212) 361-8500
ID
For 50 years this company has been making superb period fabrics. The authenticity of their fabrics, wallpapers, carpets and trimmings is acknowledged by museums. Scalamandre has been involved in the restorations at Monticello, San Simeon, and Sturbridge. A research library and consulting services are available to those persons involved in the restoration of public buildings. Free brochure.

● **Schaefer, Rick — Plasterer**
2501 Bryant St.   Dept. OHJ
San Francisco, CA 94110
(415) 826-0447
MO   RS/O
Journeyman plasterer specializing in ceilings: plaster repair, running mouldings, painting, stencilling, wallpapering. Also, replacement of exterior castings (capitals, faces, carvings). Concrete sculpture of rustic fences and curbs. Castings adapted from old photos, architect's drawings, on-site scars & pieces, and local Victorian ornament. "Spirited" imagery preferred. Will come and, with your help, save your house for an affordable fee. For estimate & poster, send $6.00 & specifics.

You'll get better service when contacting companies if you mention The Old-House Journal Catalog

---

Schmidt, Edward P. — Cabinetmaker
PO Box 443   Dept. OHJ
Glenside, PA 19038
(215) 886-8774
RS/O
Cabinetmaker will do reproduction work: furniture, doors, brackets, turnings, bookcases, wall units, and built-ins; in primitive, country, Early American, Colonial, Victorian, and contemporary styles. Pieces available in hardwoods, softwoods, and exotic species. Will also duplicate wood pieces for the rehabilitation of antique furniture and woodwork. References available. No literature, but inquiries will be answered.

Schmitt, Conrad Studios, Inc.
2405 S. 162nd St.   Dept. OHJ
New Berlin, WI 53151
(414) 786-3030
RS/O
Major midwest interior design firm. Designers, craftsmen and artisans carry through large interior design projects from analysis and proposal to final decorative treatments. Theatres, churches, banks, office buildings, etc. Longstanding reputation for quality. Call or write for appointment and brochure.

Schumacher
939 3rd Avenue   Dept. OHJ
New York, NY 10022
(212) 644-5943
DIST   ID
Schumacher has a large line of period and traditional fabrics and wallcoverings available at decorating shops and department stores. The documentary patterns have the historical information printed on back of the samples. They also have a fine line of damasks and brocades and Victorian prints, but these are decorator only. No literature.

● **Schwartz's Forge & Metalworks**
P.O. Box 205   Dept. OHJ
Deansboro, NY 13328
(315) 841-4477
RS/O   MO
Designs and executes architectural ironwork in a variety of styles, for use as gates, railings, grilles, furnishings etc. Traditional blacksmithing techniques used on all work. Custom design work. Will work with architect. Representative portfolio available for $3.50.

KEY TO ABBREVIATIONS

MO = sells by Mail Order

RS/O = sells through Retail Store or Office

DIST = sells through Distributors

ID = sells only through Interior Designers or Architects

The Old-House Journal 1982 Catalog   149

Schwerd Manufacturing Co.
3215 McClure Avenue   Dept. OHJ
Pittsburgh, PA 15212
(412) 766-6322
MO
Aesthetically pleasing, mathematically correct wooden columns. Available in Tuscan, Greek, and Roman orders, fluted or plain; round, square, or octagon shapes. Can manufacture columns to stock designs, or to your specifications. Ornamental caps: Scamozzi, Ionic, Doric, Temple of the Winds, Erechtheum, Roman Corinthian. Also — wooden lamp posts and lanterns. Specify interest for free brochure.

Sculpture Associates, Ltd.
114 E. 25th St.   Dept. OHJ
New York, NY 10010
(212) 777-2400
MO   RS/O
Fine imported tools, including rasps and carving tools. Also offer a complete line of woods, and clays. Casting materials such as plasters, plastics, and liquid metals are available. Many tools are good for scraping paint out of difficult places. Also has marble polishes and buffers. Send $1 for catalog.

Sculpture House
38 East 30th St.   Dept. OHJ
New York, NY 10016
MO   DIST
Manufacturers of handmade tools, and suppliers of material for all forms of three dimensional art. Tools are available for working in plaster, ceramics, wood, and stone. Complete catalogue with prices available for $2.00.

Second Chance
972 Magnolia St.   Dept. OHJ
Macon, GA 31201
(912) 742-7874
RS/O   MO
Specializes in hard-to-find restoration items. Inventory includes brass hardware, plumbing fixtures, fireplace tile, and old stained and beveled glass. A large collection of corbels, gingerbread, columns, entrance frames, heavily carved doors, mantels and antique staircase parts. Serves the middle Georgia area. No literature, but photographs can be supplied on request with a stamped, self-addressed envelope.

• **Sedgwick Machine Works, Inc.**
PO Box 630   Dept. OHJ
Poughkeepsie, NY 12602
(914) 454-5400
DIST
The oldest company in the dumbwaiter business, Sedgwick manufactures both electric and hand-powered dumbwaiters. Also manufactures a line of residence elevators. Free catalog.

Seitz, Robert/Fine Woodworking
Farwell Rd.   Dept. OHJ
Tyngsboro, MA 01879
(617) 649-7707
RS/O
Architectural restoration work in the Boston and southern New Hampshire area. Both on site carpentry and the use of a well-equipped shop for millwork are available. Send $1.00 for brochure; or send sketch, photo, etc., for consultation and estimate.

● = Consult ad for more details. See Advertisers' Index on the last page of this Catalog.

Selva — Borel
PO Box 796-A   Dept. OHJ
Oakland, CA 94604
(415) 832-0356
RS/O   MO
Supplier of clocks, clock kits, tools, parts and materials — including cases, hands, and movement. Quartz, battery-operated clock movements available. German Clock Catalog, $2.00, refundable on purchase.

Seraph, The
P.O. Box 500, Route 20   Dept. OHJ
Sturbridge, MA 01566
(617) 867-9353
RS/O   MO
Reproduction country sofas and wing chairs — copies of the kind of popularized furniture made by regional craftsmen in the 18th and 19th centuries: Chippendale, Sheraton, Hepplewhite, Queen Anne. Sofas from $450.00, chairs from $380.00. Frames are handcrafted and upholstery fabric is by Waverly, Greeff, Schumacher, and others. Illustrated brochure and fabric samples — $2.00.

Shadovitz Bros. Distributors, Inc.
1565 Bergen Street   Dept. OHJ
Brooklyn, NY 11213
(212) 774-9100
DIST   MO
Est. 1904. Distributors of glass, mirrors, plastic, & supplies. Antique mirror clips; insulated glass windows. Bent and patterned glass; wire glass; security glazing and bullet-resistant glass & plastic; safety glass. Ground, colored, non-glare, insulated, and obscure bevelled, tempered glass. Antique mirrors. Stained glass supplies, silicone, gloves, screening, skylights, sash chains, window guards. Glass etching. Free brochures.

Shaker Reproductions
Rear, 652 Main Street   Dept. OHJ
East Aurora, NY 14052
(716) 652-1920
MO   RS/O
Reproduction country furniture, details copied even to the dovetailing of drawers. Solid wood (pine and oak), guaranteed quality. Also brass beds and bath accessories, solid brass furniture hardware. Furniture catalog with price list $1. For accessories, specify interest and send SASE. Also send SASE for hardware brochure.

Shaker Workshops
PO Box 1028   Dept. OHJ
Concord, MA 01742
(617) 646-8985
MO   RS/O
Reproduction Shaker furniture kits, oval boxes, baskets, pegs & pegrail, lighting fixtures & tinware. Of special interest are the Shawl-Back and Tape-Back Rockers, in both child and adult sizes, identical to those made by the Mt. Lebanon, NY Shakers. Replacement chair tape also available in authentic Shaker colors. Showroom is at Old Schwamb Mill, Mill Lane, Arlington, Mass. Catalog and tape samples, $.50.

● **Shakertown Corporation**
P.O. Box 400   Dept. OHJ
Winlock, WA 98596
(206) 785-3501
MO   RS/O   DIST
A major manufacturer of shakes and shingles has red cedar shingles in 9 specialty patterns appropriate for Queen Anne and shingle-style houses. Fancy-butt shingles are 18 in. long and 5 in. wide, and are available for prompt shipment. Shakertown also manufactures 8' and 4' lengths of wood shingle & shakes panels. Free illustrated brochure.

● **Shanker Steel Corp.**
70-32 83rd St.   Dept. OHJ
Glendale, Queens, NY 11385
(212) 326-1100
MO
Company is a major manufacturer of pressed steel ceilings. Catalog, price list and brochure on how to put material up are available free.

Shelley Signs
Box 94   Dept. OHJ
West Danby, NY 14896
(607) 564-3527
MO
Signs (carved/painted) designed & executed in a traditional American vein. Custom carving work, including door panels, shells, scrolls. Folk-art style painted woodcarving of your house from a photo. Handcarved wooden plaques. Please send SASE and request for a representative slide or photo.

Shenandoah Manufacturing Co.
P.O. Box 839   Dept. OHJ
Harrisonburg, VA 22801
(703) 434-3838
DIST
Wood and/or coal stoves and furnaces; thermostatically regulated, utilitarian in design. Fireplace insert that will increase the efficiency of a fireplace. Also — add-on furnaces, to be used alone or added to an existing forced-air heating system. Free literature.

● **Sherwin-Williams Co.**
P.O. Box 6939   Dept. OHJ
Cleveland, OH 44101
(216) 566-2332
DIST
40 historic 19th-century exterior paint colors researched by Dr. Roger Moss and documented in his book "Century of Color: Exterior Decoration for American Buildings 1820-1920." Heritage colors are available in exterior latex house & trim paint and gloss oil-based house paint. Heritage color cards, $2.50.

● **Shingle Mill**
6 Cote Ave.   Dept. OHJ
S. Ashburnham, MA 01466
(617) 827-4889
MO   RS/O
High quality natural siding and roofing shingles. Special end cuts available. Custom shingles for restoration on request. Write or call for information. No literature.

● **Ship 'n Out**
8 W. Charles St.
Dept. OHJ
Pawling, NY 12564
(914) 855-5947
MO
Handcrafted copper weathervanes. Also, custom-order handlettered signage. Each sign incorporates a 3-dimensional copper animal figure like those associated with weathervanes. Heavy gauge brass bar railing. Both brochures for $.50.

● **Sign of the Crab**
8101 Elder Creek Rd.   Dept. 132
Sacramento, CA 95824
(916) 383-2722
RS/O   DIST
Manufacturer of brass hardware, fixtures, lamps, clocks, antique re-creations and nauticals. Wholesale catalog and price list to dealers. Call or write for name of distributor nearest you.

Silberman, Allen
18 Homer Avenue   Dept. OHJ
Cortland, NY 13045
(607) 756-2632
RS/O
Decorative painter specializing in stencilling. Has patterns available, can create new stencils or restore old ones. Has restored the Victorian stencilling in the 1890 House in Cortland, NY. Will travel; also will consult and/or train local craftsmen in the art of stencilling. Also conducts stencilling workshops. No literature; call or write specifying interest.

Silver Dollar Trading Co.
1446 So. Broadway   Dept. OHJ
Denver, CO 80210
(303) 733-0500
RS/O   MO
This company carries Victorian reproduction spiral staircases, street lights, mailboxes, light fixtures, fountains, and stained glass. Free catalog.

• **Silverton Victorian Millworks**
P.O. Box 877-35   Dept. OHJ
Silverton, CO 81433
(303) 387-5716
MO
Offer a variety of custom Victorian and Colonial mouldings, as well as the standard patterns. They also have window and door rosettes available in many combinations. The millwork is available in pine, redwood, or oak. They welcome any inquiries concerning custom milling. For custom mouldings, send a detailed drawing or sample for prompt quotation. Catalog — $3.50.

Skrocki, Ed
1816 Boston Road   Dept. OHJ
Hinckley, OH 44233
MO
Window glass cleaner removes black, sooty build-up on very dirty old windows. Enough for a house of windows, $9.00. No literature.

• **Sky Lodge Farm**
Box 62   Dept. OHJ
Shutesbury, MA 01072
(413) 253-3182
MO
Producers of Early American clapboards with quartersawn squared edges. Send for free brochure.

Skyline Engineers, Inc.
58 East St.   Dept. OHJ
Fitchburg, MA 01420
(617) 342-5333
RS/O
Restoration contractors specializing in steeple preservation, gold-leafing, and the restoration of historic buildings: including sandblasting, chemical restoration, and repointing. Work includes carpentry, painting, roofing (slate and copper), masonry, bird-proofing, lightning protection, and waterproofing. Free brochure. Call or write for free estimate.

You'll get better service when contacting companies if you mention The Old-House Journal Catalog

---

Sloane, Hugh L.
R.F.D.   Dept. OHJ
Bernardston, MA 01337
(413) 773-7312
RS/O   MO
Wood panelling reproduced from antique pine. Old wavy glass. No literature.

Smith-Cornell Homestead, Inc.
P.O. Box 666   Dept. OHJ
Auburn, IN 46706
(219) 925-1172
MO
Makes plaques and markers with image permanently embedded into anodized aluminum plate in bronze or pewter finish. Images can include lettering, photographs, line drawings, and logos. May be mounted inside or outside. Special rates for not-for-profit groups. Write or call for free catalog or quotation.

Smith, R.W. — Sashmaker
67 Main St.   Dept. OHJ
North Orange, MA 01364
(617) 249-4988
MO   RS/O
Sashmaker, primarily of Colonial reproductions. Replacement of 1-inch sash for various glass sizes and lites (9 over 6, 6 over 6, 12 over 12, etc.). Also stationary sash and wooden storm sash. All custom work using clear sugar pine. Call or write for cost quotations.

Smithy, The
Dept. OHJ
Wolcott, VT 05680
(802) 472-6508
MO
Hand-forged iron executed in the centuries-old manner, with forge, hammer, and anvil. Diversified work includes hardware necessary in restoration of old houses and construction of new reproductions: hinges, door latches, fireplace equipment, kitchen items, lighting fixtures, weathervanes, etc. Write for free brochure.

Smolinsky, Ltd.
203 Fawn Hill Road   Dept. OHJ
Broomall, PA 19008
(215) 353-2893
RS/O
Services southeastern Pennsylvania, southern New Jersey and Delaware with restoration contracting services. No literature.

• **Somerset Door & Column Co.**
P.O. Box 328   Dept. OHJ
Somerset, PA 15501
(814) 445-9608
MO   DIST   RS/O
Company has been manufacturing wood columns since 1906. Composition capitals also available. Column sizes from 6-in. bottom diameter to 40-in. diameter by 40 ft. long. They can also provide custom millwork such as stair parts, sash, moulding, panelling, and doors to customer's specifications. Columns brochure is free.

South Coast Shingle Co.
2220 E. South Street   Dept. OHJ
Long Beach, CA 90805
(213) 634-7100
RS/O   MO
Manufactures fancy butt red cedar shingles. Also distributes cedar shakes and shingles for roofing and siding. Free flyer — please specify.

Southern Accents Architectural Antiques
312 Second Ave., SE   Dept. OHJ
Cullman, AL 35055
(205) 734-4799
RS/O   MO
Architectural furnishings, including wood mantels, brass & crystal light fixtures, staircases, antique ceiling fans, urns, light posts, entire porches with gingerbread trim. Specialists in bath fixtures & fittings, dealing in completely restored tubs, commodes, & pedestal sinks. Complementary line of brass bath accessories & medicine chests. Photos available on specific inquiry; shipment arranged.

Spanish Pueblo Doors
PO Box 2517, Wagon Rd.   Dept. OHJ
Santa Fe, NM 87501
(505) 471-0811
MO   RS/O
Exterior doors of thick Ponderosa pine or Philippine mahogany. All custom milled to your size specifications of standard or custom designs.

Spiess, Greg
216 East Washington   Dept. OHJ
Joliet, IL 60433
(815) 722-5639
RS/O
Antique architectural ornamentation. Interior and exterior ornamental wood, mantels a specialty. Stained, leaded and bevelled glass; Antique and custom fabrication. Custom bevelling. Also handles antique tavern back bars. Good general architectural selection. No literature.

Spigel, Herman, & Chapman Ltd., Architects
420 West Bute Street   Dept. OHJ
Norfolk, VA 23510
(804) 622-7764
RS/O
Restoration architects and historic preservation planners. Dr. Frederick Herman is available for lectures. No literature; please write or call for more information.

Spring City Electrical Mfg. Co
Hall & Main Streets   Dept. OHJ
Spring City, PA 19475
(215) 948-4000
MO
Manufactures cast-iron ornamental lamp posts and bollards, and bronze fountains. Lamp posts are suitable for street use. Free brochure.

KEY TO ABBREVIATIONS

MO = sells by Mail Order

RS/O = sells through Retail Store or Office

DIST = sells through Distributors

ID = sells only through Interior Designers or Architects

Squaw Alley, Inc.
106 W. Water St. Dept. OHJ
Naperville, IL 60540
(312) 357-0200
MO RS/O
A restoration supply source, specializing in sale and restoration of oil lamps (including Aladdins), gas and early electric fixtures. Also lamp repair parts, lampshades, antique and reproduction hardware (very large stock) caning supplies, cleaning/refinishing products, bent and convex glass, mirror resilvering and sale of antique bevelled mirrors. Serves mainly Chicago area but hardware can be shipped anywhere. Catalog, $1.

Stair-Pak Products Co.
Rt. 22, Box 334   Dept. OHJ
Union, NJ 07083
(201) 688-8000
Company has designed and manufactured all-wood spiral stairways for three generations. Also Rail-Pak pre-assembled stair rail systems for remodelling or new construction. Free brochures.

Stairways, Inc.
4323-A Pinemont   Dept. OHJ
Houston, TX 77018
(713) 680-3110
MO RS/O
Manufactures custom-built spiral stairways. Metal or wood treads and handrail. Contemporary design. Their all-wood stairway is available unfinished. Free brochure.

Stamford Wallpaper Co., Inc.
153 Greenwich Ave., PO Box 561   Dept. OHJ
Stamford, CT 06820
(203) 323-1123
DIST
Documented lines of reproduction wallpapers. Can reproduce Victorian wallpapers from original documents, if the quantity is sufficient. Two lines of textures available which could accompany any pattern. No literature.

Standard Dry Wall Products
7800 N.W. 38th Street   Dept. OHJ
Miami, FL 33166
(305) 592-2081
DIST
The Thoro system is a complete line of products for waterproofing, decorating, correcting and restoring concrete and masonry surfaces. Free booklet.

Standard Heating Parts, Inc.
4615 Belden Avenue   Dept. OHJ
Chicago, IL 60639
MO RS/O
Stoker parts. Write for free brochure.

● **Stanley Galleries**
2118 N. Clark Street   Dept. OHJ
Chicago, IL 60614
(312) 281-1614
MO RS/O
They specialize in restoring and selling American antique lighting from 1850 to 1925. All fixtures are thoroughly researched so that antique shades can be matched with them. Only old glass is used, not reproductions. All fixtures are taken apart, stripped, rewired, and relacquered. Walk-in store has large selection; mail orders also taken. Call or write about specific fixtures; a Polaroid photo will be sent on request.

Stark Carpet Corp.
979 Third Ave.   Dept. OHJ
New York, NY 10022
(212) 752-9000
ID
Documented carpets for historical restorations. Also a stock line of historical Wilton carpets; machine-made and handmade rugs from over 20 countries, including Portuguese needlepoints, Romanian kilims, and orientals. Please inquire on your letterhead.

The Stenciller's Touch
232 Amazon Place   Dept. OHJ
Columbus, OH 43214
(614) 263-1420
RS/O
Design and application of Early American stencilling to walls, floors, etc. They have a large portfolio, including designs by Moses Eaton. Other motifs include Oriental, American Indian, Victorian, and Pennsylvania Dutch. Specialist in custom-designed stencils that will coordinate with client's interior space. Please call for appointment.

Stencilsmith
Leominster Road   Dept. OHJ
Shirley, MA 01464
(617) 425-4072
MO
Produces ready-to-use stencils for walls and floors. Each stencil is precut on clear durable vinyl from original handdrawn patterns. 5 Early American or 5 Victorian designs plus illustrated decorating booklet — $27.95 each. Early American or Victorian Supplies Kits include easy-to-use velour applicators, 6 tubes period color oil paint, spar varnish as paint medium for maximum durability and instructions — $19.95 each.

Stencilworks
63 17th St., NE   Dept. OHJ
Atlanta, GA 30309
(404) 892-8114
MO RS/O
Stencilling services throughout the East. All stencil jobs are custom-designed: Research and interior design capabilities available. Work ranges from restoration of historic patterns to contemporary adaptation of this traditional decoration. Lectures and classes given. Estimates possible through the mail, but further consultation usually requires travel. No literature.

● **Steptoe and Wife Antiques Ltd.**
3626 Victoria Park Ave.   Dept. OHJ
Willowdale, ON, Canada M2H3B2
(416) 497-2989
MO RS/O DIST
Reproduction Victorian style cast-iron spiral staircase. Knocks down for shipping and on-site assembly — modular units for any elevation. They also distribute W.F. Norman sheet metal ceiling panels. Illustrated folder with nearest dealer is free.

● **Sterline Manufacturing Corp.**
410 N. Oakley Blvd.   Dept. OHJ
Chicago, IL 60612
(312) 226-1555
DIST
"CONVERTO" Shower systems for adding a shower to old bathtubs. Includes tub and shower faucet, rectangular, corner, and straight shower rods. Available in chrome-plated brass and polished brass. A free brochure is available. Retail customers see listing under Barclay Products.

Stevens, John R., Associates
1 Sinclair Drive   Dept. OHJ
Greenlawn, NY 11740
(516) 420-5295
RS/O
Specializing in the restoration of buildings from the 17th century to the mid 19th century and restoration of antique street railway rolling stock. New York metropolitan region and New Haven, Connecticut area. No literature.

Stewart Manufacturing Company
511 Enterprise Drive   Dept. OHJ
Erlanger, KY 41017
(606) 331-9000
MO DIST RS/O
They manufacture ornamental iron fence and gates. Each design is custom made, with the ability to match various old designs manufactured after 1886. No cost or obligation for an estimate. A complete, illustrated catalog is available upon request.

Stringer's Environmental Restoration & Design
2140 San Pablo Ave.   Dept. OHJ
Berkeley, CA 94702
(415) 548-3967
MO DIST
Manufacturers of hand-crafted porcelain, specializing in pedestal sinks and vanity basins. Victorian design fluted base pedestal sink, and 1920's smooth pedestal sink. Bathroom accessories. Custom orders welcome. Catalog, $2.

● **Strip Shop**
2201 Tchoupitoulas Street   Dept. OHJ
New Orleans, LA 70130
(504) 522-7524
RS/O
Architectural antiques - doors, mantels, shutters, stained and bevelled glass. A quality selection of oval bevelled entrance doors. Also brass, porcelain, and other hardware to complement doors. All material is stripped and ready to be refinished. No literature.

● **Strobel Millwork**
P.O. Box 84, Route 7   Dept. OHJ
Cornwall Bridge, CT 06754
(203) 672-6727
RS/O MO
Stock and custom architectural millwork. Company specializes in the exact duplication of all styles of wood windows and doors, particularly Italianate or Renaissance styles. Full line of decorative screen doors. Doors are shipped complete; screen is in place. Brochure, $2.00.

Structural Antiques
3006 Classen Blvd.   Dept. OHJ
Oklahoma City, OK 73106
(405) 528-7734
RS/O MO
Structural Antiques has over 6,000 sq. ft. of inventory consisting exclusively of American antique architectural elements. They offer a large selection of stamped tin ceiling, barn siding, doors, stained glass windows, brass light fixtures, fireplace fronts, and other items. Services include decorating and design ideas and installation of architectural elements. No literature.

Structural Slate Company
222 East Main Street   Dept. OHJ
Pen Argyl, PA 18072
(215) 863-4141
RS/O DIST
A primary source of structural slate products for flooring, stair treads, and accent trim; slate tile for slate roofs. Free brochure.

Stryker, Donald Restorations
154 Commercial Ave.   Dept. OHJ
New Brunswick, NJ 08901
(201) 828-7022
MO   RS/O
Provides interior and exterior restoration services for residential and small-scale commercial buildings, with special emphasis on 19th century residential structures. No literature.

Studio Design, Inc. t/a Rainbow Art Glass
49 Shark River Road   Dept. OHJ
Neptune, NJ 07753
(201) 922-1090
MO   RS/O
Manufactures a large selection of stained glass items in the Tiffany style, including lamp shades, windows, mirrors and other wall decor, terrariums, room dividers, and more. All items available already assembled or in do-it-yourself kits. Custom work also available. Brochure, $2.

Studio Stained Glass
117 So. Main St.   Dept. OHJ
Kokomo, IN 46901
(317) 452-2438
RS/O
Designs and builds stained glass windows and shades. Company also repairs and restores stained glass, along with custom glass beveling. Serving the Midwest. No literature.

● **Stulb Paint & Chemical Co., Inc.**
810 East Main St.   Dept. OHJ
Norristown, PA 19404
(215) 272-6660
MO
Manufacturers of authentic 18th and 19th century paint colors for furniture, walls, woodwork — interior and exterior. Oil-based, lead-free. Exclusive maker of Old Sturbridge Village colors. Send $.50 for color cards and literature.

Such Happiness, Inc.
P.O. Box 32   Dept. OHJ
Fitchburg, MA 01420
(603) 878-1031
MO   RS/O
Restored antique stained glass windows and leaded panels. Decorative, Victorian designs. Consultation and installation for pubs, restaurants, offices, and homes. Also, custom new designs. Delivery and installation generally available. Call or write for estimates and free literature.

● **Sullivan's Antiques**
P.O. Box 132   Dept. OHJ
Santa Ana, CA 92702
(714) 541-4174
Carry old glass knobs that have never been used. Write or call for more information.

● **Sun Designs**
PO Box 206   Dept. OHJ
Delafield, WI 53018
(414) 567-4255
MO
Company offers study-plan books for a variety of structures. Gazebo: 34 designs from 8' to 20' — $6.55. Outhouse: 25 designs (can be converted to sauna, playhouse, garden shed, etc.) — $7.95. Bridges, Cupolas, Weathervanes: $7.95. Construction plans available for all designs shown in books. All PPD.

● = Consult ad for more details.   See Advertisers' Index on the last page of this Catalog.

Sunburst Stained Glass Co.
825 E. Church St., P.O. Box 5   Dept. OHJ
New Harmony, IN 47631
(812) 682-4065
MO   RS/O
Design, construction, restoration, and repair of stained glass windows, lamps, sculpture, whether leaded or foiled. Beveled glass windows available in standard and some custom patterns. Will travel for on-site work when appropriate. Services range from complete releading to minor repair to creating a new-old window — small and large commissions accepted. No literature.

Sundials, Inc.
Sawyer Passway   Dept. OHJ
Fitchburg, MA 01420
(617) 342-8671
MO   RS/O
Traditional sundials, cupolas, weathervanes. Free catalog.

● **Sunrise Salvage**
2210 San Pablo Ave.   Dept. COHJ
Berkeley, CA 94702
(415) 845-4751
MO   RS/O
Specializes in Victorian plumbing, both original and reproduction. Features valves in a polished brass finish, and sink and tub fixtures, as well as shower set-ups, in brass. Also oak and brass pullchain toilet packages, oak bathroom furnishings, and a new line of Victorian-style light fixtures. Many salvaged items too. Bath catalog, $1.00.

Sunshine Lane
Box 262   Dept. OHJ
Millersburg, OH 44654
MO
Handquilted one of a kind quilts in traditional and modern patterns. Also custom-made quilts and quilting accessories. Decorator's book with more than 60 photos of the quilts they offer is available for a $35 deposit applied to first purchase. 4-color illustrated catalog, $1.

● **Superior Clay Corporation**
P.O. Box 352   Dept. OHJ
Uhrichsville, OH 44683
(614) 922-4122
MO   RS/O   DIST
Manufacturers of clay flue linings and clay chimney tops. The clay chimney tops come in various sizes & styles. Free brochure.

● **Supradur Mfg. Corp.**
122 E. 42 St.   Dept. OHJ
New York, NY 10168
(212) 697-1160
DIST
Manufacturer of mineral-fiber (asbestos-cement) roofing shingles: an acceptable substitute for slate when replacement becomes necessary. Supra-Slate line closely approximates color and size of real thing. Also available — Dutch Lap, Twin Lap, American Traditional, and Hexagonal asbestos shingles appropriate for early 20th century houses. Free literature.

Surrey Shoppe Interiors
665 Centre St.   Dept. OHJ
Brockton, MA 02402
(617) 588-2525
MO
Clear vinyl shower curtains and plastic liners in hard-to-find sizes. Available in poly/cotton fabric. Sizes to fit converted clawfoot tubs. Brochure $.25.

Sutherland Welles Ltd.
406 West Main Street   Dept. OHJ
Carrboro, NC 27510
(919) 967-1972
RS/O   MO
Tung Oil finishing, restoring and maintenance products for wood, concrete, and masonry. Easy-to-use for both exterior and interior surfaces including walls, floors, paneling, cabinets, fine furniture. Custom stain, paint, finish, and varnish. Consultation for custom finishing. Send for Tung Oil catalog, $2.00.

Swan Brass Beds
1955 East 16th Street   Dept. OHJ
Los Angeles, CA 90021
800-421-0141
DIST
Solid brass beds, etageres, wrought iron baker racks, solid brass desks, planters, coat trees. Many other reproductions including 19th century wood carousel horses. Through retail outlets only. No literature but to find nearest distributor, call toll-free number.

Sweet William House
P. O. Box 230   Dept. OHJ
Lake Forest, IL 60045
(312) 234-8767
MO
Manufacturers of bronze historic markers indicating the name and date of your house. They also manufacture a bronze plaque with a poem about old houses. Send S.A.S.E. for free literature.

● **Swift & Sons, Inc.**
Ten Love Lane   Dept. OHJ
Hartford, CT 06101
(203) 522-1181
MO   RS/O   DIST
A primary supplier of gold leaf, roll gold and silver leaf. How-to booklet, free.

Swofford, Don A., AIA
1843 Seminole Tr Woodbrook Vlg   Dept. OHJ
Charlottesville, VA 22901
(804) 973-3155
RS/O
Architectural firm specializing in restoration, adaptive renovation, compatible new design, and maintenance- consulting. Reconstruction or new design of period buildings, both residential and commercial. Planning surveys and inventories. Passive solar heating retrofits. References and full written proposals available — no standard literature.

KEY TO ABBREVIATIONS

MO = sells by Mail Order

RS/O = sells through Retail Store or Office

DIST = sells through Distributors

ID = sells only through Interior Designers or Architects

Synkoloid Co.
P.O. Box 60937   Dept. OHJ
Los Angeles, CA 90060
(213) 268-2761
DIST
Manufactures a complete line of patching, repairing and resurfacing compounds in powder and ready-mixed forms. These products are formulated for all types of interior wall and ceiling repair as well as exterior repair of masonry, stucco, wood and compositions. The company also markets a complete line of caulks and sealants, drywall joint compounds, waterproofing paint and wall texture paint in smooth and sand finishes. No literature.

Szabo & Carrick, Architects, Inc.
3425 Kenyon St., Suite 202   Dept. OHJ
San Diego, CA 92110
(714) 224-3676
MO
Provides consultation and architectural services on a national and world-wide basis, for restoration, rehabilitation, and reconstruction projects. Only the safest and most proven preservation techniques and practices are recommended and utilized for historical masonry, stone, wood, metal, and glass materials. Feasibility studies, structural and code analysis, historical research and other investigative services. Free information will be mailed to serious inquiries.

T

T.A.G. Preservation Consultation
226 88th St.   Dept. OHJ
Brooklyn, NY 11209
(212) 748-4934
RS/O
Preservation consultation services, such as preparation of preservation plans, National Register nominations; walking tours and publications; and design services with an emphasis on adaptive re-use. Serving NY metropolitan area, including N. NJ and S. CT. No literature.

Talas
130 Fifth Ave.   Dept. OHJ
New York, NY 10011
(212) 675-0718
MO RS/O
Company sells supplies to art restorers. Several products are of special interest to those restoring old houses: textile cleaner; Wishab and Absorene wallpaper cleaners; Vultex liquid soap for cleaning stone and marble. No literature — please call or write for specifics and prices.

Taney Supply & Lumber Corp.
5130 Allendale Lane   Dept. OHJ
Taneytown, MD 21787
(301) 756-6671
MO RS/O
Manufacturers of prebuilt wood stairways and stairway parts. Free brochure.

Tatko Bros. Slate Co.
    Dept. OHJ
Middle Granville, NY 12849
(518) 642-1640
DIST MO RS/O
Manufacturers of slate floor tile for in and outside installation, Slate flagstone, structural and roofing slate. No literature.

Tennessee Fabricating Co.
2366 Prospect Street   Dept. OHJ
Memphis, TN 38106
(901) 948-3354
MO
Manufacturer of full line of aluminum and iron ornamental castings. Reproductions of lawn furniture, fountains, urns, planters. Complete line of gates, fences, balconies and all residential metal work. Will reproduce customer's designs or create new designs. Booklet of patio furniture and ornamental accessories $1.00. Full catalog of ornamental metal-work $2.50.

Tennessee Tub
905 Church Street   Dept. OHJ
Nashville, TN 37203
(615) 242-0780
RS/O
Antique tubs and pedestal wash basins dating from 1880's, completely restored. Pull chain toilets available with handcrafted precious wood tanks and seats. Brass and chrome fittings supplied. Free brochure.

Thibaut, Richard E., Inc.
315 Fifth Ave.   Dept. OHJ
New York, NY 10016
(212) 481-0880
DIST
Mural collections: Victorian, Early American, Traditional. Mural folder: $.50.

Thomas Antique Services
Star Route 2 — 212B   Dept. OHJ
Vass, NC 28394
(919) 692-6724
RS/O
Brass and copper polishing, furniture stripping and refinishing, antique restoration, brass hardware, cane, splint and rush seats. No literature.

Thomastown Chair Works
Box 93   Dept. OHJ
Thomastown, MS 39171
(601) 289-6560
MO
Manufactures a large oak rocking chair with handwoven cane seat and back, the "Plantation Rocker" of the Old South. Available in light, medium or dark oak stain, the rocker is suitable for outdoor use. Free descriptive sheet.

Thompson & Anderson, Inc.
53 Seavey Street   Dept. OHJ
Westbrook, ME 04092
(207) 854-2905
RS/O MO DIST
Complete line of stove pipe, including insulated chimney adapters. Spot-welded seam construction, heat-proof finish. Supplies insulated pipe and fittings. General sheetmetal work. Illustrated literature and price list, free.

Tile Distributors, Inc.
7 Kings Highway   Dept. OHJ
New Rochelle, NY 10801
(914) 633-7200
RS/O MO
Carries unglazed white hexagonal, black and white spiral, white unglazed random, 3/4-in. and 2-in. square unglazed white bathroom floor tiles; 3-in. x 6-in. & 6-in. x 6-in. white replacement wall tile; glazed black wall trim; replacement ceramic non-flange fixtures. Will research and try to locate ceramic tile produced before 1940. No literature, but can send specific samples in the mail. Will ship prepaid orders.

Timberpeg
Box 1358   Dept. OHJ
Claremont, NH 03743
(603) 542-7762
RS/O DIST
Manufacturers of pre-cut, mortise and tenon, pine frames. Superior insulation systems. High quality, low maintenance materials, such as cedar clapboards and roof shakes and custom-made exterior doors are included. Architectural design and engineering are also part of the package. New solar series available. Catalog — $6.00.

Timeless Patterns
465 Colrain Rd.   Dept. OHJ
Greenfield, MA 01301
(413) 774-5742
MO
Company sells patterns for 33 stencil designs. High-quality Mylar patterns can be cut, or are traceable for free-hand painting. Designs range from traditional Early American and Victorian, to original adaptations and contemporary. Includes 3 designs for stair treads, and 2 for hearth rugs. Full catalog $3.00.

Tindall, Susan M.
1130 Winonah   Dept. OHJ
Oak Park, IL 60304
(312) 383-1970
RS/O
Consultant on design, preservation and restoration of architectural terra cotta, encaustic tiles and architectural ornaments. Please call; no literature.

• Toby House
517 E. Paces Ferry Rd., N.E.   Dept. OHJ
Atlanta, GA 30305
MO
A set of seven stencils adapted from the work of Early American itinerant artist Moses Eaton. Stencils are made of clear vinyl and can be used for walls, floors, fabrics, and floorcloths. $35.00 for set. Brochure of patterns and supplies, $2.50.

Topiary Frames by John Wallace
1736 N. Cleveland Ave.   Dept. OHJ
Chicago, IL 60614
(312) 944-6329
RS/O MO
Hand-soldered topiary frames for training plants into interesting shapes. Available in all shapes and sizes, from a simple globe to a rooster or giant bunny. Hand-formed and soldered galvanized iron, sprayed with rust-proof paint. Custom work also. Free descriptive sheet with prices.

Townscape
30 Public Square   Dept. OHJ
Medina, OH 44256
(216) 725-6273
RS/O
Townscape's professional design consultants assist communities interested in revitalizing their own special 'Main Street" commercial areas and neighborhoods. By developing comprehensive action programs utilizing both statistical and visual information, Townscape is able to help cities avert the many costly trial-and-error exercises often encountered when urban design problems are dealt with on a fragmented basis. Resume/ brochure available at no charge.

• **Travis Tuck, Metal Sculptor**
RFD Lamberts Cove Road   Dept. OHJ
Martha's Vineyard, MA 02568
(617) 693-3914
RS/O   MO
Custom metalwork studio, specializing in copper weathervanes copper reproduction lamps, hand-forged ironwork (chandeliers brackets, gates, hardware), and tradesmen signs in hollow copper repoussé and hand-forged iron. All custom work in copper, brass, or iron. No literature: pieces are one-of-a-kind.

Tremont Nail Company
P.O. Box 111   Dept. OHJ
Wareham, MA 02571
(617) 295-0038
RS/O   MO   DIST
In business since 1819, this company manufactures old-fashioned cut nails that are useful for restoration work. These decorative antique nails include Wrought Head, Hinge, Rose Head Clinch and Common; also the DECOR-NAIL and many others. A sample card with 20 patterns of actual cut nails attached, history and complete ordering information is available for $3.50 ppd. Free brochure and price list.

Trow & Holden Co.
P.O. Box 475   Dept. OHJ
Barre, VT 05641
1-800-451-4349
MO   DIST   RS/O
Manufacturers of a complete line of stoneworking and masonry tools including pneumatic carving hammers, pneumatic drills, carbide tipped hand tools, and stone splitting tools. Free catalog and price list available upon request.

Troyer, Le Roy and Associates
415 Lincolnway East   Dept. OHJ
Mishawaka, IN 46544
(219) 259-9976
RS/O
Serves Indiana, Illinois, Ohio, and southern Michigan area with architectural restoration services. Information on previous restoration projects available on request.

Turnbull's Custom Mouldings
P.O. Box 602   Dept. OHJ
Sumner, MI 48889
(517) 833-7089
MO
Specialists in custom duplication of hardwood mouldings. Almost any moulding profile can be reproduced from a small sample. Free company flyer; please be specific in inquiries sent.

Twanky Dillo Forge
Sand Hill Rd. RFD 1 Box 213   Dept. OHJ
Putney, VT 05346
(802) 387-5991
MO   DIST   RS/O
Twanky Dillo Forge is the composite of two blacksmith craftsmen traditionally forging wrought iron functional objects. Special orders, reproductions, and commission items gladly accepted. Send SASE for brochure.

● = Consult ad for more details.   See Advertisers' Index on the last page of this Catalog.

U

Ultimate Energy Systems
P.O. Box 154   Dept. OHJ
Monroe, NY 10950
(914) 782-8469
MO   DIST
Distributors of multi-fuel boilers and furnaces: gas, oil, electricity, wood, coal. Combination or add-on. Literature and price list free.

Unique Brass Foundry, Inc.
1612 Decatur Street   Dept. OHJ
Ridgewood, NY 11385
(212) 381-0945
DIST   MO
Ornamental brass castings: desk accessories, knockers, etc. Also lamps, brass beds, coat racks, music stands, occasional pieces. Most business is wholesale to distributor but they will deal with retail sales by mail order, prepaid. Brass catalog and price-list, $1.

United Gilsonite Laboratories
   Dept. OHJ
Scranton, PA 18501
(717) 344-1202
DIST
UGL manufactures a complete line of products for home repair and maintenance including ZAR Clear Finishes and Stains, DRYLOK masonry treatment products, caulks and sealants, paint and varnish removers, among others. Free descriptive literature. Two booklets at $.25 each - "The Finishing Touch", a beginners guide to wood finishing, and "How to Waterproof Masonry Walls."

United House Wrecking Corp.
328 Selleck Street   Dept. OHJ
Stamford, CT 06902
(203) 348-5371
RS/O
Six acres of relics from old houses: mantels, stained glass, antiques, used furniture, antique reproductions of copper weathervanes, fabulous brass & copper reproductions. Free illustrated brochure available about the yard.

● **United Stairs Corp.**
Highway 35   Dept. OHJ
Keyport, NJ 07735
(201) 583-1100
MO   RS/O
A complete line of wood staircases, straight, circular & spiral. Available assembled or knocked down. Prefabricated and prefinished wood railing systems. Free brochure.

U.S. General Supply Corp.
100 Commercial Street   Dept. OHJ
Plainview, NY 11803
(516) 349-7282
MO
A first-rate mail order source for name-brand tools and hardware at lower prices. Catalog offers traditional tools — everything from drawknives and spokeshaves to mitre boxes and handsaws. Plus modern power tools for saving time. Catalog has over 6,000 items in 196 pages. Fully illustrated — $1.

U.S. Gypsum Company
101 South Wacker Drive   Dept. OHJ
Chicago, IL 60606
(312) 321-3852
DIST
Among the diverse products made by this major company are vinyl moulding, paints, stains, mold making materials, texture paint, masonry coatings. Free literature.

Universal Clamp Corp.
6905 Cedros Ave.   Dept. OHJ
Van Nuys, CA 91405
(213) 780-1015
MO   DIST
Manufactures a variety of clamps for repairing and restoring antiques, cabinetmaking and fine woodwork. Produces the popular "805" Porta-Press jig for assembly of mitered frames and doors. Tool completes all joints at one setting with range from 8 x 8 to 34 x 48 inches. Also makes one of the most complete tool benches, with nearly 12 square feet of work area. Available with maple or chip board top. Brochures & price list free with legal size self-addressed envelope.

Up Country Enterprise Corp.
Plantation Drive   Dept. OHJ
Jaffrey, NH 03452
(603) 532-8732
RS/O   MO
Up Country accepts orders for original designs, reproductions of period pieces, and adaptations of classic design services. They offer complete design services, working from descriptions, photographs, sketches, or detailed drawings. Have done work for Old Sturbridge Village and Smithsonian. Consultant services available. Literature $2.

Up Your Alley
784 South Sixth Street   Dept. OHJ
Philadelphia, PA 19147
(215) WA5-5597
MO
Ceramic tiles — Dutch, English, American — over 100 years old. For interior or exterior use. Photographs will be supplied on specific request.

Upland Stove Co., Inc.
PO Box 338, Dept. 17   Dept. OHJ
Greene, NY 13778
(607) 656-4156
DIST
These are the manufacturers of the all-cast-iron Upland woodstoves. Four airtight models available: 2 box stoves and 2 combination fireplace/box stove models. Quality American-made construction and materials. Available in black, brown, green. Literature and information about distributors free on request.

KEY TO ABBREVIATIONS

MO   = sells by Mail Order

RS/O = sells through Retail Store or Office

DIST = sells through Distributors

ID   = sells only through Interior Designers or Architects

You'll get better service when contacting companies if you mention The Old-House Journal Catalog

---

The Old-House Journal 1982 Catalog   155

V

Valley Iron & Steel Co.
29579 Aubrey Lane   Dept. OHJ
Eugene, OR 97402
(503) 688-7741
MO   DIST
Manufactures cast iron street lighting, using original moulds. Catalog V-12 free.

Verine Products & Co.
Goldhanger   Dept. OHJ
Maldon, Essex, UK
(0621) 88611
RS/O   MO
From U.K. authentic reproductions in fiberglass of original 18th century Georgian mantelpieces, overdoors, Ionic and Doric columns, porticos and lead garden tubs and planters. Literature — $5.00.

Vermont Castings, Inc.
6545 E. Prince Street   Dept. OHJ
Randolph, VT 05060
(802) 728-3111
RS/O   MO
Manufactures Defiant, Vigilant, and Resolute woodburning parlor stoves and Vigilant and Resolute coalburning stoves. Ideal for freestanding or fireplace installations. These high quality, cast iron stoves combine classic lines with highly efficient design. The doors can be opened or removed to create an open fireplace. With doors closed, the stoves are thermostatically controlled airtight heaters. Many accessories available. Illustrated, informative literature and price list, $1.

• **Vermont Iron Stove Works**
Box 299, 1211 Prince St.   Dept. OHJ
Waterbury, VT 05676
(802) 244-5254
MO
Company manufactures a wood and iron park bench. Vermont hardwood slats, iron end castings, and polished solid bronze medallions on the iron ends make the bench attractive as well as weather-resistant. Also available: woodstoves, porch swings, and plaza benches. For information send $1.00.

Vermont Soapstone Co.
Route 106N   Dept. OHJ
Perkinsville, VT 05151
(802) 263-5404
MO
Custom-cut soapstone available for sinks, countertops, stovetops. Also handcrafted griddles, bedwarmers, etc. Brochure and price list — $.50.

• **Vermont Structural Slate Co.**
P.O. Box 98   Dept. OHJ
Fair Haven, VT 05743
(802) 265-4933
RS/O   MO   DIST
'Slate Roofs'' — a handbook of data on the constructing and laying of all types of slate roofs. A 1926 reprint. Send $7.95. Besides roofing, company also fabricates slate flooring, sink tops, etc. Also has brownstone — typically used for replacement balustrades, cap, dentil course and lintels. Non-laminated stone with sufficient range of colors to match in restoration. Fact sheet, available: please specify.

Vermont Weatherboard, Inc.
15 West Church St.   Dept. OHJ
Hardwick, VT 05843
(802) 472-5513
MO   DIST
Full thickness individual shiplapped boards for wall paneling and exterior siding, processed to authentically reproduce the natural texture of aged barnwood. Available in three grades and two colors — Sugarhouse Gray and Autumn Brown. For restoration and reproduction work. Moulding, stain, and wrought nails available. Also, unique interior shingles: Sugarhouse Slats. Free color literature.

Victor-Renee Assoc.
6 Saxon Ct.   Dept. OHJ
Smithtown, NY 11787
(516) 724-1445
RS/O
Authentic Victorian parlour stoves. Fully restored wood or coal burning stoves with real isinglass and nickel trim. Stoves have a sophisticated compound-baffle system for efficient combustion. Restoration of all stoves provided. Selected cookstoves available. No literature.

Victoria Wallpaper Co.
43-560 Johnson St.   Dept. OHJ
Victoria, B.C., Canada V8W1M3
(604) 388-5233
RS/O   MO
Printers of restoration wallpapers. (Formerly Open Pacific Graphics.) They specialize in Victorian and Art Nouveau patterns. An illustrated brochure is available at a cost of $1.50. They also do restoration projects; inquiries are welcome.

Victorian Building & Repair
RR 1B, Box 162-A   Dept. OHJ
Compton, IL 61318
(815) 538-7001
RS/O   MO
General construction, repair, remodelling, and additions in a Victorian-complementary manner. Especially experienced in Victorian restorations, including wood siding, open porches, and millwork restoration. Design and duplication of sawn ornament. No literature; specific inquiries with SASE will be answered.

Victorian Collectibles
W66 N394 Kennedy Avenue   Dept. OHJ
Cedarburg, WI 53012
(414) 377-7608
MO   RS/O
Original American late 19th and early 20th century papers, purchased from an historical society. Inventory includes: friezes, borders, side papers and ceiling papers in a large assortment of colors. Styles include Rococo, Art Nouveau, Arts & Crafts, Scenics, Geometrics. Will also do stencilling and reproduction wall papers. No literature — will provide photo for serious inquiries. Please include yardage, style & color requirements.

• **Victorian D'Light**
533 W. Windsor Road   Dept. OHJ
Glendale, CA 91204
(213) 956-5656
MO   DIST
Company designs and manufactures electric, gas, and combination lamps and light fixtures of solid brass. Pieces designed and executed in turn-of-the-century manner, based on documented designs. Full-color catalog of 107 items that can be combined for the creation of 5000 different light fixtures. Catalog $3.

Victorian Glass Works
476 Main Street   Dept. OHJ
Ferndale, CA 95536
(707) 786-4237
RS/O
Restorers of antique furniture, complete rebuilding of wood components and all types of caning and rattan work. They also specialize in repairing and restoring most types of antique picture frames. No literature.

• **Victorian Lightcrafters, Ltd.**
P.O. Box 332, U.S. Rte. 6   Dept. OHJ
Slate Hill, NY 10973
(914) 355-1300
MO   RS/O
Manufacturers of authentic design, solid brass reproduction Victorian and turn-of-the-century lighting fixtures and desk lamps. They also carry appropriate glass shades. Fixtures are handmade to order; polished and lacquered if desired. Illustrated catalog, $2. Wholesale inquiries invited. (Formerly Stansfield's Lamp Shop.)

• **Victorian Millshop**
446 Acona Street   Dept. OHJ
Denver, CO 80204
(303) 733-5569
MO   RS/O
They make reproduction mouldings and windows based on existing period millwork. They also custom make doors and other architectural woodwork. Their knife-profiling machine can match any existing moulding or millwork. Their $2 brochure includes drawings of all their stock moulding profiles.

• **Victorian Reproductions, Inc.**
1601 Park Ave., South   Dept. OHJ
Minneapolis, MN 55404
(612) 338-3636
RS/O   MO   DIST
Designers, manufactures, and distributors of quality handcrafted solid brass lighting. Traditional designs are offered along with authentic styles from the Turn of the Century. The styling selection ranges from oil lighting, functional or electrified, thru the early electrics of the 1900's. Catalog "C" Edition 1 $5. Quality handcrafted mahogany furniture, Lightning rod/weathervanes, Chimney Pots, and Lawn ornaments. Edition 2, $3. Free lighting brochure in addition to catalog 1 and 2.

Victorian Revival
2450 Eutaw Place   Dept. OHJ
Baltimore, MD 21217
(301) 225-0649
RS/O
Sales and design services for W.F. Norman tin ceilings, ornamental plaster, Steptoe Cast Iron Spiral Staircase, and Victorian hardware and light fixtures. Catalogs are available for $3.00.

Victoriana Glass Works, Inc.
387 Bloomfield Ave.   Dept. OHJ
Montclair, NJ 07042
(201) 744-9500
MO   RS/O
Reproduction leaded stained glass for lamps, lighting fixtures, sidelights, skylights, landing and cabinet windows. Full design and execution in beveled, etched, brilliant-cut, and slump-molded glasses. Appraisals and certificates of authenticity prepared. All inquiries will be answered.

Viking Clocks
Viking Bldg, Ind. Pk, Box 490   Dept. OHJ
Foley, AL 36536
(205) 943-5081
MO   RS/O
Grandfather, mantel and schoolroom clock kits. Victorian end tables in black walnut and oak, a farmhouse chair suitable for late 19th century interiors, and a hutch table of primitive American derivation, all in kit form. Illustrated catalog with price list — $1.

Village Forge
P.O. Box 1148   Dept. OHJ
Smithfield, NC 27577
(919) 934-2581
MO
Adaptations and reproductions in wrought iron of Early American lighting. Of special interest are the well-designed iron floor lamps. Illustrated brochure and price list — $1.00 (Refundable with order).

Village Lantern
P.O. Box 8J   Dept. OHJ
North Marshfield, MA 02059
(617) 834-8121
MO   RS/O
Handmade pewter plate lanterns, sconces and chandeliers. Custom work in pewter plate, tin, brass or copper. Reproductions and restoration. Illustrated brochure and price list — $.50.

Vincent — Whitney Co.
1760 Bridgeway   Dept. OHJ
Sausalito, CA 94965
(415) 332-3260
MO   DIST
Firm specializes in hand-powered dumbwaiters. Capacities range from 5 to 250 lbs; priced from $500 to $1850. Also opener for operable clerestory windows. Free brochure; specify whether for residential or commercial use.

Vintage Lumber Co.
9507 Woodsboro Rd.   Dept. OHJ
Frederick, MD 21701
(301) 898-7859
RS/O   MO
Dismantler of barns, houses, and log houses from 18th, 19th and 20th century. They sell old lumber in rough form as well as resawn or remilled flooring, paneling and beams. Specializing in heart pine, chestnut, oak, white pine and poplar. They maintain a large stock of various lumber found in old buildings. Send $1.00 for literature.

Vintage Oak Furniture
23812 A-2 Via Fabricante   Dept. OHJ
Mission Viejo, CA 92691
(714) 768-1691
MO   RS/O   DIST
Handcrafted reproductions of oak furniture, featuring roll-top and executive desks, book cases, filing cabinets, ice boxes, china hutches, etc. Smaller items can be shipped via UPS. Literature $1.

● **Vintage Wood Works**
66 Main   Dept. OHJ
Quinlan, TX 75474
(214) 356-2158
MO
Produces a line of authentic Victorian Gingerbread Designs for interior and exterior use. Brackets, scroll-work running trims, fret work, gable eave treatments, porch railings, and signs are stocked in inventory for prompt shipment. Quotes are given for variations on standard designs, as well as for custom designs. All work is shop sanded, ready for painting. An illustrated brochure is available for $1.00.

W

Wagner, Albert J., & Son
3762 N. Clark Street   Dept. OHJ
Chicago, IL 60613
(312) 935-1414
RS/O
Established in 1894. Architectural sheet metal contractor working in ferrous and copper metals: cornice mold; inlaid cornice mold gutter; facade; and hip and ridge cap. Fabrication and installation of metal and glass gable end and hip style skylights. Specialty roofing (slate, tile). Installation limited to Chicago, IL area. Call for appointment. No literature.

Walker Industries
P.O. Box 129   Dept. OHJ
Bellevue, TN 37221
(615) 646-5084
MO
Full line of old-style bathroom fixtures, including 5 pull-chain toilets (from railroad-station style, to dovetailed mahogany). Vanities patterned after dry sinks, with copper or brass bowls. Copper clawfoot tubs with your choice of wood trim. All-china fluted pedestal sink with oval basin. Toilet seats in many woods, and an oak cover for existing porcelain tank. Color catalog $4.00.

● **Walker, Dennis C.**
P.O. Box 309   Dept. OHJ
Tallmadge, OH 44278
(216) 633-1081
RS/O
Hand-hewn barn beams, barn siding, roof slate, old hand planed beaded panelling. Also a large stock of architectural antiques: doors, wood mantels, wainscot and panelling, flooring, mouldings, plumbing fixtures, etc. Brochures available.

Wallin Forge
Route 1, Box 65   Dept. OHJ
Sparta, KY 41086
(606) 567-7201
RS/O   MO
Makes a wide range of handforged iron door hardware, boot scrapers, fireplace equipment, lighting fixtures, kitchen utensils, etc. Custom work available. Catalog and price list $.50.

Walton Stained Glass
209 Railway   Dept. OHJ
Campbell, CA 95008
(408) 866-0533
RS/O
Stained glass artisans; specialists in traditional bevelled windows. Write or call for catalog.

Warner Company
108 South Des Plaines St.   Dept. OHJ
Chicago, IL 60606
(312) 372-3540
DIST
Designs from the Art Institute of Chicago Collection, based on actual English, French, Dutch, Italian and American textiles of the 16th, 17th, 18th and 19th centuries. They have been adapted for use in today's interiors. No literature.

Warren, William J. & Son, Inc.
202 W. Magnolia   Dept. OHJ
Ft. Collins, CO 80521
(303) 482-1976
RS/O
General contractor with extensive experience with old buildings. Also provides home inspection service. Home Inspection brochure available free.

Washburne, E.G. & Co.
83 Andover St.   Dept. OHJ
Danvers, MA 01923
(617) 774-3645
MO   RS/O
Founded in 1853, they still make copper weathervanes and flag pole balls and ornaments on the original moulds. Free brochure.

● **Washington Copper Works**
South St.   Dept. OHJ
Washington, CT 06793
(203) 868-7527
RS/O   MO
Hand-fabricated lighting fixtures in styles compatible with the 18th and 19th centuries. Copper post lights, wall lanterns for indoors, outdoors, and entryways. Chandeliers & candelabras. Weatherproof kerosene lanterns, and an unusual selection of candle lanterns. Each original piece is hand-wrought, initialed and dated. U-L approved. 32 page illustrated catalog and price list, $2.00, refundable with an order.

Washington Stove Works
P.O. Box 687   Dept. OHJ
Everett, WA 98206
(206) 252-2148
DIST   RS/O
This company has been making stoves since 1875: Air-tight cast box heaters, decorative parlor stoves, cast iron Franklin stoves, wood and oil kitchen stoves, air-tight fireplace inserts. Send $1.00 for illustrated literature.

● **Watco - Dennis Corporation**
1756 22nd Street   Dept. OH-82
Santa Monica, CA 90404
(213) 829-2226
DIST
Architectural finishing and maintenance products for wood, concrete, masonry, tile and marble. Super penetrating resin-oil finishes for furniture, floors, interior and exterior wood surfaces are of particular interest to the do-it-yourself person. Free brochure.

Waterbury Foundry Co.
112 Porter St.   Dept. OHJ
Waterbury, CT 06722
(203) 753-6680
Company is one of the few sources left that still produces cast-iron sash weights for double-hung windows. Available in a variety of sizes and weights. No brochure; call for further details.

KEY TO ABBREVIATIONS

MO = sells by Mail Order

RS/O = sells through Retail Store or Office

DIST = sells through Distributors

ID = sells only through Interior Designers or Architects

● = Consult ad for more details. See Advertisers' Index on the last page of this Catalog.

Waverly Fabrics
58 West 40th St.   Dept. OHJ
New York, NY 10018
(212) 644-5890
DIST
Four Sturbridge Village collections: features documentary patterns gathered from Europe, the Near East and native American designs of the 19th century. The group consists of 13 prints, 5 upholstery fabrics and 3 all cotton damasks. Victoria & Albert Museum Collection — A group of 12 printed patterns are adaptations of documents housed at the London Museum. Also in their general line are some excellent large design fabrics appropriate for Victorian draperies and upholstery. Widely available moderately priced at department and fabric stores, or write for distributor.

Weaver, W. T. & Sons, Inc.
1208 Wisconsin Ave., N.W.   Dept. OHJ
Washington, DC 20007
(202) 333-4200
RS/O   MO
Firm has been selling decorative hardware and building supplies since 1889. Stock includes porcelain and brass furniture hardware, knobs, rim locks, front door hardware, shutter hardware, full line of solid brass switchplates, lavatory bowls, sconces, hooks, and decorative ornaments and ceiling medallions (styrene). Catalog $2.50. Literature on ceiling pieces is free.

Weir, R. & Co.
West Berlin Road   Dept. OHJ
Bolton, MA 01740
MO
Manufactures custom wood mouldings for reproduction and restoration of fine American homes. Can duplicate existing patterns for restorers. Send sample or full size drawing of desired moulding, including species of wood and quantity, for free quotation. No literature.

Weird Wood
Box 190   Dept. OHJ
Chester, VT 05143
(802) 875-3535
RS/O   MO
Company specializes in rare and unusual woods. Twenty or so varieties on hand, including butternut, rosewood. Also thick slabs, burls, carving pieces. They sell clock movements and wood finishing products too. Catalog $.50.

Welles Fireplace Company
287 East Houston St.   Dept. OHJ
New York, NY 10002
(212) 777-5440
RS/O
They service fireplaces in the metropolitan New York area. Mantels installed; chimneys repaired, cleaned and relined; gas and coal fireplaces converted to woodburning. On-site consultation, $35.00 deductible. Flyer on request.

• **Welsbach**
240 Sargent Drive   Dept. OHJ
New Haven, CT 06511
(203) 789-1710
RS/O   DIST
This 100 year old company supplies street lighting fixtures, brackets, and post. Originally designed for gas-lighting, they're now available with modern gas, incandescent electric or high-intensity electric light sources. They also make landscape furniture such as park benches, bollards and gazebos. Complete illustrated catalog available: Free to the trade; $2.00 for consumer.

• **Welsh, Frank S.**
859 Lancaster Ave.   Dept. OHJ
Bryn Mawr, PA 19010
(215) 525-3564
RS/O   MO
Historic paint color consultant. Professional microscopic techniques used to investigate, analyze, and evaluate the nature and original color of historic architectural surface coatings. Conducts on-site research for historic house museums & adaptive restorations; plus lab analysis of paint samples mailed in by old-house owners who have already ordered the Paint Pamphlet (available for $3.00). Completed projects include Monticello, Lincoln Home, Phila. Atheneum.

Western Reserve Antique Furniture Kit
Box 206A   Dept. OHJ
Bath, OH 44210
MO   DIST
Reproductions of Shaker, New England, and Pennsylvania Dutch furniture and house accessories are available in either kit or assembled and finished form. A newly expanded line is pictured and fully described in the brochure about Western Reserve New 'Connecti-Kit'. Special order items can be built for customers needing something not in regular catalog. Cost of the brochure is $2.00.

Westmoreland Cupolas
P.O. Box 7   Dept. OHJ
Delmont, PA 15626
(412) 836-8064
MO
Westmoreland Cupolas are made of redwood with mitered joints. Louvers are fastened into grooves so they won't come loose. The backs of louvers are screened to keep out birds and insects. Also makes powered ventilators that can be concealed in cupola and redwood attic louvers. Recommended flashing can be supplied with order. Brochure $1.00, refundable with order.

The Whistle Stop
PO Box 3028   Dept. OHJ
Kennesaw, GA 30144
(404) 424-1156
MO
Two plans for "The Victorian Storybook Cottage," one containing 2060 square feet and one containing 2450 square feet are available. Brochure and information are available for $2.

White Nurseries, Inc.
   Dept. OHJ
Mecklenburg, NY 14863
(607) 387-7022
RS/O   MO
Founded in 1934, this company specializes in design and restoration of 19th and early 20th century gardens. Also, appraisal and damage estimate work for tax & insurance purposes. Services by a licensed Landscape Architect. Please call; no literature.

Whitehead & Roberts, Inc.
RD 2, Box 90A   Dept. OHJ
Boonton, NJ 07005
(201) 625-1313
RS/O
General contractors, specializing in exterior and interior restoration of old houses. Serving NW New Jersey, especially Morris County. Large and small jobs. Free estimates. Please call.

Whitley Studios
Laurel Road, Box 69   Dept. OHJ
Solebury, PA 18963
(215) 297-8452
MO   RS/O
Restoration and replication of fine antique furniture. Illustrated brochure on original designed "Whitley Rocker," $5.00.

Whittemore-Durgin Glass Co.
Box 20650H   Dept. OHJ
Hanover, MA 02339
(617) 871-1790
RS/O   MO
Everything for the stained glass craftsman presented in an illustrated color catalog that is unusually helpful, amusing and free of charge. Also "Baroques" — pieces of stained glass onto which designs in black ceramic paint are fused. Can be used to create panels, or as replacements in windows. Antique-type window glass. Four retail stores: Rockland MA, Bergenfield NJ, E. Lyme CT, Peoria IL. Free catalog for mail-order customers.

Whitten Enterprises, Inc.
P.O. Box 798   Dept. OHJ
Bennington, VT 05201
(802) 442-8344
MO
Manufacturers of iron spiral staircases and ships' ladders. Also available as kits. Iron or wood treads; interior & exterior applications. Design is elegant, simple and contemporary. Staircase planning guide, $.25.

Wigen Restorations
R.D. No. 1, Box 281   Dept. OHJ
Cobleskill, NY 12043
(518) 234-7946
MO   RS/O
Will dismantle and move any house or barn. Dutch and New England barn frames available - will move to your location. Also small house frames, floor boards, old pine boards, weathered siding, mantels, etc. Free flyer.

Wiggins, D.B.
Hale Road   Dept. OHJ
Tilton, NH 03276
(603) 286-3046
RS/O
Itinerant artists. Period interiors, painted and stencilled; murals and portraits — anything to do with paint. 15 years experience, second generation in antique business. Also quality restorations of existing designs. Write for free brochure.

Wikkmann House
Box 501   Dept. OHJ
Chatsworth, CA 91311
(213) 780-1015
MO
Home renovator and wood craftsman tools. Also a line of woodworking clamps; frame and door jigs. Of special interest is their pry bar — a tool to aid in structural dismantling without destroying timbers. Catalog, $1.

Willems Painting & Decorating
731 Josephine Circle   Dept. OHJ
Green Bay, WI 54301
(414) 468-7228
RS/O
Traditional interior painting and paper services: Paper hanging, wood finishing, dry wall, color matching, wood graining, and spraying. No literature, but free estimates are given.

Willet Stained Glass Studio, Inc.
10 East Moreland Avenue   Dept. OHJ
Philadelphia, PA 19118
(215) 247-5721
MO   RS/O
One of the oldest glass studios in America. Stained and leaded glass pieces designed and executed to order. Also has extensive facilities for restoration of antique leaded glass. No literature; call for more information.

Williams & Hussey Machine Corp.
Elm Street   Dept. OHJ
Milford, NH 03055
(603) 673-3446
MO   DIST   RS/O
Manufacturer of a small Molder Planer that is capable of planing up to fourteen inches wide, (by reversing). Ideal for renovating old homes as any molding can be reproduced exactly from any sketch or sample sent to us. Planes thicknesses up to 8'. Made of heavy cast iron with ground surfaces. Send for free brochure and price sheet.

Williams, Helen
12643 Hortense Street   Dept. OHJ
North Hollywood, CA 91604
(213) 761-2756
RS/O   MO
17th and 18th century antique Dutch Delft tiles, in colors of blue, manganese, tortoise shell, white and polychrome. Also: English Liverpool tiles, 17th century Dutch firebacks and Spanish and Portuguese tiles. Free literature and price list with stamped, self-addressed envelope.

• Williamsburg Blacksmiths, Inc.
Buttonshop Road   Dept. OHJ
Williamsburg, MA 01096
(413) 268-7341
RS/O   MO   DIST
Authentic reproductions of Early American wrought iron hardware. All items are hand-finished and treated with a rust inhibitor. Catalog and price list, $2.50.

Wilson, Dan
319 S. West St.   Dept. OHJ
Raleigh, NC 27603
(919) 821-5242
RS/O   MO   DIST
Custom made garden furniture, handcrafted from selected softwoods. Chinese Chippendale planters with removable galvanized liners, Chippendale garden benches, tables and chairs. Flyer and price catalog, $1.

Wilson, H. Weber, Antiquarian
9701 Liberty Road   Dept. OHJ
Frederick, MD 21701
(301) 898-9565
MO   RS/O
Fine decorative components recycled from antique buildings. Stained and leaded glass a specialty: repairs, creations, windows and lamps bought, sold & traded. Also serves as consultant on projects involving new & antique decorative windows; available for lectures and seminars. Please write or call for more information and list of stained-glass publications.

Winans, Paul/Designer — Builder
2004 Woolsey St.   Dept. OHJ
Berkeley, CA 94703
(415) 843-4796
RS/O
Design & construction services in the San Francisco Bay Area. Specializing in renovation & restoration of old residential and commercial structures. Initial design plan through project completion. Stock and custom millwork available through this firm. Portfolio & references available during client's first consultation. No literature by mail.

Winburn Tile Manufacturing Co.
PO Box 1369   Dept. OHJ
Little Rock, AR 72203
(501) 375-7251
DIST
Manufacturers of ceramic mosaic tile, with distributors nationwide. Of special interest are their 1-in. hexagonal and 1-in. square unglazed floor tiles. Also 4-in. x 8-in. unglazed & glazed ceramic pavers. Unglazed tiles of all types — glazed tiles in limited colors available on special order. Please write or phone for name of your area distributor. Free brochure.

Window Blanket Company, Inc.
107 Kingston St.   Dept. OHJ
Lenoir City, TN 37771
(615) 986-2115
MO   DIST   ID
Insulated window curtains: Channel quilted tab-style window covering. Made of 100% polished cotton with soil-resistant finish. Filled with lightweight polyester fiberfill for sound-absorption and energy-savings. Fade resistant, water-repellent insulated cotton lining. Standard size 45'' wide x 84'' long. Custom lengths available. Easy to install on cafe or dowel rods. Color brochure and fabric swatches available for $1.00.

Windowcraft
Box 5318   Dept. OHJ
Atlanta, GA 30307
(404) 294-4296
RS/O   MO
Leaded and beveled glass panel sets in several period styles. Handcrafted sidelights, doors, and transoms. Also custom designs. Brochure available.

• Windy Lane Fluorescents
35972 Highway 6   Dept. OHC-82
Hillrose, CO 80733
(303) 847-3351
MO
Manufacturers of Victorian Era parlour or library lamp reproductions, updated with energy saving and color enhancing fluorescent bulbs. The collection includes both decorated and undecorated lamps in one basic style to complement its versatile use. Color brochure, $1.50.

Witt & Co.
3157 Lime St.   Dept. OHJ
Riverside, CA 92501
(714) 784-3600
RS/O
Contracting firm serving the Riverside, San Bernardino & Claremont area. Restoration and period-style additions, including custom-duplication of existing architectural details. No literature.

Wolchonok, M. and Son, Inc.
155 E. 52 St.   Dept. OHJ
New York, NY 10022
(212) 755-2168
RS/O   MO   DIST
Two sister companies: Decorators Wholesale Hardware carries an extensive line of reproduction hardware by quality manufactures like Baldwin, Shepherd, Artistic Brass. Locksets, faucets, and casters available as well as most furniture hardware. Of particular interest is the second company, Legs-Legs-Legs, selling an extensive line of furniture legs and table pedestals: iron, brass, wood. Also, decorative carpet rods; many wood, iron and brass shelf brackets. Free descriptive literature available — specify interest and wholesale/retail.

• Wolf Paints And Wallpapers
771 Ninth Ave. (At 52nd St.)   Dept. OHJ
New York, NY 10019
(212) 245-7777
RS/O   MO
An incredibly stocked paint store, with a large supply of hard-to-find finishes and supplies. Among the exotic items carried are: Graining brushes, specialty waxes like beeswax, crystalline shellac, casein paints, gold leaf and gilders supplies, wall canvas, and plaster patching materials. Will also handle mail orders. 54-page catalog shows much of their inventory. Catalog doesn't carry prices; must call for latest prices. Catalog is $2.00.

Wollon, James Thomas, Jr., A.I.A.
600 Craigs Corner Road   Dept. OHJ
Havre de Grace, MD 21078
(301) 879-6748
RS/O
Architect, specializing in historic preservation, restoration, adaptation and additions to historic structures. Services range from consultation to full professional services; Historic Structures Reports; National Register nominations. Building types include residential, exhibit, commercial, religious. Resume and references on request.

Wood Designs
100 Jupiter St.   Dept. OHJ
Washington C.H., OH 43160
(614) 335-6367
RS/O
Manufactures the finest quality furniture, millwork, Victorian mouldings, and panel doors in a variety of hardwoods including Walnut, Honduras Mahogany, Cherry, and Quarter-sawn Oak. No literature — call or write for additional information.

Wood-Hu Kitchens, Inc.
343 Manley St.   Dept. OHJ
W. Bridgewater, MA 02379
(617) 586-8050
DIST
Manufactures a line of solid wood kitchen cabinets, some of which are appropriate for use in an old house. Sold through distributors. Free brochure.

KEY TO ABBREVIATIONS

MO = sells by Mail Order

RS/O = sells through Retail Store or Office

DIST = sells through Distributors

ID = sells only through Interior Designers or Architects

● = Consult ad for more details. See Advertisers' Index on the last page of this Catalog.

Wood and Stone, Inc.
7567 Gary Rd.   Dept. OHJ
Manassas, VA 22110
(703) 369-1236
MO
Distributes a stone adhesive, AKEMI, for bonding together two pieces of stone, for filling natural faults, or for mending accidental breaks. AKEMI accepts iron oxide colors, so the restoration can be matched to any color stone. It can also be polished to a high gloss. Information sheet and price list free.

● **Woodbridge Ornamental Iron Co.**
2715 N. Clybourn Ave.   Dept. OHJ
Chicago, IL 60614
(312) 935-1500
MO RS/O
Steel stair manufacturer specializing in spiral and curved stairways. Contemporary and traditional styling with a variety of tread frame designs and tread surface materials. Stairs are custom fabricated to meet your dimensional specifications. Bolt-together installation requires only common hand tools. Consulting service for custom-design, and cost-free estimates available from Chicago office. Call or write for free brochure.

Woodbury Blacksmith & Forge Co.
P.O. Box 268   Dept. OHJ
Woodbury, CT 06798
(203) 263-5737
RS/O MO
Custom-made recreations of Colonial hardware, lighting devices, kitchen utensils, and fireplace equipment. Serving So. New England. Shipment can be arranged, but they have no literature. Custom orders by mail or phone.

● **Woodcare Corporation**
P.O. Box 92 H   Dept. OHJ
Butler, NJ 07405
(201) 838-9536
MO
Products for refinishing and restoring vintage homes, antiques, furniture, all aged woods and metals. Tung oil finish; copper and brass cleaner; Woodcare Clear Film (for preventing rust and tarnish); all-purpose paint and varnish remover. Send SASE for "The Restoring Guide." Technical Sales Service provided to written inquiries on home restoration problems/opportunities.

Woodmart
Box 202   Dept. OHJ
Janesville, WI 53545
(608) 752-2816
MO RS/O
Chimney & flue brushes available made of steel or polypropyl 4-3/4" to 14" diameter round or 6 x 6" to 14 x 14" square. Information sent free with a stamped, self-addressed envelope only.

Woodstock Soapstone Co., Inc.
Route 4, Box 223/908   Dept. OHJ
Woodstock, VT 05091
(802) 672-5133
MO
Manufactures a classic 1867-design wood-burning parlour stove made of soapstone. Fine-textured soapstone panels with cast-iron mouldings. A pretty, formal stove, but also functional: 10-12 hour burning time, even heat. Literature package, $1.00.

● = Consult ad for more details. See Advertisers' Index on the last page of this Catalog.

Woodstone Co.
P.O. Box 223 Patch Road   Dept. OHJ
Westminster, VT 05158
(802) 722-4784
RS/O
Manufactures reproductions of period staircases, entrances, doors, wainscoting, cabinetry and furniture along with custom moldings and wood turnings. Insulated foam-core wooden panel doors in traditional styles, multi-lite sidelites, straight & fanned transoms, and palladian windows available with double & triple glazing. High quality natural & synthetic finishes available. Free brochure.

● **Woodworkers' Store, The**
21801 Industrial Blvd.   Dept. OHJ
Rogers, MN 55374
(612) 428-4101
RS/O MO
A comprehensive source of supplies for the do-it-yourself person: hand tools, veneering supplies, picture framing, carved and embossed wood trim, books and plans, trim hardware, table and cabinet hinges, sliding door hardware, finishing supplies. Stores also in Denver and Minneapolis. 112 page catalog and price list — $1.00.

Worthington Trading Company
147 N. Main St.   Dept. OHJ
St. Charles, MO 63301
(314) 723-5862
MO RS/O
Retailers of woodburning stoves, Aladdin oil lamps, Hunter Original Olde Tyme Ceiling Fans. High quality merchandise in traditional styles. Stoves are Esse Dragon, and Petite Godin — Victorian parlor type, very ornate. Also Upland and Cawley. Serving St. Louis metro area. Will ship many items in continental U.S. Literature includes booklet "Installing and Using Woodburning Stoves" $2.00.

● **Wrecking Bar of Atlanta**
292 Moreland Ave., NE   Dept. OHJ
Atlanta, GA 30307
(404) 525-0468
RS/O
Large collection of expensive architectural antiques, especially doors, bevelled and stained glass windows, chimney pieces, lighting fixtures and carvings. Free literature.

● **Wrecking Bar, Inc.**
2601 McKinney Ave.   Dept. OHJ
Dallas, TX 75204
(214) 826-1717
RS/O MO
Varied inventory of antique architectural elements, housed in an old 18,000 sq. ft. church. Includes mantels, doors, doorways, columns, stairway components, brackets, carvings, lighting, paneling, stained and beveled glass, spiral staircases. French, English, Oriental and American examples from 17th thru 19th centuries. All materials are repaired and ready for finishing. Crating and shipping anywhere. Please inquire for specific information and photographs.

Wrightsville Hardware
North Front Street   Dept. OHJ
Wrightsville, PA 17368
(717) 252-1561
RS/O MO DIST
Heavy duty cast iron blind and shutter hinges and fastenings. Stovepipe dampers and cast-iron stove lid lifter. Free illustrated brochures — please specify.

Y

Yankee Craftsman
357 Commonwealth Road   Dept. OHJ
Wayland, MA 01778
(617) 653-0031
MO RS/O
Yankee Craftsman deals primarily in the restoration and sale of authentic antique lighting fixtures. Tiffany, Handel and other leaded-glass repairs. Custom lighting designed and executed using old lamp parts. Fine quality custom- leaded shades. Restoration and sale of antique furniture. No catalog; specific information and photo furnished free in response to serious inquiries.

Yield House, Inc.
   Dept. OHJ
North Conway, NH 03860
(800) 258-4720
MO
Quality pine furniture, fully-finished or easy-to-assemble kits. Range of designs includes Early American, classic Queen Anne, Shaker & contemporary collections. Unique gifts & accessories. Catalog price: $1.00.

York Spiral Stair
Bridge Street   Dept. OHJ
North Vassalboro, ME 04962
(207) 872-5558
MO
Spiral staircases crafted in oak or other fine hardwoods. A unique design has provided for inner and outer handrails for safety. This feature allows the stair to be uninterrupted by a centerpost. Staircases are available in diameters of 5' or 8'-6", finished or unfinished. Free brochure and price list available.

Z

Zetlin, Lorenz — Muralist
248 East 21st St.   Dept. OHJ
New York, NY 10010
(212) 473-3291
RS/O
Handpainted, custom murals, trompe l'oeil rendering. Also marbleizing — mantels, baseboards. Free illustrated flyer.

● **Zillman, Marcus P., & Associates**
1222 N. Vermilion St.   Dept. OHJ
Danville, IL 61832
(217) 446-6319
RS/O
Consultants on historic woodwork. They appraise work for insurance companies, determine cost feasibility and obtain sources for interior designers and offer a large variety of services. Seminars are offered on Historic Woodwork Preservation and Restoration. Various booklets available, including World Wood Guide. Write for free brochure.

Zynolyte Products Co.
15700 South Avalon Blvd.   Dept. OHJ
Compton, CA 90224
(213) 321-6964
DIST
Manufactures Klenk's Epoxy Enamel: a tub and tile finish, two-part epoxy coating for refinishing old sinks, tubs, ceramic tile, and appliances. Free leaflet.

If You Love Old Houses, You Should Subscribe To The Old-House Journal

THE OLD-HOUSE JOURNAL is the only publication devoted exclusively to the restoration, maintenance and decoration of old houses. Every month our plainly-written articles show you practical, economical ways of turning that old house "with a lot of potential" into the house of your dreams.

THE JOURNAL is written and edited by people who have restored old houses themselves. Their first-hand knowledge will help you *do it yourself*, turning *your* house into the kind of house photographed by those "pretty picture" magazines. Your picture-pretty home will breathe with new life from the floorboards to the finials... at costs that won't make you gasp.

THE JOURNAL will help you learn how to look at your old house with an expert's eye...will help you decide which features are worth loving restoration, and what should be stripped off and taken to the junk heap. The Journal teaches you how to be a restorer...not a remuddler.

THE EXPERT ADVICE from The Old-House Journal will help you save money when it's time to bring in contractors. You'll be able to give clear, specific instructions to them...and will be able to supervise the work confidently.

AND WHETHER you do it yourself, or have contractors do the work, you'll avoid costly mistakes.

THERE ARE EXTRA PLUSES that joining the Old-House Journal Network brings: Things like getting free classified ads, being able to use the editors as professional consultants through our "Ask OHJ" column, learning other subscriber's special techniques through our "Restorer's Notebook," and being exposed to the best books and products available for the old-house lover.

IN OUR NO-NONSENSE newsletter format, there is no paid advertising. In each 32-page issue you get solid meat...with none of the fluff that clutters most of the 4-color "home magazines."

IF YOU LOVE the look of old houses...the beauty of restored interiors and facades ...quality materials and fine craftsmanship...and yearn for the joy of making it all happen through your own efforts...then The Old-House Journal is for you. Use the Order Form on page 166, and become part of The Old-House Journal Network!

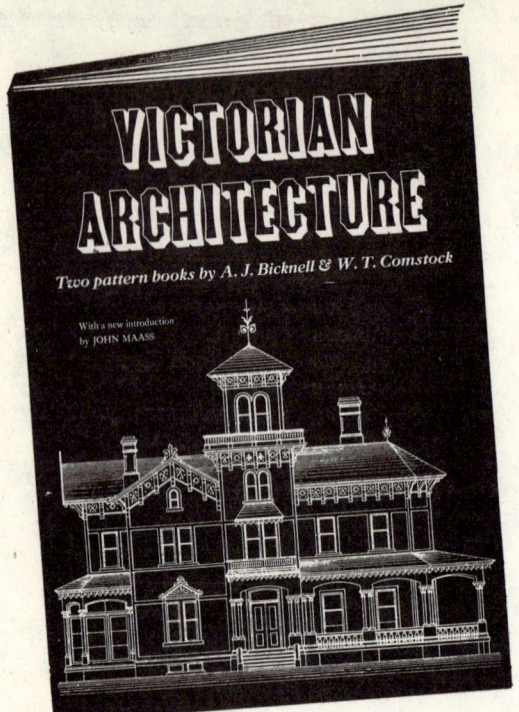

IN PRINT ONCE AGAIN!

VICTORIAN ARCHITECTURE

This "combination volume" is a great source of design ideas!

Two invaluable books of Victorian architectural details & designs are now available again through **The Old-House Bookshop** in a single softbound edition entitled *Victorian Architecture*.

This combination volume reprints in full the original 1873 and 1881 pattern books used by builders and carpenters of the 1870's and 1880's as sources for design ideas, and can unlock the past for anyone restoring a late Victorian home.

History buffs with an eye for architecture will delight in the wealth of visual information gleaned from the Mansard, Queen Anne, Elizabethan, Eastlake and Aesthetic styles, including patterns and details for:
* Complete exterior designs for houses, villas and cottages
* Floor plans
* Cornices and brackets
* Sawn wood ornaments and gingerbread
* Windows and window caps
* Doors
* Porches and balconies
* Stairs, newels and mantels
* Fences and gazebos
* Wainscotting and panelling
* Gable ornaments

Details can be used as a source for building interior and exterior woodwork, re-creating exterior gingerbread, wall stencil patterns, restoring porches, building additions... or just for pure visual enjoyment of fine design.

Included as an added treat are 16 pages of period advertisements for such products as Cannon's Patent Dumb Waiter and Minton's Tiles For Floors.

This special Limited Edition volume combines the 1873 *Detail, Cottage and Constructive Architecture*, and the 1881 *Modern Architectural Designs & Details*, by A. J. Bicknell and Wm. T. Comstock, and is identical to the hardcover version selling for $25 + postage & handling.

192 pages, Jumbo Size (10 x 13 in.)
Softbound. $15.95 postpaid.

Use Order Form on page 166, or send $15.95 to
The Old-House Bookshop
69A Seventh Avenue, Brooklyn, N.Y. 11217

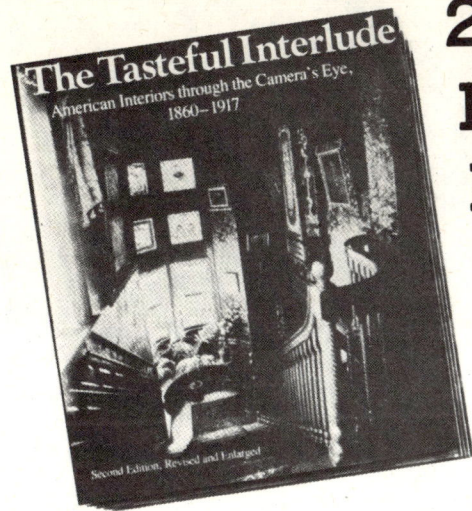

269 Original Historical Photographs In This Beautiful Collector's Edition Capture The Essence Of Victorian & Turn-Of-Century American Interiors

IGNITE your decorative imagination as you wander through what Tennyson called "the eternal landscape of the past"... enter 269 Victorian and turn-of-century rooms through the original historical photographs of *Tasteful Interlude*. These photographic portals to the past will inspire old-house owners, restoration architects, preservationists, interior designers and history buffs.

William Seale's expertly analyzed and interpreted collection traverses 57 years of evolving American interiors during the tumultuous period between the Civil War and World War I. Seale's insights enrich our perspectives on the decorative arts of the time; his words and pictures chart the reconciliation of American homes to the products of mass manufacture. He presents objects as documents, and interiors as essays in history.

Originally published in 1975, *Tasteful Interlude* has been out-of-print for 4 years. Now — actually back "by popular demand" — the second edition is available, with additional photos and commentary. You can now explore the book's gamut of residential fashions, from moneyed Manhattan drawing rooms to a seedy shanty in Colorado's silver mining country.

This broad range, from ostentatious opulence to stark simplicity provides an excellent brainstorming guide to the decorative styles of these eras. Anyone enamored with American history will surely delight in this unique expedition into Victorian and turn-of-century life and culture.

The Critics Have Said:

"One of the most useful & corrective books about the 19th century to come on-to the market."
—*Architectural Digest*

"Photographs of real rooms when they were inhabited by real people. The author should be commended for keeping an economic and geographic balance."
—*Journal of the Society of Architectural Historians*

About The Author:

William Seale, historian & award-winning author, is Adjunct Professor of Architecture at Columbia University, and former editor of *19th Century* magazine. Seale consults on restoration projects throughout the country, & is presently writing a scholarly history of the White House.

288 pages, 269 original period photographs. Softbound.

*Use Order Form on Page 166,
or send $12.95 + $2 postage & handling to:*
The Old-House Bookshop, 69A Seventh Ave.
Brooklyn, N.Y. 11217

163

What Style Is My House?

The most common question asked of us at *The Old-House Journal* is "What style is my house?" Subscribers nationwide are curious — they send us photographs all the time, trying to learn the answer.

Now The Old-House Bookshop makes available to you a comprehensive, inexpensive book that answers everything you always wanted to know about architectural styles in this country. We're excited about *The American House*, a unique, easy-to-follow illustrated guide to our rich architectural heritage. We think it's the best volume on building styles around.

Combining the clarity and focus of line drawings with a singular concentration on *style* — rather than history — the distinctions and relationships between genres are intelligibly sorted out. Introductions to each section establish the general orientation and attributes of that style. Highlighting essential form and detail, the illustrations — with bite-size stylistic explanations — then chart and clarify as never before this ever-changing lineage.

As a nation of immigrants, a host of native architectural traditions were transplanted in America, including those of the English, Dutch, German, Swedish, French and Spanish. As cultures mixed in the melting pot of the New World, formal and folk styles evolved as architects learned from one another.

The engrossing word-and-picture approach charts these changes both in the more formal styles, such as the Georgian, Greek or Gothic, as well as a vast array of not-usually-noted vernacular buildings.

Just as house design reflected many purposes, this book also serves many functions — as a convenient, complete manual of style, as a field guide for traveling house watchers, as an easy chair tour for at-home building enthusiasts, and as a popular history of residential cultural expression.

Softcover. 10 x 10". 299 pages.

To order your copy of *The American House*, just check the box on the Order Form, or send $12.95 +$2 for postage & handling to

The Old-House Bookshop
69A Seventh Avenue
Brooklyn, NY 11217

The Old-House Journal ORDER FORM

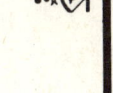

Gift Ideas For People With Old Houses

② Fold In End Flaps

① Cut Along This Line

④ Fold Flap Over And Tape Shut

NO POSTAGE
NECESSARY
IF MAILED
IN THE
UNITED STATES

BUSINESS REPLY MAIL
FIRST CLASS   PERMIT NO. 31609   BROOKLYN, N.Y.

POSTAGE WILL BE PAID BY ADDRESSEE

THE OLD-HOUSE JOURNAL
69A SEVENTH AVENUE
BROOKLYN, NEW YORK 11217

③ Fold Up Along This Line

Important

Before sealing your order:

1. Be sure that your name, address and zip code are printed clearly or typed.
2. Check to see that you have given a STREET ADDRESS — not a P.O. Box — if your order includes a Catalog, Back Issues or a Heat Gun. We ship via United Parcel Service, and they cannot deliver to a P.O. Box.
3. Verify that your check or VISA credit card information is enclosed.

② Fold In End Flaps

Use This Self-Mailer To Order:

- New Subscriptions to The Old-House Journal
- The Paint-Stripping Heat Gun
- The 1982 OHJ Catalog
- Books for the old-house lover

→ See Other Side ←

165

Order Form

Please Send The Following:

Subscriptions to The Old-House Journal
- [ ] New Subscription
- [ ] Renewal
  (Please enclose current mailing label)

- [ ] 1 Year — $16
- [ ] 2 Years — $24
- [ ] 3 Years — $32

- [ ] Master Appliance HG-501 Heat Gun — $66.95
  (N.Y. State residents add local sales tax)

NOTE: Please allow 8 weeks for your first issue to arrive

◨ The Old-House Bookshop ◨

- [ ] **1982 OHJ CATALOG**—Comprehensive buyers' guide to over 9,000 hard-to-find products & services for the old house. This "Yellow Pages" for restoration & maintenance — 25% larger this year — is the most complete, up-to-date sourcebook available. Softcover. $11.95. $8.95 to current OHJ subscribers.

- [ ] **CENTURY OF COLOR**—Authentic paint colors for your home's exterior. Covers 1820-1920; all house styles—from plain to fancy. Ties in with available commercial colors. Softbound. $12.00

- [ ] **TASTEFUL INTERLUDE**—Rare photographs of original interiors from the Civil War to WW I. Of great value to anyone decorating in a period style. Written by William Seale. Softbound. $14.95.

- [ ] **BINDERS**—Brown vinyl binders embossed in gold with the OHJ logo. Holds a year of issues. $5.25 each.

- [ ] **THE OHJ COMPENDIUM**—Collection of the most helpful articles from the OHJ's first 5 years of publication (1973 to 1977). 312 pages. Hardcover. $21.95.

- [ ] **MOULDINGS & ARCHITECTURAL DETAILS OF THE LATE 19th CENTURY**—Reprint of a mouldings & millwork catalog published in 1898. Shows doors, mantels, etched glass & many hundreds of other architectural elements used from 1870's thru 1900. Over 1,200 illustrations. 288 pages. Softbound. $14.00.

2 bonuses that come with *Century of Color:*
* a large color chip card featuring Sherwin-Williams' 40 historically-accurate "Heritage Colors."
* a certificate worth $25 with the purchase of 5 gallons of "Heritage Colors"—pays for the book twice over!

- [ ] **PALLISER'S LATE VICTORIAN ARCHITECTURE**—Largest collection of late 19th century house plans & ornamental details. Contains 2 books published by architectural firm of Palliser & Palliser in 1878 & 1887. Over 1,500 plans & details. 312 pages-Jumbo 10x13.Softbd.$21.95.

- [ ] **CUMMINGS & MILLER**—Two architectural pattern books from 1865 & 1873 show house plans & ornamental details in Mansard, Italianate & Bracketed styles. Over 2,000 designs & illustrations. 248 pages—Jumbo 10 x 13" size. Softbound. $15.95.

- [ ] **HOLLY'S HOUSE BOOK**—Style book & interior decorating guide for the 1860's thru 1880's. Contains reprints of 2 influential books by Henry Hudson Holly: "Country Seats" (1863), & "Modern Dwellings" (1878). 389 pages.Softbound. $13.95.

- [ ] **VICTORIAN ARCHITECTURE**—Reprint edition of 2 classic architectural pattern books: A.J. Bicknell's of 1873 & W.T. Comstock's of 1881. Hundreds of illustrations of houses & ornamental details in the Mansard, Queen Anne & Eastlake styles. 192 pgs.-Jumbo 10x13 size.Softbd.$15.95.

- [ ] **THE AMERICAN HOUSE**—Comprehensive guide to house styles, covering formal and folk building genres from 17th century through contemporary vanguard architects. By Mary Mix Foley. Great as a style manual or coffee table conversation-starter. 299 pages. Softbound. $14.95.

Amount Enclosed $..........   All prices postpaid.   N.Y. State residents add applicable sales tax.

NOTE: If your order includes books or merchandise, you must give us a STREET ADDRESS — not a P.O. Box number. We ship via United Parcel Service (UPS), and they will not deliver to a P.O. Box.

Send My Order To: Allow 4 to 5 weeks for delivery.

Name...

Address..

City..State.............ZIP...........

The Old-House Journal — *This page forms its own postpaid envelope.* Just check the boxes, and *clearly* print your name and address. Cut out the page and fold, as indicated on the reverse side. Enclose your check and drop it in the mail.

BECOME PART OF THE OLD-HOUSE NETWORK

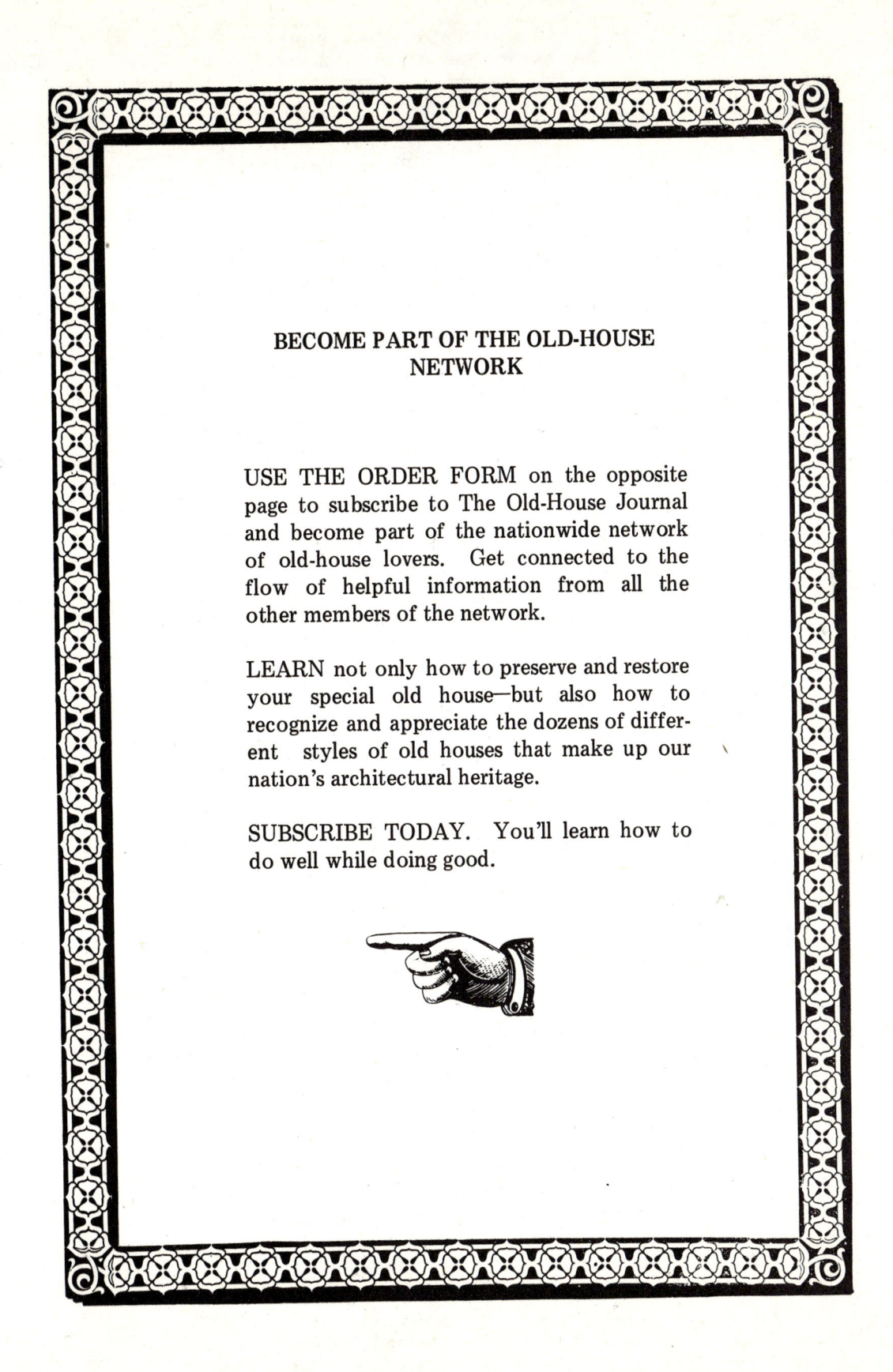

USE THE ORDER FORM on the opposite page to subscribe to The Old-House Journal and become part of the nationwide network of old-house lovers. Get connected to the flow of helpful information from all the other members of the network.

LEARN not only how to preserve and restore your special old house—but also how to recognize and appreciate the dozens of different styles of old houses that make up our nation's architectural heritage.

SUBSCRIBE TODAY. You'll learn how to do well while doing good.

INDEX TO PRODUCTS & SERVICES

A

Accessories—*see Furnishings*
Adzes 89
Alarm Systems—Fire and Security 54
Aluminum, Cast 29
Anaglypta Wallcovering 53
Anchors and Washers, Plaster 90
Andirons 70
Antique and Recycled House Parts 93-97
Antique Repairs 98
Antique Shops 98
Archeological Surveys 98
Architectural Design—Restoration 99
Architectural Millwork 19
Art Glass—All Types 44-46
Art, Original 52
Asbestos Tiles 14
Awning Hardware 31
Awnings 31

B

Balances, Window 26
Balconies, Iron 29
Balusters, Iron 29
Balusters, Porch 22
Balusters, Staircase 39
Balustrades, Roof 31
Bar Rails—*see Restaurant Fittings*
Barnboard 17
Barns, Recycled 97
Barometers, Antique 53
    (*under Other Decorative Accessories*)
Baseboards 34
Basement Waterproofing Paints 12
Bathroom Accessories 54
Bathroom Faucets and Fittings 55
Bathroom Fixtures 56, 60
Bathroom Tile 44
Bathtubs, Old-Fashioned 60
Beams, Hand-Hewn 34
Bed Hangings 49
Bed Hardware—*see Furniture Hardware*
Bellows 70
Benches, Promenade 33
Bevelled Glass 45, 46
Bird and Pest Control Products 12
Bisque Repair—*see Porcelain Refinishing*
Bleach, Wood 82
Blinds and Shutters, Exterior Wood 23

Blinds, Shutters, & Shades, Interior 53, 68
Blinds, Wood Venetian 53
Bluestone 13
Boards, Salvage 34, 36
    (*see also Salvage Building Materials, Barnboard*)
Bollards and Stanchions 33
Brackets 20, 41
Braided Rugs 52
Brass Beds 52
Brass Lacquer 82
Brass Polish 82
Brick Cleaners 12
Bricks, Handmade 13
Bricks, Salvage 13
    (*see also Salvage Building Materials*)
Bronzing and Gilding Liquids 82
Brownstone 13
Brownstone (Sandstone) Repair 103
Building Inspection 102
Building Maintenance Materials 12-13, 18
Building Materials, Interiors 34-40
Bulbs, Carbon Filament 80
Bull's Eye Windows—
    see Windows, Special Architectural Shapes
Buttresses 20

C

Cabinet Hardware 59
Cabinet, Kitchen 68
Cabinetmaking and Custom Woodwork 100
Calcimine Paint 87
Candelabra 49
Candlestands and Candlesticks 49
Caning Supplies 89
Canopies, Bed 49
Canvas for Walls 89
Capitals, Exterior 20
Capitals, Interior 43
Capitals, Porch 22
Carbon Filament Bulbs 80
Carpentry 101
Carpet Rods 61
Carpets 52
Carved and Cut Glass 45, 46
Carving, Wood—Custom 103
Casein Paints 87
Casings, Door and Window 34
Cast Aluminum, Exterior Ornamental 29
Cast Iron, Ornamental 29
Casting Materials 89

Ceiling Fans	66
Ceiling Medallions	41
Ceilings, Metal	39
Ceilings, Wood	34
Centerpieces—see Ceiling Medallions	
Ceramic Roofing Tiles	14
Ceramic Tile Flooring	36
Ceramic Tile	44
Chair Rails	34
Chair Replacement Seats	89
Chair Tapes	89
Chairs	49, 50
Chandeliers—see Lighting Fixtures	
Channels, Windows	26
Chimney Brushes	70
Chimney Collars—see Stove Pipe & Fittings	
Chimney Linings	70
Chimney Pots	31
Chimney Restoration	102
Circular Staircases	38
Clapboards, Beaded Edge	16
(see also Salvage Building Materials)	
Cleaners and Polishes, Metal	82
Cleaners, Glass	82
Cleaners, Marble	82
Cleaners, Masonry and Brick	12
Cleaners, Textile	87
Cleaners, Wallpaper	88
Clock Kits	49
Clocks	49
Clocks, Street	33
Clothing, Period	50
Clothing, Period Patterns	50
Coal Grates	70
Coal Scuttles	70
Coat Hooks	61
Coat Racks and Umbrella Stands	53
Collars, Stove Pipe—see Stove Pipe & Fittings	
Columns, Exterior	20
Columns, Interior	43
Columns, Porch	22
Commode Seats	56
Concrete Roofing Tiles	14
(under Other Roofing Materials)	
Conductor Heads—see Leaders & Leader Boxes	
Conservator's Tools	89
Consolidants, Wood—see Rot Patching Materials	
Consulting Services	98
Contour Gauges	89
Contracting Services	101
Cookstoves	71
Copper Polish	82
Corbels	20, 41
Corner Bead Moulding	44
Cornices, Exterior	20
Cornices, Interior Decorative	48
Costume, Period	50
Coverlets and Quilts	49
Cranes	70
Cresting	29
Crewel	50
Cupolas	31
Curtain Rods	50
Curtains and Drapery	50
Curtains, Bed	49

D

Damask	50
Dampers, Fireplace	70
Dating Old Houses—see Historical Research	
Decorating and Painting Services	102-103
Decorating Tools	92
Decorative Interior Materials and Supplies	41-53
Delft Tile—see Tile, Ceramic	
Design and Consulting Services	98
Design and Decorating, Interior	102
Dolls	53
(under Other Decorative Accessories)	
Door Bells, Period Designs	28
Door Framing Woodwork	26
Door Hardware, Exterior	27
Door Hardware, Interior	63, 64, 65
Door Knobs and Escutcheons	65
Door Knockers	27
Doors, Exterior	24
Doors, Interior	34
Doors, Sliding—Tracks and Hardware	68
Doors, Storm and Screen	17
Downspout Fittings—see Gutters & Leaders	
Drapery and Curtains	50
Drapery Hardware	50
Drapery Trimmings	50
Drapes, Insulated—see Window Coverings, Insulating	
Drawings, Original (House)—see Prints & Original Art	
Dry Sinks and Liners	65
Dumbwaiters	35
Dutch Tiles	44

E

Electric Switches, Push-Button	80
Encaustic Tile	44
Energy-Saving Devices	70-71
(see also Fireplace Devices)	
Engraved, Glass	46
Engraving, Brass—see Plaques & Historic Markers	
Entryways	26
Epoxy Resins—see Building Maintenance Materials, Rot Patching Materials, and Casting Materials	
Escutcheons	65
Etched Glass	45, 46
Exterior Building Materials	12-18
Exterior Ornament & Architectural Detail	19-33

The Old-House Journal 1982 Catalog 169

F

Fabric 50
Fabric Cleaners—*see Textile Cleaners*
Fabric Restoration—
    see Antique Repair and Restoration
Fancy Painting—Gilding, Glazing, etc............. 102
Fanlights 26
Fans, Ceiling 66
Faucets & Faucet Parts, Bathroom................. 55
Faucets & Faucet Parts, Kitchen 68
Fences and Gates 31
Fenders, Fireplace 70
Finish Revivers 82
Finishes, Interior—Specialty Paints 87
Finishes, Oil 82
Fire Alarms 54
Firebacks 70
Fireboards—*see Fire Screens*
Firegrates 70
Fireplace Acccessories 70
Fireplace and Chimney Restoration 102
Fireplace Dampers 70
Fireplace Devices 70
Fireplace Parts 70
Fireplace Tools 70
Fireplaces, Manufactured 70
Firescreens 70
Flatting Oils 82
Floor Registers 36
Floorcloths 52
Flooring, Parquet—Installation 103
Flooring, Stone and Ceramic 36
Flooring, Wood 35
Folk Rugs 52
Fountains 32
Frames—*see Mouldings, Interior*
Framing, Door and Window 34
Franklin Stoves—*see Stoves*
Fretwork and Grilles, Wood 36
Froes 89
Furnace Parts 71
Furnaces, Coal-Fired 70
Furnaces, Wood-Burning 70
Furnishings 49-53
Furniture Hardware 61
Furniture Kits 52
Furniture, Lawn and Porch 32
Furniture—Period Styles 52
Furniture, Reproductions—Custom-Made 52
Furniture Stripping 103

G

Galvanized Metal Roofing 14
Garden Ornament 32
Gargoyles 33
Gas Lamp Mantles 79
Gas Lighting Fixtures 80
Gas Logs 70
Gates and Fences 31
Gazebo Plans 89
Gazebos 32
Gilding and Bronzing Liquids 82
Gilding Services 102
Gingerbread Trim 20
Glass, Antique 45
Glass, Art—All Types 44-46
Glass Bending 46
Glass Cleaners 80
Glass, Curved—For China Cabinets 44
Glass, Curved—Window 26
Glass, Leaded and Stained—Repair 45
Glass, Leaded and Stained—Supplies 89
Glass Shades 80
Glass, Window—Handmade 26
Glazing Services 102
Glazing Stains and Liquids 82
Globes, Glass 80
Glue Chip Glass 46
Gold Leaf 82
Graining Services 102
Graining Tools 89
Granite 13
Grates, Coal 70
Grilles and Fretwork, Wood 36
Grilles, Hot Air Register 36
Grilles, Iron 29
Gutters and Leaders 20

H

Handrails, Iron 29
Handrails, Staircase 39
Hangers, Picture 52
Hardware, Awning 31
Hardware, Cabinet 59
Hardware, Custom 28, 64
Hardware, Drapery 50
Hardware, Exterior 27-28
Hardware, Furniture 61
Hardware, Ice Box 68
Hardware, Plumbing, and House Fittings 54-69
Hardware, Shutter 28, 68
Hardware, Trunk 68
Hardware, Window 68
Hardwood Strip Flooring 35
Hardwoods Suppliers 36
Heart Pine Flooring 35

Heat Gun......................................59, 90
Heat Shields.....................................70
Heating Systems, Central—Solid Fuel..........70
Heating Systems, Solar..........................71
Hewing Tools....................................89
Hexagonal Ceramic Tile..........................44
High-Tank Toilets...............................56
Hinges, Door................................27, 63
Hinges, Shutter.................................28
Historical Research.............................99
Holdbacks.......................................28
Hooked Rugs.....................................52
Hooks, Coat.....................................61
Horsehair Fabric................................50
Hot-Air Guns....................................90
House Inspection Services......................102
House Moving...................................102
House Parts, Salvage............................93
House Plans.....................................89
Houses, Recycled................................97

I

Ice Box Hardware................................68
Ingrain Carpets.................................52
Inlays and Veneers..............................40
Inspection Services............................102
Interior Design................................102
Iron, Cast—Ornamental..........................29
Iron Furniture..................................32
Iron, Wrought—Ornamental...................29, 31
Ironing Boards, Built-In—
    see Dumbwaiters & Built-Ins
Ironwork, Exterior...........................29-31
Isinglass for Stove Doors.......................71

K

Kerosene Lamps and Lanterns.....................80
Key Blanks......................................68
Kitchen Cabinets................................68
Kitchen Faucets.................................68
Kitchen Sinks...................................68
Kits, Clock.....................................49
Kits, Furniture.................................52
Kits, Needlework................................52
Kits, Stained and Leaded Glass..................89
Kits, Stencil...................................92
Knockers..27

L

Lacquer, Brass..................................82
Lacquering Services............................102
Lacquers, Clear and Colored.....................82
Ladders, Library................................68
Lamp Posts and Standards........................80
Lamp Shade Kits, Glass..........................89
Lamp Shades.....................................52
Lamp Shades, Glass..............................80
Lamp Wicks and Lamp Oil.........................80
Lamps, Antique..................................72
Lamps, Exterior.................................80
Lamps, Kerosene.................................80
Lamps, Reproduction...................74, 76, 79
Lamps, Street...............................33, 80
Landscape Design...............................102
Lanterns..80
Lanterns and Lamps, Exterior....................80
Lanterns and Lamps, Kerosene....................80
Latches.................................27, 28, 64
Lawn Furniture..................................32
Leaded and Stained Glass Supplies...............89
Leaded Glass....................................45
Leaded Glass Repair.............................45
Leaders and Leader Boxes........................20
Leather Replacement Seats.......................89
Leather Wallcovering............................53
Lectures and Seminars...........................99
Letterdrops.....................................27
Library Ladders.................................68
Light Bulbs, Carbon Filament....................80
Lighting Fixture Parts..........................80
Lighting Fixture Restoration...................102
Lighting Fixtures and Parts..................72-81
Lighting Fixtures, Antique......................72
Lighting Fixtures, Gas Burning..................80
Lighting Fixtures, Reproduction.......74, 76, 79
Lightning Rods..................................32
Limestone.......................................13
Lincrusta-Walton Substitute—see Anaglypta
Linen...50
Linings, Chimney................................70
Locks, Door.................................27, 65
Log Houses—see Recycled Houses, Barns and
    Other Structures
Lumber Suppliers................................36

M

Magnifiers, Portable	89
Mail Boxes	32
Mail Slots	27
Maintenance Supplies, Exterior	12-13
Mall Furniture and Equipment	33
Mantels	47
Mantles, Gas	79
Marble	13
Marble Cleaners and Polishes	82
Marble Flooring	36
Marble—Replacement Pieces	48
Marbleizing	102
Markers, Historic	32
Masonry and Brick Cleaning Compounds	12
Masonry and Supplies	13
Masonry Paint Strippers	12
Masonry Paint-Stripping Services— *see Masonry Repair and Cleaning*	
Masonry Paints	13
Masonry Repair and Cleaning	103
Masonry Sealers	13
Masonry Tools	90
Materials Analysis	99
Mechanical Doorbells	28
Medallions, Ceiling	41
Medicine Cabinets	54
Metal Ceilings	39
Metal Ornament (Sheet Metal)	32
Metal Polishes and Cleaners	82
(see also Rust Removers)	
Metal Replating	103
Metal Roofing	14
Metal Shingles	14
Metalwork Repairs	103
Mica for Stove Doors—*see Isinglass*	
Microcrystalline Wax	88
Milk Paints	87
Millwork, Architectural—Exterior	19
Mirror Resilvering	103
Moisture Meters	89
Morris Chairs	50
Mortar Analysis—*see Materials Analysis*	
Mortise Locks	27, 65
Moulding and Casting Supplies	89
Moulding, Corner Bead	44
Moulding Planes	90
Mouldings, Exterior	22
Mouldings, Exterior Wood—Custom	20
(see also Architectural Millwork)	
Mouldings, Interior	48
Moving Historic Structures	102
Murals, Wallpaper	53
Musical Instrument Repair	103

N

Nails, Handmade	90
National Register Applications— *see Consulting Services*	
Needlework Kits	52
Newel Posts, Staircase	39

O

Oil and Wicks, Lamp	80
Oil Finishes	82
(see also Tung Oil)	
Oriental Rugs	52
Ornaments, Interior—Plaster and Wood	41, 48
Ornaments, Sheet Metal	32
Ornaments, Wrought Iron	29, 31
Overdoor Treatments	37
Outbuilding Plans	89

P

Paint Analysis	99
Paint Removers, Masonry	12
Paint Stripping Chemicals	12, 87
Paint Stripping Gun	89
Paint Stripping Services	103
Paint Stripping Tools	90
Painting and Decorating Services	103
Paints, Exterior—Masonry	13
Paints, Finishes, Removers and Supplies	82-88
Paints, Period Colors	84
Paints, Specialty	87
Panelling, Wall—Wood	40
Parquet Flooring	35
Parquet Repair and Installation	103
Patching Materials and Fillers, Wood	88
Patching Plaster	90
Patterns, Period Clothing	50
Pedestals and Plant Stands	52
Pest Control Products	12
Photography, Architectural	103
Picture Frames—*see Mouldings, Interior*	
Picture Hangers	52
Pigeon Control	12
Pigments and Tinting Colors	87
Planes, Wood—Moulding	90
Plans, Gazebo	89
Plans, House	89
Plant Stands and Pedestals	52
Planters	32
Plaques and Markers	32
Plaster Analysis—*see Materials Analysis*	
Plaster Casting Materials	89
Plaster Mouldings	48
Plaster Patching Materials	90

Plastering, Ornamental 103
Plastering Tools.........................90
Plasterwork, Decorative..................49
Plastics for Casting 89
Plating, Metal 103
Plumbing Fixtures.......................56
Pocket Door Hardware 68
Pokers 70
Poles, Drapery 50
Polishes 82
Porcelain Knobs—see Door Knobs and
    Cabinet Hardware
Porcelain Refinishing Materials 87
Porcelain Refinishing Services 103
Porch Furniture.........................32
Porch Parts 22
Porticoes—see Overdoor Treatments
Portraits, House—see Prints & Original Art
Post and Beam Houses—see Recycled Houses,
    Barns and Other Structures
Posts, Lamp 80
Posts, Porch 22
Posts, Salvage—see Salvage Building Materials
Power Tools 90
Preservatives, Wood.....................13
Prints and Original Art 52
Prisms 80
Pull-Chain Toilets 56
Putty, Colored..........................87

Q

Quarry Tile—see Ceramic Tile & Flooring, Ceramic
Quilts and Coverlets 49

R

Radiators...............................68
Railings, Iron..........................29
Recycled House Parts 93
Recycled Houses and Barns...............97
Reed Organs, Harmoniums, & Melodians—Repair—
    see Antique Repair and Restoration
Refinishing Products 82-88
Registers and Grilles 36
Renovation & Restoration Supply Stores ...97
Replating Services 103
Researching Buildings—see Historical Research
Restaurant Fittings, Period Style........53
Restoration Consultants 99
Restoration Services 98-101
Retinning, Copper—see Metal Replating
    and Metalwork Repairs
Rim Locks...........................27, 65
Risers and Treads, Staircase............39
Rocking Chairs 49, 50

Rollers, Stencil—see Wallpapering & Decorating Tools
Roofers, Specialty.....................103
Roofing Materials 14
Rosettes, Ceiling—see Ceiling Medallions
Rot Patching Materials 87
Rug Kits—see Needlework Kits
Rugs and Carpets.......................52
Rust and Corrosion Removers............87

S

Salvage Building Materials 18
Salvage House Parts 93
Sandstone 13
Sandstone (Brownstone) Repair 103
Sash, Window 26
Sconces—see Lighting Fixtures
Scrapers, Paint........................90
Screen Doors...........................17
Scuttles, Coal 70
Sealers, Masonry 13
Sealers, Wood 87
Seats, Chair—Replacements..............89
Seminars and Lectures..................99
Shades and Blinds 53
Shades, Glass..........................80
Shades, Insulating—see Window Coverings, Insulating
Shakes, Wood 14, 16
Sheet Metal Ornament...................32
Shingles, Metal 14
Shingles, Special Architectural Shapes...16
Shingles, Wood 14, 16
Shower Curtains—Special Sizes 60
Shower Rings 60
Shutter Hardware....................28, 68
Shutters and Blinds, Exterior Wood 23
Shutters and Blinds, Interior 53, 68
Siding, Barn...........................17
Siding Materials 16-17
Siding, Salvage—see Salvage Building Materials
Signs, Old-Fashioned...................32
Silk 50
Silver Plating 103
Silver Polish..........................82
Sink Bowls, Replacement 60
Sinks, Bathroom 60
Sinks, Dry 65
Sinks, Kitchen 68
Slate 13
Slate Flooring 36
Slate Roofing Tiles 14
Slater's Tools.........................90
Sliding Door Tracks 68
Slumping, Glass 46
Soap Dishes, Period Styles.............54

continued

Solar Heating Systems......................71
Spindles, Porch............................22
Spiral Staircases..........................38
Stained and Leaded Glass Kits..............89
Stained Glass..............................45
Stained Glass Repair.......................45
Stained Glass Supplies.....................89
Stains for Glazing.........................82
Stains, Wood...........................13, 87
Stair Rods.................................61
Staircase Parts............................39
Staircases.................................37
Staircases, Spiral.........................38
Stamped Metal Ornament.....................32
Stanchions and Bollards....................33
Statuary...................................32
Steel Ceilings.............................39
Steeples—see Cupolas
Stencilling...............................103
Stencilling Supplies.......................92
Stone......................................13
Stone and Ceramic Flooring.................36
Stores, Renovation and Restoration Supplies....97
Storm Windows..............................71
Stove Heat Shields.........................70
Stove Parts................................71
Stove Pipe and Fittings....................71
Stove Polish...............................82
Stoves.....................................71
Strap Hinges...............................27
Straw Matting..............................52
Street Lamps...........................33, 80
Streetscape Equipment......................33
Strippers, Masonry.........................12
Strippers, Wood............................87
Stripping Tools............................90
Stripping, Paint—Services.................103
Structural Materials—Interior..............40
Stucco Patching Materials..................13
Supply Stores for Renovation Products......97
Switch Plates..............................68
Switches, Electric Push-Button.............80

T

Table Bases—see Pedestals & Plant Stands
Tapestry...................................50
Telephone Parts, Old—
    see Antique Repair and Restoration
Terne-Metal Roofing........................14
Terra-Cotta Mouldings......................22
Terra-Cotta Roofing Tiles..................14
Textile Cleaners...........................87
Textile Restoration—
    see Antique Repair and Restoration
Texture Paints.............................87
Tiebacks...................................50
Tile, Asbestos.............................14
Tile, Ceramic..............................44
Tiles, Encaustic...........................44
Tiles, Roofing—Terra-Cotta and Ceramic.....14
Tiles, Slate...............................14
Timber Frame Houses—see Recycled Houses,
    Barns and Other Structures
Tin Ceilings...............................39
Tinting Colors.............................87
Toilet Seats, Wooden.......................56
Toilets, Period Styles.....................56
Tools...................................89-92
Towel Racks................................54
Towers, Roof—see Cupolas
Transoms...................................26
Treads and Risers, Staircase...............39
Tree Grates................................33
Trunk Hardware.............................68
Tung Oil...................................87
Turnbuckle Stars...........................32
Turnings, Custom..........................103

U

Umbrella Stands and Coat Racks.............53
Upholstery Tools and Supplies..............92
Urns.......................................32

V

Varnishes..............................13, 88
Vases......................................32
Velvet.....................................50
Veneers and Inlays.........................40
Venetian Blinds, Wood......................53
Ventilating Equipment......................71

W

Wainscotting 40
Wall Canvas 89
Wall Panelling, Wood 40
Wallcoverings Other than Wallpaper 53
Wallpaper Borders 53
Wallpaper Cleaners 88
Wallpaper, Custom Duplication 53
Wallpaper Hanging 103
Wallpaper, Period Reproduction 53
Wallpaper Restoration 53
Wallpaper, Scenic 53
Wallpapering and Decorating Tools 92
Washers and Anchors, Plaster 90
Water Heaters—Alternate Fuels 71
Waterproofing Compounds 12
Waxes, Specialty 88
Weathervanes 32
Whitewash 87
Wicker Furniture 52
Wicker Repair Materials 89
Wicks and Oil, Lamp 80
Wide-Board Flooring 35
Window Balances 26
Window Coverings, Insulating 71
Window Frames and Sash 26
Window Framing, Interior 34
Window Glass—Curved 26
Window Glass—Handmade 26
Window Grilles 29
Window Hardware 68
Windows, Special Architectural Shapes 26
Windows, Storm 71
Wood Baskets 70
Wood Carving 103
Wood Fillers 88
Wood Flooring 35
Wood Grain Fillers 88
Wood Mouldings—Custom 20
   (see also Architectural Millwork)
Wood Patching Materials 88
Wood Preservatives 13
Wood Sealers 87
Wood Shakes and Shingles 14
Wood Stains 13, 87
Wood Turning 103
Woodworking, Custom 100
   (see also Millwork, and Furniture,
   Reproduction—Custom-Made)
Woodworking Tools 92
Wrought Iron Ornament 29, 31

Advertisers' Index continued from next page.

Toby House 92
Travis Tuck, Metal Sculptor 33
United Stairs Corporation 37
Vermont Iron Stove Works 33
Vermont Structural Slate Co. 13
Victorian D'Light 77
Victorian Lightcrafters, Ltd. 76
Victorian Millshop 27
Victorian Reproductions, Inc. 76
Vintage Wood Works 23
Walker, Dennis C. 97
Washington Copper Works 81
Watco-Dennis Corporation 84
Watercolors 58
Welsbach 81
Welsh, Frank S. 100
Williamsburg Blacksmiths, Inc. 28
Windy Lane Fluorescents 75
Wolf Paints and Wallpapers 87
Woodbridge Ornamental Iron Co. 38
Woodcare Corporation 83
Wrecking Bar, Inc. 96
Wrecking Bar of Atlanta 97
Zillman Associates 22

The Old-House Journal 1982 Catalog   175

ADVERTISERS' INDEX

Advertiser	Page
AA-Abbingdon	39
A-Ball Plumbing Supply	60
A.E.S. Firebacks	70
A.S.L. Associates	88
Abatron, Inc.	87
Able/Stanley Wood Carving Co.	41
Abraxas International, Inc.	65
Addco Architectural Antiques	35, 93
Agape Antiques	70
Alcon Lightcraft Co.	76
American Delft Blue, Inc.	43
American General Products	39
Antique Street Lamps	80
Architectural Antiques Exchange	94
Architectural Iron Co.	29
Architectural Paneling, Inc.	48
Architectural Restoration & Design Assoc.	98
Architectural Terra Cotta & Tile	44
Arriaga, Nelson	50
Art Directions	94
Ascherl Studios	80
Ball and Ball	69
Barclay Products Co.	55
Beall, Barbara Vantrease Studio	44
Beauti-home	68
Benjamin Moore Co.	85
Berridge Manufacturing Co.	15
Biggs Company	49
Bishop, Adele, Inc.	92
Bix Process Systems, Inc.	85
Black Wax—Pacific Engineering	88
Bona Decorative Hardware	60
Boseman Veneer & Supply Co.	40
Bow & Arrow Stove Co.	71
Bradbury & Bradbury Wallpapers	53
Broad-Axe Beam Co.	34
Broadway Collection	62
Buecherl, Helmut	102
ByGone Era	93
Campbellsville Industries	20
Canal Co.	96
Carlisle Restoration Lumber	36
Cascade Mill & Glass Works	25
Cedar Gazebos, Inc.	32
Ceiling Fan Company, Inc.	66
Charles St. Supply Co.	91
Chemical Products Co., Inc.	85
City Barn Antiques	72
City Lights	73
Classic Illumination	77
Colonial Lock Co.	28
Combination Door Co.	16
Condon Studios—Stained Glass	47
Constance Carol, Inc.	51
Country Curtains	51
Country Floors, Inc.	44
Crawford's Old House Store	26, 44, 65, 91, 97
Creative Openings	17
Cumberland General Store	71
Cumberland Woodcraft Co.	23, 41
Daly's Wood Finishing Products	84
Dean, James R.	37
Decorator's Supply Co.	43
Deft Wood Finish Products	84
Deseret Industries Manufacturing	52
Devenco Louver Products	53
DeWeese Woodworking	54
Diedrich Chemicals	12
D. Diehl Restoration	100
Dixon Bros. Woodworking	52, 101
Dorothy's Ruffled Originals	50
Dovetail, Inc.	42
Dutch Products & Supply Co.	44, 74
FMP	34
Fan—Attic, Inc.	66
Farm Builders, Inc.	17
Feather River Wood & Glass Co.	24
Felber, Inc.	42
Fine Tool Shop, Inc.	90
Focal Point, Inc.	42
Folger Adam Co.	28
Frog Tool Co., Ltd.	92
Fuller O'Brien Paints	85
Furniture Revival and Co.	88
Gates Moore	74
Greg's Antique Lighting	75
Guerin, P.E.	63
Haas Wood & Ivory Works	101
Hallelujah Redwood Products	20
Henderson Black & Greene, Inc.	26
Hexter, S.M., Co.	51
Hill, Allen Charles AIA	99
Hilltop Slate Co.	13
Historic Preservation Alternatives	98
Hobt, Murrel Dee, Architect	98
Holm, Alvin/Architect AIA	100
Hope Co., Inc.	82, 85
Horton Brasses	60
House Carpenters	91
House of Webster	71
Hyde Manufacturing Co.	92
Ice Nine Glass Design	46
Illustrious Lighting	79
Itinerant Artist	91
JMR Products	18
Jennings Lights of Yesterday	54
Kayne, Steve—Hardware	63
Kenneth Lynch & Sons, Inc.	22
King's Chandelier Co.	75
Kingsway	39
Kohler Co.	55
Lavoie, John F.	26
Ley, Joe/Antiques	96
London Venturers Co.	76
Mad River Wood Works	15
Marshall Imports	88
Maurer & Shepherd, Joyners	24
McNair, John, Construction Co.	71
Metals by Maurice	81
Michael's Fine Colonial Products	23
Millham, Newton—Blacksmith	63
Morgan Woodworking Supplies	40
Mosca, Matthew	98
Mountain Lumber Co.	36
Nast, Vivian	45
New England Brassworks	54
Newstamp Lighting Co.	74
Norman, W.F., Corporation	14, 40
Ocean View Lighting	75
Old House Inspection Co.	99
Old-House Journal	59
Olde Bostonian Antiques	95
P & G New and Used Plumbing	54
PRG	88
Peg Hall Studios	91
Period Lighting Fixtures	75
Period Pine	95
Pocahontas Hardware & Glass	47
Porcelli, Ernest	46
Progress Lighting	78
Purcell, Francis J. II	48
Putnam Rolling Ladder Co.	68
Reggio Register Co.	36
Remodelers' & Renovators' Supply	101
Renaissance Decorative Hardware	65
Renovation Concepts, Inc.	96
Renovation Products	16, 19, 23
Renovator's Supply	Inside Front Cover
Restoration Hardware	64
Restoration Works, Inc.	60
Rheinschild, S. Chris	56
Ritter & Son Hardware	64, 68
Ritter & Son (Flora & Fauna)	32
Robillard, Dennis Paul, Inc.	19
Robin's Roost	79
Robinson Iron Corporation	30
Roman Marble Co.	47
Roy Electric Co., Inc.	73
Royal Windyne Limited	67
St. Louis Antique Lighting Co.	74
Saldarini & Pucci, Inc.	41
Saltbox	74
Santa Cruz Foundry	33
Scalamandre	Inside Back Cover
Schaefer, Rick—Plasterer	101
Schwartz's Forge & Metalworks	30
Schwerd Manufacturing Co.	21
Sedgwick Machine Works	35
Shakertown Corporation	18
Shanker Steel Corporation	40
Sherwin-Williams Co.	86
Shingle Mill	15
Ship 'n Out	33
Sign of the Crab	56
Silverton Victorian Millworks	19
Sky Lodge Farm	16
Somerset Door & Column Co.	22
Southington Specialty Wood Co.	37
Stanley Galleries	73
Steptoe & Wife Antiques	38
Sterline Manufacturing Co.	61
Strip Shop	93
Strobel Millwork	49
Stulb Paint & Chemical Co.	84
Sullivan's Antiques	65
Sun Designs	89
Sunrise Salvage	57
Superior Clay Corporation	31
Supradur Manufacturing Corp.	15
Swift & Sons, Inc.	82

For T through Z see previous page.